# A BLIGHTRESS OF WRATH

## A CONDUIT OF LIGHT SERIES

### BOOK THREE

## CHELSEY ANN TOMPKINS

This book is a work of fiction. Names, characters, places, and plot are the product of the author's imagination. Any resemblance to actual events, locales, or persons, living or dead, is coincidental.



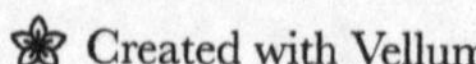 Created with Vellum

*For those who have lived through the dark and found themselves on the other side.*

# CONTENT WARNINGS

This is a book with adult themes including self harm, body dismemberment, surgery, thoughts of suicide, suggestion of attempted suicide, pregnancy, childbirth, child loss, stillborn child, death, spousal loss, grieving, potential drowning, and sexually explicit scenes between consenting adults.

# PRONUNCIATION GUIDE AND MAIN CHARACTERS

## PRONUNCIATION GUIDE

### Characters

**Adaynth**— UH-DAY-EN-TH
*(the first Baron, Visalia's companion)*
**Clairannia**— CLAIR-AWE-NEE-UH
*(medicus conduit)*
**Figuerah**— FIG-AIR-UH
*(iumenta conduit)*
**Ilyenna**—ILL-YEN-UH
*(lapis channeler/conduit, Thevin's mother)*
**Karus**— CAR-US
**Lanna**— LAWN-UH
*(daughter of the Lady of the Spire)*
**Lia**— LIE-UH
*(the Fortress cook, lapis conduit, sister to Visalia)*
**Moira**— MOY-RUH
*(faerie of Felgren)*
**Mychael**— MY-KAY-EL
*(training channeler, medicus affinity, loves Pompeii, former Hyrithian guard)*

**Philius**— PHILL-E-US
(*Karus's adopted brother, Prince of Hyrithia, training channeler*)
**Pompeii**— POM-PAY
(*Overseer, loves Mychael, Pah-Pah*)
**Revich**— REV-ICK
**Saelyn**— SAY-LIN
**Thevin**— TH-EH-VIN
**Visalia**— VIS-ALL-E-UH
(*the Blightress's given name*)

## Places

**Arcaynen**— ARE-CAY-NEN
**Hyrithia**— HIGH-RIH-THEE-UH
**Lythglyn**— LITH-GLIN
**Radyx**— RAD-ICKS
**Viridis**— VER-IH-DIS

## Conduits/Magic

**Agricola** (*agriculture*)—AH-GRIH-COLA
**Cosensian Magic**— CO-SEN-SEE-AN MAGIC
(*magic wielders giving their power to one person through touch*)
**Iumenta** (*animals*)—EYE-YOU-MEN-TAH
**Lapis** (*stonework*)— LAP-IH-S
**Medicus** (*doctors*)— MEH-DIH-CUS
**Rhyzolm**— R-EYE-ZOLM
**Wieldwryn** — WHEEL-D-RIN

## MAIN CHARACTER DETAILS

### The Blightress (Visalia)

The original magic wielder was born in a forest around 900 years before this story takes place. Her parents treated her poorly, but when her sister, Thalia, was born, she found more purpose in her life. She fell in love with a childhood friend named Adaynth. Understanding she would live forever, Visalia gave some of her power away in three places. The forest she grew up in, Felgren Forest, was given her power so that it could never die. This had the unforeseen effect that the forest then gave power to others. These magic wielders are called *channelers* and they can train in Felgren and take trials to become *conduits*. Visalia also gave some of her power away to the two she loved most: her sister Thalia (Lia) and her companion, Adaynth (first Baron). With the loss of their child at birth, Visalia became the Blightress, plaguing the land with Blight. Adaynth passed his power on from Baron to Baron to train channelers in Felgren.

Hundreds of years later, the Blightress discovered Karus (previously named Ash'Arah) while she grew in her mother's womb. The Blightress felt a connection to this growing babe and gave some of her power to Karus, resulting in the Blightress's mind connection to the powerful magic wielder. Her current goal is to take back the power she gave away to the Baron and channelers on the isle to rule over Arcaynen with Karus at her side as her daughter.

## Karus (previously Ash'Arah)

Growing up as an adopted child of the Queen of Hyrithia, Karus spent her first twenty years as the sister to Prince Philius. When Karus was taken from Hyrithia by Baron Heimlen, she discovered more about the power she could wield. When she and Heimlen attempted to destroy the Blight in Felgren, she held the *Simulair Solum* spell for too long and forgot her past. After seven years, she woke completely from this loss of memories when the Blightress spoke to her in her mind. When she met the Blightress in person, it did not go well. Karus refused to accept any kinship with the Blightress, choosing instead to become a second Baron with her companion, Baron Revich, and find a way to destroy the heart of the Blightress.

## Baron Revich

Growing up as an orphan mining rhyzolm in the Hallow Marshes, Rev was manipulated by Baron Heimlen to become his predecessor with only the continuation of power in mind. But Revich is kind, loving, logical, and fiercely devoted. He disregarded his mentor's advice, becoming the first Baron to lead with his heart.

Baron Revich has loved Karus since his rhyzolm first gave him a hint of what she looked like, and now they are companions and share their roles as Barons. In A Baron of Bonds, we learn that the world has been told that he died the night Saelyn was born. In the last chapter of A Baron of Bonds, we discover that is not true, and Baron Karus has plans to save him, though we do not know where he is or why he is gone. (Sorry about that.)

## Saelyn

Introduced in A Baron of Bonds, we learn that Saelyn is the daughter of Baron Revich and Baron Karus. She is powerful, able to reverse time by one minute and conjure other magic unheard of. Felgren Forest has always felt like her true home, and her name has been whispered on the wind her entire life. She has grown up lonely with a somewhat troubled relationship with her mother who grieves the loss of her father. However, Pah-Pah (Pompeii, the Overseer of the Fortress) has been like a grandfather to her, and her best friend, Thevin, has been a bright spot in her life throughout the years. She is, in fact, in love with him. However, when he confessed he feels the growing love between them, she refused to admit the truth of her own heart, fearing Thevin would one day tire of her and leave her forever. She has very recently learned that her father is still alive. (Again, sorry about that.)

## Thevin

We don't know much about the only child of the companions Ilyenna and Talon. He was born a few months before Saelyn and spent every Felgren summer as her best friend. He eventually fell in love with her, and when he tried to confess this the day before her seventeenth birthday, she refused to allow them to be anything but friends. We do not know what he does with his parents outside of Felgren, but it was hinted in A Baron of Bonds that he has been through some harrowing experiences.

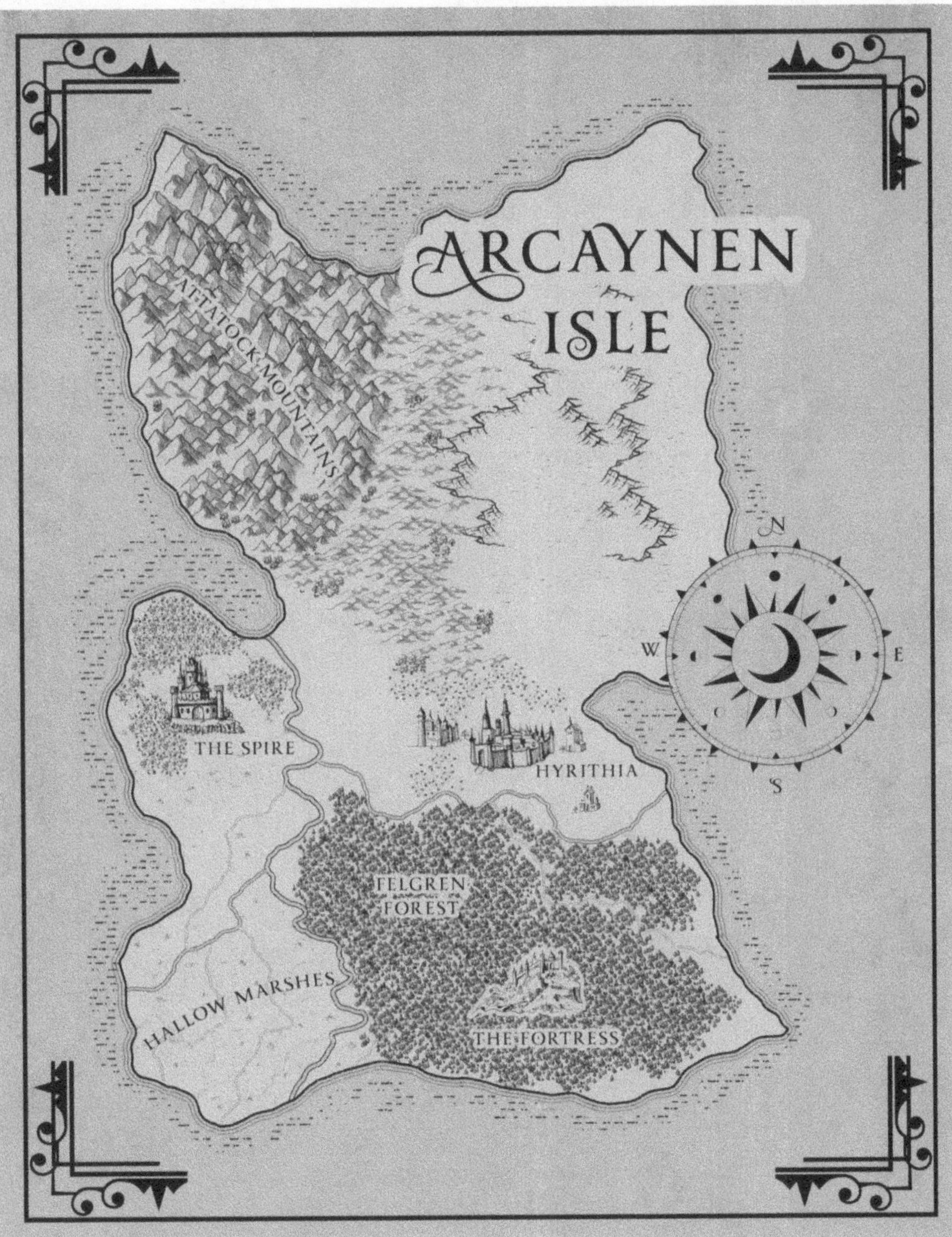

ARCAYNEN ISLE
ATTATOCK MOUNTAINS
THE SPIRE
HYRITHIA
FELGREN FOREST
HALLOW MARSHES
THE FORTRESS
N
E
S
W

# PART ONE
## SEVENTEEN YEARS AFTER

*The silence is cold.*
*In the absence of his voice, his warmth, I am left out in the frigid wind.*
*No words to soothe what aches.*
*No body to warm mine, to heat, to please.*
*I don't light the fire in our hearth.*
*It's been as barren as my soul since the day he left.*
*I sleep in our rooms, but I do not dream.*
*I bathe in our bath, but I am not clean.*
*I dress by the bed, but I am not clothed in him…*
*As it should have been.*

# CHAPTER 1
# SAELYN

"Saelyn, my Little Love, your father *lives*." My mother lifted my chin as I frowned. "And our time has come to save him."

I stepped back on the balcony, refusing her touch. "What do you mean my father lives?" I shook my head. My body chilled with her words in the beginning of the summer storm. "My father is dead. He's been dead since the night I was born seventeen years ago."

My mother's eyes brimmed with tears. It was rare to see them turn from the black eyes of a Baron to the brilliant green they now glinted. She swallowed in hesitation, wringing her hands in her black skirts. "It was necessary to let you believe this. I had to—"

"*Let me believe this?*" I spat. "You lied!" I swept my gaze north. "Where is my father? Why does he need to be saved?"

"There is so much to tell you. I've been waiting seventeen years to tell you all of it, and—"

"You've been *waiting*? *Waiting for what*?" I didn't understand. I couldn't. My heart had been ready to soar. I had been ready to confess my love for Thevin this night of my birthday celebration, and he had stopped me. Before I could push to confess my feelings further, my mother had given me this weighted truth.

"I made a promise to your father," she said, reaching for me. "He wanted you to have a childhood. To have a life without the knowledge that he was forced to be gone from it. He loved you, Saelyn. He loves you now. I can feel it."

I bit my lips together, backing away from her again. I had lived my seventeen years in a lie. What truth did I really hold? I knew nothing. Nothing about life, about love, about my own mother and father. It wasn't fair.

"If you'd sit, Little Love, I will help you understand—"

"Is my father in immediate danger?" I interrupted.

"No," she returned with a shake of her head.

"When do we leave?"

She sighed heavily, recognizing my anger. "Tomorrow morning. We leave for the Spire."

I tried to keep the surprise from my face and nodded. "Who knows my father lives?"

"Pompeii. As well as three others."

"*Who?*" Anger spread through me.

"Friends of mine. And one other. They have not seen you since you were very young."

"Lucky, I guess, they got to see me at all."

"Sae—"

"I'm going to let Thevin know we're leaving in the morning. That's what you said earlier, isn't it? He and his parents are leaving with us?"

My mother nodded, her eyes back to black, her countenance back to the hardened stone I recognized. I turned to leave.

"I understand if you do not wish to sleep in my rooms tonight, but stay with Pah-Pah or Thevin instead. I do not want you sleeping alone anymore."

I whipped around. "And why is that, Mother?"

Her jaw clenched. "I do not trust that she has not found a way to get to you."

"Who?"

"The woman who is the reason he left. She is called the Blightress."

# CHAPTER 2
# THEVIN

I took another long pull from the bottle of wine I'd snuck off with, wholeheartedly prepared to be drunk by the time Sae got to our grove of maple trees.

*I don't want to forget it,* she'd said to me, and I'd stopped her.

I'd all but said the exact words I had felt every day for the past year, and she had stopped *me* then. I wanted her, but more than that, I wanted her to be real. I'd never let her compromise or settle for me like she was attempting to. She'd told me she didn't want to risk our friendship. She had worried that someday I'd leave her, arguing I'd be able to live without her smile.

But that was never going to be an option for me.

The next pull on the bottle was longer, and I gulped continuously.

I'd been drunk twice before. Both times my parents had discovered me outside a tavern in the Spire, heaving my guts out. I'd only wanted to wash away what I'd seen in those days. The horrors of war were a heavy burden on my nineteen-year-old shoulders.

On anyone's shoulders.

The rain continued its pelting through the trees, but our fort held strong. We had built it together two summers ago as our stronghold against the summer storms that frequented Felgren Forest.

Well, I had built it, and she had directed me. I had gathered the logs and laid them at an angle. I had tied them together with willow branches, filling the gaps between with mud and moss so it remained warm and dry. She'd chosen the charred maple tree as the site for our little sanctuary. It grew over a rocky outcropping that led to a small stream.

We hadn't yet visited our fort since I had arrived in Felgren, so I sorted through the things she'd left to show me. Each summer when I visited with my parents, she'd have new things to share—stones she'd found, leaves she'd collected that she thought were particularly interesting. I picked up a bundle of dried daisies bound in yellow ribbon. I remembered giving them to her on the last day of summer when I'd had to leave again. It had been the hardest leave yet because I had accepted the reason I'd so badly wanted to stay.

It had taken a few nights that year for me to sort out my feelings. At the end of every summer, I felt the urge to stay in Felgren, but I'd always thought it was the forest I was missing. Then I began to imagine my future after the war, and Saelyn was always at my side. I dreamt of taking her to the cities of Arcaynen that were still intact. I imagined what it would be like to watch her experience life outside of the forest for the first time. I wanted to show her everything, but I also wanted to follow wherever she wanted to lead like a moth to the most enchanting flame.

She'd said we'd just stay friends.

Friends stayed in each other's lives, so just friends we would be.

I heard the sound of her lumen before I saw him. A massive beast, he was easily the largest of the wolf pack with thick, black fur, a snout longer than my arm, and silver eyes.

She all but tumbled off him as I rose to greet her, patting the mossy roof. "You'll be happy to hear our fort has—"

Sae fell into me, her black cloak soaked, her face pressed into my chest like she wanted under my skin. I felt her body shaking as she wrapped her arms around my shoulders, and I sobered immediately.

"What is it?" I squeezed her back, winding my hand across her head, holding her cheek to my chest. She continued to shake, sobs leaving her throat. "Are you hurt? Tell me that at least."

She shook her head, and I checked that off my list of worries for the moment. "Come inside. I have some wine left and your favorite meat pies. I even snatched you a square of strawberry cake."

I led her inside our forest dwelling and Boros followed, settling himself on one side of the enclosure. I helped her down onto the tattered blanket, unrolling the entrance flap and lighting another lantern.

She remained quiet, staring off into nothing as I unclasped her cloak and placed a warm, clean blanket around her shoulders.

I liked taking care of her. I missed taking care of her when I had to leave. But this silence was frighting and instead of offering her food and drink, I sat in front of her, lifting her chin that was pointed at her boots. "Talk to me, Sae."

Her red-rimmed eyes had turned to brilliant lighting blue. Her cheeks and nose were splotched with tracks of dried tears.

I reached out to her hands. "Was it your mother? What did she say to you?"

"She said…" she gulped and I felt the shiver that ran through her body. "She said my father is alive. She said we leave tomorrow for the Spire and that we are going to save him."

I narrowed my eyes to mere slits, cocking my head. "Baron Revich died seventeen years ago. Everyone knows that."

She scoffed, lowering her head again. "Apparently, that's not true. My mother has lied all these years. Hardly anyone knows." Her head snapped back up to me. "Your parents don't even know."

"It doesn't make sense," I pressed. "Why lie? Why wouldn't she go after him?"

"I don't know yet. Maybe I should have stayed to listen, but I didn't want to hear any more." She glared at the flicker of the lantern. "She kept this from me my entire life. Pah-Pah did, too. I feel so betrayed by them both. And my father? Is he hurt? Is he fighting?"

I knew he wasn't. Unless there was more to the story, Baron

Revich was known as a martyr, not a man fighting in this war. "Did Baron Karus say where he is?"

"With someone called the Blightress."

My blood went cold, and I sobered further.

Sae watched my reaction, not missing a beat. "Who is she, Thevin?"

I took her hands from her lap and squeezed them. "She's the cause of all of this. She's the one who started this war."

# CHAPTER 3
# SAELYN

War.
I knew little of it and even less about its origins. What I did know was that it had been raging outside of Felgren my whole life, and now, I wondered if it had been raging the exact entirety of it.

I wiped the tears off my cheeks. "Will you tell me?"

"I'm not supposed to te—"

"I don't care what they've told you to hide from me, Thevin. I am not a child." I straightened my spine, squeezing his hand back. "If I am to leave for the Spire and help save my father, I need to know all of it. Everything you know."

"I'm under a direct order from Baron Karus to never say a word to you about life outside of Felgren." One side of his lips lifted and his eyes sparkled. "Good thing I'm not very good at following orders."

I wasn't sure that was true. Thevin always followed the orders I'd given him since we were fifteen.

He rubbed his face, pulling a hand through his golden curls. My stomach tightened at the movement. I hadn't forgotten what had happened between us, what had torn in his confession of his feelings and my rejection of them. And when we had danced at my party, and I'd been ready to take a risk with him? Then, he'd told me to forget all about it.

"I can't tell you much about how it started. Most of us don't know." His jaw tightened in muscle that ticked as his icy blue eyes caught mine. "But I can tell you how it's going."

I suddenly wasn't sure I wanted to know. Just by the look on his face, I knew I'd been kept ignorant to all of it for seventeen years for a reason. Was I so fragile?

My mother must have thought so.

"I'm sorry, Thevin," I whispered, barely audible with the pounding of rain that continued its slew on the eaves of our hideout.

He shook his head. "You don't need to be sorry."

"But I am. I can see it in you now. You've been out there fighting, haven't you?" I scoffed and pulled my knees to my chest. "I've just been here. Doing nothing while my father and best friend are out *there*."

"Before I tell you about this war, Sae, there's something you should know. Everyone else knows and you'll find out soon enough."

I mumbled into the tops of my knees, "There's nothing you can say that could shock me more than finding out my father is alive."

"There might be."

I frowned.

"This whole war is a fight over you."

# CHAPTER 4
# THEVIN

How do you tell your best friend she's the center of so much death and destruction? Probably not like I did.

"Fuck, I shouldn't have started there."

"Can we go?" she muttered, pulling the blanket tighter over her shoulders.

Her body shook from the summer chill or the news I'd just clumsily dropped—either way, I wanted so badly to pull her into my lap and wrap my arms around her.

"Sure," I said instead.

I stood and held my hands out to her. She took them and pulled herself up while Boros stretched, waiting for her command.

"My room," she started. "Will you stay and talk to me there? My mother doesn't want me to be alone, and now…I guess I know why."

*By the Baron*, she didn't know anything at all. She didn't know what we'd face outside of this protected forest. She didn't know about the monsters, the decimation. She didn't know how my chest hurt from the idea that I'd get to stay with her tonight and just be near.

I helped her onto the back of Boros and jumped up myself. He turned his head to glare me, but followed Sae's order to get back to the Fortress anyway.

I held her close to my chest, both of our heads bent low to avoid the downpour of summer rain. In the fifteen minutes it took to get back to the looming black towers, I planned out what I'd tell her. I'd need to be methodical. I'd need to let her in slowly—two things I happened to be good at.

Boros stopped at the steps that lead to the kitchens, and I hopped off before helping Sae. She ruffled his ears, telling him he could go back to the den. He swiveled his enormous head toward me.

"He still doesn't like me," I said grudgingly, offering my hand, palm up for him to sniff.

He did so and huffed loudly, nudging his head at Saelyn's side.

"You probably smell too different. You smell like,"—she gestured to the green shield of light protecting Felgren—"out there."

I nodded, knowing what she didn't, but soon would.

Boros raised his head and howled. His call was answered by several lumens in the depths of the trees. He gave her one last nudge and ran off under the darkening sky.

I inched open the door to the kitchens to glance inside. I saw the cook speaking to Pompeii while several kitchen maids ran in and out with trays of food.

I closed the door again and grimaced. "They must have moved the party into the Fortress. Pompeii is there. I'm guessing you don't want to see him?"

She tilted her head back to the sky, her hood falling in the movement as she put her hands on her hips and sighed in a loud groan. Then, catching my eye with hers, she raised a brow. "Blend?"

"Blend," I repeated.

She pulled her cloak from her shoulders and placed the tips of her fingers on my cheek.

Her touch was ice I wanted to melt. I wanted to take her hand and wrap it in my own, protecting her from…everything.

She paused, holding back her spell, giving me a smirk.

"*Dissemulen*," she mumbled, and I felt the same blur around me she'd projected before. We had used this spell countless times to get us out of the Fortress undetected. She'd also used it to get us back in before we were caught. She had explained it to me as a spell of non-detection. Unless we were being actively looked for, no one would really notice us. We'd blend into the bustle of the Fortress with ease.

My mouth ticked up as she used the spell on herself. Her body blurred like a faint smear of paint, but her face had always been clear to me each time. Sharper, if anything.

I pulled the door open again—just enough so that we could both slip inside. The trick was to act like you belonged. I hadn't even the smallest lick of magic, but I had cunning. Doing what I did with my parents, it was a necessary skill. I picked up a tray of bite-sized squares of Sae's favorite cake and headed toward the door which led to the dining room. I glanced behind me as Sae grabbed a pitcher of wine, following me out of the kitchens undetected.

Party guests littered the dining hall. They mingled and laughed, completely unaware that the daughter of the Baron slid past their smiles and chatter. We entered the foyer to find it had been made into a dance floor. Dozens of people who had come from all over Arcaynen moved around the open room in twirls of elegant gowns and quick feet.

I checked on Sae behind me as I headed towards her room. I could see her face clearly in the crowd as she moved through it in a swift gait. She kept her eyes down as much as possible, even though the party guests wouldn't look her way unless they were looking *for* her.

I turned left at the Baron's study and into the corridor that led to a few rooms on the first floor. One of them was Baron Karus's room where Sae sometimes slept next to her mother. Another at the very end of the branching hall was the room my parents shared with me when we visited. It was a bit cramped, but we were used to occupying the same space on our assignments, so just having a roof over our heads was enough for the three of us. At least in the Fortress, I got to sleep on a couch instead of the hard ground. Every other room in the Fortress was co-habited with channelers or conduits, and because I was neither, I didn't get my own space.

Sae moved ahead of me in the quiet hall, standing before her door and whispering, "*Redisyn mi domen.*"

Saelyn was a talented channeler. Even I knew that.

She'd never been allowed to train with the others, but she'd done what she could for herself anyway. I'd always loved that about her. She had explained the spells she created like this: since she could derive magic from Felgren, she could shape it herself. She could combine words from the magical language and use them to create something new. She'd done this many times, including when she'd crafted a spell to unlock her door. One that meant, *I've returned. Let me in.* I knew there were others, but I didn't know if she understood what that meant about her power. I doubted she knew creating her own spells was a *Saelyn* thing. Not a channeler thing.

We slid into her room and took a breath. She set the pitcher of wine down on her desk and fell back onto her bed, letting go of the blend spell around us and covering her face with her hands.

I set down my tray of strawberry cake and sat beside her, nudging her arm. "Hey. Scoot over."

She wiggled to give me some room, and I took it, folding my hands at my chest.

The ceiling of her room had been painted to mimic the sky. One side was an ode to the blooming dawn with rays of golden yellow. The other, a scene of the moon, full and silvery with speckled stars that seemed to glow if you stared at them too hard.

"She said my father didn't want me to know."

I turned my head to watch her.

She wiped her eyes and continued. "She said he wanted me to have a childhood without the burden of knowing he was out there alive somewhere." She wiped her nose with a humorless laugh, covering her face again.

I itched to touch her. Instead, I cleared my throat. "I don't know a lot about your father, but I do know a lot of what you're about to see. If we're leaving for the Spire tomorrow, I don't want you to go not knowing what you'll face."

"Me either."

"I mean, I'll be there to protect you, of course. And your mother can protect all of us, but…"

"Tell me, Thevin."

"Are you sure you don't want some cake first?"

She laughed and sat up, pulling a blanket off the back of her desk chair and mumbling, "*Incendo*."

Her fireplace burst into light, and I picked my soaking wet self up off her bed to help her lay the blanket out flat by the fire. Without a word, she retrieved a cup from her bedside table and poured some wine while I brought over the tray of cake. Each little square had been topped with a brilliant red strawberry.

"We'll have to share," she said, taking one long gulp of wine before offering me the cup.

I shook my head. "I've had enough for tonight."

She heaved a sigh too heavy on the night she turned seventeen and pulled the cup close to her chest, staring into the fire.

I stole a moment and watched her face. I wished I could handle this better. I didn't regret telling her how I felt about her—she should know the truth of my feelings. But I did regret not telling her sooner. If I had told her the moment I returned to Felgren this summer with my parents, we'd be past this awkward stage after my confession, and it would be easier to to sit with her in the dancing firelight to discuss the war that coated the rest of the isle in a blanket of fear.

I didn't know exactly why Baron Karus waited seventeen years to tell her only child about her father's true fate, but I could guess at why she was taking Saelyn with us to the Spire.

"Has your mother ever spoken to you about training to become a conduit?"

Sae's eyes flicked back to my face, resting on my mouth before glancing up to my eyes. "No. She said someday she'd be able to start my training, but that she was too busy now to do it. I stopped asking after I turned fourteen. Why?"

"I don't know for sure, but I have the feeling she was waiting until now." I leaned back on my hands and sighed. "We need you. She probably understands that more than I do."

"Need me how?"

"People like me—the ones who cannot wield magic—we can be useful, but not to the extent of people like you. We both know you're powerful, but I don't think you realize the depth of it."

She took another long drink of wine. "Then tell me, Thevin. Tell me of this war. I am listening."

# PART TWO
## SEVENTEEN YEARS BEFORE

# CHAPTER 5
# KARUS

**B**riefly, I wondered how I knew.

I wondered if I was sure.

But as I pressed Revich's hand to my belly, I had no doubts our child grew within me. I let out a cry of disbelief, laughter, and joy. Every emotion swept through our bond, together and all at once, shifting across our faces.

He didn't say anything. He didn't need to.

He beamed at me with such love, such devotion, I cried again and inhaled sharply when his other hand lifted to my cheek, brushing into my hair as he bent to my lips and kissed me.

"Karus?" I heard Clairannia at my side before I broke our kiss and turned to her.

"Can I…?" she questioned, gesturing to where Rev's hand lay over my womb.

I nodded, bringing her hand above Rev's.

"*Vennae*," she murmured, watching my face. Her own lit with glee. "It's there. I can feel both of your hearts beating." Turning to the small crowd of party guests, she announced, "The Barons are having a child!"

The cheer of the crowd filtered through the clearing where we stood in cries of surprise, congratulations, and laughter.

Figuerah had her arms wrapped around me a moment before Clairannia joined, my hand still clasped tightly in Rev's.

I struggled to hear the words that spilled forth as the world around us erupted into a dozen conversations echoing at once. I heard Pompeii's voice somewhere behind me followed by Mychael's, and though we were pulled separate ways, Rev did not let go of my hand.

Moira fluttered before my face, grabbing my cheeks as tears streamed down them. All three of my friends began talking at once—

"—start to make a list of what you need to eat—"

"—don't know how you'll get there, but I'm coming, too—"

"—more, Karus. Remember when I said you were *more*—"

"—told you so, but I did warn you, Karus—"

"—certain routes we should take, and I'm the best option we have to get—"

"—grow from flower buds, so I didn't know why you felt like a bud somehow—"

"*Please!*" I stepped out of their reach. "Give me some room to breathe!" I put a hand over my chest, closed my eyes and inhaled.

I heard Revich speaking quietly to Pompeii and Mychael as more of our party guests started the music over again and danced around the clearing.

I caught Lia's stare in the small crowd. Her grey eyes watched me with a sorrowful stillness. I cocked my head in her direction, questioning. She plastered a thin smile on her lips, shaking her head before moving through the crowd.

I brought my attention back to my friends. "Clairannia, I'll take that list of foods to eat when you have it. And yes, you warned us plenty about what could happen if we kept skipping the styris tea. This child was not intended, but it is wanted and loved." She nodded emphatically, unable to hide her glowing excitement.

"Figuerah, I don't know how we're getting to the Attatok Mountains to pick up the new channelers now, but we'd love if you'd help us." I gestured to the two green portals. "Revich's portals allow one beating heart to enter before they close. I won't be able to enter one until he can fix that or I have this child."

Figuerah took her companion's hand, confirming, "When you're ready to leave, Nyeimah and I will guide you there."

"Moira." I turned to my faerie friend in her gown of crimson petals. "You were right. And you were the first one to recognize what was happening. I'd love to see that field of flowers where faeries are born someday."

A sharp toothed smile lit her face.

Revich tugged on our clasped hands, and I turned just in time to see Mychael step through one of the portals. In a moment, he was gone. Rev made a motion with his other hand and the second portal disappeared in a flash of light.

He pulled me to his chest, cradling my head into his neck as he addressed the crowd. "Thank you everyone, for your congratulations. We are just as shocked as you are of this news. Karus and I will now excuse ourselves. Please enjoy the rest of the party and celebrate for us. Mychael has gone to explain our situation to Geyrand and Vivianna, and I will retrieve him soon."

Wrapping his arm around my waist, Rev pulled us toward the Fortress, giving a final wave to our people who cheered, calling for the celebration to last the night.

As the music faded behind us, I let my emotions seep to him. Through our companion bond, he'd be able to pick up on everything I was feeling. I laid my head on his shoulder as we walked in the late spring evening.

I sent him my surprise, my excitement, my awe in how our lives were forever changed. But strongest, I sent him my love. I sent the spring breeze of Felgren through his hair, over his cheeks, ruffling the linen of his sleeves. I summoned the scent of strawberry blooms from where they grew near the Fortress; his favorite fruit. I grew him a trail of creeping ivy that wove through the path before us; his favorite color. I bent the trees to the west so that the setting sun could shine on his face; his favorite warmth.

"You're my favorite warmth," he murmured in my ear, pulling me closer while we walked.

The dense line of trees thinned, and the cold stone fortress we'd made into our home rose from the forest. When our boots met the bottom of the dark staircase, he turned my shoulders, cupping my face. I closed my eyes and tilted my head, leaning into his grasp. He gently pulled my head back, urging me to look him in the eyes.

Not a fleck of black rose through the ocean blue. Not a single hint of the power of Baron peered out from his gaze. These were Revich's eyes. His mother's eyes. Hopefully, the eyes of our child to come.

He filled his lungs, confessing, "I do not love you more. That would be impossible to do."

I laughed, shaking my head and pulled his wrist to my lips to kiss. Once again, and just as gently as before, he moved my face back to look at him.

"But I want you to know something," he continued. He brushed his lips across mine, passing over my cheek, my jaw, my neck, before his hands left my face, sliding down to my waist as he lowered to his knees. He bent his head to my stomach, declaring, "Karus, I promise to spend my life loving you and our child. I will do whatever I must to keep you both happy and safe. This is a vow I will not break."

He lifted his head to meet my eyes as I wove my fingers through his black waves. He continued, "I could not love you more, but our child...our child I will continue to grow to love. Everything has changed. Everything I thought before...everything I thought I wanted..." He shook his head, sliding his hands up and down my waist. "All of it feels so insignificant."

I lowered to the first step, sitting so I could pull his face to mine. "It's alright, my love. It will take time to adjust, but we still want the same things. We will still be able to do the same things for this world that we've been working toward." I kissed him, adding, "We'll just have even more reason to do it."

I pressed his head to my chest where he murmured, "We're having a child."

"We're having a child."

"We're going to be parents together."

I kissed the top of his head, laughing. "We're going to be parents together."

He wrapped his arms around my back, kissing my cheek as the sun slivered into a thin line of gold, broken through the trees across the horizon. "Will you wait here with me for a little while?" he murmured.

I breathed in the forest, his scent of pine and earth more recognizable to me now than my own. "Baron Revich, I would wait with you forever."

~

*"IF YOU DOUBTED OUR FATES WERE TIED, LITTLE SPROUT, YOU CARRY even more proof."*

My eyes shot open in the lingering dark. The fire in our hearth continued to burn and glancing at the clock on Rev's bedside table, dawn was still hours away.

His face was nestled into my belly, his arms wrapped under and over me. I attempted to slow my pulse so that he would not wake.

The Blightress spoke to me in my mind for the first time since I had faced her in the conduit trials. They'd been almost two months ago, and not a snarl nor threat had come from her.

I had known that wouldn't last.

I had known she'd seek me out again, but I didn't know if I'd be able to push her out completely now that I carried the power of a Baron.

I heard her tsk at my thoughts. *"Karus, we are even more entwined now that you've taken half of the power of Baron. When will you accept this?"*

I squeezed my eyes shut and addressed her there in the corner of my mind where her vines of obsidian wove through the space in a knotted web. *"I won't."* I swallowed hard. *"I won't ever accept it. You murder, you steal, you kill the forest you gave power to. Why would I allow you into my life? What reason have you ever given me to do so?"*

Revich stirred.

*"I only kill those who deserve death. Your father arrived in my lands to hurt me, and I killed him for it. Baron Ereyth was weak and would have hurt those channelers more than help them."*

Revich stretched his arms out around me and rolled to his back, pulling me with him. I followed his movements, doing my best to keep him sleeping while I tried to understand her words.

*"Baron…Ereyth? The Baron who went mad and murdered his channelers after their Offerings? You killed him?"*

Over one hundred years ago, that event had set off a spiral of distrust toward any future Baron of Felgren. Though the Lady of the Spire and Madame of the Mountains at the time had decided to continue to let their channelers be taken to train in Felgren, the Queen of Hyrithia had not. And so, for a hundred years, no channeler born in the city could be given an Offering. That was until Baron Heimlen created a deadly disease in Hyrithia, offering the cure if the Queen handed him me.

*"He deserved it. He had abused his channelers before. I know some of what goes on in the heads of Barons."*

I didn't like that. *"So, you're calling yourself a hero now? And I should just forgive you for what you've done because you have good intentions?"*

*"My intentions are for us, Little Sprout. Come to me. Bring your lover if you must, but come. We can be together as intended. I see how you wish to help your people. I can aid in that. When my power is restored, we can help the people you love together. Mother and daughter ruling the isle side by side in a greater realm than we could ever achieve on our own."*

*"By stealing people's power to wield for ourselves?"* I pressed the palms of my hands to my eyes, wishing I could shut her out entirely.

*"It is my power. It has been taken from me."*

*"You gave it away to the forest! You cannot just take it back."*

*"What choice did I have?"* her dark voice seethed. *"I was young, I was foolish and reckless. I made a choice that I thought would make me loved. Instead, I broke, and centuries later, I found you. You were always meant to be mine. Beloved? Why do you think that name suits you so well?"*

*"Because I chose—"*

*"Because you are loved. You have been loved by me when you grew in Arah's belly, just as you love the babe in yours. Everything I have done was for*

us. *Everything I continue to do is for* us. *For our family, Karus. And you will see. I will do what I must to make you see.*"

Revich's hands brushed my face as tears fell freely down my cheeks. He pulled me to his chest, rocking me in his arms as my body trembled.

"*I cannot love you. I am sorry for you, but I cannot love you, Visalia.*"

Silence.

My words to her lingered in silence.

"*Speak to him. Speak to Adaynth, and then tell me how sorry you really are.*"

Revich held me tighter to his chest, letting my last tears fall. My face pressed into him where I'd never leave as long as he let me stay. And he'd let me stay forever.

The Blightress had gone. Her last words to me had come hard and chilled. Words I'd rather not follow.

I wiped my hand under my nose and whispered into Revich's soft, black waves, "How can we make the world better for our child? What can we do for her, so that she grows more loved than we ever were?"

He smoothed the hair from my face, pulling his thumbs across my wet cheeks. "Her?"

"Yes. Her."

His face lit. Even in the dark, I saw joy produce from his eyes so blue. For the first time since I'd met him, I watched as his power poured from his skin. It lifted in smokey tendrils of a deep blue that hazed around his body.

"A girl? You're sure?"

I nodded. I didn't know how I knew we were having a daughter. I just knew.

"Karus." He spoke my name as he meant it. His beloved. That was why I had chosen it. His love, Clairannia and Figuerah's love—those were the reasons beloved fit me so well. What love had the Blightress ever shown me? Hers was possession, a desire to own me as her daughter. That was not love, and I knew it.

I kissed him deeply, pulling myself back to a place where I had a solid ground. A place where my soul had taken root in the threads which bound us by fate. This man was my fate. He was the path I'd chosen years ago, and the Blightress would not take that from me nor our child.

"You're glowing. Look." I smiled down at him, placed in his lap, straddling his hips.

He shook his head, not even glancing down as his power radiated from his skin. "Ah, Karus. It was bound to happen to me, too." He kissed my jaw, catching my final tear that swelled there from the words of the woman who I knew would never stop pursuing what she longed to possess.

"She said—"

He slid his thumb to my lips. "Is it urgent to know?"

I smirked, heat pooling in my lap. "No."

"Then let me love you, Karus. Let me love the reason I glow."

# CHAPTER 6
# REV

**M**y love cried out for me in the early hours before dawn, before we'd have to take the steps toward our responsibilities. She called my name, writhing beneath my mouth. Her fingers pulled on my hair, urging my tongue closer to the warmth I pressed it to.

*By her breath*, I'd never tasted anything so sweet or lush as the desire that poured from her body because of me.

Our fire had never extinguished. Our passion had always burned. Even in the seven years she'd been gone from me, it had been there, waiting. A beacon so great, I could not escape its light.

How I had wanted her then. How I had wished to hold her, touch her, protect her from what had been done.

I gripped her hips, pressing them to the bed as she approached the release I'd give her. She'd become voracious, a fiend in my arms, greedily taking what she knew was hers to take from my lips, my teeth, my tongue.

It was a challenge to hold her there like that. Her moans seeped through my skin, and my body did not want to wait. It wanted to consume. It wanted to take her every inch of life and meld it to mine, weaving the threads of our bodies to mirror the threads of our bond.

My beloved shuddered beneath me as I pressed her legs open wide, sinking my tongue into what was mine to taste, mine to enjoy.

She pulled me to her mouth with nails that dug into the skin of my arms. Her tongue slid across my own, and I shared the delicate result of how I loved her.

Pushing me to sit back against the headboard, she slipped herself on top of me, sliding up and down my hard length while she gripped the headboard for balance.

Her hips rose and fell, bucking against me as she took her turn to love me. She was so beautiful and wild. Born an ethereal creature, I held no doubts fae blood flowed through her veins. Everything—even down to the last strand of white hair on her head which had taken over most of the original chestnut hue, was so very, very alluring.

She rode hard, her head tilting back as she shook the bed in her pursuit of another end from me. I tucked my arms around her, lifting her up. A whimper came from her throat, but I caught the protest on my lips.

I wasn't done with her.

I never could be.

I lifted her off the bed, her legs wrapping around me, and I carried her before the fireplace, murmuring between our lips the spell to kindle the flames before I laid her down on the soft, woolen rug.

I loved her best on the floor.

I loved her best sprawled out below me, my hands seeking to thread through hers, holding them down above her head. I loved her best closest to the ground where we both had come from in some way. Where we both took our power from the roots and the soil in Felgren. We'd both been channelers before we'd been Barons, and I sought to love her closest to where our lives had begun.

She sucked in a breath as I slid into her fully. Her knees pressed to my sides as she bucked her hips, doing her best to summon what she was ravenous for.

Pulling her bottom lip between her teeth, she looked at me pleadingly, a desperate moan of my name pulling from her panting breath.

Still pinning her hands to the floor, I withdrew myself before easily slipping back inside her. Her hips bucked up against me harder this time with the demand of more.

"Say it, Karus."

I didn't have to wait long before a pleading *please, Rev* came from her lips.

Karus was a woman who could never be tamed. Her glow could never extinguish, and I'd be a fool to try to control her. But in those moments where her ecstasy relied on me, I held a power over her she had only ever let *me* wield.

And I wielded it well.

My pace picked up as I gave her what she'd begged me for a hundred times. If there was anything I wanted control over, it was this. It was the rhythm of my hips driving into her repeatedly while she bucked and writhed beneath my body. It was the flash of green in her eyes overtaking the black eyes of a Baron.

"Rev," she panted as I thrust hard again and again, just as she liked it.

No. She loved it.

It was her last call to me that I was about to finish her into a state of limp euphoria, so I buried my face into her neck as I let go of any of the wait I had promised myself, spilling into her heat while her body slackened around me.

I let her fingers free and steadied myself above her on my elbows, sliding my hands through her hair to hold her head.

I kissed her deeply, fully, barely letting her come up for air as I tried to extend those moments of lust for her long after our bodies were spent.

She lifted her hands through my hair and pushed me to lay on my side, draping that long, smooth leg over my hip.

My back to the fire, I watched her green tendrils of magic pull the blanket off our bed and settle over our skin, streaked in the best kind of sweat.

I wrapped my arm under her head and pulled my forehead to hers. "Whatever it is she said to you, I'll keep you both safe, just as I promised."

She nodded, pulling the cover up over our shoulders, brushing her lips across mine before closing her eyes and falling into a few more hours of sleep.

# CHAPTER 7
# KARUS

"**B**eets?" I scowled at the array of food in front of me, curated by the one and only Clairannia.

"Yes, Karus, beets. Every one of these foods feeds your body which feeds your babe."

I glanced at Figuerah. She sat across from me next to her companion, Nyeimah, with a face contorted in disgust.

"Just don't eat too many of those," Clairannia continued, digging into a plate full of the breakfast I wish I was eating. "Beets can stain your teeth and make your pee pink."

In a tinge of nausea, I covered my nose and mouth for a moment. "There's no concern of eating too many, Clairannia. I'm not sure I'll be able to eat them at all."

I picked up my fork and moved around some of the other foods on my plate. My eggs had been scrambled with spinach, my strawberries had been chopped and mixed in some kind of tangy yogurt, and a vegetable hash had been fried in the form of purple potatoes, beets, onions, and carrots.

Not a single cinnamon bun graced my plate or the table. Not even a gravy and sausage meat pie.

I had months left of this.

Exhaling swiftly out of my lips, I stabbed a forkful of beet and potato and brought it to my mouth to chew, closing my eyes to get it down while catching up to the conversation of which route was best to take to the Attatok Mountains. Our new channelers were still there, waiting for us to arrive.

"I don't think so, either," Figuerah was saying. "Going too far east is risky. We should take the Carrow Road to the west of Hyrithia. It's not as straight of a journey, but it's definitely safer."

Clairannia asked, "When is Revich returning from retrieving Mychael?"

I forced a swallow from the mush in my mouth. "Later tonight."

She filled her fork full of cheesy eggs and continued, "Have you discussed which of the channelers here you're taking with you to the mountains?"

I speared a bit of egg on my fork, trying to convince myself to eat it. "We're bringing all of them."

Clairannia sputtered, "All six? Why?"

I laid down my fork in defeat. "There isn't enough time. We can't waste the weeks we'll be gone now that I cannot travel through Rev's portals. We're adding so much time onto the journey, and they need to have some training before we return with the new channelers from the mountains and the Spire. I offered for Rev to go without me, but he refused." I took a sip of my tea. At least Clairannia had let me have that with sugar and milk, just as I liked it. "I know it's unusual, but they'll have to train with us outside of Felgren."

"All of this is unusual," Figuerah added. "Two Barons. One of them a woman." She shook her head, sipping her own tea. "I for one, don't mind the upheaval of tradition one bit."

Clairannia nodded. "I'm just surprised, that's all. In another month or so, Karus, you should be feeling better—like your old self. I can come to you as far as Lythglyn, but then I must get back to the Spire. I'll see you there in a few weeks anyway."

I wrapped my arm around her shoulder. She tilted her head to mine, and I kissed the top of her thick black hair.

She lifted her head with a contagious grin. "Now, let's start discussing the nursery."

M‌Y BROTHER AND I WALKED THE PATHS OF FELGREN IN SILENCE.

All the other channelers were either nursing headaches from drinking too much at the celebration the night before or nursing the ones who were sick.

Surprisingly, Philius informed me he hadn't had anything to drink, even though drinking had been his favorite pastime when I'd reunited with him just months ago in Hyrithia.

Our boots crunched over pinecones and dry needles along our path. We hadn't chosen a destination—only a decision that we needed to clear some of the silence between us.

"Are you—" he began, just as I started, "It's okay—"

We chuckled and fell back to the quiet.

I cleared my throat. "You go first."

"Congratulations," he offered, folding his arms across his chest.

The noon sun beat down over the cloudless sky, filtering through the shifting leaves of the trees. The welcome shade cooled our path in a reprieve from the late spring, which stubbornly refused to give way to summer.

I gave a snort, saying, "Thank you. But I know you have much more to say than that."

"You haven't been listening to what I've been saying."

"So say something I will listen to, Big Brother." I grinned up at him, a good six inches taller than me.

He shook his head and his black coils bounced in the movement. He rubbed his face, and I once again thought of Heimlen. I'd guess I always would every time I saw the blackened hands of my brother. The residual evidence of the Black Fever, which had almost killed him, swam down his wrists in a spill of black ink against his mahogany skin.

I looked away quickly. The last thing I needed was to linger on a subject which made me furious.

"Be careful." He paused. "No, you won't listen to that. Be smart."

I laughed into the breeze, pushing his shoulder lightly.

"I mean it, Karus. I see that you won't leave Revich—"

"*Baron* Revich," I interrupted, only concerned about my companion's title when it came to my princely brother using it.

"Fine—*Baron* Revich. You're less likely to come back to Hyrithia with me now, but please, Karus. Be smart. Think all of this through. You passed the conduit trials, you passed the Baron trial." He glanced at me with a smirk. "I knew you had all of that in you, but the Blightress…" he trailed, his eyes furrowing along with his mouth.

"What do you know about her?" I pulled at a long blade of blooming grass along the path.

"Nothing before I saw the Blight. Only what you've told me anyway."

I remembered that day. Philius had been asking to see the Blight which had played a hand in the disease that had killed countless channelers in Hyrithia. The look on his face at the edge of the endless abyss in Felgren had been so strange.

I let the silence continue to fall as we walked.

He finally cleared his throat again and said, "I heard her that day. Or really, she heard me."

"*What?*" I cried, turning his body to face me. "Why didn't you say anything until now?"

"I wasn't sure at first. But I went back."

"Dammit, Philius!" I heaved a sigh and rubbed my eyes, ready for a nap. "We told you not to go there without us." I glared at him, putting my hands on my hips. "Have I told you the story of how the Blight tried to take me once?" I gestured in its general direction in Felgren where it had slowed to a snail's pace in growth, but still consumed hundreds of acres. "It is dangerous and powerful. Just like her. Talk about being smart," I lashed.

"I know, I just…I had to be sure. When you and Revich—" He paused and corrected, "*Baron* Revich took me, I asked the Blight what it had stolen from me. But I only asked in my mind. I just was…wondering, you know. Ever since I was sick and you were taken…nothing has been right."

I stepped forward and pulled him into a hug, not wanting him to see the tears that brimmed in my eyes. "What did you hear back?" I murmured into his shoulder.

He gave my body a quick squeeze and let go, turning back to the path and motioning for us to keep walking. "I thought I heard a voice in my head. I thought I heard the word *nothing*, but I wasn't sure."

"What about when you went back? *When* did you go back?"

"A few days before the party. After you'd passed your trials, and I knew for certain I would never be able to convince you to come back to Hyrithia with me."

He kicked a rock and was silent for another moment. I didn't push. I knew the best way to help my brother was to listen. All our lives we'd both been told what to do, where to go, and who we were, but none of that had been true for me. So, I waited. I waited for Philius to tell me his truth.

"I've always been the future king," he started. "A placeholder until my future queen bears a little girl. I was fine with that. I accepted it. Then you were taken. Nothing made sense anymore." He shrugged. "You're my sister. You were always supposed to be there, too. I thought maybe you'd become companions with Geyrand and have babies of your own."

I kept my mouth shut and stared out at the line of trees.

"I know. I know you didn't love him like that, but I guess in my head, I just assumed everything would fall into perfect place like we were told, and when it didn't…" He sighed, moving to sit on an old stump of a fallen tree off the path. "I felt like such a fool. One minute you were gone, the next we were told you were dead, and I couldn't save my sister from the circumstances of her being taken in the first place, so… I turned to drink. A stronger man would have found another way to cope."

I sat beside him, smoothing out my black skirts. "You didn't have the support you needed, Philius." I elbowed his arm. "But you do now."

He glanced to me in a frown.

"I mean it. You have me, and you have your fellow channelers who have really warmed up to you the past few weeks, considering what you were like when you got here. You have Baron Revich as well. You may not particularly like each other, but he does care about your future, and he does believe in you. I believe in you."

"The Blightress said she can train me."

"*What!*"

"When I went back, asking in my mind who was speaking, she revealed herself. She told me that the Black Fever had brought us closer as channeler and the origin of magic and that she wants me to come to her white stone palace and train."

"What the *fuck*, Philius!" I jumped up and faced him, my temper raging. I didn't even attempt to control it. "You're just telling me this *now*? Why did you wait so long? What did you say to her?"

He lifted his hands as if to placate me. "I'm sorry! I'm sorry! I really am. I just needed to process what I'd had learned about myself and that woman."

"*Process*?" Shoots of green, long and spindly, shot out from the base of the fallen tree, reaching toward the sky in new life fueled by all the power I now held as Baron. I closed my eyes and breathed deeply, taking several long inhales. My brother still sat, smartly keeping quiet.

I tilted my head back, letting the feeling of warmth and love wash over me.

Rev.

He'd felt that little outburst of anger and was sending his love back to me through our bond.

I took one more breath and nodded, biting my lips together and addressing Philius again. "What did you say back?"

He warily glanced at the shoots of saplings still slowly growing at his boots. "Remind me not to make you *really* angry."

"What did you say, Philius?" I repeated through my teeth.

"I asked who she was. She told me I already knew."

I rolled my eyes.

"Then, I asked her why she'd want to train me at all since I don't seem to have strong magic."

"And?" I huffed.

He shrugged. "She said I do…I'm just not training with the right person."

I laughed sardonically. "Oh, really?" I glanced toward the north as if I could see her there in her swampy forest and palace of white stone. "Did you tell her no?"

"No."

"*Philius*."

"It's not like I plan to actually do it. But I thought maybe I could get more information out of her. Maybe I'll learn something we can use in this plan of yours to get to her heart and destroy it. So, I asked her where I could meet her if I decided to accept her offer."

My nostrils flared and red petals of demorte flower bloomed at my feet.

"She said I could just open my mind to her and she'd be there to listen to my answer. I don't have to be near the Blight to speak to her."

I frowned. "You can speak to her in your mind at any time?"

"That's what she said."

"Have you tried?"

"No."

"Try it. Right now."

"And say what?"

I bit my bottom lip, staring down at the crimson blooms around my boots. "Ask her what she wants out of training you. Tell her you don't want any harm to come to your sister."

He rubbed his face and bent forward on his knees grimacing up at me. "I just ask that in my own head?"

"If she's really there, you should be able to tell. Like a little space inside that doesn't belong to you alone."

He quirked a brow.

"Just try it, Philius."

He scowled and closed his eyes.

I waited in the silence, chewing my bottom lip.

After a few minutes, his body rose, quick and ridged.

There she was.

Keeping his eyes closed, his face tightened into furrowed brows and a deep frown.

A few minutes more and his eyes flashed open, the golden hue large and brilliant in the midday light.

He opened his mouth to speak then closed it again, looking to the north as I had just done.

"Tell me," I whispered.

"She knows. She knows all of it. Your plans—everything."

"Fuck," I swore, ignoring the concern radiating to me through Rev.

"Fuck is right," he agreed.

~

"And so I said, 'Humans need more time to think about things, but I'll ask.' and then I flew here to tell you, and that's been my morning. What about you, Karus? You seem angry or something."

I wished I could fly as fast as Moria.

I wished I could portal.

It would be so much easier if I could just create a portal like Rev and transfer across Felgren back to the Fortress in an instant. Better yet, I wished I could portal like the Blightress with no restrictions on how many beating hearts could go through. I reached down to grab more of my black skirts as I ran, cursing myself for not bringing the lumens with us.

"I'm sorry, Moira," I huffed in response. "I'm going to have to speak to you more about this later. I need to get to Pompeii." She flew at my shoulder, keeping up with my jog back down the path Philius and I had walked. He'd stopped calling for me to wait for him and was now just keeping pace behind me.

"I wish you had wings, Karus. Maybe you just haven't grown them yet. You're part fae after all, and fae tend to change, you know. Over time we become new."

I scrunched my face, glancing at her above my shoulder.

"It's true!" she giggled. The sound echoed through the trees. "You have fae blood, so maybe you'll grow some, and we can fly through the forest together, or," she gasped, "maybe your parasite will be born with them!"

I glanced at her again, relieved to see the tall black towers of the Fortress ahead. "My *what*?"

"That thing you're growing. It is a parasite, isn't it? Clairannia said it would take parts of you and consume them."

I slowed to a walk, instinctively pressing a hand to my belly. "Moira," I puffed, "that's not…that isn't…" I rubbed my face. "You and I need to sit down and have a real talk about this. But not now. I'm sorry, my friend, but I really need to speak to Pompeii." I nodded toward the front doors of the Fortress. "Meet me here before dusk?"

She shrugged. "Sure. Bring——"

I waved her off. "Yes, yes, bring bread and butter. I will."

She waved at me and then fluttered to Philius, flying around his head several times while he failed to swat her away. Her laugher lit again before she flew off in a streak of shimmering wings.

"She's annoying," he puffed, catching his breath.

"She's particular," I retorted, waving at Pompeii who stood on the black stone steps in his usual green livery. "Go inside and gather the other channelers in Viridis for me, would you?"

"I want to hear——"

"No, Philius. I don't know what this is and cannot risk you hearing what I'm about to say."

He scowled but nodded. "It'll be hard to get Rell and Renn out of bed. They're probably still green."

"Help them then. You know what they need."

"Alright. Best I can do is get them to Viridis in forty minutes, but they might be uselessly hungover today."

He nodded to Pompeii and headed up the stairs into the Fortress.

"Baron Karus," Pompeii greeted, offering a hand to help me climb the steps. "You're quite flushed. I came as soon as I felt your call." He grinned and whispered conspiratorially, "You're getting better at this Baron-Overseer communication, you know. I was only tugged halfway out of my chair this time."

I chuckled, taking his hand, though only out of politeness. It would be a while before I needed help climbing stairs. "I'm glad I didn't send you to the ground like before. Let's head to the study. I need to speak with you on something urgent."

He waved me in first through the massive wooden doors of the Fortress. I strode across the foyer in haste to the study Revich and I shared. A few of the servants dipped their heads toward me, addressing me as Baron. I smiled at each warmly, though still feeling a bit out of place with the title.

Pompeii followed me into the study, and I moved behind the desk. I opened the leather-bound book I was currently using to journal my time as Baron, finding the next blank page. I motioned for Pompeii to sit across from the giant oak desk.

"I hope everything is alright with Baron Revich and Mychael," he started, lowering to the chair.

"They are just fine and will return together this evening as planned." I dipped my quill in the bottled black ink and wrote the day's date at the top of the page. "I need to ask you something strange."

He rose a brow, but nodded.

"It's important that you do not ask me further questions. I cannot answer them. You will understand why in just a moment."

"The mystery is intriguing, Baron."

I bit my lip. "I am going to say this once, and then you and I will not speak of it again until I can speak to Revich. Do you understand?"

He nodded. "Of course."

I glanced to his chest where I knew a dark bruise remained from the disease that had almost killed him just weeks ago. We called it the Black Lung—a disease that had spread from the Blight which I had grown from the Blightress's Blight in Viridis.

"I want you to search your mind and tell me if you can feel

something that does not belong. Then, I want you to try to speak to it, but only in your own thoughts."

He frowned. The black kohl across the lids of his honey golden eyes puckered in the movement. I'd never seen him this unnerved.

He took a deep breath, nodding in acceptance of his task.

I watched him carefully as he closed his eyes, his back straight in the chair, his golden complexion warm in the beams of sunlight filtering through the window behind me. His neat graying hair had been pulled into a tight bun at the back of his head as usual, and his beard and flicked mustache were trimmed as neatly as ever. Pompeii had been a well put together man every day I'd known him, except for the few weeks he'd been slowly dying to the Black Lung disease.

I waited in bated breath as the seconds ticked by.

And then, there it was. The jolt of realization.

His eyes flashed open, his frown deepening as his eyes flickered across my face and then across the room. He swallowed and nodded to me slightly.

I gave him a nod of encouragement and he took a deep breath, closing his eyes again. A few moments later, he shot up from his seat with his mouth agape as if he was about to speak.

I shook my head.

He clamped his mouth shut, a tick rippling in his jaw.

"Thank you, Pompeii. You may return to your duties."

He cleared his throat. "You are welcome, Baron Karus. I—" He stopped, pulling on the hem of his emerald green jacket embroidered in threads of gold. "I will wait for your call."

I watched him turn and leave in haste, closing the door behind him.

*"Such a clever Little Sprout."*

I knew she'd be there, reaching out to me in my mind once I had figured out the truth.

I gulped. *"Can you speak into the minds of every magic wielder or just the ones diseased by the Blight?"* I responded in my own thoughts.

*"Does it matter what I answer?"* she crooned. *"I know you well enough to guess that you'll investigate further."*

*"And what will I find?"*

"*I have a special…connection to those who've had the Blight living inside them. Think of it as a…parasite of sorts.*"

My heart raced. "*How* dare *you.*"

I heard her laugh as if she stood in front of me. "*Moira is such a funny little thing, isn't she?*"

"*I've locked you away in my head. I know you cannot read my thoughts.*"

"*I once read your thoughts, Karus. Before you cleverly shut me out from them. It's how I know you so well.*"

"*But you are in the minds of the fae?*"

"*I can enter the mind of any creature I've made.*"

I shelved that thought for later, replying, "*Lia?*"

"*Ah, yes. My sister has not let me into her mind in several centuries. Perhaps you could talk her into remedying that for me?*"

"*She is clever as well if she shut you out centuries ago.*"

A slow grin pulled at my lips in the silence of her reply.

"*Do you really think this plan of yours will work?*" I could hear how she tried to hide her anger. "*Have you thought of what might happen if you succeeded?*"

"*You'd leave us alone and we could live in peace?*"

"*And you? If I am gone, what part of you dies, too?*"

I clenched my jaw. "*I'd gladly give up my power if it meant——*"

"*I do not speak of your power, Little Sprout. I speak of you. If you destroy the heart of the one who made you, you destroy your own.*"

"*You're lying.*"

"*Perhaps. Though I have not lied to you since we first spoke. When I woke you from those terrible, terrible years, Karus. Ask yourself why I would choose to lie now.*"

"*To save yourself. And you did not make me. My mother and father made me.*"

"*Nonsense. I nurtured you just as much as Arah while you grew in her womb. I could nurture your own child if you'd like me——*"

"*You will not even speak of her.*" Black ink spilled over the page of my journal, toppled from my sudden rage.

"*Her?*" She chuckled, "*My, my, how history loves to repeat itself.*"

She didn't know. The Blightress didn't know my child was a girl before I had accidentally said so. That was hope that what she said was true, and I really had blocked her out from my thoughts.

I took a deep breath. "*Neither of us are the replacement for the child you lost.*"

"*On the contrary, Little Sprout. This is more proof that you very well could be. Just think of all we could do together. I have no doubts she is very powerful indeed.*"

I shivered in the silence I let creep in. My hands, clammy and sweaty, closed the journal, and I rose in haste, covering my mouth. "*You will have nothing to do with her. I will never speak of her to you again.*"

I cut our connection before she could reply, flying out of the study door and careening right down the corridor off the foyer that led to our rooms.

I barely made it to the basin of our washing room before I retched into the porcelain bowl.

## CHAPTER 8

# REV

Taking a moment to lean against the door to our rooms, I watched Karus sleep. Her face was turned to me as if she'd fallen to her exhaustion, waiting for me to come home.

She lay with her knees to her chest and her arms tucked in underneath her hair. Drool trickled down her cheek, which was exactly how I knew she'd fallen asleep quick and hard.

I waited there, wanting to give her more time to rest, considering the rage and fear that had filtered through her not long ago. I also wanted to run to her and pull her into my arms, telling her everything would be alright, regardless of if that statement was true.

I slipped my hand into my pocket to palm the rhyzolm. It was the only way I could feel our daughter. It hummed and thrummed, buzzing in my hand, stronger each day.

Our daughter. Our little girl.

I wiped my cheek.

Somehow, I'd gone from a desolate heart to one overflowing with love in the span of less than a year. Just months ago, I'd been watching Karus as her memories returned, hoping beyond anything that she was coming back to me after seven years without her.

And now?

Now we were bonded companions, and she carried our child. She'd become my partner in the Baronship, and she'd finally found her true place in this forest by my side, holding half the power of Baron, though far more powerful than me.

*By the breath of my beloved*, I loved her.

I couldn't wait any longer. I was at her side, smoothing the hair back from her face where white strands stuck to her lip.

She turned, falling to her back and stretching her arms over her head.

Her black eyes fluttered open and she brought a hand to her mouth to wipe her cheek. Her smile was slow coming as she blinked up at me, the dark of her irises just as slow to flicker into a brilliant emerald green.

"You're not supposed to be back until this evening," she yawned, pulling on my arm to join her.

I slipped my hands over her back, tugging her to my chest, kissing the top of her head. "When I felt those emotions of yours, I focused on getting back sooner."

She grunted.

"Geyrand and Vivianna are well. They are a happy family," I sighed. "I asked them to leave like we discussed."

She pulled away to catch my eye. "And?"

"They're waiting another week for Vivianna's recovery, and then packing up for Hyrithia."

She nodded, snuggling back into me. "Good."

"It was difficult to convince Geyrand to leave. In fact, it was Viv who really did the convincing. I'm not sure I had much of a part of it. Once she understood the danger of the Blightress living in the north, she started packing." I chuckled, "It was Mychael who took over cooking for a day."

"I think I could use some of his lemon ginger soup, honestly," she murmured.

"Have you been able to eat anything today?"

"Not really."

I kissed her temple and left the bedside to get her water.

"Thank you," she rasped, gulping from the cup.

"What was it that upset you earlier?"

She finished the drink, wiping at the corner of her mouth. "The Blightress has a mental connection to anyone affected by a disease created by the Blight."

My brows rose. "You mean the Black Fever and…"

"The Black Lung, yes," she finished. "Both Philius and Pompeii can speak to her in their thoughts. She knows our plans to train more channelers and get to her heart to destroy it. We have to assume she knows everything Philius and Pompeii know."

I rubbed my mouth. "That explains why Pompeii left so quickly when I asked after you. What about the channelers? Did you—"

She nodded quickly. "I did. None of them could find a place in their mind where she resides." She sighed heavily. "She didn't know that our child is a girl. I'm hoping that means I have successfully blocked her from my own thoughts, but I need to speak to Lia. The Blightress said Lia blocked her out centuries ago."

"Smart woman," I muttered, pulling open the sack I'd brought with me.

"That's what I said." She grinned, taking the pear I held out to her—the last of Geyrand's crop. Biting into the fruit, she spoke around her chewing, "I don't know what this means. Can we risk taking Philius with us? Can we risk this plan at all now?"

I wiped at a bead of juice on the corner of her mouth and replied, "Let's think about this. She knows we plan to train more channelers to destroy her heart and hopefully, dampen her power. If we can weaken her…" I caught Karus's gaze. "I won't take any more risks." She looked at me in surprise, but I continued, "She's threatened enough of you and our lives. I won't be satisfied until I myself feel that she has stopped breathing. Neither of us can defeat her as she is. She's too powerful for that. I felt it when she came to me during your trials. If we can weaken her, we—"

Karus cupped my cheek, nodding. "Alright, Rev. I'm with you on this. Destroy her heart, weaken her power, and then…" she drew a full breath. "Then we kill her."

∼

A DETAILED MAP OF ARCAYNEN ISLE WAS SPREAD OUT BEFORE US ON the white marble floor of Viridis. The garden library had once housed the most maps on the entire isle. Now, it contained only a handful of rolled pieces of parchment in long tubes tucked into the shelves. Three quarters of the stacks were mere crumbling dust when I had searched for the maps I knew Viridis used to hold. But the Blight, which had ravaged its way through Viridis for years, had taken its toll on this section.

"This trail"—Ilyenna pointed—"is no longer there. The Carrow Road was widened before I was born and this one lost its use."

Ilyenna, Clairannia, Figuerah, and I knelt on the hard floor, peering over the only complete map of Arcaynen I could find. Even outdated by a hundred years, it was the best we had.

"You're sure?" I questioned. "Because that road would certainly be the fastest route from Lythglyn to Radyx." I pointed to the small city at the base of the foothills of the mountains where Madame Zoreyah would meet us in one week. We would gather some of her channelers and others in the Spire to train in Felgren, building our forces against the Blightress.

Ilyenna nodded, cupping her swollen belly as she leaned forward, tracing the trail with her finger. "Even when it was used, it was difficult to traverse. The word Tectus means—"

"Hidden," I finished, nodding. Then glancing to her face, I put a hand on her shoulder. "Sorry. I don't mean to interrupt. Please, go on."

She gave me a sheepish grin and continued. "Yes. Tectus Trail means hidden trail in the magical language. It was carved out by sheep herders who traveled from the foothills of the mountains to the Spire to sell wool."

Figuerah added, "The story goes that the trail was outlawed by a Madame a hundred years ago, after the mother of one of the channelers killed by the mad Baron jumped from the highest cliff to her death. It's said to be haunted by her spirit and no one goes there."

Clairannia asked, "The Baron who killed his channelers after their Offerings?"

"Yes. Baron..." Figuerah looked to me to fill in the name.

"Ereyth," I answered. "Baron Ereyth was the man who killed his channelers right after he'd gathered them from their Offerings in Hyrithia." I sighed and rubbed the back of my neck. "Karus recently learned the Blightress had a hand in that as well."

Clairannia gasped. "The Blightress actually killed them?"

"No. Not according to her, anyway. The Blightress told Karus she killed the Baron after he murdered his channelers. She claimed it wasn't the first time Ereyth had hurt women."

"Why would she care what he did?" Ilyenna asked, sitting back and tucking her feet underneath her.

"I don't know," I answered. "All I know is that event began the Treaty and Baron Thalius had already been training as Baron Ereyth's replacement for a year. Baron Thalius was the one to sign the Treaty and adhere to it."

"No channelers could be taken from Hyrithia?" Ilyenna questioned.

I huffed, staring down at the map. "Not until Karus anyway."

"Baron Thalius…" Figuerah started. "Where do I know that name?"

I didn't glance up as I mumbled, "Heimlen's predecessor."

Figuerah's hand reached for mine and squeezed. "Then we got you. Then Karus." She smiled, her honey eyes sparkling as Clairannia placed her hand over mine as well. "The best Barons Felgren has ever seen."

I chuckled, pulling my hand out from under theirs and squeezing them both back before standing and shoving them into my pockets. "Thank you for your help. It's settled for certain then. We leave in the morning. All eleven of us."

"You're still bringing Philius?" Figuerah asked, folding her arms at her chest. "You said the Blightress can access his mind. What if Karus cannot teach him to block her out before we leave? What if he lets slip something important?"

I bent down to roll up the map, sliding it back into its blackened wood tube. "She can help him. She's the only one who's been able to help him in anything so far. We won't discuss important details around him. We'll keep him in the dark, but he needs to train, Figuerah."

She scoffed. "What he needs is a boot to his royal behind."

I laughed, catching Clairannia's snicker. "Perhaps. But I believe in him. He has a part yet to play here. I can feel it."

Figuerah sighed, pulling an arm around Clairannia's shoulders. "If you're done with us, Rev, we've got a nursery to help plan."

Clairannia squealed excitedly and began talking about a certain painting she had in mind for the ceiling of the baby's room.

I tucked the wooden tube under my arm, hoping Viridis would let me leave with it. I turned to Ilyenna who stood, gripping the railing overlooking five floors to the garden courtyard below.

I tugged at her sleeve, saying, "Don't hold that. I don't trust the integrity of these rails anymore." I gestured around as she let go and took a step back. "While we're gone, this is Pompeii's project. He's already ordered workers from the Spire to come replace what's been lost to the Blight."

She hummed in agreement. "The rails on this floor are solid. It's the third floor to the east you need to replace first." She pointed across the hall to the blackened rails below.

I glanced back at the section she had been holding. Quirking a brow her way, I stepped to the golden metal and gripped the rail, shaking it hard. It didn't budge.

"How could you—"

"It's my lapis magic, Baron Revich." Her hand hovered over the rail, revealing a wake of shining gold. Her blonde curls bounced over her plump, pink cheeks and her smirk turned into a grin, gracing her pale skin with one single dimple folded into her light freckles.

I offered her my arm as I turned toward the stairs to escort her out of Viridis, thinking of all she could do to help the mining town I had grown up in. "Ilyenna, have I ever talked to you about the Hallow Marshes?"

# CHAPTER 9
# KARUS

Sipping my lemon ginger soup, I quietly regarded Lia. She reminded me of a honeybee flitting from task to task, hardly a pause in her flutter around the kitchens.

We hadn't given her much time to prepare food for eleven of us to travel across the isle, and when I'd mentioned that we'd be able to pick up more supplies in Lythglyn, Radyx, and the Spire, she'd mumbled something about the actual quality of supplies we'd find there.

I blew on another spoonful of soup and smiled at her as she glanced my way, probably to check that I was actually eating, well aware I had little appetite.

Servants came in and out of the kitchens, some of them occasionally snagging some fruit or bacon off the communal tray as they carried on with keeping the Fortress running like her little worker bees.

Lia addressed her primary cook. "Jesslyn, I'll have you feed the chickens, please. I've not had the time, and they're likely in a ruckus fit about it."

Jesslyn nodded and replaced her apron with a different one before heading out the door that led to the forest.

I admired Lia even more now that I knew she was the Blightress's sister, just as old, living her endless years here in the Fortress instead of out there as the lapis conduit she once had been. She had arrived back in her birthplace of Felgren around the time Heimlen had been chosen as the next Baron. I wondered if he'd ever questioned how the cook of the Fortress never seemed to age and had lived just as long as the hundred years he had.

"Whatever reason you're watching me, love, it'll have to wait until I can get this dough in the oven. Eight loaves extra I have to bake, and I haven't even begun to gather the cheese from the cellar."

Realizing Lia was speaking to me, I cleared my throat and answered, "I'm sorry. I didn't mean to stare, but I do need to speak with you."

She continued kneading the sticky white dough and nodded. "I have the feeling I know who it's about." Sprinkling flour over the surface, she tucked the ends of the dough underneath, shaping it into a round pillowy bundle before placing it on a tray and covering it with a cloth. She then pulled more stretchy dough from a large bowl and began to repeat the process. "I've made a list of the cheeses I need to pack over there." She nodded to a piece of paper by the stove. "If you'd like to help, you can collect them, and I'll be able to speak with you sooner."

I forced down one more sip of soup and brought my bowl to one of the kitchen maids who took it from me to wash.

I picked up the list of cheeses on my way out of the kitchens. The cellar doors were nestled into the ground at a slant as two worn wood slats with iron hinges. I'd seen them plenty of times, but never had a reason to enter the cold storage under the Fortress. Bending down to pull the handles, they creaked loudly and fell back with a resounding thud.

I skimmed the list again and murmured, "*Illuminare*" bringing my ball of green light to hover over my hand and glow in a steady pulse that matched the beat of my heart.

I began my descent into the cold cellar, shoving aside memories of the last time I stepped underground. The black stone steps were worn in the middle, representing the hundreds of years of footfall from hundreds of years of the Fortress's servants.

Each step echoed into an open space below—so dark, even the soft glow of green couldn't penetrate my path downward. I stopped for a moment, laughing to myself. It was just a cellar. No danger, no looming monsters or deathly plants to ensnare me. No ancient woman claiming me as hers and forcing me into abyssal black for two weeks to wander.

I rolled my shoulders and tightly gripped my list with its neatly sprawled letters. In a deep breath, I whispered to myself, "I'm just here for cheese."

The bottom of the space loomed ahead in a long, narrow walkway with wooden shelves housing a countless array of jars, bins, and bottles. As I found the last step, I held my light up high to see that the cellar ended in a stack of oak barrels.

As I had suspected, Lia kept a well organized pantry. The long wooden shelves were labeled, making it easy enough for anyone to find what they needed in this space under the Fortress.

I walked along the shelves, growing used to the damp, musky smell. I held my light up to each one, reading the labels in perfect swooping letters. Lia's cellar hosted various herbs and spices, along with jars of lard and honey, and bowls of stones in many colors. I was curious what uses she found for all of them, knowing she used her lapis magic in her cooking. I wandered all the way down the cramped aisle, ending at the enormous stacked barrels. The cheeses, eggs, and milk were kept at this end, and I shivered in the cold, understanding why.

I unhooked a linen sack from its peg along the shelves and began to fulfill the list. By the looks of it, Lia planned for twenty people instead of eleven to be traveling for two weeks across the isle. I carefully laid the last block of my favorite white, crumbly cheese on top of the others. My task completed, I pulled the strings of the sack and hauled it over my back. The weight surprised me, and it swung lopsidedly, banging into one of the stacked barrels.

I sucked in a breath as the barrel teetered, then toppled to the stone floor, spilling a mound of flour across the aisle.

Cursing in disbelief at my clumsiness and the fact that Lia was going to scold me endlessly, I righted the barrel and looked around for a broom. Instead, my gaze caught the iron hinges of a door where the barrel had been neatly stacked against the wall.

*I should ask Lia what this is,* I thought, reaching out to touch the old wood.

*I should call to Revich,* I mused, as I used my trailing power to lift the few barrels still stacked, leaving the door just sitting there, waiting to be opened.

I leaned on its heavy surface, listening for any sounds and using my iumenta magic to feel for any sign of life on the other side, finding nothing.

I sighed, knowing I couldn't do this. At least not alone, and at least not without asking Lia first. I'd made enough choices in my life without thinking them through, and as I pressed my hand to my belly, I knew I couldn't afford another one.

I turned around instead, trying to decide how best to tell Lia about the spilled flour. I jumped in a gasp, grabbing at my chest to see her there, standing in front of me, her orb of dull gray light pulsing above her palm.

"Lia! I'm sorry about all of this. I'll get it cleaned up and get your pantry back to what it was."

My cheeks reddened, and I stepped to move around her when she asked in a low murmur, "Would you like to see, Baron Karus?"

I glanced at the hidden door behind me. "See what exactly?"

"A story of the past long forgotten."

"Lia…" I started. "What have you hidden down here?"

She shrugged. "It was not mine to hide. I only blocked the door to avoid questions from the kitchen maids. But you are Baron of this Fortress, and you will understand the meaning of what I can show you."

She maneuvered around the barrels, stopping at the door. Pulling at the ring of keys at her skirts, she found the one she needed and turned it into lock. The door swung inward, opening into another long corridor.

I swallowed my nerves, stepping in behind Lia, following her steps with my light down the hall. We entered a small, circular room, bereft of any warmth at all. My breath flowed from my mouth in puffs of what looked like green billows against the orb I held. A singular desk and chair looked about to crumble to dust against the curved wall, but it was the stone pillar in the center which held the secret of the space. The white sandstone I'd seen once before, rose from the floor in a solid block, meeting the height of my chest.

As I reached out to touch the dusty surface, Lia finally spoke. "It held her heart."

I frowned in a silent chill.

She continued, "Visalia's heart was brought here centuries ago by Baron Adaynth. He suspended it here, above this pillar." She paused and I swept my hand over the gritty white surface. "That is until she took it back."

"Tell me what happened." I glanced around the cramped space, guessing we were somewhere underneath the foyer of the Fortress. "Tell me the story of your sister."

## CHAPTER 10
# REV

After I'd escorted Ilyenna back to her room to rest, and checked in with the channelers nursing headaches, I headed back toward Viridis. I needed a place where I could sit and think through our plan in peace.

Just as we had planned months ago in Hyrithia with the leaders of the isle, we would gather our extra channelers and train them quickly. We needed to destroy the Blightress's heart before she showed her next move and became too powerful to stop.

I palmed the massive rhyzolm at the ancient doors of Viridis and murmured my name into the dark corridor. A viridescent portal bloomed, and I stepped through. The waves of lavender and jasmine on the breeze welcomed me back to the sanctuary I had missed all those seven years Karus had been gone from herself. She was right to push for its return. She was right to trust that I'd make sure she made it out of the *Simulair Solum* spell she had used to destroy the Blight, which had desecrated this place months ago.

I eyed the spaces that needed the most work, agreeing with Ilyenna that those bannisters on the third level looked more than weakened. They looked as if they'd crumble to dust at the slightest touch.

I shoved my hands into my black pockets, squeezing the rhyzolm for the tenth time in the hour since I'd left Karus, urging her to try to get something in her stomach. I felt her somewhere near the foyer of the Fortress, or at least, I felt our child there. She was the only living thing I could sense anymore with the rhyzolm.

I stepped down the marble stairs into Viridis's courtyard. Peeling white birch trees and mounds of flowers greeted me while bees buzzed and birds flew above. All was as it should be in the garden library of Felgren. Wandering my way through the paths, I sat against a tree, pulling on a wide blade of grass and holding it taut between my hands. I blew into it, and a loud whistle floated on the breeze. Pompeii had taught me the trick when I'd first arrived in Felgren as a young man determined to prove himself worthy of the title of Baron. I hoped to someday teach the skill to my daughter.

I leaned my head back against the tree, arms draped over my knees, promising myself I wouldn't let my exhaustion catch up to me as my eyes drifted closed. My thoughts wandered to what Karus had told me she discovered this morning. The Blightress was in the minds of anyone diseased by the Blight. How many survivors of the Black Fever were there? Thousands of lives had been lost from the disease Heimlen had created in order to get Karus to Felgren, but we needed numbers on the amount of survivors who now bore the mark of the fever in black hands and wrists.

The Blightress had told Karus the power of Baron came from her. Lia confirmed it, so was she there somewhere in my own mind?

"You won't find her here."

The voice startled me, and I opened my eyes to find I was no longer lying against a tree in Viridis.

I blinked rapidly and rubbed my face before squinting in the dying light of a sunset that filtered through the trees of my child-hood home. The muddy town of Mire lay in the distance, with its marsh forest and wood cabins trailing smoke from chimneys.

Instead of a birch tree in Viridis, I found myself leaning against one of the great marsh trees from which rhyzolm was mined. A man sat across from me, around the same age as myself, his eyes closed to the orange sunset. His dark brown hair was cut short with a longer length on the top that curled across his widow's peak. He wore a Baron's clothes, and when he opened his eyes, a dark hazel gaze stared back at me.

"Why am I here?" I asked, reaching into my pocket for the rhyzolm to find that it wasn't there.

The man shrugged. "You're the one who brought us here, not me."

I gripped the tree root to rise, and his hand shot out to pull me back down. "Where's Karus?" I demanded.

"She's fine, Revich. She's with Thalia in the cellars. You're dreaming in Viridis. Nothing to get all heroic over."

I studied him. "I know you."

His laugh came in a boom, and he swept his hands down his face, responding, "I would hope you know me."

"If I'm dreaming, why are you here with me? You've never been in my dreams before."

He shrugged again. "You were the one asking questions before you fell asleep. You must have found that place."

"What place?"

"That dark cavern you love to keep locked. The one where the true amount of power you hold resides." He rose a brow. "The place where I gave you everything I've given all Barons, and you decided you wanted to hand over half of it to your lover."

I took a deep breath, filling my lungs with the scent of my upbringing—moss and mud. I leaned forward, holding out my hand.

His lips tilted upward as he took it.

"Rev," I said with a shake.

"Adaynth," he replied.

I took my hand back, resting my arms at my knees. "So, Adaynth, first Baron of Felgren, do you live in Karus's dreams, too, or just mine?"

He chuckled, letting his head fall back against the massive tree root. "I live in the minds of all Barons. It's where I've been since my body gave out, and I discovered a way to keep my power from going back to Visalia."

I nodded slowly. "Do you talk to Karus in her mind, too?"

He shook his head. "Not since the day you put her through the Baron trial."

I nodded again. "How do we stop the Blightress? How did you do it before?"

He stared up at the tall trees with spindly leaves at the top. "It won't work like before."

"Then help me figure out how to do it now. She has threatened to take our child. She has threatened to take our power." I leaned forward, trying to catch his eye. "Tell me what to do."

"She's broken."

"I don't care what she is—how do I stop her from destroying our lives?"

"I don't exactly know."

"What *can* you tell me, then? What happened between the two of you hundreds of years ago that made her into this?"

"Our daughter died at birth. Did you know that? Of course you did." He took a breath, folding his legs and leaning forward.

I swallowed heavily. "I'm sorry. I truly am, but I won't let her take mine. I won't let her take Karus. I will do anything, Adaynth. I will do whatever it takes to—"

"I kept her heart locked under the Fortress for about eight hundred years."

Shocked into silence, I frowned at the first Baron across from me.

"You didn't know that, now did you?" He laughed, shaking his head. "Absurd, isn't it? I remember the day I told her she had my heart just as well as the day she forced her own from her chest and handed it to me." He swept his fingers through his hair. "Blood and all. She couldn't die by it, and she told me she couldn't live by it either. She said that to me on the day our child was stillborn. The woman I loved ripped her beating heart from her chest, Revich, and gave it to me like it was nothing." He wiped a hand under his nose and sniffed, catching my eyes with his. "That is what I mean when I say she is broken."

A shiver ran through me, and we sat still in the silence of the

Hallow Marshes. Time passed. Minutes went by. I carefully observed him as he gazed out into the marsh. There was more to this story that he wasn't telling me. I could feel it there between us, hanging heavily in what he didn't say.

"So you kept her heart with you?" I asked under my breath. "Beneath the Fortress?"

He cleared his throat in a rasp. "I did. When I had the Fortress built to have a place to train channelers, I kept her heart beneath it. Without it, she'd changed. She wanted to find a reason why our child was dead." He looked back at me stating, "There wasn't one. Regardless of who she decided to blame, there wasn't a reason for what happened to us. She grew cold. She grew dark and angry—wrathful. When I would visit her, she began to speak of taking back all the power she'd ever given. To me. To Lia. To Felgren. She created the Blight then. It was unlike anything I'd ever seen."

"How did you—"

"The sun." He nodded toward the last sliver of light on the horizon. "I discovered that warmth and eternal rays of light around her heart could hold her power at bay. It was an accident, really. The story goes that the great Baron Adaynth took up his mantle as savior and stopped her. But that wasn't it. No,"—he shifted, running a hand through his hair that fell over his face—"I just wanted her to be warm again. I saw her as often as I could, but she wouldn't let me touch her after our child's death, so I gave her my warmth the only way I knew how. I kept her heart under the Fortress and used everything I had to hold the *Simulair Solum* spell around it. She never once asked where I had taken her heart, and I never revealed it."

I suppressed a chill, finally getting answers to legends we'd only guessed at for hundreds of years. "You kept the *Simulair Solum* spell around her heart to dampen her power?"

"Yes. I used my love for who she once was to strengthen it. And it worked for so long. Even when I'd had enough of living in the flesh without her and gave up my body, I discovered I could reserve some of my power to hold her heart there." He sighed, shaking his head. "That was until Ereyth."

Hatred sifted through his expression. "I knew he wasn't strong enough to withstand her. I knew she'd been attempting to get her heart back from the Fortress. For what reason, I didn't know at the time. Now I understand it was to regrow her power. Ereyth was weak, preferring channelers based on their bodies rather than their talents." He shook his head. "When he let her into his mind, I tried to force her out, and then we held a silent battle. She won. She convinced him to find her heart in the Fortress and bring it to her on the night of the Offerings in Hyrithia. Ereyth desired more than power—he desired her, and she promised him many things. On the night he murdered his channelers in his madness, she hunted him down and killed him, taking her heart with her. I saw her there in his mind right before he died. She smiled at me like she knew I could see. Then the power shifted to Thalius, and I didn't know what happened to her heart after that." He glanced at me. "I do now."

"You've seen it? In Karus's mind?"

"No, but I've heard things here and there. Enough to know she's grown it. It beats in rage, Revich. It fuels her."

"So what do we do now? Can we destroy it?"

"I don't know. You can certainly try."

I nodded. "Can she be killed?"

"She doesn't think she can."

"Do you think she can?"

"She's already dead in my eyes, Revich. She died a long time ago."

I swiped my hand over my mouth, hiding the surprise of that admittance. "What else is she capable of?"

Adaynth cocked his head and held out his hand. "Would you like me to show you?"

Taking a deep breath, I nodded and reached out again to grip his hand in mine.

～

DESOLATION.

Desolation of a vast, empty land.

No, not empty.

Wrath and fear seeped from every inch of the Blight around us.

Every crater of pitch black, every strangle of abyssal dark vines, emitted a hatred so thick, I could choke in the dense pressure of it.

I'd never gone into the Blight except for the one occasion Karus ran through it to save Moira from a sure death. Back then, I hadn't taken in just how devoid of life the Blight really had been, or how it was now, deep in the depths of Adaynth's memories.

"This isn't even her worst," he warned, standing next to me in the desecration of his memory's Felgren Forest.

I surveyed the Blight some more. Enormous black vines, the width of tree trunks, wound over the soil which bloomed in white patches of death in a sure sign of decay. Thorns, sharp as knives, rose from each one as the vines moved, encasing the once-living trees in an embrace of death. Mist wove through my hair and across my cheek as a beckoning—a pull to lay down into the damp soil and dissolve into the earth just as thoroughly, just as slowly, as the creatures who had once roamed the forest had done.

The stench alone was enough to bring bile into my throat, and I swallowed back the vomit. The decay of bodies and blood poured through every inch of my skin, choking me in a successful attempt to force me to retch. I covered my mouth and nose, inhaling short bursts of breath to avoid taking in the scent of rotting decay all at once.

"This is what she did before her heart had grown," Adaynth murmured, arms crossed at his chest. "This is nothing compared to what she is capable of now. Revich,"—he grabbed my shoulder, forcing me to look at him instead of the silent rage around us— "do you hear me? She can do more than this. Before I dampened her power through my warmth, she was beginning to create…things. Beasts and creatures that had not existed before."

"The fae?"

"Yes, but more than that. The fae creatures as you know them are mere children compared to what she was attempting just before…" he choked a moment, coughing into his sleeve. "Just before I was able to stop her for a time."

I shook my head, surveying the hatred around us once again. "We cannot stop this as we are now. We will need time to train more conduits before we can rid the isle of this. How do we get more time?"

Something ticked in his jaw for a moment before it was gone.

"What is it?" I pressed. "You're keeping something else from me."

"I've done something. Something I wasn't sure was possible, but she asked, so I tried."

"Who asked?"

He flicked his gaze to mine. "Karus. That day she accepted the power of Baron, she asked for the power to make you safe, happy, and loved, Rev, and I *tried*. I did what I could."

I swallowed back my rising anger. "What did you do?"

"I don't think you'll ever know. But this"—he gestured around us—"this can be stopped." He sniffed, his face blurring before me. "This does not have to be your future. Either one of you."

The dull glow of Viridis grew as my eyes fluttered, and I tried to keep my focus on the first Baron's face.

"If you're strong enough to stop it."

My eyes shot open under the birch tree as I woke in the library. I panted, inhaling the fresh scent of grass and newly grown blooms that surrounded me in the garden where I had sought rest for just a moment.

I reached into my pocket to find the rhyzolm. Karus was still in the foyer of the Fortress. Or the cellar, according to Adaynth.

*If you're strong enough to stop it.*

I knew I was. Whatever choice came before me, I'd choose the one which kept Karus safe. Which kept our child safe. There was no other choice for me, regardless of what that meant for my own future.

# CHAPTER II
# KARUS

As Lia told the story of Visalia's stillborn child, I pressed my own hands protectively over my belly.

"By the time I arrived," she finished, "Visalia's babe was dead. There was nothing anyone could do."

"And she was overdue? By how long?" I asked.

"Four weeks, give or take."

"It was a girl?"

"Yes."

"Visalia never recovered."

"She did not."

"She tore out her own heart and gave it to him."

"Yes. It was then that I left. I couldn't watch my sister turn into a monster."

My lip trembled. "You left her? In her darkest hour, you left your sister?"

Lia shifted on her feet, her head bent. "I…I struggled to watch the two people I loved most fall apart. She blamed Adaynth for the child's death. I,"—she patted down the skirts of her apron—"I didn't stick around to find out why. I know it was wrong. I know I should have stayed, but—"

"You just *left* her?" I scoffed. "How could you do it? She'd just lost her child, Lia, of course she was broken."

"I have spent time at the bedsides of countless mothers since then to do what I could to make up for—"

"But you left her!" I lashed out.

"I was young. I didn't know what would become of her or what she would be capable of after that. I know I should not have left."

"Visalia experienced the darkest moments of her life without the sister she loved. What happened to her is no excuse for what she has done and continues to do, but I see her more clearly now." I turned toward the door, adding, "I see you both in clarity."

I rushed back through the long corridor, picked up the sack of cheeses, and with a wave of my hand, gathered the flour on the stone. I didn't bother finding a broom, and I didn't bother to look behind me to see if Lia would follow.

I climbed the steps out of the cellar, filling my lungs with fresh Felgren air, scattering the flour into the wind. I burst into the kitchens, dropping the cheese on the small table, and followed our bond straight to Revich in Viridis.

**CHAPTER 12**

# REV

I let my hands slide along the titles in the Felgren Origins section of Viridis. After waking, I'd headed straight there, searching for the book I'd never read, but Karus had told me plenty about.

It was the only book in all of Viridis we'd ever found about the Blightress, full of the tales parents whispered to their children at night to keep them in bed. My own mother and other townsfolk had spoken some of these stories, detailing the deeds of evil woman who would steal you in the night and show you her wrath if you misbehaved. I was promised these stories were not true and that the Blightress did not exist. She was recognized as merely a herald of your misfortunes if you gave into your anger.

I sensed Karus enter Viridis and find her way to me. Her arms wrapped around my waist and her cheek rested on my back. I took one of her hands, bringing it to my lips to kiss the inside of her wrist, finishing the last few lines of the rhyme I was reading.

"Lia left her," she whispered solemnly. "Visalia pulled out her own heart from her chest, gave it to Adaynth, and Lia decided to leave her."

I marked my place with a piece of ribbon and closed the book.

Pulling Karus to my chest, I tried to ease what I knew she feared. "No one is going to leave you. Not me, not Clairannia or Figuerah." I kissed the top of her hair. "Not even Moira, though I could see her wandering off for months, not realizing that counted as leaving."

She gave a snort into my shirt.

"I spoke to Adaynth," I said softly, leaning against the shelf, holding her tightly. "He came to me in a dream. He told me their story and showed me the Blight as it was when he was alive. He kept her heart below the foyer."

"I know," she mumbled. "I was just there with Lia who told me everything, too. Is it terrible I feel some pity for the Blightress?" She lifted her head, searching my gaze with green eyes in a thick ring of black. "Everyone she loved, everything she had hoped for was ruined." She shook her head. "I understand that at least. I understand how she broke and how she turned to anger as a comfort. What she has done is wrong, what she is doing is wrong, but…"

"I know. I feel it too."

"What if we can help her heal? What if we can find a way to soften her hatred and fear?" She tapped the cover of *Legends of the Blightress: A Collection of Tales Passed Down Through Centuries* in my hand. She recited from memory,

> *"Without anger, she laughed in mirth.*
> *Without love, she left them bleeding.*
> *Without hope, she walks the earth.*
> *Without fear, her heart is fleeting."*

She continued, "What if what she truly fears is being alone? Being unloved? I hate her, but I pity her. That could have just as easily been me."

"No, Karus, you could never be what she is." I cupped her face, lifting her gaze to mine. I knew my eyes had filtered to blue when a smile pulled at lips. "I am your sky, remember? Even in the darkest of nights, I'll be there, waiting for your light to return. I'll hold you up forever, just as I've always done. You have my love, my heart." I pulled her head back to my chest, kissing the top of her head. "You always will."

She sniffed, wiping the tears on her face. "I'd like to name our daughter after you."

I raised a brow, pulling her back to ask, "What's the female equivalent of Revich?"

She laughed, biting her lip. "No, not Rev. Sky. I'd like to name her as the magical language for sky. A reminder of who her father is and the role you'll play in her life, too."

I slipped my hands through the back of her hair, pressing my forehead to hers and declaring, "Saelyn is a beautiful name, and I promise, my sun, my moon, I'll hold her up, too."

# CHAPTER 13
# KARUS

Watching all the people I loved pack their things into the two carriages at the edge of Felgren caused a lump in my throat I couldn't swallow. The turmoil of emotions from the last six weeks since the trials had me constantly breaking down into sudden joy, sudden fear, and sudden tears of sadness. I turned my back on the scene to say goodbye to the forest I loved, the lumens I loved, the Overseer I loved, and Lia, whom I was disappointed with, but still cared for deeply.

Parvus bit the hem of my black Baron skirts, pulling me away from the line of trees that marked the edge of Felgren.

"I know, I know." I sighed, scratching behind his ears covered in a thick moss. I stared into his eyes which had grown more angular and redder in the weeks since the Blightress had helped heal the lumens from their fall into the underground tunnel.

He whined looking up at me, his tongue pulled into his mouth for once. I wiped a tear and bent to his face where I held it. "It's only two weeks. It will be nothing to you. And no, you cannot come with. You and Rauca need to stay here and get better."

I scratched his neck, feeling the vines growing beneath my fingers.

Figuerah approached, assuring, "Madame Zoreyah might know what to do about this change in the lumens. We'll ask her about it when we get to Radyx."

She had examined both of the giant wolves thoroughly, finding nothing wrong with them except the vines, thorns, seeds, and moss that bloomed over their coats of fur each day.

"Everyone is saying their last goodbyes and we're ready." She squeezed my hand and gave a last hug to Parvus before joining Clairannia in one of the carriages.

Lia stepped up beside me, holding out a pine green silk band with one and a half moons embroidered across the front. "I have something for you, love."

I took it, smoothing my hands over the intricate design.

"I had just enough time to finish it last night," she added. "Do you like it?"

Holding the growth band for my child, I nodded, pressing my lips closed to stop the tremble I felt all the way to my heart. I'd wear the band all throughout Saelyn's growth, adding moons until I gave birth. Then we would wrap the band around her crib to bring peace and good health in her first year of life.

"It's beautiful. Thank you, Lia." I handed it back to her and turned so she could tie it around my waist.

"I wasn't where I should have been all those years ago." She sniffed behind me, finishing the bow. "I won't make that mistake again. So, I'll be here when you return for all of it. I promise you."

I pulled her into a hug and held on tightly. Somehow, she felt like more than a friend, but family. "How do I know I've kept the Blightress out? How can I be sure she isn't there right now, inside my thoughts?"

"You must shove her away. Put her in the darkest corner of your mind. Close the door on her, and she cannot get through. I know you have the strength to do this."

"I feel her there," I murmured into the breeze. "But I have covered her corner in webs. In ice. In a dark place. She can speak to me, but if I don't respond, she goes away."

Lia pulled back to look at me. "She used to speak to me often. I decided that if I did not respond, she would stop."

"Did she?"

"Eventually, yes."

I bit my lips, hesitating on my next question. "Can she be healed, Lia? Maybe we don't need to destroy her, maybe we just need to—"

"She's been broken longer than she's been good. Remember that."

I straightened my shoulders, nodding. "I haven't seen Moira today, so if she returns, please let her know when we'll be back."

"I will."

I smiled and left her side, walking the path that led to where Pompeii and Mychael embraced each other as they said goodbye. Mychael whispered something in his ear, and I slowed my pace to give them privacy as they shared a long, deep kiss.

I bent down to pull a few yellow blossoms growing in a patch along the dirt path, waiting until the last possible second to leave. I hadn't been so hesitant in leaving at our companion celebration, but now, so much had changed.

I was growing our child.

I couldn't go through Rev's portals.

The Blightress lived in the minds of those touched by diseases of the Blight.

She'd had a stillborn child, and Lia had left her.

The most haunting of all, the Blightress had ripped her own heart from her chest and gave it to Adaynth. He had kept it warm for centuries before she convinced Baron Ereyth to steal it back for her. We'd learned so much and had even more to do.

"*Baron Karus.*" Pompeii's voice interrupted my somber thoughts. I lifted my eyes to say goodbye, but he was still far ahead, his back to me, watching Mychael climb into the seat next to the carriage driver.

I jolted upright at the discovery that he was speaking to me in my mind.

"*Bring him back.*" He turned his head, still fifty feet away, catching my gaze with golden eyes lined in kohl. *"Please, Karus. Bring back the man I love."*

I swallowed, replying through my mind, *"The Blighted trees in Viridis…I grew those."*

He nodded, looking back to watch everyone gather into the carriages. Rev leaned against one of them, patiently waiting for me.

*"I grew the Blight that caused the Black Lung. The Blightress gave me that power. We are both in your mind."*

*"Yes. I found you there with her, but seeing how pale you grew upon the confirmation, I didn't want to upset you more."*

I held onto my buttercup stems tightly, following the path to reach his side. "I promise not to pry into your thoughts," I spoke upon the wind gusting around us. I watched Rev smile in the breeze as it blew through his hair.

Pompeii said with urgency, "I don't care what you do to my mind, just bring him back." He faced me, pressing his hands to my shoulders.

"We're not even going to her heart yet, this is just to—"

"Do not underestimate her determination." His usually pleasant face broke into something hard. "I have heard her cries of rage. I have dreamed of what this forest once was. She will not stop, and she will not let anyone get in the way of what she wants."

He glanced once again to the carriages. Several heads of the people I loved and must care for, stuck out of the carriage doors, waiting for me to finally join them. "Bring all of them back."

"This is quite the ominous goodbye," I said in a nervous laugh. "But I promise."

He pulled me into an embrace and admitted, "It's the only goodbye I can give you."

A shiver ran up my spine and he let go, stepping aside so I could continue on to join everyone else.

"Ready?" Rev asked, taking my hand.

I took one more look at Felgren. The thick tree line was a stark contrast to the edge of frozen earth that marked the border of the forest, telling the story of winter settling over the rest of the isle.

I pulled my warm cloak tighter over my shoulders and nodded

to Pompeii before brushing Rev's hair behind his ear, planting a quick kiss on his lips. "Ready."

~

A DUSTING OF SNOW COVERED THE FIELDS OF GRASSES AND ROWS OF broken stems from the wheat grown in summer. I watched a few flakes fall outside of the carriages we'd commissioned to take us all the way to Radyx.

Inside our carriage, Clairannia and Figuerah spoke to Rev about their plans for our daughter's nursery, catching him up on the details of the sun and moon painted ceiling they had planned. I had let them take over the details, thankful that I wouldn't need to plan them myself now that I was Baron and considerably more busy training channelers.

Revich added his own thoughts, and my mind drifted to our task at hand. Mychael sat with our carriage driver at the front, and behind us, Philius sat with his. That carriage held Renn, Rell, Ilyenna, and Nyeimah with Talon sitting on the bench at the back.

We all agreed to take our turns outside of the carriages along the way. Clairannia and Figuerah had assured us there were no real dangers on our first stop to Lythglyn, especially not to two carriages full of Barons, conduits, and channelers. If anything, we were the safest travelers there could be, and I wondered what Pompeii had been so concerned about.

Perhaps I'd ask him more this evening when we arrived at Lythglyn and test the distance between our connection. I was tired of ignoring my power and dismissing what I could do. I held the power of each type of conduit magic: iumenta, lapis, medicus, and agricola. I was and had always been adept at using each type of magic if I'd just admitted it. Now that I was Baron, I could easily control the earth, the wind, and the water of the isle. There was only one soul more powerful than me.

The Blightress had been left. I could not turn a blind eye to that. She'd been broken, and she'd been left by those who should have stayed to love her. I thought of Philius. I thought of myself, of

Revich. We'd all seen the darkness at some parts of our lives, and yet, we'd never been abandoned. Revich and I had made it through and Philius was getting there, so what was it that made us so special? Why did we get the nurturing we needed in those darkest times and Visalia did not?

Baron Adaynth said he kept her heart safe, kept it warm, loving her still, but was that enough?

Rev had watched over my care for years, speaking to me each day, checking on any sign that I was finding my way back to my memories. He had given me space to heal, looking consistently for the rhyzolm in the hope that it could help my memories return. Did Adaynth do any of those things?

I should ask.

I should reach out to him in my mind.

I didn't want to. I didn't particularly like him and our first introduction weeks ago, when I had passed the Baron trial, didn't exactly emit warm feelings between both of us.

But he said he'd try.

He told me as I accepted half the power of Baron that he would try to give me the ability to keep Revich happy, safe, and loved. I didn't feel any different on that front. I didn't notice any new power or any new way to do those things for him.

I turned my head toward Rev, still resting my body against the window of the carriage. I missed why they were all laughing, but seeing the three people I loved most, warmed my heart in the slight chill of winter that pressed on the carriage. Rev held my hand in his lap. He squeezed my fingers and winked, murmuring, *Caloren* to warm the cabin. My heart fluttered, always prone to fall at the attention he gave me.

I took a deep breath and closed my eyes, listening to my loves speak quietly in the jostling of carriage wheels over frozen roads. My thoughts drifted to the first days of falling for Rev.

*"Show me what you can do."*

The memory of his words drifted on the warmth of that spring day years ago, and I took a moment to adjust to the dream I found myself in. Rev wasn't there beside me by the small stream with the charred maple tree above the outcropping of rocks, but someone else was.

"Which one of us called this meeting?" I asked, glancing at the first Baron who leaned against the blackened tree above the stream.

"You have not so forcefully pushed me from your mind as of late." He shrugged, sweeping his hair back from his face where it fell across his forehead. "I took the opportunity to see how the second Baron fairs."

"Do you know the story of this place?" I asked, bending down to glide my hand across the cold water.

"I know more about this place than you, Karus." He lifted himself off the tree and jerked his head in its direction. "I know the story of the origins of this tree."

"A tale you'd like to tell me?" I gave him a small smile, attempting to be polite to the man who shared a space inside my head.

"Centuries ago, a fae and human planted this tree together in hopes that their love for each other could grow and be nurtured in this forest as a symbol of unity."

I smiled, admiring the massive maple tree even more.

He hopped down, splashing into the water and walked toward me, adding, "That was until you burned it down."

My smile faded into a glare. "Why is it, *truly*, Adaynth, that you dislike me so?"

"I told you before. I see Visalia in you."

"Yet, I am not her."

"So you've said."

I stood, brushing the wisps of white hair back from my face. "You find your self-worth in what? Keeping her broken heart locked away beneath your black fortress?" I scoffed. "Tell me, what did you do to kill your child?"

"I did not kill our child."

"Why does she insist you did?"

"Because."

I splashed through the stream to reach him and gritted through my teeth, "Because *why*?"

"You think you know her? You think you've got her figured out?" He sneered. "You know nothing of what we went through. You know nothing of who she was before she fell to her own sorrow. You don't know loss, Karus. You don't know what it is like to watch the person you love most fall to their own pain, blaming you the entire time for the whole of it."

"Then *tell* me. Help me understand her better so that I can stop her from taking everything I love."

"You know everything you need to know. I cannot provide any more insight to her."

"Bullshit," I spat, stepping closer.

He grabbed my shoulders, shaking me. "You know what's bullshit? I can feel her there, in your mind. She occupies the same space I do and because Revich decided he *needed* to give you half of my power, the power that *I* gave him, I now live there inside of you, too. *With. Her.*" His nostrils flared and his hazel eyes turned glassy. "I feel her there. I know her presence like I know my own soul and *that* is bullshit. Because of you, I share with her a place I never wanted to. Because of you and Revich's somehow undying love for you, I've had to relive parts of my past that I have kept at bay for fucking *centuries.*"

He jostled me again, letting go in a huff. "And don't you think for one second, for one minuscule moment of time, that I wouldn't leave your mind if I could. But I am now bound to it, just as I am bound to Revich's, and I will continue to be until the day you both die and my power moves on to the next Baron. You will die. I will keep living. You will fade into nothing, and I will jump to the next, and the next, and the next, doing my duty to this forest. My legacy will live on, and you will fade into mere memory, then history, until not a single soul on this isle recalls anything about you all."

I huffed a laugh. "And what a Baron you've turned out to be. Admiring your own legacy more than the people who are working to change lives. Tell me, Baron Adaynth, what have you done to bring more prosperity and happiness to the people here? What whispers have you let seep into the minds of the countless Barons you've given power to? What attempts have you made to soften their hearts, hmm?" I closed our gap, refusing to back away from him. "Tell me what you said to Heimlen to try and convince him to choose another way to get me here. Tell me what you said to show him that murdering thousands was the wrong choice!"

His nostrils flared, his silence telling.

"I thought as much," I pressed. "You have all this power? All this ability to siphon into one Baron then to another, and yet, all you do is stay silent because you are a coward. All you do is sleep in these minds and scoff at the people now trying to change what has always been." I drew a deep breath, feeling the fast blink of my eyes as I began to wake. "Tell me why she blames you. Help. Me."

"Karus. Karus, wake up."

My eyes flew open and I shot upright, holding my chest with one hand, smoothing over my belly with the other. Rev held my cheek tilting my face to meet his. "Just a dream. It was just a dream." He pulled me to his warm body.

"We've stopped?" I gasped, searching out the window for Clairannia and Figuerah.

"Just to change carriage positions. Talon and Philius will join us here. Clairannia and Figuerah will ride outside for a while."

"No, no I'd like to instead if that's alright with them. I think a bit of cold will help me stay awake."

He kissed my forehead before bending to step out of the cabin. He called to Clairannia and Figuerah who were stretching with Nyeimah and the others.

I took a moment to be still in the silence of the carriage. I didn't dare address Adaynth in my mind. I didn't know if it would open a channel to the Blightress as well. He was hiding something. I felt it there, speaking to him.

Rev popped his head back inside, offering his hand. "Come, my love. Let us ride on the back of this carriage together all the way to Lythglyn." He glanced behind him, then back to me as I placed my palm in his. "If this is an attempt to get me alone for your wicked desires, consider me a willing pawn."

I laughed, falling into his arms where he caught me. "Baron Revich, I wouldn't dare."

He kissed me lightly, wrapping a hand around the back of my neck to whisper in my ear, "Yes, you would."

I would.

Of course, I would.

For a moment, I held him there. Time stopped, voices faded. My lover, my companion, my heart, my life, my bonded soul and I stood on a dirt road, sodden by winter's biting chill, surrounded by those we loved and cared for, and I kissed him in the moment we shared.

Just us.

Only us.

"You're glowing," he murmured on my lips in what I knew was a smile without ever seeing it. I could hear it in his voice as I'd heard it a thousand times in his arms.

"You make me glow, Baron Revich."

"She glows?" I heard Nyeimah's question somewhere near us.

"Yeah, she does that," Figuerah answered.

"Why don't you glow for me?" Nyeimah pouted.

I peeked over Rev's shoulder in a smile as Figuerah replied, "I'll glow for you tonight, if you'd like."

Clairannia's laugh burst from her chest and her cheeks reddened as she hopped back into the carriage.

Once everyone was into their seats, Rev gave the order to keep moving. He wrapped his cloak around both of us, and I leaned my head on his shoulders, reciting my dream.

He grunted when I spoke of the feeling that we didn't know the whole truth. He added, "I also felt like Adaynth was hiding something when he came to me in my dream."

"And another thing," I paused, settling in closer. "Pompeii discovered I'm in his mind as well."

Rev frowned, asking how that could be.

"The Blighted trees in Viridis," I explained. "I made those trees. I grew the Blight that you accidentally created the Black Lung with."

"Fuck."

I nodded my agreement. "He was incredibly concerned about the safety of Mychael on this trip. I've never seen him like that."

"I think he cares for Mychael more than he's admitted to. I'm sure that frightens him."

"Well, we won't let anything happen to our channelers. Of course we won't. Lia told me that if I keep the Blightress locked away in my mind, she cannot reach me. Now I just need to teach that to Philius and we'll be even safer."

We heard my brother's laughter booming from the carriage behind us.

"He's loosening up." Rev nodded toward the sound.

"I think he's adjusting to the responsibility of becoming an uncle."

"It's about time he adjusted to any responsibility, so I approve."

I mumbled my agreement and we continued on down the frozen road to Lythglyn, filling the chill with the sound of our excitement for the future we believed would be ours.

# CHAPTER 14
# REV

Lythglyn lay out below us as our carriages crested a small grassy hillside. Lanterns glowed as tiny specks of flame, beckoning us to follow for warmth, food, and a bed.

It was the town at the halfway point between the Spire to the east and Hyrithia to the west. The Attatok Mountains sprawled jagged across the distant horizon as our next destination. We would leave Clairannia here as we headed north to Radyx, and after a few days, we would head to the Spire to gather the last two channelers.

Our carriages entered the city gates, passing through the mostly empty streets. We pulled up to the cleverly named Lythglyn Inn, all of us hopping down to stretch our legs and eat one last supper together before Clairannia would go her own way. We talked, we laughed, we ate, and we listened to the music before saying our goodnights and heading to our rooms upstairs.

In the morning we met again for breakfast in the much quieter common room. Karus stared at her porridge, hands in her lap, only able to take a bite or two and mostly sipping tea. Clairannia spoke of the Spire and all the places she wanted to show us of her home. By the time breakfast was over, the three best friends were struggling to say goodbye, so I gave them some space, helping Mychael and Talon with the horses.

When I returned to the common room, I found Karus, Clairannia, and Figuerah somehow embracing in a three-way hug. It was perhaps the one thing Heimlen got right. He'd hunted for two other channelers whose personalities would suit what he knew of Karus, and he'd done well.

Clairannia watched them go to the carriages, her lip trembling. I approached, bringing her in for our own goodbye embrace. "We'll see you very soon."

She squeezed her arms around my chest and let go, wiping under her eyes. "I know. Just…make sure Karus is eating. I know she won't stick to the foods I've encouraged, but make sure she's eating something, Rev."

"I will."

"She told me." Her gaze cast downward and she folded her arms at her chest. "About every terrible thing Baron Adaynth said to her. I'm worried about her going so far north. It feels wrong that she's headed right toward the Blightress's lands."

"She's got protection," I murmured, then nudged Clairannia's shoulder with my elbow. "Besides, she's close to the most powerful thing on this isle."

She nodded, twisting her lips. "I know, but she hasn't found her limits yet. And we don't know if Saelyn is weakening her or providing her with more magic. Ilyenna's babe is certainly pulling from her. When I examined her, she told me how much her magic has changed."

"Is that common? That the child changes the mother's power?"

"Yes. It varies by channeler or conduit, though. Some are almost completely drained. Some become far more powerful for even months after they give birth. No two are ever the same. I won't be able to tell with Karus until she is a few months further along." She looked up to me with hardened eyes. "I'll be there. When Saelyn comes, I promise to be there." She reached out and patted my shoulder.

I gave her one last hug, planting a kiss on top of her thick black hair and left, joining the nine others, leaving Clairannia behind.

~

THE CARROW ROAD WAS A BLEAK PLACE. WE'D LEFT OUR DRIVERS IN Lythglyn, and I drove one carriage across the rutted road while Nyeimah drove the other. Mychael sat next to me, taking a lesson on tree growth while Karus worked inside the cabin with Philius, Renn, and Rell. Figuerah was at the back of their carriage, giving special attention to Talon, training him to call different types of birds to his outstretched arm while Ilyenna picked up some extra sleep.

"Good shape on that one," I praised to Mychael sitting beside me. "And what about a chestnut leaf?"

He waved off the image of an oak leaf, cupping his hands together, then spreading them apart to reveal a wisp of white magic in the shape of five long ellipse-like leaves with lacy veins and jagged toothed edges.

Mychael closed his hands, chuckling. "I don't think I'll be pursuing agricola magic, Baron. I don't seem to be particularly adept at it. Why is it so important to learn about the types of trees in Felgren if that's not the path we'll choose after the trials?"

I called my power to hold the reins and folded my arms at my chest, sitting back against the carriage bench. "I'll tell you a secret." I winked his way, then closed my eyes, laying my head back as well. "It's not really about what tree leaves you can identify or remembering which trees have the most growth in the summer months. It's about knowing the place your power comes from. The better you understand all parts of Felgren, the better you can harness what it gives to you. Part of Philius's struggle is that he cannot let go of where he believes he and Karus should be. He doesn't accept what she accepted long ago, and so the channeling line of connection between him and Felgren is stunted. It's part of why you have become stronger than he in the little time you've been training."

Mychael sat with that truth for a moment before clearing his throat. "When I first saw you and Karus in Hyrithia, I thought of how great it would be to live your lives. To live in Felgren, training in magic, riding enormous wolves." He paused again, letting the clop of hooves hang in the air. "Before your offer, I didn't think I held enough power to ever be chosen, so I forgot about it most of the time. Solla was always so much better at it anyway."

I opened my eyes and looked him over. He rarely spoke of his companion who had been killed by the Black Fever seven years ago. "I'm sure she would have made a great conduit," I encouraged.

"She would," he chuckled. "She always kept that little hope that she'd be given an Offering. Even as we got older and knew people our age are never taken to Felgren. Even as we were deciding if we wanted a family, she still insisted she would go if asked."

"And did you? Start a family, I mean."

"Neither of us ever really wanted children. We thought of adopting for a little while, but decided it wasn't something we were missing in our lives."

"I'm sorry you lost her," I found myself rasping, surprised at my own sudden emotions.

He eyed me with a small smile. "Thank you. I've found peace in remembering I got to know her. I got to be in her life and witness her living it. It took a few years, but then I was able take comfort in that. She'll always live in here." He pointed to his chest. "Pompeii likes me to talk about her. He says talking about her life will help me keep moving forward with mine."

I quirked a brow. "If Pompeii gives you advice, I'd take it."

He smirked. "Oh, I do. I didn't expect to…to find someone like him. But just like I told him before we left—we don't know what our future holds when we take the uneasy step of moving toward the unknown, but we do know what our future holds when all we do is stand still."

"And what's that?"

"The same life we've always lived."

I nodded. "I'll have to remember that one."

A loud bang erupted from the cabin, followed by shrieking laughter. I pulled the horses to a stop, signaling to Nyeimah to stop as well behind us.

The door flew open and Philius ran from the cabin, dousing the flames at his shirt sleeves. Mychael jumped off the bench, running to his side to help.

I hopped down, brushing against Karus who tumbled out of the cabin and fell to more laughter against my chest, Renn and Rell still cackling inside.

"What was that about?" I asked, checking her over for burn marks before looking over the twins.

"He was practicing—" she wiped at her eyes, bursting into laughter again.

"He's alright!" Mychael announced. Tendrils of white rose from his fingers, wrapping around the Prince's arm while he murmured a healing spell Clairannia had taught him.

Karus took a deep breath, her lips still spread wide, her laughter still contagious as I found myself chuckling too.

"He was practicing *Illuminare* with Renn and Rell and said he'd be able to make a larger orb of light if I'd just channel some of my power to him." She sighed, shaking her head. "So I did, and obviously, he couldn't hold it. It burst into flame instead. Thankfully, it only got him."

"His spell lit on fire?" I questioned, beckoning Philius over so I could have a look at his wound.

"Not at first," she replied, pulling back his burned sleeve. Philius winced with his arm outstretched. She looked up to him, in approval. "You held that spell for five minutes straight. That's a record."

"What's the point if I can't hold it without lighting myself on fire?" he gritted as Karus ripped the rest of his sleeve and healed the welts further.

"Philius," I called, "Light that bush on fire over there." I nodded toward a lonely withered shrub along the side of the road.

"Now?"

"Yes, now."

He summoned a ball of orange light, small as a button above his hand. Huffing a breath, he flicked it toward the bush. The glow died out inches before it hit the dry stems. I placed my hand on his shoulder, letting my power flow through his vest, his shirt, all the way to his skin, using Cosensian Magic to give him more of what he needed to produce the same flame as before.

I nodded for him to try again and he did, this time producing a much larger ball of light, the size Karus and I used for the same *Illuminare* spell. He tried again, flicking his wrist toward the bush. Once again the light dispersed into nothing but orange smokey tendrils.

"Mychael! Renn, Rell!" I called. "Come place your hands on Philius and focus your power to him."

One-by-one they touched his back, and I joined them as we sent our magic through him. The orb of light grew to the size of his head and his brows shot up in surprise as all of our power aided his own.

"Try again, Philius," I ordered. "Make the flames and light that bush on fire."

He nodded in silence, focusing intently on the light he held. Once again he flicked his hand, sending the orb to the bush where it splintered in a flash of light, a slight spark flaring before disintegrating into nothing but gray smoke.

The scent of burning barely filtered through the air as Renn and Rell whooped and hollered, patting him on the back with words of praise.

"I almost had it," he shrugged, a smile pulling at the sides of his mouth.

"You'll get there," Mychael encouraged, slapping his back.

I nodded his way. "Well done, Philius. Let's take twenty minutes to stretch our legs. Mychael, inform the other carriage please."

I slid my hand into Karus's and led her across the frozen brush away from eyes and ears. She was quiet, head down and frowning.

I slid my hand into my pocket, palming the rhyzolm, acknowledging what I'd already suspected.

When we were out of earshot, Karus finally spoke, "Saelyn's giving me more power, isn't she?"

She stopped with her hand over her growth band.

"Clairannia said it'd be one or the other. Our child will either make your magic stronger or weaker."

"That's what you were trying to find out, wasn't it? It wasn't whether Philius could light the damn bush on fire, it was whether a Baron and three channelers could help him do what just one Baron could."

I nodded slowly. "If the Blightress finds out how even more powerful Saelyn has made you—"

"She won't. I-I won't do that again. I'll be more careful." She chewed on her lip, hands on her hips as she turned to keep walking. "Philius thinks he has her cornered in his mind. I told him exactly what Lia told me, and he said he'll concentrate on that, but…we need to be careful."

I grabbed her hand. "Our daughter might be far more powerful than either of us. The Blightress cannot know that. Saelyn will need to be hidden while we train channelers to destroy her heart. It will just give the Blightress more reason to take you both."

"She's determined enough now. I can't imagine there's more she'd try to do."

"Think of it this way; if the Blightress knows how much more powerful you've become, she might do something drastic, knowing we really have a chance to destroy her heart with what you can now wield. Our only hope here is that she doesn't know our numbers, and she doesn't know our strength. She doesn't know when we'll attack either. In fact, I've been thinking…what if we use Philius as bait once the time comes?"

Her head twisted to me. "Use him as bait?"

"Yes. Let him think we're somewhere else and then go for her heart. If she can read his thoughts, she'll think she's safe. If she can't,"—I shrugged—"we're no worse off."

"But he can't know. We'd need to lie. And lie convincingly."

"We have time to come up with something, but this might be in our favor. Till then,"—I pulled on her waist—"maybe I should be the one to work with him."

"I'll give you Philius if you give me Mychael," she bargained.

I laughed into the damp cold. "Alright, but keep in mind, he's already fairly smitten with Pompeii."

She pinched my arm. "Your teasing about how handsome he is never gets old."

I chuckled, kissing the top of her head.

"How much longer do you think we have for today?"

"The foothills are just an hour's ride ahead. It will be much slower then because the Tectus Trail is no longer used.

"Can I handle the cart for a bit?"

"You want to?" I asked in surprise.

"I'm in the mood to try something new." She shrugged.

I pulled her all the way into my arms, lingering at her ear. "Do you think you'll feel the same tonight?"

I felt her heart begin to race through our bond. "If you're teasing me again, Revich—"

"I'm not. I've been longing to love you under the stars since that night after the Baron trial."

"What do you have in mind?" she purred, sliding her hands across my chest, my stomach, lingering her fingers through the band at my waist.

"Now, why would I go and spoil the surprise?" I tilted her chin up to face me, watching her black eyes hint at a Felgren green.

She reached for my lips, steadying there and whispering, "Which one of us caves first, Rev?"

I snorted. "Now who's teasing who?"

"Hey, Barons!" An echoing call came from the carriages behind us. We both turned to look, though I was sure to let my hand linger across her waist.

Philius had his hands cupped around his mouth, shouting, "We need to move! Look at those clouds!" He pointed north at the dull gray billowing ahead.

I waved a hand to signal we were headed back while Karus pinched my backside. "Looks like a chilly night ahead."

I jumped, laughing with her and swinging my arm underneath her legs. She kicked in mock protest as I ran us back to the carriages, replying, "I'll be sure to keep your bed warm."

# CHAPTER 15
# KARUS

We managed the storm fairly well considering how it turned into an outright blizzard. Figuerah took over the reigns for Rev after he'd taken them from me when I'd varied between staying awake and pitching forward in a doze.

Clairannia had said that my constant exhaustion would wear off in a few more weeks and Ilyenna confirmed this. She only took naps occasionally, having more energy and a beautiful blush that brushed a rosy pink across her freckled cheeks.

Little more than a trade route, the Carrow Road was devoid of towns, though small cattle farms dotted the hillsides around us every once in a while. We debated whether we should stop at one and try to pay the farmer for a warm room to sleep. Talon eventually won that argument, insisting we couldn't go any further with the horses in such cold.

We came across a small sheep farm not far off from the road and steered our horses down its frozen path, just managing to get both carriages to the barn that rose above a small stone cottage. Revich knocked on the door, explaining who we were and our destination to the old companions inside. But it wasn't until we showed off our conduit rings that they believed us and agreed to let us stay for the night and ride out the storm.

Figuerah and Talon unhitched the horses and brought them into the barn while the rest of us piled into the small common room of the stone house, which we learned had only one bedroom and washing room.

"We've plenty of blankets for the lot of you, so don't you worry about that," the old woman, Shey, said as she handed us mugs of hot tea. We'd all gathered around the fireplace after hanging our wet cloaks nearby to dry. We cut our bread, cheese, and apples for a small dinner while Shey's companion, Wellyn, spoke of the longest winter ever recorded.

"Wasn't just the snow that killed off most of our ewes that year, but the ice." He drew a long breath and nodded toward Shey. "How many did we loose that winter some years past?"

"T'was fourteen, dear," she answered, settling into the rocking chair we'd made sure to leave for her while the lot of us sat on the stone floor. "Yes, that was something. And so many ewes dead with no explanation. Just off and frozen one morning. No rhyme or reason 'bout it."

I narrowed my eyes at the fire. "How many years ago did you say?"

Wellyn leaned back in his own chair, rubbing a dark wrinkled hand over his stubbly chin. "Let's see. Must have been seven winters past. Since our favorite ewe was bought that spring and she's got to be seven now, isn't that 'bout right, Shey?"

"Yes, yes. Seven years ago was that horrible, horrible winter. Ice coated every tree and the mountains didn't thaw for some time." She caught Figuerah's eye and nodded directly to her. "A chill that stuck with you, even as you warmed by the fire! Took some time for it to thaw away and many farms couldn't make it through. Why, just a bit of a ways down the road, the young couple and their family had to pack up and leave for Hyrithia to make a living. You'll pass their farm when you leave in the morn', empty as it tis."

Rev's piercing gaze fell on me while Figuerah stole short glances.

They knew what I knew about the origins of that winter.

I didn't look their way as I turned to the old couple asking, "How long do these storms typically last for you out here?"

Shey sipped her tea. "Oh, this one'll last through the night, my dear. But clear up by morn'. Typical this time of year. You'll be nice and warm in here through the night. Though I'm sure you're used to better accommodations in that forest of yours."

"What about your barn?" Rev asked, sliding his arm around me. "Karus and I wouldn't mind sleeping there and freeing up more space in this room."

I eyed him, wondering what plans he was concocting.

Wellyn cleared his throat. "Well, suppose the loft could make do, but some of the slats in the roof are broken. Been meanin' to get those fixed so it might be a bit cold up—"

"We have magic to keep it warm, thank you," Rev replied quickly, pinching my backside and pulling me closer when I squeaked in response. "I'll take a look at those slats while we're there."

"That's very kind, Baron Revich. Thank you, lad."

As the hour grew later and the stories of farming grew longer, Rev and I gathered our blankets and murmured our goodnights, trekking out into the winter storm that still raged, blowing jagged flakes into our faces as we raced to enter the side door of the barn.

"*Illuminare,*" Rev called, lighting the inside of the stone room, disturbing the animals. Our horses neighed in stalls at the back corner while a few dozen sheep called out at the disturbance, inciting a riot from our sudden appearance.

"*Compaynen,*" I soothed, calming them instantly to settle down huddled into their beds of hay. I stepped forward, blankets in hand and looked around. The pale stone bricks stacked around the open room appeared to be taken straight from a quarry and were covered in decades of grime. "Is this what you had in mind for trying something new?" I asked, glancing over my shoulder at Rev who surveyed the room himself.

"No. But up here?" He nodded toward a narrow wooden staircase that led to the loft of the barn.

I followed him up the rickety stairs to bales of hay stacked five high, enclosing the space with a fine layer of dust and straw strewn about the floor. A thin layer of snow had settled in the middle of the loft, and glancing up, I saw the sky through broken slats of the roof.

Without a word, Rev used his blue tendrils of power to sweep away the snow, laying a few blankets down over the creaking floor-boards. He laid himself on them to face the opening above, folding his hands behind his head.

I barked an incredulous laugh. "You want to sleep there? Under a blizzard?"

"Where else can we stay warm and see the stars?" he asked softly.

I laid down beside him, curling up to his solid body, looking up into the open sky. "How can we see the stars through this storm?"

Silver flakes fell in the silence, drifting down from the dark grey clouds. I followed them with my eyes as they settled softly onto his black waves, his dark lashes, melting across his warm cheeks. I raked my fingers through his hair, pulling myself up to smile over his full lips, brushing the straight line of his dark brows, the sharp edge of his jaw. In the still quiet, I admired the man I loved. I soaked in every detail, solidifying to memory the face of the man I'd share any space with. Barn, forest, fortress, inn— wherever this man slept, I only wanted the space to sleep beside him.

"Well, Karus,"—he closed his eyes, his lips pulling into a mischievous grin—"that's entirely up to you. If you can cause a winter to rage over months and months outside of Felgren, what makes you think you can't blow away this little storm?"

I cursed. We knew it was true. Of course we did. The winter that came to Arcaynen Isle seven years ago was the same winter I had caused in Felgren the night my memories disappeared from holding the *Simulair Solum* spell so long. And where that long winter lost its grip on the isle after only a few months, inside Felgren, it had lasted years.

I hovered over his face, touching his lips. "How is it that I can control the weather, Revich?"

His jaw ticked, and he pinned me with a sharp look. "You are not her. Just because she gave you some of herself does not mean you will have her history."

I closed my eyes, forcing the storm from the sky. I moved the clouds with my wind. I cleared the snow from the ground with my warmth. I drained the puddles with the inhalation of my breath, pulling the cold water into the earth, letting it flow down to the roots in the soil.

When I opened my eyes again, he was no longer watching my face. He stared at the place in my chest where my heart beat in a steady pulse. I caught his hand in mine as he reached out to touch me.

"This is yours." I patted our hands against the space of my ribs where my heart was caged behind bone and sinew.

"I'll never let you fall like that." He nodded to my chest. "Your heart stays right here where I can always feel it."

I kissed him and fell beside him again, draping a leg over his waist. We watched the night sky, now clear of its storm with a hundred stars twinkling across the black.

"I wonder what stories they'll tell now," he said, murmuring a spell of warmth to wrap around us. "What stories will come of the night they hosted a handful of magic wielders who blew away the storm and thawed the frozen earth?"

I chuckled. "Perhaps I'll have my own rhymes and songs one day."

"Oh, I'll encourage it," he teased.

We held each other for a long moment, enjoying the stillness and the silence in the warmth of our embrace.

Rev broke the quiet. "Adaynth said he granted your request. When you asked him to help keep me safe and happy before taking the power of Baron, he said he'd done it. He also said he didn't think I'd ever know what that meant."

I frowned, tracing the leaf pattern on his black vest. "Do you think it has to do with Saelyn?"

"That was my thought, too, but I don't know how. It was that night, you know. When we made her."

I nodded. "I know."

With a wave of his hands, a blue fiery wall rose around us in a magical cage, ending at the open roof, enhancing the brilliance of the stars.

I laughed into his chest. "I remember this."

"It's a favorite memory of mine," he remarked casually. "Loving you within the cage of my power is something I think of often, and I'll admit, Karus," he whispered in my ear, sending a shiver down my neck, "I've been meaning to get back to that moment."

"This time with a skylight?" I asked, working my fingers over the buttons of his vest as he unclasped my cloak.

He chuckled softly, his warm breath pebbling my skin. "This time with more time and just the stars to guess at how I love you."

# CHAPTER 16

## REV

**D**awn came and I took my time loving her again. I kissed her softly, delicately, in a sear over her skin with my promises of forever, my dedication to her body, my ode to her altar.

Her knuckles whitened as she gripped the blankets tightly in her fists, moaning my name with her face buried deep into the wool. On my knees, I slid my hands over her back, worshiping all of her before me, my world arching in pleasure, begging me for more.

I'd give it.

I'd give everything I had.

I bent forward, picking up momentum and sliding my fingers underneath her body. At my touch, she rocked against me, guiding my fingers exactly to where she needed me. She called out into the gray blankets with a muffled curse on her lips. I left a trail of kisses on her spine before rising up behind her once again to give my offering.

I pressed my fingers into her hips, no longer holding back to let her pleasure build. Instead, I let it ignite, flare, and burn me as I lost all sense of self, of coherence, only existing in that moment where time stood still, and I worshiped her thoroughly.

Her scream of release coincided with mine, and I slumped forward, holding her body to my own for just a few moments longer, unwilling to leave her just yet.

She slumped forward, breathing heavily, turning and pulling me to her chest as she wrapped her long legs around me. Her lungs heaved as she smoothed the hair back from my face, tucking it behind my ear.

I glanced upward at the broken slats to see the faintest hint of a purple sky that drove away the dark. I rested my chin on her breast, laying my kisses there, searching her face for a response. Her eyes were closed, but a smile tugged at her lips the moment I pulled her peaked flesh into my mouth.

"How do you find the stamina, Baron Revich?" she asked in a sultry murmur.

"I've had some seven years to dream up scenarios of what I'd do to you when you returned." I pressed my body into her hips, bringing myself up over her face and tracing under her lips. "This is just me fulfilling some of those dreams."

She laughed and shook her head squinting at the sky above. "We have a little more time. Let's make it count."

~

I FIXED THE ROOF OF THE BARN EASILY ENOUGH. FINDING A LADDER on the bottom floor, I hauled it to the loft with some nails and a rusted mallet. Karus fell silent, brushing the bits of hay off the blankets as she lifted them high into the air then snapped them taut to fold neatly. Something sifted through her mind, so I waited for her to tell me what it was.

We headed downstairs, checking on the horses and giving them water and some grain we'd brought with us. The morning light lit the cold earth as we left. A wide expanse of snowless ground surrounded us in a circle around the farm and the pastures.

"Did you see the storm leave us last night, Barons?" Shey greeted us as we stepped into the cottage, looking for some much needed food. She handed us plates of eggs and toast, ushering us to the fireplace to sit near Figuerah and Nyeimah.

Figuerah swallowed a gulp of tea adding, "Yes, it's the strangest thing, Barons. The storm stopped abruptly last night and left Wellyn and Shey's farm completely untouched by the cold." She jabbed Karus in the arm with her elbow.

"How interesting," Karus muttered through her eggs, then smiled at Wellyn. "I hope the subsiding storm allows your sheep to graze longer in the fields today."

He rubbed his hands together, watching out the window. "I suppose it will. Strange weather pattern indeed. I'll have to excuse myself and help your friend. The sheep should be out by now."

I cocked my head. "Friend?" I glanced around the room, realizing who was missing. "Philius? Did you send him out to open the back door of the barn?"

Wellyn shrugged on his coat at the door. "That's right. The tall one with all the curls bundled at the top of his head."

Mychael joined Wellyn at the window, already buttoning his cloak. "He left twenty minutes ago." He turned to me. "You didn't see him?"

I shook my head and set down my half eaten food, pulling open the door with Karus right behind me.

"Philius!" she yelled into the morning air.

She brushed past me, running toward the barn. I was right behind her, calling with her as we entered. All of us began a search over the entire grounds, calling his name into the frozen air, rioting the sheep and upsetting the horses let out to pasture.

"He's gone," Mychael puffed beside me.

"Help me gather everyone," I huffed back.

The nine of us gathered in front of the cottage. A taut surface of panic fell over us as we met each other's gazes, each thinking but unable to voice what we truly feared.

"He can't be far," I started. "He has thirty minutes on us. He didn't take a horse and the snow beyond the circle around the farm is deep. Ilyenna, Talon, you start on the perimeter at the road.

Rotate clockwise and the rest of us will set up around the remaining area."

"What are we looking for?" Ilyenna asked, already turning to leave.

"Footprints," I replied. "Call out when you find his prints. Do not follow. Stick to the perimeter. We meet back here in fifteen minutes."

I took Karus's hand in mine and we headed to the other side of the barn where the foothills met a deep ravine that then climbed upward into the side of another hill.

Karus stalked the edge of the snowfall with me. We searched carefully for any sign of her brother, whom she cursed at continuously in a muttering of obscenities I knew came from a place of fear. She cursed again with something about bringing the Lumens with us next time then halted, grabbing my arm and pointing. A set of tracks led through the snowfall into the steep hillside.

"Let's call everyone back," she said as she turned around, headed for the house.

I stood for a moment in the calm of dawn, my eyes tracing over the path Philius must have taken. A deep foreboding had me clenching my teeth, knowing Philius had taken a route that would lead straight to the abandoned Tectus Trail.

# CHAPTER 17
# KARUS

Philius was gone. I warred with the thought of reaching out to the woman who haunted a dark corner of my mind—the woman who I knew was the reason for his leaving.

I debated it in my own head a dozen times before glancing to Rev as we all trudged through the snow, melting our path little by little with magic. He shook his head once, knowing what I was thinking without me ever having to say it aloud.

"We both know it's the Blightress." I confirmed my thoughts in a grumble, pulling back a particularly thorny blackberry branch and hauling myself up another foot along the hillside.

"More reason not to contact her. Whether Philius went by choice or by her command, she wants you to reach out to her."

He took a moment to glance behind us to see how the rest of our party faired. Ilyenna and Talon were right behind us while Renn, Rell, and Mychael drafted the middle of our line, Nyeimah and Figuerah at the end. We'd gathered everyone together and packed a meager amount of food, planning to return to the farm if we did not find him by midday.

"Maybe we should hear what she has to say. Maybe we—"

He cut me off as he used his power to pull back more of the

underbrush, and I used mine to melt the snow. "No. This is either a trap or she really does want to train him in her own way. If the first, we need to keep her out of your head. If the second…"

He trailed off, stopping for just a moment to let his black eyes darken. "If the second, he's already lost to us. I need you to think about that and what it means for you and him."

I scoffed, "Philius is a stubborn ass, but he's not interested in actually training with her. He told me he wasn't, and I believe him." I knelt against the steep ground, balancing by holding onto a jagged rock jutting from the side of the hill. "*Liquiren*," I spoke in frustration, my hand flat on the snow. A brilliant surge of green power spilled from my fingertips, racing across the rest of the hill to melt what snow was left. I lifted my hand, bringing the snowmelt up above us and flicked my fingers to the side. The gush of icy water flew down the hill, splashing into the ravine below.

Rev's brows rose. I shrugged and kept moving, able to see the path to the top of the hill a little easier.

When we reached the top, I surveyed the Tectus Trail while Rev helped pull the rest of our party to the narrow path. The trail had been cut into the side of another hill that rose before us. I searched the snow, looking for Philius's prints to direct us. They led north and upwards.

"Reform the line," I called as Figuerah took Rev's hand to help her up onto the road. "We continue up this trail and do not break our line. The Blightress is unpredictable at best, vicious at worst, so eyes open."

"And what if Philius left on purpose?" Figuerah demanded, taking a moment to catch her breath. "What if we find him on her side?"

Nervous murmurings crept through the line of magic wielders, and I shared an apprehensive look with Rev.

He gripped my hand tighter and addressed them. "If any of you would like to go back at this point, do so now. You may return to the farm and wait for us there. It's your choice, not ours."

The eyes of seven stared unflinchingly back at the Barons of Felgren in silence.

He nodded, continuing, "It's more than likely the Blightress used her connection to Philius through the remnants of the Black Fever. This feels like a trap to capture Karus or any of you. But we will not leave one of our own behind. Be on your guard and let the more experienced of us protect you should you need it. Do you all remember how to shield?"

An agreement of nods rumbled through them. Even Nyeimah was able to produce a small bit of her silver magic to use.

"Good," Rev continued, "Now we follow this trail. We have a few hours yet before it becomes too dangerous to continue."

"This trail is haunted, Baron Revich," Ilyenna called, cradling her swollen belly.

I mimicked her movement.

"It's just a trail, Ilyenna," he returned, continuing upward, keeping my hand in his.

I hoped he was right.

～

PHILIUS'S BOOTPRINTS IN THE SNOW WERE THE ONLY INDICATION OF life along the abandoned trail. No animal prints, no foliage along the path, no evidence revealed that this trail was regularly traversed by anyone or anything. We climbed for another hour in our line with little said and cloaks pulled tightly around our shoulders. Revich led us, sending a warming spell behind to help with the ever-pressing chill of silent, cold earth. Snow fell lightly on our shoulders, but not enough to cover Philius's tracks.

We couldn't be too far from him, though it'd be hard to catch up unless he stopped. The trail thinned and we had no choice but to take it one by one, sticking close to the left side of the rocky hill. The trail dropped off into a treacherous fall on the right if we dared veer too close to the edge.

We neared the crest of the hill, and I held on to the sharp rocks beside me to keep pushing forward. Icy stone, coarse and jagged, met my fingers, and I pulled my hand back as if burned. My heart thundered in my chest as a deep well of cold flowed over my skin.

"What is it?" Rev faced me, grabbing onto my waist and calling for a halt.

All eyes fell on me as I tried to catch my breath, reaching out to the rock once more. I picked at the layered stone, ignoring the break of my fingernails, using both hands to pull chunks of the rock away. Pieces split into long rectangular flakes, and I let them fall to the snow at my boots. I bent down to look into the divot I created along the rock wall, confirming what I had just felt down my fingers. A subtle golden light pulsed, and I followed it, using my fingers to dig. Ilyenna gasped behind me as the root came free from the rocky depths. It was black like the Blight with a golden light that flowed down the thick of it to a well-timed, steady heartbeat.

"I felt it," I said, staring at the root that Rev reached out to touch. "I felt it through the rock." I grabbed his arm. "The Blightress is here. This is hers." My eyes shot up above us, unable to see what was at the top of the hill, knowing that whatever it was, our lives were about to change once more.

"Shields up," Rev called, holding his own hand out in front of him as a thin glow of his fiery walls encased his body. "Be on your guard. Follow orders," Rev commanded. "If we say run, you run. You get back to the farm, regardless of who joins you."

Talon grumbled, "I thought we weren't leaving any of our own behind, Baron."

There was a murmur of agreement.

I smirked and raised my brows at Rev who frowned. I turned back around, agreeing, "No, we don't. Stick together. I made a promise to get all of us back to Felgren, and I plan to keep it."

I looked back at Rev with a grin, suggesting more confidence than I felt.

His face turned to stone. "I love you," he said, his black eyes flicking blue.

I frowned at his tone. "And you'll love me still when we have Philius back, so don't you dare say it like a goodbye."

He chuckled and nodded, turning around and leading the way up.

I kept my hand along the rocky wall as we climbed.

*Thump, thump.*

*Thump, thump.*

The heartbeat I knew well was much slower than what thrummed in my chest as the horizon view changed, and we reached the top of the hill's summit. The snow became deeper, encasing the ground in a layer of sharp ice. The sound of our footsteps would have alerted anyone listening as the loud crunch sounded over and over from the nine bodies approaching the massive grove of trees ahead.

They loomed at the crest of the hill in an endless array of ragged black branches and pulsing lights at the trunk of each. Dim colors hummed in green, red, blue, silver, and gold—every color I'd ever seen a channeler or conduit produce rose and fell in the hazy morning sun.

"His prints lead into this grove," Rev called in front of us.

"These trees look Blighted," I admitted, crunching through more ice to approach the nearest one. I heard the unsheathing of a sword just behind me and turned quickly to see Mychael gripping one in his hand. "I don't remember you bringing any weapons with you to Felgren," I remarked.

"This is borrowed," he said at my back. "This sword has been in Pompeii's family for centuries. He insisted I take it with us." He shot me a playful grin. "He also said I'd be more useful in physical combat than magic on this adventure if needed."

I chuckled, knowing Pompeii was probably right. Mychael hadn't been training in magic nearly as long as he trained as a Hyrithian Royal Guard.

Rev addressed all of us. "Mychael, Rell, Ilyenna, and Figuerah, you follow Karus's footprints. The rest of you, follow mine. We stay in two lines and keep the noise minimal. Step where Karus and I step. We stay close, we stay together."

I moved next to Rev, planting my boots in the snow at the edge of the trees that seemed to circle around a center. I felt the pulse continuously in my bones, and as everyone followed orders, I closed my eyes for just a moment to focus.

The power flowing from these strange trees was immense. This didn't feel like the Blight. It felt stronger, different from what we'd seen the Blightress produce so far in her rage across the isle.

I opened my eyes and frowned.

It wasn't just immense power that I felt, weighted and heavy in the air in this grove of dense trees. It was the *potential* of power. I jerked my head to Rev, meeting his eyes.

"I feel it, too," he spoke low, inaudible to our people behind us.

"Rev…" My breathing came at a rapid pace, my bones chilling further as the truth hit me.

"I think so," he agreed, already understanding what we were about to see.

I turned to address those in our care. "We feel…individuals here." I nodded to Rev. "Whatever we are about to see, try to keep your emotions under control. We are finding Philius, and we are leaving with Philius. Is that clear?"

Varying nods of agreement came through their thin shields of light.

Revich took my hand in his and with a nod from me, we stepped forward into the line of trees.

# CHAPTER 18

# REV

Only our boots crunching through the ice broke the silence. The trees grew tall with dark trunks dusted in snow. The sky was harder to see through the tops of dark pine, needles sharp and threatening as we entered the line of trees.

I had guessed at what we'd find, but the truth in those trees was far worse than anything I could have imagined. Graphed into each trunk was a face, a body, limbs of people—channelers, conduits possibly—it was too difficult for even me to tell.

Each body was sunk in varying depths of the black trees with vines that wound over and through their skin, arms, legs, and torsos. Some frozen faces could be seen, eyes closed, some were too far into the depths of their tree to even discern if it was a man or woman, old or young.

Ilyenna retched somewhere behind me and Talon rushed to her. I twisted my head to see her stop him with a hand and a look. She shook her head, wiped her mouth, and stood straighter, following the steps through the ice.

I stole a glance at my beloved only to see what she was feeling plainly on her face.

Cold, searing anger engulfed her. With hands closed tightly at her sides, her jaw clenched as she studied another of the trees. Its black carcass pulsed a purple light. The red hair of the trapped woman lifted slightly in the cold breeze, her face frozen and partially consumed by the rough bark.

"This is what she does with them," Karus whispered so only I could hear. "She takes them and feeds off their power like this."

"Yes."

"There are *hundreds* here." Her voice broke for just a moment before she swallowed and continued. "How long do you think she's been doing this?"

I shivered, passing by a tree pulsing in a golden glow. The only sign of the channeler inside was the shape of a hand reaching out through the coarse bark. "The Tectus Trail hasn't been used since Baron Eyreth murdered his channelers."

"Less than a hundred years, then." She paused, glancing behind to the rest of our people, each face grave and heartbroken for their brothers and sisters in magic. "What if one of these is—"

"These are too old. These trees have been here a long time. We both can feel it. If she plans this fate for Philius, we have not come across him yet."

"Can they be saved?" she asked, voicing the question we all were undoubtedly thinking.

"I hope so." I reached out to touch the cheek of an old woman, her face the only part of her exposed in the ragged trunk of the tree. Her lashes were encased in ice, frozen to her face. Her white magic pulsed from the center of the tree where her heart was buried deep beneath the wood. She didn't flinch. She didn't open her eyes or show any evidence that she could ever exist outside of her cage at all.

We trekked on, passing tree after tree, magic wielder after magic wielder, silent as a graveyard. Possibly, that was exactly where we were. I felt each one's power as we passed, but not as a single hub of magic. Instead, each tree felt like a nodule, a branch's point which led back to a whole somewhere, feeding the Blightress with unchecked power.

Even more so than before, I understood while crossing through the grove of people that the Blightress was unmatched. Karus and I together could never defeat her as she was now, siphoning the power of hundreds, here at the top of a nameless hill at the base of the Attatok Mountains.

I also understood that she had led us here because she wanted us to see. Her reasoning frightened me most, and I gripped Karus's cold hand tighter in my own.

"Stop," Figuerah whispered harshly at the end of Karus's line. Her eyes danced to Talon, who lowered his head, brows furrowed.

He nodded to her and she spoke. "There are creatures ahead. Some kind of animal that feels like,"—her eyes darted to Karus—"they feel like lumens."

As if they'd heard, a howl pierced the air, flying through the grove, eerie and vicious.

"We need to hurry," Karus urged. "Figuerah, Talon, up front."

They did as she commanded, moving swiftly to the front of the lines, shields out, and hands before them.

"*Compaynen*," Figuerah called through the sea of trees. Her golden power flowed from the tips of her fingers, winding through what we still had yet to face in a spell of calming.

We trudged faster, caring less about the crunch of ice as the howls continued in a beckoning for what we would face next. A clearing loomed ahead as we passed tree after tree, body after body, pulsing in that dim glow.

We broke through to a clearing, finding Philius unconscious in the snow, his puffs of white breath the only indication that he was still alive. Three massive lumen-like beasts circled his body. Their heads were shaped from elongated vines, their limbs no more than branches of black trees. Though these creatures were akin to the wolves of Felgren, nothing protective or sweet lay in the aggression of their movements. Behind them, a pulsing black portal loomed. Its inky surface rippled like water in the light snowfall.

"*Concess*," Figuerah commanded in a spell to cease the beasts' movement. They ignored her spell and continued circling Philius as if in wait for a command from someone else.

Talon stepped closer, easing slowly toward Philius, low to the ground, his eyes on the beasts. He whistled low in a sound of ease, approaching the beasts with Figuerah beside him.

I kept my eyes on the portal, knowing exactly where the true threat lie.

Talon reached for Philius's cloak, pulling his hand back just in time as one of the creatures snapped at his fingers in a vicious snarl.

"We don't have time for this," Karus warned, striding forward fearlessly and giving orders. "Figuerah, keep their mouths shut. Talon, Mychael, grab Philius on my mark."

She looked my way and I nodded, shaping a viridescent portal to send Philius back to Felgren the moment we had him.

"You *must* teach me that," she insisted, building her power into a green ball of light and bringing it back to her chest, readying her magic to fly forward.

"We get out of this, I'll teach you anything you want," I promised, sending my own power low to the ground to wrap around Philius and help get him to the portal.

Renn, Rell, Ilyenna, and Nyeimah circled the clearing, shields intact, spells ready.

"On my mark," Karus started, "Three, two—"

The black portal shimmered and its maker stepped onto the snow in a graceful sweep of black robes. "I do appreciate you bringing such powerful magic wielders to me, Kar—"

I opened a second portal in front of her, leading to the depths of the sea, and in an instant, she was gone. The shimmery green of my portal did not close as usual, however, and before I could investigate why, Karus brought me back to focus, saying, "Now you *must* teach me how to do that."

The beasts lifted their heads to howl, but Figuerah kept them clamped shut in a spell of golden vines just as Karus sent her ball of light forward.

It split into three arrows, deftly aimed right for the heads of each creature. The sharp points hit their marks swiftly, soundlessly, all three of the massive beasts falling to a thud in the ice.

"Now!" Karus shouted.

At her command, Mychael dropped his sword in the snow,

pulling with both hands on Philius, Talon doing the same. I wrapped my magic around his middle, pulling the unconscious prince to the second waiting portal. In an instant, we shoved him through, sending him back to the Fortress. The portal closed upon itself just as long, frozen fingers wrapped around my throat behind me, black nails cutting into my skin.

A beautiful voice whispered, "Have you forgotten, Baron Revich? Your portals allow only one beating heart through." She paused, scraping her nails down my neck. "And my chest carries none."

## CHAPTER 19
# KARUS

I caught the flash of black at Revich's back, as I heard the Blightress's voice. "It seems I've underestimated your cunning, Baron Revich. You've already stolen away my prize. Pity." The Blightress squeezed Rev's throat tighter, one hand wrapped around his windpipe, her nails sending thin trails of blood down his skin. She held his back to her chest and her iridescent eyes shifted to me. "I do hope Saelyn inherits the trait."

Without another thought, I called to the tree behind her, glowing an eerie dark purple in its center where it consumed the power of the channeler it held. A thick branch whipped around her throat, pulling her upwards slightly. She choked and pulled at the black wood encircling her neck, keeping one hand wrapped around Revich's throat.

"Let him go or I pull up," I threatened through gritted teeth.

A gargled laugh came from her, though I did not miss the surprise in her face as she replied, "Do you really think to stop me with my own syphoner trees?"

"Most creatures on this isle cannot live without breathing," I spat. "Should we see if you're one of them?"

I yanked on the branch and she squeezed Revich's throat harder. She had bound his arms to his sides with black vines reaching through the snow at his feet.

"He'd be dead before you had the chance to see just what I could survive, Little Sprout, so here are your two choices."

"Karus…" Figuerah's voice came as a warning, and I stole a glance behind me to see the three beasts slowly rising, their head wounds healing over into thick vines of Blight.

"You can walk with me through that portal," the Blightress offered, jerking her chin to where the black abyss remained. "Or, you can let your lover die, and I'll drag you through instead."

I didn't miss the flicker of movement on Revich's face or the way his eyes darted across the small clearing to each of our people, landing on Figuerah and giving the slightest nod disguised as a struggle to be free.

The Blighted beasts left their circle, easing slowly toward Talon, Mychael, and Rell.

I answered, "Your creatures leave first. Then, you let Revich go, and I will enter that portal."

She tsked and gave her response. "You speak as if you have the upper hand here, whereas we both know I could destroy every one of you without a thought more, so I suggest you get into the portal, Karus."

I pulled at the branches around her throat with my power, and she attempted to lift herself higher.

"Let. Him. Go," I seethed.

"GET IN THE PORTAL!" she screamed, her fury pulling at my own in a vicious rage of all we had left to see through in our story together.

The beasts pounced, and I turned in time to see Rell falling to the ice. The creature dragged her toward the portal, her shield no match for the beast's jaws.

"No!" Renn screamed, pulling on her sister's arms. Ilyenna yanked Renn away, slamming her to the icy ground before she could follow her sister as Rell was pulled into the darkness.

I let the rage take ahold of me, simmering through my veins and siphoning from that charred maple tree of my mind, demanding Adaynth give me everything from that place where I kept him locked away. Fire poured from my hands like liquid heat, spreading over the ice and snow, melting a path to the syphoner trees and flickering over the grove, licking its way up each one.

Another beast pounced on Mychael, dragging him along the ground. He reached for his sword and cut over the black vines at the beasts's throat. It yelped, releasing him. He rose and rushed to Talon who fought against the last beast.

My flames burned hotter, and I shaped my green light into a dagger, slicing down the Blight holding Revich's arms at the same time I lifted the branch around the Blightress's neck higher.

The Blightress let him go, digging at the tree limbs wrapped around her throat as she was lifted into the air, slamming into the tree alight in my flames.

Revich grabbed my hand, pulling me toward the center of the clearing, rotating his arms to produce five shimmering portals, calling for everyone to get out.

Figuerah raced toward Nyeimah, ducking just as two enormous black cats bounded over her head, pouncing on the Blight beast still dragging Talon toward the black portal. Snarling rippled through the air as the muri fought against the Blight beasts, biting, maiming, slicing through flesh and vines alike.

Ilyenna pushed Renn through one of Revich's portals, and it closed in a resounding *thwap*. She then bolted for Talon, bringing him into her arms for a moment, before urging him toward another portal.

Hand-in-hand, Revich and I flew to Mychael at the base of the Blightress's portal, pooling together our magic in an attempt to pull him back. Blood trickled from his jaw where the beast had sliced through his flesh, leaving an open slash from his cheek down to his collar bone.

I pulled on my fire, now burning fiercely through the syphoner trees and set the creature aflame. It yelped and retreated quickly toward the portal, refusing to let go of Mychael in its jaws.

The scent of burned flesh hit my nose as a hand gripped my chin, claw-like nails digging into my cheeks. "You've brought this upon yourself." The Blightress shoved my face away, erecting a wall of iridescent light in her wake, forcing Rev and me to fall back into the snow.

"No!" I cried as she palmed Mychael's face, lifting him with inhuman strength and tossing him into her dark abyss. His scream washed over me while I pounded on the shimmering wall separating us from the darkness that two of our channelers had been pulled into. Her creature dove through and she turned her head back to me. It was then that I saw the charred flesh that puckered and blistered over the side of her face, the ring of bruised skin at her throat, and the blood that flowed from her burns down to the top of her breasts. At that moment, I understood why she did not want us to follow. The fire burned bright around us, decimating her syphoner trees, killing her power source and weakening her enough that she would not risk a further fight.

"He didn't listen," she growled, spitting blood into the snow and wiping under her lip.

Revich pounded his fists at the wall of iridescence, calling out the *Simulair Solum* spell. The Blightress flinched and shielded her eyes. The withering sound of the Blight beast behind us met our ears, but we kept our gaze on the darkest threat.

She continued, eyes focused on me. "I begged Adaynth to take her out. To cut me open and save our daughter's life. I knew I'd gone too far, carried her too long. I knew her life was dwindling with each day she remained in my womb.

"When I tried to cut her out myself, he used the power *I* gave him to tie me to the bed. He refused to let me go and she was born dead. He could have saved her. There was a chance he could have saved me, too, but he didn't listen, Karus, and I am done waiting." She pointed a long finger at my belly, flecked in blood. I backed up, wrapping my hands around myself. "That child is mine whether you come along or not. She holds power that comes from *me*. She. Is. Mine."

"You will not touch her!" I shouted, my flames crawling over the snow, climbing up the sides of her portal. "She is ours! You cannot—"

She backed into the portal and the iridescent wall shattered, fracturing into a thousand shards. Revich pushed me to the ground, covering me with his own body, shielding us in a flickering blue flame of his power.

# CHAPTER 20
# REV

"Are you hurt?" I huffed breathlessly, hovering over Karus, digging into my pocket for the rhyzolm.

I felt our daughter, strong as ever, and let myself breathe a sigh of relief.

"She can't have her," Karus choked, covering her face.

"She won't."

"Saelyn is not hers. Rev,"—she gripped my arms, shaking me, her eyes an abyss of black as she raged, "she cannot have her. She can't. She can't. She can't."

Her sobbing filled the air with the low crackle of the dying fires around us.

"Karus," I whispered, pulling her into my lap, cradling her head and rocking her back and forth. "She won't take her. She's ours. I would never let that happen."

Her cries fell into seamless rage as she pounded at my chest over and over, screaming, pulling at everything I could give her—my clothes, my heart, my life, our bond, my very soul which had become one with hers a long time ago.

I took all of it.

The brunt of it.

The full force of it as she ripped my vest, screaming her words of what the Blightress could not do into the smoke-filled sky. Her voice carried through the scorched grove as if those words on that wind would reach the Blightress in a declaration that she was wrong.

Time passed.

I didn't count the minutes, which felt like hours, and when Karus's voice was finally hoarse enough that her vehement words were merely a raspy whisper, she wiped at her face, gulped in a breath of air and rose from my lap.

Figuerah, Nyeimah, Ilyenna, and Talon stood nearby, each with their own tears, watching the Barons of Felgren hold onto the hope that their daughter would be saved.

Karus wiped her sleeve under her nose. "We don't know where she has taken Rell and Mychael, but we can guess at what she'll do with them. We'll be going to the Blightress's heart sooner than planned. We're going to get them back."

I surveyed the charred syphoner trees. I needed to see the extent of the damage done to the channelers inside, but as I studied them closer, I understood the truth. Not a single light continued to glow in the circle of trees surrounding the clearing, each no more than smoldering wood and dying embers.

"The Blight beast?" Karus asked.

"It's dead," Figuerah answered, patting the head of the sleek black muri sitting beside her. "This one ripped its head from its body. We'll bury them separately."

"Burn them," Karus murmured. "Burning the Blight will kill it, too."

Figuerah nodded, catching my gaze. "The channelers in Radyx…"

"Revich will continue on by portal with you to Radyx. Ilyenna, Talon, and I will return to Felgren to inform Pompeii and take care of Renn and Philius."

I pulled Karus to me, countering, "I'm not leaving you." I looked to the companions. "Figuerah and Nyeimah, you will leave for Radyx by portal where I will join you in two days to retrieve the channelers. We push this timeline forward. The Blightress has shown her hand and what she's capable of. Tell Madame Zoreyah we need more channelers. I'll explain to Lady Lamoral and The Queen as well."

I gestured toward two remaining portals. "These will take you both to Radyx. I'm sorry, but I cannot send your Muri as well."

Nyeimah kissed the top of both of the beast's black heads, saying, "You don't need to. These are wild beasts. Figuerah called them to our aid and they came."

Figuerah offered her thanks to both of the large cats and they sauntered off into the trees. Karus wrapped her arms around the iumenta conduit and let go first, giving a quick hug to Nyeimah as well before taking Ilyenna's hand and moving toward the trees.

Figuerah frowned as they left. "I'll explain the urgency. We need to spread the word about these beasts." Figuerah gestured to the desecrated syphoner trees. "And about what the Blightress has done to those she has stolen."

"Make your words count. I'll be with you soon."

I embraced her quickly, stepping back to let the companions step through their portals.

"Baron, I—" Talon's voice caught in his throat as we followed Ilyenna and Karus. "I'm sorry. Rell, Mychael…" He brought his fist to his mouth, pressing hard to his lips before stammering, "I want t-to go after them."

I put my arm around his shoulder as his voice broke, and his body shook in silent sobs. "We won't let this be their end. They deserve better." I gestured to the syphoner trees. "They all deserve better, so let's fight for them. Let's find a way to bring them home."

He wiped at his face and sniffed into the cold air. "What do we do now?"

Karus watched our exchange, and I stared back into those eyes filled with black, filled with anger, and hatred, and fear. I took a deep breath in, slowly, letting her see my chest inflate. She followed, filling her own lungs before we both exhaled together. She turned back around, still holding onto Ilyenna's hand, who wiped at her eyes continuously. I looked back at the man beside me, murmuring into the midday air, "We hold onto hope, Talon, and we defy the dark."

~

WE MADE THE LONG TREK BACK TO THE FARM IN SILENCE. ONCE A line of nine, now only four, met Wellyn and Shay at their stone cottage, the sun beginning its descent behind the hills. Karus explained that the four of us would be leaving at dawn, taking our four horses back to Felgren immediately. She offered them the carriages as payment for hosting us for so long.

She didn't explain. She didn't go into detail of what we'd seen, and as Karus and Ilyenna were ushered into the house with Shay promising a warm bath, I took a moment to warn Wellyn of what awaited on the Tectus Trail, urging him to consider packing up and moving to Hyrithia or the Spire.

He didn't believe me at first, listening with a deep-set frown about how the Blightress lived and was searching to regain her power. It wasn't until Talon angrily shook the old man that the truth began to settle in.

"But she's a myth," he insisted. "We all know the songs and legends."

I nodded. "Passed down through centuries. Her real story is a tragic one, which I will not repeat here. All you need to know, we've told you. What you do with that information is up to you."

He patted my shoulder, heading back into the cottage. "Thank you, Baron Revich. For telling me the truth."

I stood before the door, my hands in my pockets, one squeezing the rhyzolm tightly. Talon followed the old man, taking a glance back at me, but I shook my head. He closed the door behind him. Alone, in the dusk of winter's chill, I sat on the stone steps, head in my hands, and wept.

~

Karus hardly spoke as we rode back to Lythglyn. The four of us were faster by horseback than by carriage. We kept our horses at a trot, aware that though Karus was not far enough along for concern, Ilyenna should not ride hard with her almost five moons of growth.

I held Karus again that night at the inn. Her tears streamed freely down her face with sobs of how we lost two of our channelers to a terrible fate and were left with the Blightress's threats to take our child.

No words could soothe her. No amount of kisses I placed on her temple could cease her tears, so I held her instead. I rocked her in my arms, singing the only lullaby I could remember from my mother.

> *"Sweetly does sing,*
> *The wren to the tree,*
> *Calling into the summer breeze.*
> *Softly does hum,*
> *The bee to the sun,*
> *Flying into the summer breeze.*
> *Shyly does bloom,*
> *The babe in the womb,*
> *Growing into the summer breeze."*

She laughed into my chest, now bare and wet, soaked with her tears. "Your mother sang that to you?"

I stroked the wet strands of white from her cheeks. "Yes. I remember her voice only through that song. She'd sing it to me when the night felt especially dark. She'd hear me cry out and slip into my bed, my head in her lap, and she'd sing it over and over until I fell asleep. She'd still be there in the morning, ensuring I made it through the night without being afraid."

"That's beautiful."

"When Saelyn comes, I want that to be the first song she hears. A gift from my mother. I think she would have liked that."

"Rev," Karus broke, her voice still hoarse, barely audible as she met my lips with hers. "She would be so proud of you."

I swiped at another tear falling down her cheek. "She would have loved you. I don't remember a lot of her, but I know that much."

We fell into silence. Her head rested on my chest in the dark, the only source of light a few slivers of wood still burning in the fireplace. I watched the moon as it danced across the sky, feeling Karus's head grow heavy as she gave way to her exhaustion.

I reached down to cover the hand at her belly with my own, pouring love and hope into our child, ensuring myself that what I had repeated over and over in this room, and back in the snowy clearing, was true. Saelyn would not be taken from us. The Blightress would not have her. I had used hope as a weapon before. I knew how to wield it once again. I knew that a man with hope was still alive.

# CHAPTER 21
# KARUS

"*He is gone.*"

Pompeii's voice broke into my thoughts as we neared the boundaries of Felgren.

I didn't want to lie. I didn't want to embellish what little hope I had that we'd return Mychael and Rell to this forest to train once more.

I breathed deep, squaring my shoulders on the back of my black horse, raising my chin with trembling lips. Pompeii could not see me, but I needed to pull myself together. I had learned by now that to be Baron was to believe myself stronger than I was.

"*She took him,*" I replied in my mind. "*We are not giving up. We are gathering ourselves, and then we will make an attempt at her heart and be able to look for him. I promise you, we are not giving up.*"

Silence.

My stomach churned, and for a moment, I thought I'd retch over the side of my horse.

Revich's head swiveled to me as he reigned his horse closer. "What is it?"

"Pompeii. He...he knows."

Rev drew his eyes back to the line of trees in the distance and pushed our party forward.

~

I STEPPED INTO FELGREN AGAIN WITH A HESITANCY I HADN'T FELT since Heimlen had brought me to the forest more than seven years past.

The trees fell to their own sorrow. The wind felt weighted and mournful as the four of us returned without those who deserved to be there.

Once again, my heart raged, urging me to do what I would have done if not for Saelyn. If she had not been at risk, I would have fought for our channelers with every inch of my life. But it was not just my life at stake, not just Rev's when I had chosen not to follow.

There were three of us to consider now, and I would not risk the safety of our daughter for anything or anyone.

And it hurt.

Pompeii was there, just inside the tree line, dressed immaculately in his emerald livery. The only evidence of his pain was a difficult one to notice. He had not dressed his eyes in the black kohl he kept swept along his upper lids.

Rev reached him first, pulling his old friend and Overseer into an embrace. The hug was short with Pompeii pulling out of reach and addressing me as soon as I caught up to them.

"Baron Karus," he began, "there has been an incident, and you are needed back at the Fortress."

He gestured behind him. A black lumen stepped up to his side, sniffing the air. He was massive, easily the largest lumen I'd ever seen. His eyes were a silvery metallic, and he padded up to my side, his head bent to sniff my belly before he looked up to my face. With a huff, he turned to offer his back.

"Where are Parvus and Rauca?" I asked, petting his dark fur.

"They are missing."

"Fuck," Rev exhaled, shaking his head and running his hands down his face.

Talon and Ilyenna's lumens rushed to them, jumping and whining in their greeting.

"Parvus?" I gazed out into the trees as if Pompeii was wrong. As if I'd see him and his mother, Rauca, bounding over the underbrush to greet us at any moment. I would brush my hands across his ears and check for more signs of seeds, moss, or vines. His tongue would loll from the side of his mouth and he'd give me that impatient whine before turning for me to hop onto his back.

But he didn't. And he wouldn't. The silence that followed between the five of us only fueled my worry. We'd accepted it, then. Mychael was gone. Rell was gone. Our lumens were gone as well, and we knew exactly who had called them to her.

I exhaled in a quick release, focusing on what Pompeii needed from me. I climbed onto the back of the lumen he called Boros with Rev settling in behind me. This lumen was the only one I'd ever seen large enough to carry two riders.

All five of us seated, I asked Pompeii as we began our ride through Felgren back to the Fortress, "Why am I specifically needed?"

"It's Prince Philius. He's—" Pompeii cleared his throat, continuing, "With the help of Renn, he has cut off his own hands."

# CHAPTER 22
# REV

More curses escaped me.

I squeezed the sides of Boros, urging him to run faster through the forest trails, taking the quickest, but less trodden one that led right to the Fortress doors.

I needn't bother, though. Karus was already whispering words of magic in his ears, giving him some of her power so that he moved easily and seamlessly through the underbrush. She called to the wind to help guide his way, the air moving swiftly as he bounded over logs, bushes, and fallen debris with ease.

What would have taken over an hour, became merely half of one as we reached the tall, black towers of the Fortress. Pompeii, Talon, and Ilyenna would still be far behind us.

Karus all but leapt from the massive black beast, faltering only slightly on her skirts as she picked them up, bounding across the path that led to the stone steps. I knew how quickly she moved because I ran just behind her the entire way, ensuring any slip, any stumble, I'd be there to catch her.

She burst into the foyer, calling out to Lia who came immediately, her face stricken with tears.

"This way," she said, ushering us through the dining hall doors.

We followed Lia at a run, passing through the warm kitchens, then through the doors that led to the servants' quarters. We headed to the only empty room. It had once been Sylva's, Heimlen's lover and life source. Karus burst into the room without a knock, arriving at the bedside within seconds. Philius lay there, his face gaunt, his wrists wrapped in clean white bandages.

"Philius!" Karus yelled, shaking him awake. His eyes flew open and he reactively reached for her. He stared down at his bound wrists instead, shaking slightly at what he had done.

"Why?" Karus shook her head, gripping his arms.

"It's how she did it," he rasped. "The Black Fever was still there, inside of me through my diseased hands."

My stomach rolled at his admission. I heard Renn move before I saw her in the corner of the small room. Her arms were crossed at her chest, her red curls unbound and falling limply at her shoulders. Her light brown eyes were rimmed red and tears streamed heavily down her freckled cheeks.

"How did this happen?" I asked her, turning so that Karus and Philius could speak in private.

She lifted her chin in a defiance I had never seen on her young face. "He asked me to. So, I did."

I hid none of my anger as it slid from my voice. "How did you do it, Renn?"

Her eyes widened slightly at my tone and she returned, "An axe. We went out into the forest, and we got rid of *her* in his mind."

I bent my head, in a deep exhale. When I looked back to her face, her lips trembled and she took a crying, shaking breath. "She took my sister. She took my friend. She took over Philius's thoughts and forced him into those trees of people!" She was shouting now, pointing at Philius. "We solved that problem without you! I would have done it earlier if I'd known what she'd do!"

I pulled her to me as she cried in heaving sobs at my chest.

"She's right," Philius said. "This is the solution we came up with and it worked." He lifted his face back to Karus. "She's gone from my head completely. I couldn't let her do this again." He reached out to her. "Hear me when I say I'd rather die than let her take over me again like that. I didn't remember anything. When I found myself back here and Renn told me what had happened, we had to *do* something."

Renn silently cried in my arms, and I brushed at her hair, understanding the depth of despair she held.

"Get up," Karus demanded. "Get dressed." She turned from Philius's bedside, stopping at Renn in my arms. She pulled the hair back from Renn's face, quickly fixing it into a long red braid down her back. "Wipe your face and get something to eat. I need you at the back door of the kitchens in an hour." She swept her gaze to me briefly, then turned to everyone in the room, including Lia at the door. "As soon as the others arrive, we head to the Blight and destroy it. This is our forest and no part of the Blightress will remain here."

She swept out of the room and all eyes locked on me. I pulled a handkerchief from my vest pocket and handed it to Renn. "I need to speak to Baron Karus. Will you be alright?"

She nodded, wiping at her nose. "I'll be doing what she says."

My eyes darted to Philius who nodded, then to Lia.

She said, "I will do what I can to help, Baron Revich."

I bit back a reply. I would be outnumbered in this and Karus knew it.

"Excuse me," I murmured, letting go of Renn and exiting the room, following the hall into the kitchens. Karus was there, filling a plate full of food from the communal tray.

"What are you doing?" I asked, refraining from letting the anger seep through my words.

"I am eating, Baron Revich," she responded, setting her plate down at the small table and cutting into a slice of cold ham.

"We don't need to do this right now. Let's think about it and what our options may be."

"No," she countered. "The Blightress will not sit and think about her next move. She is two steps ahead of us and will not expect this. As soon as the others are here and fed, we leave. We destroy the rest of the Blight in this forest. They may not be trained in Cosensian Magic, but you know we don't need much. The Blight will be gone by morning."

"You'd risk all of them?" I ran my hand through my hair, sliding into the chair next to her. "What if she sends an army of those beasts out from the Blight and attacks us all?"

"She could do that at any time. And the best way to stop her from such a threat is to destroy the Blight in this forest."

I sat back in my chair, rubbing a hand over my mouth, watching my love, the mother of my child, as she speared a piece of ham she'd cut so carefully and brought it to her mouth. Her hand shook. Her eyes were dangerously close to letting those formed tears spill over, but her back was straight. Her chin high.

In all the years of Baron I had on her, I'd never had someone to make decisions with. I'd had to make hard ones. I'd had to sit and eat with the weight of what was heavy on my shoulders, but I'd done it alone.

I gripped her wrist as she went to take another bite. Her body froze while she decided if she'd take my help, if she'd accept that we did this Baronship together, made our choices for our people together.

Her black eyes finally met mine and her lips quivered.

"We do this together," I whispered, leaning in, holding her gaze as her tears finally spilled over her lashes, falling in long shiny trails to her chin where they dropped into a splash over her plate. "You breathe, I breathe. You live, I live."

She let out a cry and nodded, attempting to focus her face back into a solid expression.

She couldn't. And I didn't want her to.

"It's time," she trembled, taking a stuttering breath.

"I know," I murmured, pulling on her wrist to bring her onto my lap. I wrapped an arm around her waist and tucked her arm around my neck, cradling her head to lay on my shoulder.

Her weight fell onto my body, immediately comforting my soul as I held her, welcoming more of her tears, gathering all of the pain she emitted through our bond and holding it there for her within my own chest, my own heart.

Karus was my companion, my partner, my love, and though I knew loneliness, I swore in those moments of time when she needed to fall apart, that my beloved never would.

# CHAPTER 23
# KARUS

Of all the choices I'd made, this was the one I feared the most.

Not attempting to destroy the Blight seven years ago with Heimlen.

Not following the Blightress into the dark tunnel of her making, not taking back Viridis, not the trials.

This.

It was one thing to risk yourself.

It was entirely another to risk the people you loved.

I stood at that black line I knew well. I knew it in myself, in my own soul so marred with the choices I had made.

The edge of Felgren and the Blight was clear as day.

Here was life.

Here was death.

Here was renewed hope.

Here was endless despair.

In some ways, I understood. The Blightress had been held down, tied to her own bed so that she could not cut the babe from her womb and save her daughter. I would have attempted it, too.

Her lover hadn't listened to her, her sister had abandoned her. Was there any doubt I would have pulled my own heart from my chest?

That was the question I feared to answer.

Could I have become exactly what she was?

"I'm not leaving you, Karus," Rev breathed in my ear behind me, feeling all the turmoil I let fly through our bonded hearts. "I'll repeat myself; you are not her."

Why did I need to hear those words so often?

I turned my back on the hundreds of acres of Blight still left in Felgren and addressed the people I cared for in this forest.

"What we are about to do will be draining. Cosensian Magic is difficult to use, let alone hold for the period of time we need to do this. Do not let go. Do not hold back your channel of power from this forest. Let it flow down this line. Give it to me, and we will see the end of this Blight upon our home."

I finished my speech, tying a braid down my back, tucking my white and chestnut strands away from my face. I nodded to Moira, jerking my head toward the thirty Growers she'd been able to gather in the last forty minutes. "Are they ready?"

She screeched into the wind and thirty heads of varying foliage from the massive fae creatures nodded.

"Let's begin," I called, turning around to face that endless black. Rev tensed behind me. I could feel it in the way he gripped my arm as I held my hands out to hover over that black line. "*Simulair Solum*," I called. The green orb in my hand instantly burst to a simulation of the same sun that beat down upon our faces in the midmorning light.

The unsettling hiss of the Blight shrinking away sounded around us in a chorus of death as the thick, thorned vines shriveled and fell to ashes. I took one more glance behind me with an encouragement I hoped all of them could feel in my dark gaze.

They spread out behind me in a V shape, both Rev and Lia holding onto my arms. Gripping Revich's shoulder was Talon, followed by Ilyenna. Pompeii held onto Lia while Renn held onto her, also gripping Philius's arm. We didn't know how Philius would be able to conjure power now that he couldn't use hands to summon it from his fingers, but he insisted he be there as well, and I would not deny him.

I wouldn't deny any of them, seeking retribution in their own ways for what the Blightress's influence had brought into their lives.

The Growers walked up to the line, fanning out beside us and planting their limbs into the space where the Blight nearby withered away to death. Already, shoots of green sprouted where they touched the ashen earth.

"I love you," I murmured, taking one last glance at Revich just behind me with a small smile.

"And you'll love me still at the end of this, so don't you dare say that like a goodbye, Baron Karus."

I laughed, my eyes filling with the green I knew appeared because his jaw tightened and he swallowed. Without a word, he cupped my cheek with his free hand, bringing my lips to his for one last kiss before we descended into what would become our future path.

I closed my eyes and let the heat of the power I held radiate over my face. The warmth kissed my skin, flowing through my hands and spilling into my body, fueling my resilience, fueling my assurance to myself that we would all make it to the other side of this Blight, and it would be destroyed from our forest forever.

I focused on the sun I held and sent my love, my promise to Saelyn growing steadily in my womb that I did this for her. I did this for her future here in Felgren. The one she deserved and the one I'd fight for every single day of my life.

When I opened my eyes, I let the power of those behind me flow. Brilliant colors of blue, silver, purple, gold, and green swirled over the ball of light in my hands as it grew in size, engulfing what I could see. Even sparks of orange flame flickered around the corona, and I smirked with the proof that my brother's magic was still with us.

I took my first step forward into the Blight and heard her voice in my head. *"Do not force my hand, Little Sprout."*

I shuddered, despite the warmth that flowed through the

resounding hiss of the Blight's death. I spoke to her, taking more steps into the decay. "*It is you who has forced mine.*"

I let it grow, let it build just to the point where I could carry the weight of what I had long, long ago been chosen to bear.

Before I cut her off completely, I let her in on the secret I'd been keeping. "*I could have loved you. Saelyn could have loved you. But now, I will do everything in my power to end you.*"

# CHAPTER 24
# REV

Heimlen had called my love for Karus my weakness. He would have said the same of Saelyn.

The man who had mentored me haunted my thoughts at the line of Blight as I held onto the woman I loved.

He had tried to teach me that we were Barons. We led alone, we died alone.

Years ago, I'd decided to fuck that tradition and give my heart to the woman I didn't want to live without.

Then I'd lost her.

I would not lose her again.

To ancient evil, to the spell we both knew could kill her, to beasts of abhorrent power, to time, to death.

So, instead of turning around and pulling her back to the Fortress and our rooms by force, I found the hand of hope once more in my life to help her destroy what had taken root in our home.

Heimlen had claimed loving her made me weak.

I knew it made me strong.

I heard the first Blight beast before I saw it as it trampled through the Blight to my right. I'd been ready, already sifting through all the scenarios of what the Blightress would attempt once she realized what we were doing. Destroying the Blight here in Felgren would weaken her power, if only for a short time.

All black limbs and red glowing eyes, it leapt into the air, pouncing on the Grower at the far end, bringing it down into the forest floor. I pulled back on some of my power, churning the earth where the Grower fell, swallowing them both into the ashen soil below. Instantly, I siphoned enough power to shield our people, Moira, and half the line of Growers. It was a risk to pull any of my power away from Karus, who picked up her pace, holding onto the sun the size of our rooms in the Fortress. Another vicious snarl sounded to our left as two more Blight beasts emerged from the shadows, taking down one, then another of the Growers within seconds of their appearance.

"Talon!" I called. Understanding my urgency, he conjured his golden light behind us at the beasts, forcing his power across their bodies. Tendrils of magic wove over and through the beasts' wooden sinew, striking through them at the last word of his spell. Each fell to the ground, and the Growers regained their footing, running in a mass of twigs and leaves to catch up to their brethren, continuing their growth back into the soil.

The ashes behind us were covered in the beginnings of new life from the Growers, a promise that what was broken could be renewed. I prepared for the next round, hearing the howls in the distance, but was not ready for the blackened trees ahead as they pulled their roots from the earth, forming into the sharp limbs and features of the trees Karus had told me about when she'd been pulled to the Blightress's lands.

Easily fifty feet tall, the Blighted trees rose in an unnatural stiffness that cracked and snapped with black sap oozing from their gargantuan maws. I understood Karus's horror at these creatures as an ear-piercing bellow echoed through the forest. One of the abominations swept its limb forward, striking three Growers at the end of the row, launching them into the trees behind us.

"Pompeii, Renn! Help the Growers!" I called, pushing more, sending more of what I could to Karus.

A blast of purple and red power flew from the both of them, winding over the new growth of saplings the Growers had planted in the wake of the Blight's death. Their agricola magic grew the small trees to massive ones, their branches winding around the jagged limbs of one of the Blight trees, rooting it to the earth in a haunting screech of anger. The other Blighted tree darted around the new growth with a surprising dexterity, raging and running right for Karus. Before it could take another earth-shattering step, it splintered in two, the swipe of an azure axe slicing through one tree, then the other, both husks falling in crashing thuds to the ground.

Lia caught my eye and I winked, returning what power I'd taken to destroy them back to Karus.

She carried the sun steadily, despite the battle around her, and picked up her pace, each of us running out behind her, none of us letting her go.

Two more Blighted trees formed from the darkness around us, smashing into the line of Growers. Moira cried out in the destruction of her kind, but stayed inside the shield of power I carried, leaving her faekind behind in the wake of their demise.

Five more Blight beasts burst from the Blight ahead, their bodies slamming into my shield, knocking them back. Karus's sun disintegrated them the instant they hit the solid earth. Another four hit the shield again, this time with what looked like a long-dead muri at their side.

I held onto the shielding spell with ease, knowing there was only one who could break it.

And then, she was there in a billow of black shadows as if summoned by my confidence, slicing through the last line of Growers with ease. The last ten outside of my circle of blue light fell to pieces on the ground, dead before they could even look her way.

"Fall back with me!" Lia shouted, letting go of Karus and breaking through my shield to face her sister. Pompeii, Renn, and Philius followed, splitting from the group. Karus stumbled slightly from the loss of power, but kept her focus forward, sending her sun upwards, her growing streaks of white hair billowing around her face.

"Go!" I yelled behind me at Talon and Ilyenna, pointing toward Lia who held her hands out before her, pulling every stone she could find from the ground and hurling them toward the Blightress and the array of Blight beasts surrounding her. They flew through the air, captured in Lia's silvery tendrils of power, hitting the iridescent shield the Blightress held.

Karus stopped running, turning for a moment to look back at the scene behind us. "We have to help!" she shouted over the sound of snarls and roars from the Blight beasts and Blight trees that tore at my shield, fueled by the Blightress's presence. With one last swipe of thorns and branches against my shield, it finally broke, exposing us to the creatures. Karus's sun held them at bay as we resumed our pace, never escaping the fight that raged behind us.

"We destroy this Blight, she'll be too weakened to stay!" I called to Karus, pulling more of my power to surround just the two of us in a new shield.

A high-pitched scream pierced the air, and we stopped to look back as Renn fell to the ground beside Philius, her body wrapped in black vines grown up through the ashes, pulling her into the earth. With a spark of light, the scent of fire and burning flesh wove through the air as the vines encasing her body burned. Pompeii was there, pulling her away as Philius knelt to the ashes, the wrappings at his wrists now black from the fire burning with his power.

The Blightress's haunting laughter surrounded us, calling more creatures to her side. "What a foolish attempt at defiance. This forest is mine. You all are *mine*." She bent to the black ashes, flattening her hand on the ground. Inky tendrils of Blight rose, some of them disintegrating instantly as they were met with Karus's sun. Blight beasts leapt at Talon and Ilyenna, knocking them to the ground, distracting Lia enough for the Blightress to blast through her silvery shield.

"The Blight will just keep growing!" Karus yelled, holding the sun with one hand and grabbing my forearm with the other. "Conjure the spell, Rev! We can fix this!"

Her sun rose above our heads, still growing in the mass of destruction, reducing the Blight to ashes even as the Blightress grew more of her dark stain on our forest.

"*Simulair Solum!*" A great ball of warmth hovered above my free hand, not even half the size of the one Karus held.

"Now!" she called, and I sent my own sun up to hers. It touched the surface and then slipped through to form an impossible mountain of unwavering light that burned my cheeks and lips just by standing under its rays.

I pulled Karus to me as I felt her fading, falling to my knees with her in the ashes. She gripped the back of my neck with one hand, jutting the other up into the air, sending our joined shape of blistering light and heat further up above the trees. Then, wrapping her hands at the base of my jaw, she actually smiled in glorious brilliance and murmured above my lips, "Without hope, she walks the earth." Her gaze shifted to the blistering sun still rising above the trees. "But I have hope, Rev. For this forest, for Saelyn, for us. She can't take that away. She never will."

Her raw, blistered lips met mine, and we both let go of the weight. The sun above us, swollen to the size of the clearing we'd made in the Blight's destruction, burst at the touch of her mouth on mine, exploding in a boom that reverberated through the forest, raining down fire and light that flew through the Blight as swiftly as a Felgren wind.

# CHAPTER 25
# KARUS

A cry of rage and pain echoed through the burst of light, fading just as the Blightress did, just as all the Blight and her creatures quickly disintegrated to ash in our forest.

I kissed Rev deeply, pouring my power over his lips, healing them and mine all at once, shifting my fingers from his sharp jaw up through his black waves covered in ashes.

In the last declaration of my power, I had filled that blazing sun with hope. Hope that we'd see this forest as it should be. Hope that Rev would kiss me again, love me again, and many more times after that, as it should be. Hope for the child we'd made growing in my belly, an innocent life who deserved more than to witness pain and destruction of the isle in the fight to come against the Blightress.

The flaring tendrils of the sun burned all around us in the wake of the Blight's final demise. Rev wrapped his arms around my back, pulling me further into his lap, returning my kiss with one of his own—hungry and demanding.

I pulled back from his mouth, my heart racing, my body responding to his urgent kiss as it always did when we were in the aftermath of some dangerous event we'd just faced. I wrapped my arms around him, pressed my cheek to his and whispered in his ear, "I love you still."

He groaned, pulling my face back to his, pressing me back into the ashes we'd left in the outcome of the sun we'd made together.

The Blightress was gone, her beasts gone, her plague upon the forest gone—disintegrated completely in the smoldering pockets of flame and light still simmering on the surface of the earth around us. I could no longer feel the Blight or hear the heart of it beating relentlessly as it had done for years.

He kissed me wholly, fiercely, as if we were the only ones left in our forest.

We weren't.

"Is this what humans do after exhausting their power?" Moira lilted from somewhere above our heads.

Revich streamed a myriad of curses across my lips before sitting up and pulling me up with him, rising from the ground to survey the damage. We were at least thirty feet away from the others who thankfully hadn't seemed to notice how entwined we'd become since lighting hundreds of acres into little fires.

I rushed to Philius and Lia hovering over Renn who lay unconscious on the ground. The right side of her face and shoulder were burned in a streak of raw flesh.

"I didn't mean to—" Philius started, unable to finish in his grief, rising and walking away.

"*Vennae,*" I murmured, closing my eyes and searching through her veins for a pulse. It was there, but weak. "We have to get her back to the Fortress," I urged, calling to Rev.

He was already there, creating two portals in swift movements of his hands.

"I'll take her," Pompeii said, helping me pull her to her feet, still unconscious.

"These lead straight to the room Philius occupied in the servants' quarters." Revich took Pompeii's place, lifting Renn easily.

"I should be able to heal these wounds," Pompeii assured us as he stepped into his portal to wait for Renn on the other side.

We lifted her to the portal, careful of her raw wounds and gently pushed her through, hoping Pompeii was ready to catch her. The portal closed in a rush of power as her body disappeared.

I surveyed the damage, feeling Pompeii's gentle tap through the Overseer-Baron bond on my shoulder, assuring both of us Barons that he had Renn safely in that room. Talon was holding onto Ilyenna tightly as they caught their breath. Lia was bent to the earth, inspecting the ashes that fell while the few Growers left sifted their limbs into the earth, slowly returning life to the soil.

"Philius!" I called, catching up to him as he paced through the new growth.

"I burned her!" He brought the stubs of his wrists to his head, ready to scream into the still smoldering forest.

I caught his arms in mine, mumbling the spells of healing he needed to close the wounds. "You saved her from that Blight. It was going to pull her under the surface."

"I didn't mean to. I didn't—."

"I know," I soothed. "She will know, too, when she wakes."

"The Blightress," he breathed, "she's gone?"

"Yes."

"She just left without more of a fight?" he asked, in a grim purse of his lips.

"I think—" I started, opening my mind to her, just to see if she lingered there. "I think she's wounded. She didn't suspect that I could destroy all of the Blight at once, and I couldn't have without Revich's help. When the Blight is destroyed, she feels it. Just like when I burned those syphoner trees. She—"

"What are we waiting for, then?" Philius whipped around with the glint of hatred in his golden eyes. "Let's go now. Let's go to her heart and be rid of her."

"I—"

"You know how to get there. You've been before. So let's leave. While she's recovering. She won't expect us. We can rid the land of her now. We don't need to wait."

I couldn't lie, the same line of thought had already crossed my mind, but seeing Renn burned and the aftermath of destroying the

Blight, I hesitated in admitting to Rev what the rage in my heart wanted to do next.

"It's not up to us. We all have to agree because all of us will be taking a risk."

"I'll talk to them."

"No!" I grabbed his vest as he lurched forward. "Let me. Your temper never won any arguments against anyone but the Queen." I sighed heavily, checking his wrists one last time to see that his wounds were healed over.

Revich and Lia were deep into a conversation, so I took a moment to dampen the pockets of flame around us. They'd sprouted here and there around what was now a clearing in the midst of healing. The Growers left were working hard, their spindly bodies bent to the ashes, pushing limbs into the ground and slowly sprouting buds of bushes and saplings of trees. Moira leapt from each new circle of growth, spinning and twirling, her own fae magic encouraging the growth and blooms of red, yellow, and white which opened for her as she danced.

Philius stayed close as I smoothed my black vest and skirts and wiped at the black remnants of Blight.

"I'm with you, Soot." Philius muttered so only I could hear.

I grunted a laugh, my lips pulling into a smile. It was the nickname he'd given me as a child. Instead of calling me Ash, he'd call me *Soot*, just to get under my skin as brothers tend to do.

"I haven't heard that in a long time," I replied in a heavy sigh, hands on my hips, gripping them tightly and gazing up into the trees stained with black.

"Too long." He crossed his arms awkwardly, pausing slightly with how to tuck the stubs of his wrists underneath. "I'm here as a reminder of where you came from."

I shivered and stared at my brother for a moment in a distant memory of us as children, running through the tall grasses of the Hyrithian Plains. Hand-in-hand we'd taken on invisible foes and leapt greatest distances, and we'd done it together.

I'd never hold his hand again.

I cocked my head, filling my lungs and looking down at my boots to recuperate my thoughts.

They all gathered silently. Without needing to call them to me, my people circled in front of me. Each stood in varying states of dishevelment and exhaustion, waiting to hear what I had to say.

Philius stood to my left, followed by Talon and Ilyenna, still holding onto each other. Ilyenna's silent tears streamed down her face as she cupped her growing belly.

Lia next, looking the most exhausted I'd ever seen her. Her black hair, always swept back into a bun at the nape of her neck, had now fallen out completely, flowing down her shoulders in beautiful waves of onyx. She looked younger, tired, but if I looked hard enough, I'd guess she wasn't a day over forty.

My eyes followed the line, landing on Rev. I knew he gripped the rhyzolm in his hand even though he'd shoved them both into his pockets, standing there like a pillar of chiseled marble. I saw through the ash and grime, right to the man who would need the most convincing to do this.

His eyes warred.

Black, blue, black, blue—an unending swirl of color fading in and out like ocean waves on a starless night.

"The Blight is gone from this home we share," I started, honing my anger into strength. "But there is one more task I ask of you."

Five sets of eyes locked on me, and I stood taller, straighter, no longer a channeler brought to the forest to save it, but a Baron leading in the fight to protect it. "The Blightress did not expect us to succeed in ridding Felgren of her poison. She is feeling the effects of the Blight's destruction, possibly still healing from the syphoner trees we burned days ago. She is weak."

Revich shifted slightly, and in the subtle movement, I knew he knew what I would ask next.

"We can leave now. I know the way to her heart underground. The tunnel will lead us to a portal. It does not fade. That portal will lead to her heart. We can destroy it while she is weak. She will not expect that from us." I nodded to Philius. "He no longer has a connection to her, and she is in the far corners of my mind. The

Blight is gone and she does not know of what I speak to you now. I ask if you will come. I do not command it as one of your Barons, I ask it of you as one of your family."

A smile tugged on Philius's lips as he stepped closer. "I will come with you, Baron Karus."

Lia pulled her hair behind her, twisting the long length in her hands and tucking it into a bun at the nape of her neck. "I will not leave you now, Baron Karus."

I nodded to her, biting down on the sob that begged to leave my chest.

I looked to Talon and Ilyenna. They shared a silent conversation and Ilyenna nodded slightly. Talon kissed her temple and turned to me. "We will come with you, Baron Karus." He glanced to Rev, adding, "We hold onto hope. We defy the dark."

Revich's jaw feathered, but he didn't look away from me. His nostrils flared, his eyes darkened to black, the war of blue a battle lost. He did not hold my stare as a lover, he analyzed me as a Baron. For perhaps the first time since we'd met all those years ago in the foyer of the Fortress, he looked at me as Heimlen had. As a woman with power, with potential, with a stubborn spirit and strong will.

"I will speak to Baron Karus alone," he ordered, holding my gaze—the one I, too, refused to break.

Neither of us moved, neither wavered from the pull of our hearts, ever that thread of the bond we shared, now hot and drawn tightly as if we each tugged on the other side, attempting to bend the other to our will.

The rest of them left, wandering off to watch the rebuilding of Felgren.

I stepped closer and he followed, closing the gap between us that had never felt right. We stood, chest to chest, him slightly taller, me with my hands on my hips, refusing to give into wrapping them over his shoulders and pulling him closer.

He kept his hands in his pockets in a show of defiance of what we both wanted and what was right and natural, our bodies always finding their way back to the other.

"What is your objection, Baron Revich?" I asked calmly and quietly, setting the formality of the conversation to come.

"My objection, Baron Karus, is that this is not a task we are ready for. We bring with us, who? Three channelers in various stages of skill, an ancient lapis conduit, and two Barons? We planned for a small army of channelers and conduits to do this. I see no evidence we are ready."

"The question is not if we are ready, but if she is at her most vulnerable. She is weak. I feel it. I feel her cowering there in her palace of white stone. I see her there on the floor in agony at the destruction we've done here." I kept his stare while jutting my chin. "Look around and see her pain. Now is the time to strike when she is writhing on the floor and least expects it."

"I have looked around, and do you know what I see?" His voice came in a clipped growl. "I see an impulsive channeler who wants revenge. I see a frightened couple that would go to the ends of the earth for either of us and follow us blindly to their demise if we so asked. I see a tired woman who fears making the same mistake she made hundreds of years ago. I see my partner, my companion, a Baron of this forest, the mother of my child, pushing herself beyond her limits by way of pain and anger. I see her most clearly of all."

I raised my chin, clamping my mouth shut and swallowing hard enough that it hurt. I gave him my love, pure as the first night we spent together. I was angry, frightened, determined to go to that heart and destroy it for good, but more than that, I delved deep into my own soul, finding his there with mine, sending that image to him through our bond.

He jerked, blinking rapidly.

I opened my mouth, breathing deep and lifted a hand to his chest, covering the fabric—the skin and bones—which protected his heart. "We all go or none at all. Whatever you choose, I'll love you still."

The moment I reached out to him, his hand was there, pressing my fingers to his heart. "The only reason I'll agree to this is because of our daughter. I go for her. If I did not feel her so strong and steady through this stone,"—he pulled the green rock from his pocket, and I watched in awe as it hummed in his hand, buzzing across his palm—"then none of us would be going. We do this for the future of the children of this forest, of this isle, and no other. We do not do this for ourselves, for revenge, for blind loyalty, for some regret we have to face—no. We do this for Saelyn. For Ilyenna's child. For all the children who are and are yet to be. They deserve a world in which this threat is just a history they hear in lyric and song before they drift to sleep."

He dropped the rhyzolm back into his pocket and pulled my hand to his lips. "I'm afraid becoming a father has made me as reckless as you."

I laughed, taking my hand from his lips and sliding it through his hair, letting my body fall into his chest, delighting in the feel of his strong arms that slid around my waist. They always would. He'd always be there to hold me, even at our times of tension.

"I love you," I whispered, hovering my own lips just below his and glancing from his brilliant blue eyes to his mouth.

He tightened his hold on my body, my heart, pulling that tether as close as our bodies were in that healing forest we loved. "And you'll love me still." He grinned and winked, the gesture melting me into a puddle at his feet, where I'd gladly worship for days on end as soon as we had rid the isle of the woman who haunted it.

"And I'll love you still," I agreed, pulling him down to join my lips in a kiss that we lost ourselves to as lovers, Barons, and deciders of the shadowed path we'd chosen.

# PART THREE
## SEVENTEEN YEARS AFTER

*It should have been us.*
*It should have been everything we worked for, wanted, dreamed.*
*I do not hold the hand of hope.*
*I fight in the dusk of fear, simmering in rage and agony.*

# CHAPTER 26
# SAELYN

T hevin spoke softly, quietly, easing me into the reality of the world I would face outside of the forest that raised me. I'd been sheltered all my seventeen years. I knew that. But I did not realize the depth of the false life I lived in Felgren.

How could I have known the horrors that awaited just outside my mother's shield of crystalized green shards? How could I ever have imagined the dire need for my mother's army of magic wielders to defeat this Blightress?

I watched Thevin in silence, taking in what he told me about the creatures he had faced, the friends he had lost.

I didn't know loss—I knew loneliness and discontent.

Thevin, however, knew them all. He'd faced each one in his life and somehow still came back every summer—happy, carefree, teasing me and falling...for me.

It could be that I was different enough in his life that he wanted to cling to those summers to avoid what he knew was the truth. And with that thought, a new fear rose within me. What if he did not want to be with *me*, but he wanted those warm summer days instead of his cold, dark ones? What if he wanted the innocence of a young woman who didn't know the horrors he knew?

"Thank you for sharing this," I whispered in a rasp as he finished his last story of battle. I pulled the blanket tighter around my shoulders, breaking my gaze from him to watch the flames dance in my hearth. "Thank you for telling me the truth." I reached out and took his hand. "I'm so sorry, Thevin. I'm so sorry you've lived with these burdens, and I wasn't there to be your friend through all of them."

He glanced at me and then around the room. "You've always been with me, Sae. I've always had this place to hope to come back to." He wove his fingers through mine and kissed the back of my hand. "I've always had you to come back to."

My heart raced at his touch. But that inkling of fear grew, fueled by my own inexperience of life. Something told me what he hoped for was just a dream. Something told me that if I was willing to take the risk of becoming his, I'd need to first prove to him that I was more than just a girl trapped in the safety of a forest.

I could do what he did. I could fight. I had power, I was strong, and I could show him that I was more than a simple girl who danced through wildflowers. Then, he'd see a different side of me. Then, he could decide if I was what he truly wanted or just a dream to chase away the nightmares he faced.

"Tell me what you're thinking," he urged, and I took my hand back from his.

"I'm thinking I'm ready. I'm thinking it's about time I leave this place and become useful. I'm thinking," I paused, watching his lips tug upward. "I'm thinking it's time for bed."

I rose from the floor, flicking the blanket into the air and back onto my bed, pulling down the sheets and fluffing the pillows. He reached the other side of the bed and grabbed one along with the blanket.

"I'll take the chaise," he muttered, tossing the bedding he'd hoarded onto the long lounge chair.

"You don't want to sleep in the bed?" We'd slept in my bed together plenty of times as children.

He fell back onto the chair, arms behind his head, kicking his boots to the floor and crossing his feet at the ankles which fell past the length of the chaise. "I won't get a wink of sleep with the way you toss around while you sleep."

A decorative pillow, embroidered with a field of yellow buttercups, hit him square in the face, jolting him from his cool indifference. He sat up, tossing his blanket aside.

"Fine," I said cooly, "sleep on your lounge chair, but don't come crawling to me when you fall off in the middle of the night." I laughed, pulling my night clothes from the armoire. When he didn't respond to my playful jab, I looked over my shoulder to see him sitting up, elbows on his knees, rubbing his hands over his face, muttering something to himself.

Cursing words that would give me a scolding from Pah-Pah, I padded to his side, sitting next to him. "It must have been hard for you," I spoke lightly. "To relive all of what you've seen out there." I laid my head on his shoulder. "I'll take the chaise, you take the bed. I'll fit better on this thing anyway."

He peeked out from his hands. "I'm not taking your bed from you. And on your birthday of all nights."

"My bed is enormous." I gestured to the gargantuan thing. The large headboard and footboard were carved from a maple tree with etchings of flowers, trees, and delicate creatures with wings. "I promise to stick to one side and leave you completely to the other." I nudged his arm. "You won't even know I'm there."

He laughed, rich and full, tilting his head back in the moment and leaving me confused as to what was so funny. I stood up, taking my night clothes with me and headed to my washing room calling, "I've won this argument. Besides, we need good rest before our journey tomorrow, so come wash your face and brush your teeth!" The last word I shouted before I closed the door. I shimmied out of my cerulean gown, quickly stepping into my soft cotton pants and pulling my nightshirt over my head. A soft knock came and I kicked aside my dress, opening the door for Thevin to join me. I began to braid my long, black waves back as he leaned against the door frame with his arms crossed.

He looked me up and down and chuckled.

"What?" I asked, finishing the plait and tying it back with a strip of ribbon.

"I've just never seen you in pants."

I glanced down, wondering if my choice in nightclothes made him uncomfortable. "I don't like sleeping in a nightgown anymore. My skirts get all tangled up in my legs."

He followed me to the basin and took the jar of mouth paste I handed him. "More evidence of how much you move around when you sleep."

I scowled his way before splashing my face with water and finding a fresh towel to dry my skin. He scooped up the minty paste and began brushing at his teeth with his fingers.

"Sorry I don't have another brush." I shrugged, starting on my teeth as well.

He finished and spit into the basin, watching it drain into the small hole at the bottom. He wiped at his own face and said, "It's fine that you wear pants. Most women outside of Felgren wear them."

I spit my own paste into the basin, cocking my head. "During the day?"

He nodded, turning to leave. "It's easier to fight an enemy when you have free movement of your legs."

I thought about that for a moment while extinguishing the flame from the sconces on the bathroom wall. Thevin was already in the bed, lying flat on his back, hands once again behind his head as he stared up at my painted ceiling. I dimmed the fire to a low crackling with a white wisp of my magic and slipped under the covers, far away to the other side.

"Happy birthday, Sae," he murmured softly.

If I'd been a braver person, I'd have reached for his hand again. I wanted to touch him. I wanted to curl up onto his chest and feel what it was like to be held by the best friend I loved. Instead, I tilted my head to catch a glimpse of his features in the soft light. His eyes were closed, and I could just make out the long, light lashes, the upturned curl of his lips, and the sharp line where his jaw turned, meeting the base of his ear. I could study his face all night and never tire, which was ridiculous and had me chiding myself all over again.

"Thank you," I whispered back, turning away from him completely and curling my legs to my stomach. I closed my eyes, determined to prove myself to him, to my mother, to the world, and retrieve my father from the clutches of the woman who had broken everything.

# CHAPTER 27
# THEVIN

Sleep came quickly as an easy sort of slumber—some of the better sleep I'd had since returning to Felgren.

I'd lied about why I didn't want to sleep next to her. Her tossing and turning never bothered me when we were just childhood friends, and I'd slept in far worse circumstances.

I didn't want that tug on my heart I knew would come when I woke up to see her there beside me, curled up in a ball, her wild hair almost entirely freed from the braid she'd forced it into the night before.

I looked away quickly when I woke and pressed my palms to my eyes, forcing myself to calm down from the urge to pull her to me and wake her with light kisses.

Those were out of the question.

Far, far out of any question, and dammit, I needed to pull myself together.

She'd had a long night learning her father was somehow still alive and that her mother wanted to save him. I couldn't fathom why, seventeen years after his supposed death, Baron Karus had chosen now to admit he lived. This knowledge would change things. If the Wieldwryns knew about Baron Revich's survival, new tactics would need to be implemented when the Dimming came to pass.

I allowed myself one last longing glance at the best friend I was hopelessly in love with and slid silently out of her bed.

Though I was tall and strong, I was also trained for silent steps, a shadow who could slip in and out of a space without so much as a shift in the air. While the Wieldwryns were soldiers trained in magic, the Runners were used as a covert group of soldiers with no magic abilities whatsoever. The Four used us to get their army behind enemy lines and pull them out again when the tides turned.

It'd been that way for over a decade. Baron Karus was just one of the Four on the isle. She played her part in training soldiers sent to hold back the line of Blight trees, Blight beasts, and… I ran my hands through my hair, looking back at Sae. The girl I had laughed with while riding lumens grew into woman right before me, and it had taken all of a year to even notice.

I'd been involved with a few women in the past few years, but any pursuits of someone to share my bed had faded away at the end of last summer when I had admitted to myself that there was only one person I wanted to wake up next to.

I silently slid into the washing room, cursing my lack of magic in the dark. For whatever reason, the Fortress sported very few windows—Sae's room included—and from glancing at the clock on her mantle, it was dawn.

I managed to splash water on my face, brushing at my teeth and spitting the taste of sleep from my mouth. I needed to get back into my parents' rooms this morning and pack my few things, change my clothes, and—

"Why are you up so early?"

Sae's question in a yawn startled me. Some Runner I was. She'd somehow gotten out of bed and all the way to the washing room without me hearing.

"I slept hard. I'm usually up this early."

I stepped back into the room, thankful she'd started the fire again so I could see. I grabbed my shirt and pulled my arms through, beginning to fasten the buttons at the bottom.

Her cheeks flushed and I realized she'd likely never seen much of the male body. I couldn't even remember the last time we'd gone swimming together in the Great Stream of Felgren.

"I should start packing," she muttered, spinning on her heels to avoid me.

I hid my chuckle at her embarrassment, refraining from teasing her on the day she'd be leaving her home for the first time. I finished my shirt and headed to the chaise, pulling on my boots.

She began yanking skirts and dresses from her drawers, folding them neatly on the bed, muttering to herself something too low for me to hear.

"The Spire has…" I slipped on my last boot and stood. "A different style of clothing than Felgren. You'll see what I mean when we get there."

"Are you suggesting I'm going to stand out like a sore thumb in something like this?" She held up one of her gauzy dresses lined in pale pink lace.

"I like that one."

"I look like a child in most of these." She bit her lower lip, scrunching her face.

My gut lurched at her expression. I was in so much trouble.

"What about this?" She tossed the dress back into the wardrobe and pulled out a black skirt and cream top with ties up the front. She held the pieces up against her body for me to weigh in.

My heart tugged for the third time this morning. She was adorable standing there—hair a frizzy mess pulled up on top of her head, sleep still dragging at her eyes.

I nodded convincingly. "That one." I cleared my throat and headed to her door in a rapid dash. "I'll see you at breakfast." I left before she could say anything more and slammed the back of my head against her closed door, releasing a breath and wondering how I was ever going to get through this.

~

BREAKFAST WAS A SOMBER AFFAIR.

My parents had pelted me with questions as soon as I got to their room to start packing up what I had just unpacked only days ago.

They wanted to know everything Sae had told me and everything I knew about Baron Revich. I'd shrugged more than once, reminding them they'd actually trained with him, not me.

They asked about Sae's power and what I knew of it. I told them what little I did know or at least most of what I knew, explaining that, yes, I had always known she was more powerful than most.

When we'd arrived at breakfast, packed and ready for the day's journey, Baron Karus and Pompeii were already seated. They sat across from each other at the ridiculously long dining room table, chewing silently. My parents stopped in the doorway, staring at the Baron, waiting for…something.

"There were reasons you could not know," the Baron spoke softly, her black eyes focused on the three of us.

"*Reasons?*" my father scoffed. "Like what?"

"Talon." My mother used her light voice to calm him as she often did.

The Baron answered with, "We will discuss further details on the matter when we arrive at the Spire for the meeting of the Four and the commanders."

"Further *details* on the matter?" My father ignored my mother's steady calmness as he brushed forward, sliding into the chair next to the Baron, continuing, "You told us Revich was dead. You told the world Revich was dead and seventeen years later, you spring it on everyone—on your own *daughter*—that we need to change the Dimming to accommodate saving him?"

Pompeii cleared his throat. "You speak to the Baron of Felgren, Talon, lest you've forgotten."

"I don't give a damn," he snapped.

My mother gasped and my brows rose in shock. I'd never heard such words or disrespect from my father.

"Talon," Baron Karus soothed, placing a hand on his shoulder.

"There are threads here I don't expect you to yet understand, but I'm asking you to trust me."

He pulled his shoulder back from her hand, demanding, "Why haven't you saved him?"

He asked what we'd all been thinking since the truth was revealed. The air in the room tightened and silence remained.

Baron Karus's eyes hardened staring at my father. They seemed to have a wordless conversation that lasted long moments, interrupted when Sae opened the dining hall door, dressed in her black skirts and cream corseted shirt.

She smiled at me and then glanced around, her face souring when she caught sight of her mother and the Overseer she called Pah-Pah.

The Baron rose to greet her daughter, offering her a seat on her other side. We sat in silence, only the tiny clinks of our forks and plates heard and echoing off the walls of green and gold.

Finally, Baron Karus set down her fork and knife, turning to her daughter. "Pompeii will help you finish packing. You will also need to say goodbye to Boros. We leave in two hours for the Spire."

"We can't bring him with us?" Sae asked.

"We are leaving by portal, and no lumens will be joining us. The people outside of Felgren use horses."

"But Boros is just as big as a horse, I don't see why he can't—"

"Lumens are not welcome outside of this forest. He will frighten the people who do not know him. He cannot come."

Saelyn paused, her eyes flicking to me. I nodded slightly.

"Because of the Blight beasts?"

The Baron's dark eyes shot to me, and I coughed into my delicate tea cup.

She lifted her chin slightly and asked, "What have you told her, Thevin?"

Before I could contain my coughing fit, Sae replied, "I asked him to tell me what's out there so I'm ready to face it. I know about the war you've kept from me, and I know why you did."

The Baron's eyes did not leave my face as she softy questioned, "Why did I keep it from you, Saelyn?"

"Because this Blightress wants my power. That's why you never trained me, isn't it? She'd find out somehow and would want to harness the power I can wield."

"Is that true?" my mother asked the Baron, setting her hand on my back and patting lightly as I drank from my cup to clear my throat.

All eyes on her, the Baron took a deep breath and said, "Yes."

"This changes everything," my mother admitted, her shoulders slumping as she moved eggs around on her plate. She shook her head and looked back to the Baron with tears. "Why did you wait? Seventeen years, Karus. Why didn't you fight for him? We would have helped you."

The Baron closed her eyes and took another deep breath.

I watched Sae carefully. Her entire world had been turned upside down in a matter of hours. It didn't help that I foolishly confessed my feelings for her less than two days ago, either. Of all the people at this table who had mourned Baron Revich's life, I felt for Sae the most.

I glanced to my own father who stared at the Baron with a furrowed brow as she gathered herself. I couldn't imagine my life without him. Couldn't imagine who I would have become without his guidance, his ever-insistent adage that had gotten all of us Wieldwryns and Runners through the worst of it.

Hold onto hope. Defy the dark.

My father spoke then, pushing his chair back to leave. "We loved him, too, Karus." He took my mother's hand and squeezed my shoulder. They left without another word.

Sae reached out to her mother, taking her hand. "Is everyone going to be angry with you?"

"Many, Little Love."

"Then I won't," she promised. "I just want him back. For all of us."

I caught Pompeii's side glance. He nodded toward the kitchen door, and I rose to follow him through, giving the powerful mother and daughter time together before they left their home.

## CHAPTER 28
# SAELYN

My attempt at goodbye to Boros went poorly. So poorly in fact, that he followed me back to the Fortress, disregarding any commands I gave him. He sat next to me, my traveling bag in one hand, my other occupied, stroking the top of his head at my chest. His silver eyes pleaded up at me, and he gave a slight whimper—the first I'd ever heard from him.

"You can't come," I reminded him, planting a kiss on his long, black snout. "The people out there won't understand that you're a good boy." He nudged my arm to keep petting his ears.

We stood at the bottom steps of my home—all of us. The entire staff and guests from the party the night before were crowded around five portals glowing a bright emerald in the morning sun.

I was fascinated more than frightened to be leaving, especially by portal. My mother typically only made them to bring more channelers to our home to train or when she brought a few leaders to the forest for occasional meetings of which I was never allowed to attend.

Each summer, Thevin arrived with his parents at the edge of the forest where she would lift the shield just enough to let them in. But these portals I had watched her unfold were enticing. I studied her movements as she pulled her hands from the ball of green light she'd created, forcing open a few portals which would lead to a part of Arcaynen I'd never seen.

The Baron of Felgren finished her words to Pah-Pah and they embraced. He murmured something in her ear, and I recognized the break in her, noticed the grip she had on his arm as she nodded with a trembling chin.

She kissed his cheek and addressed the crowd. "The shield over Felgren will be weak for as long as we are gone." She nodded to Pah-Pah. "Pompeii will work with each channeler here to produce what shield you can. Stay alert. Do not enter the deep forest alone. Report back to your Overseer of any oddity you may come across." She gazed out at her people for a few moments, the sharp flicker of her portals glowing behind her. "I do not know when we will return. The Dimming is coming. As you have likely heard by now, Baron Revich is alive."

A hushed band of whispers filtered through the crowd, but my mother continued. "If all goes well, we will return with Baron Revich and the Blightress will be defeated once and for all."

I dug my fingers into Boros's fur. It seemed as if every eye shifted to me, the one this war apparently needed and the daughter of the long-thought-dead Baron. My role was set, my future already predicted, and I had no say.

Thevin shifted on his feet next to me. The back of his hand brushed mine as I gripped my travel bag to the point of white knuckles. I relaxed at his touch, not even daring to look at him.

There was one other task I needed to complete. It was a choice I would make for myself—convincing Thevin, who claimed to possibly love me, that I was more than just a girl of the forest he came to see every summer to escape from the horrors of war. I could be strong, too. I could be powerful. I could prove to all these people that I was capable of doing great things, powerful things, and I could help save my father and help with whatever the Dimming was.

I rolled my shoulders, giving one final squeeze to Boros before taking a few steps to Pah-Pah to say goodbye. Two flashes of light and Thevin's parents were gone, leaving through their portals to the Spire.

Thevin grinned my way, his one beautiful dimple appearing in the smile, and he turned his back to the portal saying, "See you in a minute," before falling back and disappearing completely.

I laughed and hoped he fell out of it on his backside.

I caught Pah-Pah's chuckle as well as he pulled me in for one of my favorite hugs. He kissed the top of my head and sighed. "I love you. You are powerful, you are beautiful, you are your father's daughter. He would be so proud of you, Sae. I always will be."

We swayed for a moment while the crowd dispersed, and my mother waited for me to join her. I lifted my head at his chest and squeezed, replying, "You'll be proud of me still, Pah-Pah. They don't know how powerful I can be." I winked and he laughed in a rich tenor.

"I don't doubt it."

My smile faded as I pulled back, still clinging to my bag, still holding his arms. "I'll bring him home." His face fell immediately, but I continued. "I promise. I'll bring all of them home."

His golden, kohl-lined eyes darted to my mother behind me.

"Come, Saelyn," she called, lifting her hand to take mine, watching Pah-Pah. "I, too, have promises to keep."

I kissed his cheek one last time and turned to her portals. "Will you teach me how to make these?" I asked, my eyes flickering over the glow of light that matched my height and build.

"I will, Little Love. Your father taught me, and I'll teach you." She squeezed my hand. "Ready?"

I nodded and took a last step out of my home and into the world beyond.

~

LIGHT BLINDED ME, AND I COVERED MY EYES WITH MY ARM, LANDING on solid white marble, catching myself on my knees. My bag skittered across the floor, the sound accompanied by a murmur of voices all around.

A calloused hand I knew well slid over mine as I braced myself. "I fell, too. Though not nearly as gracefully."

I blinked in the bright light to see Thevin grinning ear-to-ear in front of me, his golden, cropped curls flipped casually to one side, his other hand reaching out to help me up from the floor.

"Are you alright?" I heard my mother ask, patting my back.

I stood, nodding, and dusting off my black skirts, pulling the hair from my face and taking Thevin's hand for balance as I fixed my boot that had come loose in the fall.

I caught his stare, but he left quickly, moving to where my bag lay across the circular, open hall at the edge of an outlook upon a great city.

A gasp caught in my throat at the sight. High above the vast citadel, I could see each purple roof, each canal, water a clear blue, that wove through the white stone buildings like threads of a tapestry.

The structures rose high into the air, each domed roof a variation of purple, pink, and blue. Each building a cascade of white stone arches and ornate carvings dressed in long flowing vines of green, some blooming petals of every color I'd ever seen.

I held onto the edge of the stone column, careful in leaning over the side of the short railing along the curved arch which led back into the room. If there'd been clouds in the blue sky, we'd be inside them so high up in what I assumed was the famous Spire the city was named for.

Thevin stood within arm's reach, his brows raised as he observed the city below.

"I didn't—" I started, attempting to reign in my awe and giddiness at the view. "It's beautiful," I finished simply.

"It is," he agreed, his gaze turned to me, rather than the city.

My cheeks flushed, and though I'd deny it if he teased me, I knew it wasn't from the sharp breeze at my face.

"Thevin!" A yelp came from the wide, open room behind us, and we turned as a breathtaking young woman came running, her arms wide, matching Thevin's as she jumped into them, laughing and kissing his cheek.

"I thought you weren't arriving until the end of Felgren Summer!" she chastised playfully, stepping away from him only to shove his shoulder.

Her golden curls were bound in a braid that had been woven over the top of her head, bundling into a knot at the back. Her eyes were a pale blue, her lips pink and thin, a becoming feature on her pointed face.

Thevin rubbed his shoulder, feigning offense. "Plans changed. And you don't need to push me off the Spire because of them."

The beautiful girl laughed, her voice steady and confident, ringing through the domed hall. "Like I wouldn't catch you before you fell." She moved a hand to the sheathed sword at her side.

He chuckled and turned to me. "Sae, meet Lady Lanna of the Spire, daughter of Lady Lamoral."

My stomach might as well have been dropped out of the archway. I struggled to settle the immense unease I'd felt at the reunion I'd just seen, for I'd never seen Thevin interact with someone my age, let alone this Lady of the Spire who seemed to know him very well.

I bit the inside of my lip and stepped forward, plastering a small smile on my face, bowing my head slightly with my hand out to greet hers.

She winked and pulled my hand toward herself, wrapping her arms around my waist and squeezing once. She didn't let go, even though my body stilled in the shock and scent of her jasmine perfume. "I have been waiting, and waiting, and waiting to meet you, Saelyn of Felgren." She planted a kiss on top of my head and stood back, taking my hands in hers as she looked me over.

"You've been waiting to meet me?" I asked, dumbfounded at who exactly this young woman was.

She gave a halting scoff, turning to Thevin who stood nearby, his arms crossed, doing his best to suppress the amusement on his face. "Let me guess..." She jabbed a thumb at Thevin. "This piece of work hasn't said a single thing about me to you in all those months he's spent in Felgren." She glared at him. "Tanning and lounging— getting into all kinds of mischief with you." She leaned in close and murmured, "Please tell me it's true that your wild lumens don't care for him at all."

"I wouldn't go that far," Thevin started.

"Oh, hush, you," Lanna scolded, pulling her arm around my shoulder and swinging us away from him.

She had a good four inches on me, almost as tall as Thevin, and I guessed she was older than both of us by a few years at least. She smiled down at me, weaving us through the crowd of people I didn't know. I searched for my mother and found her just ahead of us. The Baron spoke to an older man, about the age of Pah-Pah, who wore thin robes of gossamer silver, completed with a white high collar.

"Hello, Baron Karus," the Lady Lanna said, nodding to my mother.

My mother bowed her head back in greeting, her eyes darting between the both of us, landing on the hand that still gripped my shoulder.

Lanna addressed the man, "Viceroy Mediyr, meet Saelyn, daughter of the Baron of Felgren."

He bowed, sweeping his hand out in a gesture of honor. When he rose again a kind smile grew across his golden skin. A short, white beard curved around his chin and jaw in the exact style I knew well from Pah-Pah. His clay brown eyes were lined in that same black kohl and crinkled at the sides of his face.

*By the Baron*, I hadn't been prepared for this. In mere minutes, I'd seen my first city, met who I assumed was royalty, and was being introduced to the most powerful people on Arcaynen Isle.

My mother took my hand, pulling me from Lanna's grip.

"It's nice to meet you, Viceroy," I stated, mimicking a confidence I wanted to portray, though I felt foolish and irritated I'd been brought here with no warning as to what I'd face.

"Lady, Viceroy," my mother said, "we'd like to take some time to settle in before the gathering begins tonight. Lanna, would you mind showing us to our rooms?"

Lanna gripped her hands behind her back and nodded once. "Happy to, Baron."

We slipped away, my hand still held in my mother's as I gawked at the enormity of where I'd been led to. The top of the Spire was only the beginning of the massive structure's beauty. Lanna led us across the circular room, gathering Thevin and his parents along the way, talking endlessly in front of us about the sights she'd show me while I visited her city.

I couldn't look at everything fast enough as we descended the white stone stairs that wrapped around the Spire. My gaze flew across every surface, including the back of Lanna herself. It all happened so quickly, I hadn't noticed that she wore a loose white shirt and form-fitting black pants. The fabric gripped tightly to every one of her curves and strong legs, tucking into tall black boots that laced up the front to her knees.

I'd never seen such a display of one's body in public, and I understood then what Thevin had been waiting for me to see. I took my eyes from the hanging purple wisteria blooming in what must be late spring to frown back at Thevin behind me.

His twinkling eyes were already on me as he followed down the steps next to his parents, his hands tucked into his pockets. He raised a brow as if to say, *See, I told you.*

I gestured to my own corseted shirt and long black skirts with a grimace and he laughed, causing Lanna to pause her talk about the canals and look at us.

Her eyes darted between the two of us, and my mother squeezed my fingers once.

The Lady of the Spire grinned wickedly, her mouth open and her tongue brushing her teeth. "Uh-huh," she muttered and jerked her head to the side. "Through here." She addressed my mother. "Your rooms have been prepared for your planned coming weeks from now, Baron Karus."

"I do apologize," she responded. "Thank you for having them ready for our early arrival. Your city and tower are breathtaking. I wished through all those times I projected myself from Felgren that I could see it in person."

Lanna smiled wide and gestured to the doorway that led back into the great tower. Talon, Ilyenna, and Thevin stepped into the long hallway, heading to their rooms.

"I'd like to speak to Lady Lanna privately, if you don't mind finding our room yourself, Saelyn."

Thevin turned instantly, calling, "I'll help her find it."

His face held a delighted grin, and he cocked his head for me to follow him.

I let go of my mother's hand and turned, catching some of their conversation as I continued down the dim hall.

"How is your mother?" she asked.

Lanna sighed. "Same as always. Nothing's changed."

Thevin led me to a tall, copper door, turning the knob and pushing it open.

There was hesitation in my mother's voice with her next question. "How are things here, really, Lanna?"

I heard them walk away as I stepped into the room I'd share with my mother while we were in the Spire. More white stone, more high, domed ceilings—it was an incredible construction and an enormous suite with columns dotting the room, climbing to the ceiling in patterns of whorls.

We'd entered a sitting room with chairs and short tables set in conversational arrangements. I stepped onto the balcony which, instead of leading to another city view, led to what must have been the open center of the spire. More balconies just like it littered the stone alcoves, circled around the core of the Spire, all the way down to the bottom floor where I could barely make out people walking below.

"I wasn't expecting all this detail," I said, leaving the balcony to take in the room.

"I could have warned you, but I would have missed your face in seeing all of this,"—he gestured around, letting his hands flop down to his sides—"for the first time."

"Hush, you," I teased.

He tilted his head back and laughed.

I sighed, tracing my hand across a porcelain tea set in the shape of seashells. "Why didn't you ever mention Lady Lanna?" I asked quietly with an attempted casualness.

"I wanted to." He folded his arms at his chest and leaned

against a pillar. "I was under direct orders from your mother to say nothing about any of this, remember?"

"I thought you weren't good at following orders."

He sighed, tilting his head back to lean against the carvings. "This order, I understood. If you knew what was happening outside of Felgren—*who* was outside of Felgren—maybe you'd want to leave and that was just too dangerous, Sae."

"I see."

He stepped toward me. "There's still so much you don't know."

"Because I needed to be protected or because I wasn't strong enough to handle it?"

"It wasn't my choice," he spat.

"It wasn't mine, either," I gritted back, reflecting his temper.

He had come close, and I found that I had stepped forward as well, our bodies just inches apart. Everything unsaid between us hung in the salty sea air that permeated everything I'd seen so far.

My face softened. I knew because he inhaled deeply and his eyes paused on my lips. I wanted to kiss him there, in the great spire, in this new place I could never even fathom existed in my wildest dreams.

For the hundredth time, I wished I had gone back just one minute in time to when we had danced in my rooms. I wished I had told him then that I'd felt the same, that I'd risk all of what we had if it meant I'd get to call him mine.

I wished I had confessed just what he meant to me as we met in the forest clearing dance floor on the day of my party. I should have told him then, but I had hesitated, just as I did right there in that Spire room, warring with myself if I should say what I felt or first try to show him that I was strong, too. I wasn't some damsel in the forest, waiting for him to return each summer so we could frolic in the fields of yellow blossoms, regardless of how often we had done just that. Regardless of how much waiting I really had done for him to return to me.

"Ask me, Sae," he said.

I blinked, chasing away my thoughts of shouting so the entire city could hear just how much I loved him. "Ask you what, Thevin?"

"Ask me what I'm thinking."

My grin crept in easily and my heart thudded. "What are you thinking?"

"I'm thinking it's time for you to see the world."

# CHAPTER 29
# THEVIN

It wasn't the ease of being able to slip out of the Spire that surprised me. It was Sae's willingness to do it. The moment I'd even suggested such a thing, she'd bolted, heading straight for the pen and parchment by the door, jotting a quick note to her mother and leaving it where it'd be seen on the table in the middle of the room.

I'd been even more surprised when she took my hand then, pulling me to the door and back onto the famous staircase that wove around the outside of the Spire, leading down to the inner courtyard.

I kept up with her pace, both of us out of breath by the time we reached the bottom, both of us laughing, bracing our hands on our knees.

"Blend?" she'd asked, wiping the hair from her face before I could do it for her.

I nodded, glancing around. "Blend."

She murmured her spell, touching my face, then hers.

She was clear as ever, and I meant to ask her why the spell didn't work on me when she instead pulled me along, deeper into the inner courtyard.

Her face wasn't known in the Spire, but mine could be, and we weren't exactly following orders leaving like this. I cringed thinking of what Baron Karus could do to me when she found out I'd taken her very well-kept secret, powerful daughter around the last safe stronghold in Arcaynen.

Even with that possibility, it was worth the risk of the Baron's ire. I wanted Sae to live. I wanted her to see the world, or at least this part of what was left untouched by war. Outside of Felgren, this city was my favorite place to rest, to eat, to thrive with fewer cares for the horrors outside of it.

She leaned over the pond at the center of the courtyard, pointing to the orange and white fish swimming gracefully along the sides, poking their mouths above the water, hoping she'd brought food.

"Look at these!" she exclaimed, the note of excitement lifting in the air, but no more than a passing murmur to those around us with her spell.

I took her hand, pulling her up, letting my fingers slide through hers like we did when we were ten. "Just wait."

THE CITY BUZZED WITH GOSSIP. WORD HAD ALREADY SPREAD OF THE Baron's early arrival and how she did not arrive alone. Thankfully, the citizens of the Spire didn't know what Sae looked like or who she really was other than the Baron's daughter, and with her magic that blended us into the background, we passed through the streets without a second glance.

I took her straight to the Hatchery, showing her just how large the aurum fish could become after decades of care. The Hatchery acted as a hub for the canals that ran through the city walkways, allowing the giant fish to swim through the Spire and find their way back home.

Sae reached into the deep pool, her hand gliding over the brilliant gold scales of an aurum fish twice the size of a lumen. She laughed, shaking water from her fingers, and then gasped as a man jumped into the pool, followed quickly by a hollering woman. They rose to the surface and began to swim, taking long backward strokes, brushing up against the massive fish who seemed to play alongside them.

"Can we?" she asked, not taking her eyes off the couple.

"Did you bring the right undergarments?" I teased, thinking of the times as children when we had spent days swimming in the Great Stream in our most threadbare clothing.

She scrunched her face, hands on her hips. "Guess not." She cocked her head, eyeing the clothes of the swimmers. "Can you find me a clothing shop?"

"You need coins to buy new clothes."

She reached into her pocket and dangled a purple bag in my face. "You really think Pah-Pah would send me to his home city without some coin?"

I quirked a brow. "Alright, let's get you some new clothes."

I led her out of the Hatchery, following one of the canals westward, keeping an eye out for the blue roofs. I pointed out how they changed in color as we headed west. "It's how you know what part of the city you're in. West, blue,"—I pointed again— "east, purple, north, pink."

"And south?" she asked, her head tilted back to see just the edge of the varied blue shingled domes that glinted in the midday sun.

"South is green."

"I still think I'd get lost living here," she laughed.

"I'm sure there's a spell to help you find your way."

She shrugged and I pointed to a door set into the white stone building I'd led her to. I pulled on the copper handle, gesturing her inside.

"If there is, I don't know it. I've never needed a wayfinding spell in Felgren." She mumbled to end the spell at her face, sweeping a hand over mine as well.

"Doesn't surprise me in the least," I admitted.

We stepped inside the shop and a middle-aged woman with long black hair braided across the top of her head greeted us. "Good afternoon, may I help you find something?"

"Yes, please," Sae started. "I'm looking to dress in the fashion of this city. Preferably pants and boots." She held up the bag of coins. "I'll also need swimwear for myself and my friend, if you have it."

The shopkeep raised her brows, eyeing the hefty bag of coins. Her eyes brightened, looking us both over. "Right this way," she offered, gesturing to a dress form fitted with a similar style to what Lanna typically wore.

It was the Lady herself who'd single-handedly changed the common clothing in the Spire in the last five years. She'd complained endlessly to me about how unfair it was that just because I was male, I got to wear pants that allowed me the swiftness I needed to perform as a Runner in the Four's armies. But Lanna, the daughter of one of the Four, could only wear long, bulky skirts and couldn't run nearly as fast because of it.

I set myself down into a sleek cobalt chair, setting my ankle over my knee to watch Saelyn pick out and purchase clothes for the first time in her life. I hoped I'd get to be a part of a lot of her firsts.

~

"So we just…jump in?" Sae asked, bent down on her knees, her hand back to swirling in the water of the Hatchery.

I'd been keeping my cool fairly well, considering.

Considering since we'd left the shop, her new clothes bundled neatly in a package, she'd told me all about her new attire. The new corseted shirt, the black leather pants—just like Lady Lanna's she'd informed me—the tall black boots…

And now, here she was, dressed in what she assured me that woman had said was swimming attire appropriate to the Spire's fashions.

"I think so," I managed, avoiding the sight of her mid thighs and knees, exposed completely along with most of her shoulders and arms.

The cut of the swim wear was bold, flattering, and I noticed I wasn't the only one in the Hatchery taking my fair share of glances.

We had bundled our clothes on the edge of the deep pool, my own swimwear exposing my entire torso and most of my calves.

Sae hadn't said a thing when she'd gasped at the scars across my chest. I'd gotten them last winter during a particularly brutal surprise attack on the Hyrithian border from a band of wild Blight beasts.

Three long, white slashes across my right pectoral had been difficult to heal, and honestly, the medicus conduit assigned to me in that tent just outside of the Blight Line had more important soldiers to work on at the time. She'd done a quick job of it and moved on, unbothered about how my skin would heal over and scar forever.

There were a few other swimmers in the pool that spanned at least two-hundred feet in diameter and at least fifty feet deep. I peered down, searching for the aurum fish when a splash of cool water hit me in the face.

Sae's head popped up above the surface and she pulled the hair back from her cheeks, sputtering water from her mouth. Her eyes matched the color of the pool—ocean blue and…stunning.

If fae existed in the sea, and she was one of them, I wouldn't be the least bit surprised.

She laughed at my expression and kicked backward, her hand trailing over the golden body of an enormous aurum fish.

"Well?" she called. "Are you coming with me to see the world or not?"

The moment was perfect, staring out across the water at her bobbing up and down, her black hair pulled back and her eyes sparkling like the morning sun on the Great Stream in Felgren.

It didn't matter anymore that she didn't love me the same way I loved her. I only cared that she wanted to share her life with me.

Her experiences, her adventures.

If I spent my life loving this woman I couldn't have, I'd still be a happy man. I knew that truth and grinned wickedly as I stepped back, ran forward, and splashed beside her into the pool.

# CHAPTER 30
# SAELYN

We swam for hours, taking breaks occasionally to lie in the sun that seeped through the Hatchery skylights in long amber rays. Thevin told me stories about his time at the Blight Line—the missions he'd been given as a Runner, working closely with his parents who were both conduits with prized power.

Never once did he mention the scars across his chest.

Never once did he touch them as I longed to do.

Those were parts of Thevin I hadn't known, but wanted to.

I wanted all of it, soaking up every one of his stories like our skin soaked up the warmth of a spring sun.

Guilt pricked her nasty little head a time or two when I occasionally wondered if my mother was worried about us. But she had that damned rhyzolm with her always and would be able to find us if she really needed to.

"This world you've shown me is wonderful," I said at the end of laughing until we cried at his story about Lanna's mishap with a particularly ornery Horned Vintras in the Attatok Mountains.

We were lying on our backs, arms behind our heads, looking up to see the occasional group of white birds soar across the blue sky.

"There's so much more to see. Even the dark parts of this isle are something to behold. But," he wavered, "nothing I've seen compares to Felgren. The trees, the fields, the streams. The sun when it shines down from the sky like a warmth I've never known or will ever know anywhere else." He closed his eyes and sighed.

I turned my head his way. I wanted more than any swimming, or exploring, or adventuring, to follow the line of his arched nose with the tip of my finger.

He peeked one eye open as if he could feel me studying him. "What?"

"Do you think there's hope?" I sat up, pulling my frizzy damp hair over my shoulder. "Do you think we can defeat the Blightress?" I set my chin on my knees, pulling them to my chest. "Do you think there's any chance of saving my father?"

He followed my movement, pulling his arms around his legs. "Hold onto hope. Defy the dark. That's what my father always says before we leave to any frontlines. He said it comes from something your father told him a long time ago. Before either of us was born." He wrapped an arm around me, pulling me to him so I could rest my head on his shoulder. "I think your father was a great man. *Is* a powerful Baron. And if anyone can bring him home, it's your mother and his daughter."

A tear fell down my cheek before I could stop it.

I didn't want to stop it.

I wanted to shed tears for my father. For what he'd missed while he'd been gone from us for so long.

"Sometimes I miss him." I wiped my cheeks, sniffing. "Even when I was told he was dead, somedays I'd find myself at his portrait, wondering if I'm like him. Wondering if he'd be proud of who I've become without him. I wonder if he would have trained me himself or would have taken me,"—I gestured to the pool in front of us—"fishing."

"Baron Revich liked to fish?"

I laughed, replying, "Yes. Yes, it's one of the few things I know about him. My mother once told the story of the day she knew she could no longer hide her feelings for him. He'd been fishing of all things."

Thevin laughed, the sound echoing through the cool breeze and flowing through the open arches of the room. "Maybe he'll teach you someday, Sae." He tilted his head to mine. "Someday, when he's back with you, father and daughter, fishing in Felgren."

I pressed my chin to his shoulder. "You'll have to join us."

"Oh, I will," he chuckled. "I wouldn't miss watching you catch a slimy fish for the world."

"I bet I could catch a fish before you could," I teased back, nudging his arm.

He tilted his head with a gasp in mock astonishment. "Before *me*? Never."

"I can do a great many things better than you, my dearest friend Thevin."

"Name some."

"Running, climbing, lying…lumen riding?"

He covered his hands with his face, feigning embarrassment. "I've forgotten all those things. But I still think I could catch a bigger fish than you."

"We'll have to wait and see," I laughed.

"Why wait?" he asked, rising and stretching his arms over his head, then around his body.

"What are you doing?" I stood with my hands on my hips.

"Catching the biggest fish." He grinned and his single dimple flashed just as he ran toward the pool and dove in.

"*The-vin*!" I yelled, shaking my head and crossing my arms.

He popped up out of the water, flicking his head like a lumen after a rainstorm. "Watch me catch the biggest fish!" he called, capturing the attention of several onlookers nearby.

I ran to the edge of the great pool, following his sleek form as he dove back under the water, swimming straight for the largest aurum fish we'd seen flowing lazily. Its scales were pure white with one small patch of brilliant orange at the end of its tail. It was easily ten feet long and darted from Thevin the moment it noticed him headed straight for it.

I laughed, sitting on the edge of the pool with my feet in the cool water. I cupped my hands to my mouth and shouted, "Go for something smaller on your first try!"

I doubted he heard me, and regardless, he didn't follow my advice as he chased after the massive beast. I giggled to myself watching his body glide through the water. He at last came up for air, flicking his hair again and wiping his face, taking long deep gulps.

He smiled at me, then looked around for something else to catch, giving up on his initial trophy. We eyed the next largest fish at the same time as it rose close to the surface nearby. With another flash of his smile, he turned his body, diving once again toward the entirely orange fish, not quite as long as the last, but still bigger than Thevin. The fish glided at the surface, unafraid of the man swimming toward it. In a flash, Thevin just managed to grab ahold of its dorsal fin.

The fish thrashed in a panic, but Thevin held on with both hands, showing off for my amusement.

I rose in slight concern and shook my head, giving way to laughter and ready to jump in to join him.

The fish thrashed its body to knock off its rider, but Thevin held on, cutting through the water like a knife and lifting a hand to wave at me.

I waved back, about to tell him he'd proven himself enough, when the massive white aurum from before circled around them in agitation, flicking its tail across the water.

"Thevin!" I cried, "Let go!"

He realized the real danger just as I did. The white fish twisted and smacked its tail sideways across the water, hitting Thevin squarely in the chest.

I screamed his name, watching his body go limp, his hands releasing the fin as he began to sink into the ripple of waves across the surface.

I didn't think—I dove, gliding into the water and using my momentum from the jump to propel straight for Thevin's body slowly lowering in the depths.

The white aurum fish wasn't done, however, as it circled back toward him for more punishment. I didn't have time to act, didn't have breath for a spell. I paused under the water, releasing my hands back over an orb of white, pulling them apart, just as I'd watched my mother do to form the portals that led us to the Spire.

It was my one chance, my one thought to send that fish… somewhere.

I had barely enough time to set a destination, let alone think twice if I was powerful enough to form a portal like I'd seen my mother do that morning. The only thought that passed through my mind was the fact that I should have reversed time instead of jumping into the pool to save him, and now, I didn't have the breath to do it.

A flash of white light wove through the water, blinding me and the aurum fish. It swerved away at the last second, avoiding whatever it was I had just formed under the waves. I swam as fast as my legs could push me toward Thevin, wrapping an arm around his chest to heave both of us to the surface.

People lined the edge of the pool, some already in the water, swimming toward us. A man took one of Thevin's arms and we swam him to the hands of the people waiting to pull him out.

"We need a medicus conduit!" I huffed, rising from the pool with the help of more onlookers.

They laid him flat on the white stone. His eyes were closed, his chest unmoving.

I heard the shouts, the cries for help repeating through the open space, trickling out onto the side walkways. I shoved the hair out of his face and turned his head to the side. I pushed down on his chest in a panic, pleading, "Come on, Thevin. Breathe, dammit!" I pushed over and over, pressing so hard I could have cracked his rib and not cared.

My mind sifted through every medicus conduit spell I'd ever read about in Viridis, coming up with nothing to force water from lungs. I pushed and pushed, panicked, raging, crying for someone to save him, to please *help me save him.*

Dainty, wrinkled hands, the color of sand, slid gently over mine, squeezing once and then guiding them off his chest. A ruby conduit ring graced one finger.

I gasped and looked up to see earthen rich brown eyes look into mine with just as much surprise as I held. The woman looked back down at Thevin, gripping the back of his neck with one hand and shoving the palm of her other at his sternum. Her voice was high and light as she said, "*Visaquae,*" jabbing her palm into his chest.

A flash of red and then water from his lungs sprayed all over me, and I gave a shuttering gasp, releasing my breath and holding his head as he coughed continuously onto the wet stone. He turned to his side, heaving in big gulps of air over and over, more and more water flying out of his mouth.

I cradled his head in my lap, soothing my hand over his back and repeated *thank you* again and again to the stranger in a medicus conduit's all-white attire with a jeweled red flower pin attached to her vest. She sat with her legs folded, her hands at her knees and watched me carefully—knowingly—as if she'd seen me before.

"You look just like him," she sighed to herself while the crowd around us cheered and clapped.

"Wh-what?" I stammered.

"Your father," she amended. "You look just like him."

"You knew my father?"

She nodded sweetly and her small lips curled upward. She held out a hand for me to shake. "I knew Baron Revich, Saelyn. My name is Clairannia Lynns. It's nice to meet you again."

We arrived back at the Spire thirty minutes later, Thevin's arm over my shoulder that I insisted he keep there, refusing to let him walk on his own, no matter how often he mumbled something about being just fine.

"You'll need rest," Clairannia said. "If a bruise forms on your chest, find me or another medicus conduit and they'll be able to heal it."

I'd been quiet, thinking about this conduit who knew who I was and recognized me based on my father's features.

"He's alive," I blurted, guiding Thevin toward the first steps of the winding Spire staircase. "My father, I mean."

Clairannia stopped. "What?"

"My mother told me yesterday. At my seventeenth birthday celebration."

"She told you?"

"You knew?"

Clairannia's mouth tightened to a thin line. "Yes. I knew."

I frowned. "So you're one of her friends, then. One of the three who knew besides Pah-Pah."

She tilted her head. "Pah-Pah?"

"She means Pompeii," Thevin explained.

Clairannia nodded, handing me the bundle of clothes she had carried and rushing up the stairs. "I need to speak with the Baron. Please go to your rooms and stay there until your mother comes to retrieve you." She ran her hand along the stone stair rail, sprinting up each step, calling back, "I'll explain to your parents, Thevin. Nothing more than a misadventure."

"She's a mysterious one," he said as we carried on.

Halfway up the tower and out of breath, we found our hall of rooms, spilling into the one I would share with my mother. I helped him onto one of the bright yellow chairs and he sank back into it.

I fell into the one opposite, tossing our things onto the short table between us. "I can't believe you did that." I rubbed my face, swiping my damp hair from my forehead.

"I did it though," he mused. "The biggest fish anyone's ever caught."

I bit my lips together, stifling my smile.

He watched me try, bursting into laughter the moment he saw me grin. We laughed until it hurt, wiping tears from our eyes.

"You're in so much trouble when your parents find out," I giggled, grabbing the package and clothes on the table to go change.

He chuckled once more, shaking his head and grabbing his own discarded clothes. "No. I've been through worse."

I opened my mouth to ask if he meant the scars on his chest, but he rose instead, headed toward one of the rooms. I followed, stepping into the other room, taking a moment to appreciate the large bed and small furnishings in yellows and oranges. I entered a smaller closet to change out of my swimwear and step back into my black skirts and cream corseted shirt. I decided to save my new clothes for another time, not ready to risk my mother having something else for the day to scold me about.

I tucked my new clothes onto the shelves next to the skirts and dresses I'd brought from Felgren, already unpacked and neatly stacked, along with a few other items that I didn't recognize.

I heard his soft knock and opened the door for him to come inside. One look at his face had me grimacing. "You need a nap."

He nodded, stumbling for my amusement to my bed and falling face-first, dressed in his original attire.

"Are you hungry? How do I get food here?"

He mumbled into the sheets, "There's a bundle of flags by the balcony. Slide the orange flag into the slot on the rail and someone will bring up food."

My brows rose in surprise. "What other colors are there?"

He lifted himself higher into the bed, pulling the white quilt over himself. "Purple for laundry, white for a message, and black for emergencies."

"Clever," I muttered, already heading out the door to find the flags. They were bundled into a large pail near the balcony. I pulled the orange one and placed the stick into the slot on the rail, just as he'd said. The bright fabric flew in the inner spire breeze, and I noticed a white flag flying a few stories below.

I waited at the door to our rooms, curious how long it would take for someone to see it. Within ten minutes, a servant arrived carrying a tray of fresh fruits and cheese.

"I apologize, miss, but the midday meal has already been served and dinner is being prepared in the kitchens." He smiled wryly, setting the tray on a table in the room.

"Thank you very much…" I said, holding a hand out to greet him properly as Pah-Pah had taught me.

"Yezron, miss." He took my hand briefly.

"Thank you, Yezron. I'm Saelyn, daughter of—"

"Of the Baron of Felgren, yes, I know. Everyone on staff will know who you are, miss. You only need to place your flag there and we will prioritize your needs."

"Oh, there's no need for that, but thank you." I gestured to my room. "My friend, Thevin, is tired and needs rest. I expect my mother to arrive back here soon, before the gathering tonight."

"Yes, we all know Thevin, too," he chuckled. "If there is anything more you need, please do not hesitate to wave the white flag. I can send messages throughout the Spire. Amaya will be up in two hours to help you dress for the gathering and dinner."

"That won't be necessary, I can dress myself."

He nodded once, explaining, "The Baron has already commissioned a gown for you to wear tonight. It arrives soon and, forgive me, but the dress customs here might be quite different than what you're used to. And difficult to put on yourself, if I may suggest."

My cheeks flushed. "Alright. Please have Amaya come help. Thank you again."

He held up his hands and backed toward the door. "It is nothing, miss."

"Saelyn."

"Miss Saelyn." He bowed turned to leave.

I looked over his suit—far different than anything I'd seen Pah-Pah wear in Felgren. It was all white with different textures and patterns sewn into the shirt sleeves like lace. A high collar was stiff and high on his neck against his olive skin. I stole a glance behind me to where Thevin was probably already asleep.

"Wait," I urged, stepping forward before he could close the door.

He opened it wide and asked, "Yes, Miss Saelyn?"

"Would you mind..." I bit my lips together, remembering my goal here was to prove that I was no simple girl of Felgren. "If Amaya is able, please ask her to come up as soon as possible. I have some...questions about your customs that she might be able to answer."

His face lit in a brilliant grin, displaying a mouth of white teeth. He nodded again and said, "But of course, Miss Saelyn. I'll send her right away."

"Only if she's free!" I added as he shut the door and I crossed my arms, ready to write a list of what I needed to know in order to show myself just as capable as any other seventeen-year-old here.

I peeked into my room to confirm my suspicions that Thevin had already fallen asleep. He had—completely knocked out from his "misadventure" across my bed.

I sat down near the tray of food, shoved a strawberry into my mouth, and began to write.

# CHAPTER 31
# THEVIN

Saelyn's snorting laughter woke me in her bed. I hadn't meant to fall asleep right away, but apparently I did, clothes intact. I stretched my arms over my head and searched for water. After gulping a full cup, I ran a hand through my hair and opened the door a sliver, trying to guess at who Sae was laughing with in the main room. I assumed it was a woman—someone with a low voice that I didn't recognize as anyone Sae would know in the Spire.

I glanced back to the clock in the room and cursed. The evening had already begun, and I was never going to hear the end of my parent's scolding if I wasn't dressed in time for dinner. I entered the main room soundlessly, spying Sae sitting on the balcony while a servant I recognized, but couldn't remember the name of, shoved pins into her hair.

The woman was mid-sentence when she spotted me walking toward them. A cool smirk lifted over her mouth as she greeted me. "Hello, sir, I hope you slept well."

Saelyn all but jumped out of her seat, the last few curls of her long, black hair bouncing over her shoulder as she darted across the room to me, grabbing my arms. "You slept for *three* hours!" She shook me slightly, her dark blue eyes lined in copper kohl. The color somehow made her eyes look bluer, brighter, reminding me of the sea at the edge of the Spire's white stone cliffs.

"I love this," I brushed my fingers just below her eye, careful to not disturb what the woman had artistically added.

Sae's smile widened and she raised her chin. "Thank you. Amaya is very talented."

I moved my hand up to touch the woven braid in her hair, thick and sparkling with silver pins in a crown over her head. She swatted my hand away, scolding, "You'll mess it up!" Grabbing my shoulder, she turned me toward the door. "You only have an hour before dinner and the gathering after. Go get yourself together and run a comb through your hair." She shoved me playfully, and I pretended to stumble across the room, hand over my heart in mock distress.

I reached for the door but it opened for me, the Baron of Felgren surprised to see me there. She gave me a short-lived small smile, and I stepped aside for her to enter.

"Your parents are waiting for you," she said, jerking her head to the hallway where, indeed, both of my parents, already dressed for dinner, eyed me with a special disappointment I knew well.

I sighed, gave one last smirk to Sae, and closed the door behind me as I left.

"I assume you know what we have to say," my father started, his arm around my mother's waist as they headed to the door of the rooms we'd share.

"I can guess," I muttered under my breath.

They opened the door and we stepped inside. One glance told me it was similar to the rooms we usually used in our short stints in the Spire, gathering new channelers for the Baron to train.

It would take months for us to find them. So few channelers had been born in the last two decades, and the rest were conscripted in the war already.

I leaned against the door, my arms crossed, bracing myself for what I was about to hear.

My mother poured a cup of tea at the sideboard, adding a little sugar before bringing it to me. I thanked her and held it warm in my hands as she settled in next to my father on the coral couch in the center of the room.

He gestured to the chair across from them and said, "Sit, Thevin."

Reluctantly, I crossed the room, bringing my much-needed tea with me.

Once I was settled, my father leaned forward, asking, "Are you alright?"

I took a quick sip of tea before answering, "I'm fine."

"I can't believe you did that today," he said, focusing his dark eyes on my face.

"It was just an accident. I was lucky Sae was there to pull me out of the water and that conduit, Clairannia, was nearby to help me breathe again. You know I've been through worse."

"It's not that, son," my mother began, "of course we are relieved you are not drowned at the bottom of the Hatchery, but taking Sae out of the Spire for hours…" she trailed, shaking her head. "This isn't like Felgren. You two cannot go about like you have normal lives. She's the Baron's daughter. She's actively being sought after by the Blightress herself, and she doesn't understand the extent of any of this."

"She deserves to see the world." My voice hardened in my rising anger. "She deserves to live her life, and if I can help her do that, I'm going to."

"Her mother was worried—"

I cut my father off with a wave. "Her mother is always worried. Always calculating ways to keep her daughter from any harm, which keeps her closed up like a precious stone in a box. If anyone should see what this world is like, it's her. She should be out there with us. She should be given the opportunity to understand what we fight for. What her father fought for."

"And you've told her? What it's like on the front lines?" my mother asked in her quiet way.

"Yes. She's heard it from me. But she needs to see it. If we could just take her to the Blight Line—"

"It's not our choice," my father cut in. "That's up to the Baron, and a decision will be made at the gathering tonight."

I let out a deep breath, gulping down most of the tea. "I'd better get ready." I rose and headed toward my room.

My mother murmured something to my father and then followed, her steps light on the stone floor. "May I come in?" She stood at the open door as I chucked off my shirt, headed toward the washing room.

"Yes."

I loved my parents. They'd given me a hard task in life, but had loved and cared for me every step of the way, allowing me to find and learn my place in the isle, never berating me too hard when I made mistakes. They had let me live where Saelyn had not been able to. Adventuring through Felgren wasn't like adventuring outside of it. I knew that. Of course, I knew that.

"Your clothes are laid out for you in the closet," she said, pulling at the hem of her ruby silk gloves that slid past her elbows.

I nodded, headed there before her next words stopped me. "Does Saelyn know your feelings for her?"

My heart thudded in my chest and I turned. "She knows enough."

"And her response?" she pressed.

"We're friends, Mother."

"You're more than that."

"We're not," I said curtly. "We're best friends. Nothing more."

"She cares deeply for you and you, her. We all see it."

I scoffed and called back to her from inside the closet. "What you see is two people who've been friends for a very long time. She wants it to stay that way, and I'm fine with that."

"She just needs time, Thevin. Don't give up on her."

I stuck my head out from the closet. "I'm not giving up on her. If anyone here is on Sae's side, it's me." I continued to dress, donning the velvet cerulean jacket and flicking up the high collar of my shirt. The pants I'd been given were a midnight blue, a contrast to the hue of the jacket. I left the shirt open slightly at the chest, as was the fashion and rolled back the sleeves of my jacket, showing off the silk pattern of yellow leaves underneath—another of the Spire's customs.

My mother followed me to the washing room. "She'll need you before long when she truly understands just how different life is outside of Felgren." Clearing her throat, she added, "Outside of the Spire."

I splashed my face with cool water, patting it dry and grabbing the comb to manage the curls at the top of my head. "She has me," I responded, catching the stare of my mother in the seashell mirror. "There's nothing more I can do than be there for her, and I'm going to keep doing that."

She nodded once, stepping closer to smooth the lines of my jacket. "She has a good friend. The best kind there is."

Her words stung, grating against my skin.

Because I wanted more than that. I'd take what I had with Sae and be happy with it, but if my parents could see how I felt...I knew they couldn't be the only ones.

I decided I didn't care. Let them pity me. Let them wonder why Sae didn't want our relationship to change. I'd wondered the same over and over since the night a few days ago when I'd laid it all out, letting her choose to take the risk or not.

"I'm ready," I finally replied, pulling at the collar one more time and taking one last glance in the mirror.

"You look handsome." She smiled at me and the soft lines around her eyes crinkled, for once showing her age.

I looked mostly like her with the same blue eyes, the same golden curls. But where her skin was pale, mine held a darker hue. I'd always tanned easily, and every summer my skin became darker in the Felgren summer sun, closer to my father's.

"And you're beautiful as always, Mother." I kissed her cheek and stepped past, ready to move on from our conversation and go to dinner, pretending my heart wasn't a wounded, bloody mess.

# CHAPTER 32
# SAELYN

My mother dismissed Amaya before I could protest and gestured to the balcony chair to finish my hair. I slumped into it, bracing for the impact of her scolding.

She was already dressed in a long black gown with a sheer white collar. The vested front would still identify her as a Baron, though I doubted that was needed with her famous black eyes and flowing white hair.

"You are beautiful, Little Love," she started, her voice soft and kind.

I swallowed. "Thank you, Mother."

She heaved a heavy sigh, and I felt the tremble in her fingers as she pinned another curl into the top of my dark braid. "There's so much I still need to tell you. I'm sorry I haven't had much time, but after the events tonight, we can rest here and talk of the past." She finished my hair and smiled down at me, the slightest flicker of green forcing its way into the depths of her dark stare. "You must have questions."

"Of course I have questions. I—" I stopped, lifting my chin, remembering my promise not to be angry with her. "I am ready to listen when you're ready to speak."

Her face fell slightly, but she nodded. "Come, let's get you into your gown."

Following her into my room, she pulled a gown from the closet, admiring how it sparkled.

I tilted my head as she unfastened the buttons in the back. "Aren't you going to scold me? For leaving with Thevin today?"

She smirked, helping me out of my skirts. "Not this time. I hope you both had an adventure today you'll remember always."

Shocked, I opened and closed my mouth like an aurum fish. "And Clairannia told you everything that happened?"

She nodded, gesturing for me to step into the delicate fabric. I tiptoed into the sheath of the dress and she carefully pulled it up over my shoulders. It was a daring piece, but as Amaya had assured me, at the highest fashion of the Spire.

My mother fastened the buttons at the back, explaining, "I did speak to Clairannia, and yes, I understand what happened today. You and Thevin are young. It's past time you get to go on adventures outside of Felgren. Besides, the Blightress doesn't know you're here, and this city is safe."

I was rendered speechless, not at all expecting this response. I grinned back at her through the dressing mirror as she finished the last button and swept her hands over my arms. "I'm excited. For tonight, I mean." I studied myself in the mirror, admiring the color of the fabric, the placement of the braid woven in a crown atop my head, and the way the curves of my breasts and hips accentuated the long lengths of my waist and legs. I wasn't quite as tall as my mother, but taller than most women I'd met.

She smiled back at my giddy reflection. "Now let's talk about the events of the night."

"Oh, I already know!" I exclaimed, searching the closet for my soft velvet shoes that made me at least two inches taller. They were tricky to walk in, but Amaya had shown me how to adjust my weight on my feet. "Amaya already went over everything I need to know. She's been a wonderful help!"

"Everything?" my mother asked. I caught the disappointment in her voice. "Even the Ceremonial—"

"Dance, yes, all of it. The dinner, the toasting, the gathering of the Four." I paused. "Though, she knew less about that, but had some general ideas of what happens."

"It's just a formal meeting of the Four. Although, one of us will not be there."

I finished the buckles at my shoes and nodded, reaching out my hand to her. "I'm ready when you are, Mother."

She gave me a dazzling smile, took my hand in hers, and we left to begin our evening.

~

We entered a room toward the top of the Spire with more arched open windows that surrounded what I assumed was a dining hall. A long table glistened with dinnerware in various shades of the roofs of the Spire. A few dozen people milled about, some with drinks in hand, waiting for the dinner to begin.

Lady Lanna spotted us at once, hovering near the doorway as if in waiting. She sprinted toward us, her arms wide, her mouth open in surprise at my gown. "Saelyn!" She pulled me into a genuine embrace. "Our fashions are most becoming on you and you alone!" She vaguely gestured behind her, murmuring, "You are the most beautiful creature here by far, and I believe I'm not the only one who would say so." She winked as if I understood her comment and greeted my mother with a kiss on the cheek.

"The Viceroy is looking for you as always, Baron Karus," she informed us, pulling my arm into the crook of her elbow and leading me away.

I studied the women of the room, confirming that the gown I wore was in the standard of fashion. I stumbled slightly in my shoes and Lanna caught me, whispering, "I hate these damned shoes." She lifted the sheer hem of her silver gown to show me the similar style on her own feet. "My mother refuses to let go of this tradition, but when *I* am Lady of the Spire…" she trailed, shrugging.

"Is your mother…unwell?" I inquired, taking a glass of something that smelled like citrus from the servant who passed us.

"Very," Lanna answered, her eyes darting around the crowd, obviously in search of someone. "She's a stubborn woman, though, and is hanging onto life by a thread."

I eyed her in surprise. "You and your mother have a…strained relationship?"

Her laughter boomed through the room and several eyes glanced our way. She led me to one of the windows where we could see the shades of green painted on the roofs, designating the south Spire. "My mother is…" she began, pulling her lips to the side, "an interesting woman. She did her best to force the fight from me, but never succeeded."

"Oh, I'm sorry," I said. "She couldn't accept your independence?"

"No," she laughed, pulling at the sword strapped to her waist, somehow appropriate, even in her long silvery gown, "She literally could not force the fight from me. She tried to raise a Lady of the Spire and got a soldier instead."

It was my turn to laugh with her.

"I see you two are getting along swimmingly." The voice I'd know anywhere came from behind me. I spun in my heels, my face still in a laughing grin as I looked upon Thevin.

His mouth opened in awe and his brows rose. "Saelyn," he breathed. "You look…" his words faltered and he closed his mouth, swallowing.

Lanna leaned over my shoulder and laughed, "Doesn't she, Thevin? Doesn't she look…" she trailed off in a jest.

I gave a stinted laugh, but Thevin didn't respond, nor did he move as his eyes flickered over my gown.

"Oh, dear," Lanna muttered, "I do believe Viceroy Mediyr's daughter is calling me." She squeezed my arm once and winked, her body flowing into the crowd seamlessly. I watched her go, biting the inside of my cheek.

I wasn't expecting Thevin's reaction at all.

I glanced back to him, only to find his eyes caught at the sheer fabric that did little to hide the shape of my legs. I shrugged nervously. "Did your parents chastise you much?" Nervous laughter escaped me. "My mother wasn't angry at all, if you can believe it." I met his silent stare, now assured my dress had been too daring, too revealing, even though the style was common among the women in the room. I frowned down at the sheer sparkling powder blue fabric and then looked back up to Thevin. "Is this not right?" I glanced around. "Amaya said it was the latest—"

"Ask me what I'm thinking," he whispered low, his words barely audible under his breath.

I laughed in relief. "What are you thinking, Thevin?"

"I'm thinking you should only wear this color. Nothing else will do."

I laughed again, nudging into his shoulder where he caught me, surprising me by pulling me into his arms. "You're beautiful, Saelyn," he continued in my ear. A shiver spread through my body, shaking me slightly as he pulled away, kissing my cheek as he went.

Now. I should tell him now. I should confess I loved him.

My heart raced in my chest and my cheeks burned, but I didn't care as I started with, "Thevin, I've been wanting to tell you—"

He shook his head, grabbing my hand. "Come on. Let's find our seats." He pulled me toward the table where guests were beginning to sit and settle for the meal.

"But, I—" I tried again.

Instead of listening, he yanked me harder, avoiding the conversion that was well overdue. I ran my tongue along my teeth in annoyance, even as the dinner bell chimed and the room quieted to a low murmur.

Thevin pulled a saffron cushioned chair with a low back for me to take, and I sat in a puff, sighing and folding my hands into my lap.

Another ding sounded and the man at the end of the table, whom I recognized as the Viceroy, stood to begin a speech. Thevin and I sat somewhere in the middle of the table across from his parents and my mother. Lady Lanna looked bored next to the Viceroy while a pretty young woman sat across from her, making a face. Lanna held in her snicker and the speech began.

I hardly made out a word of what was said, still fuming and now set on a course to end this between Thevin and I.

I'd tell him tonight.

I didn't care if he didn't want to hear it; I was saying those words.

Damn the timing, damn the odd desire I had to prove I could be just as strong as Lanna, and was more than a simple girl from Felgren Forest.

He would know by the end of the night that I loved him and could do with that truth whatever he wished. I wouldn't wait any longer to take the risk I had dreamed of since I was fifteen years old. It was time to put aside my fear and live for the future.

# CHAPTER 33

# THEVIN

The flickering of my mother's eyes across the table didn't help. Her piercing blue stare fell on me consistently throughout that endless dinner, and I shifted uncomfortably for the hundredth time. It was difficult enough to keep my eyes off Saelyn in that damned dress, let alone keep up with the conversation around me after trying to focus on that droning speech of Viceroy Mediyr's.

I wouldn't be surprised if not a single person at this table heard what he had to say, instead focusing on the daughter of the Baron in her pale blue shift that shimmered in the waning sunlight, lighting her up as if in awe of her beauty. Every line, every curve of her body was held in shape by the pale blue fabric that clung to her backside, and torso, and breasts. The cut of the top curved wide to show the world just how perfect she was. Her long legs, accentuated by the high shoes she wore, were left bare of any fabric but the sheer tulle. Her calves, her knees, her creamy thighs—anyone could see the shape of all of it, and I was sure I wasn't the only one looking.

I was plenty experienced with the beauty of a woman's body, but when I had seen Sae speaking with Lanna, I'd just stood there, dumfounded. I was well aware of the fashion of the Spire, which tended to more acknowledge a woman's body than hide it, but when Sae wore that gown—that color—the palest blue that set her dark hair and pale skin into the ode of a brilliant summer sky…

I chewed my food by habit alone, unsure of what I'd eaten, my skin too tight, my seat too hard, my heart bickering with my mind on what action I should do next—answer the question Saelyn had just asked me or turn her chin and kiss her.

"Huh?" I responded like an idiot, decidedly not caressing her cheek to kiss her lips in front of all these people.

"I said, how is your chest?" she repeated for me.

"My chest?" I looked down at my blue jacket to see if I'd spilled something.

She cocked her head in irritation. "From that tail slap you received today from the enormous white fish you swam with?"

Her annoyance snapped me out of my stupor long enough to respond in my usual casual flirtation. "Not sure, we'd better look together tonight."

*By the breath of the Baron in front of me*, my cheeks heated as Sae opened her mouth wide, looking around the table to see if anyone else heard.

I recovered from my own shock and playfully nudged her arm. "I'm joking, Sae. It's fine. A little bruising. Nothing permanent."

"You should see a healer then, like Clairannia said."

I forced another bite of what looked like some kind of root vegetable. "They're rare these days and busy with real work. It will heal on its own."

She twisted her lips but nodded.

By the time dessert was served, I'd had just about all I could take sitting next to her, hearing her laugh at something the guest on her right said about her spoon. I scoffed under my breath, doubting it was as funny as Sae made it seem. Surely, she was just being polite.

I took my pitiful longing gaze away from her and rose, excusing myself to step away for just one relaxing moment to breathe. More people were finishing their food and rising to mingle before the Song of Remembrance and Ceremonial Dance began. I stepped away to an open ledge furthest from the table. Leaning over the balcony's edge, I inhaled the dusk air which settled on the city like a warm blanket in a soft bed, or a warm body, its simple presence there to tell you you're not alone.

"Why don't you just tell her?"

I exhaled into the breeze, long and slow. Quiet as ever, Lanna sidled up next to me, mirroring my leaning over the rail while flicking her pocket knife rapidly between her fingers.

"If that falls, you could kill someone," I muttered, rubbing my face.

"Good thing I'm quick with my fingers." She winked and slid the knife between her forefinger and middle, flicking it into the air to spin before snapping it back into her palm just before it fell beyond her reach.

"Show off."

"So?" she insisted, "Why don't you confess your feelings to Saelyn? Get it over with. Like ripping a bloody bandage from your skin." She patted my chest where she knew my scars remained.

I flinched as she smacked my bruise, shuffling away slightly so she couldn't tease me about this afternoon.

"She knows." I shrugged, even though my heart fell to my stomach.

Her brows rose and her mouth turned downward. "After all that moping last winter, you finally told her?" She gave a grunt when I didn't respond. "That bad, huh?"

"No, it wasn't bad, she just…" I stole a glance behind me, Lanna's gaze following. Sae lingered at the table, this time deep in conversation with her seat mate, a young male channeler I'd met on occasion who was due to train in Felgren in the next rounds. "She said she didn't want to risk our friendship," I finished. "And that was the end of it."

Lanna huffed. "Why do I feel like that's not even close to the end of it?"

"It is." I eyed her, my words heated. "She was very clear on what she wants from me and that is only friendship. So I will give her friendship. And I will make it through more of these damn dinners where she wears something like *that*,"—I jabbed a thumb behind me—"and I will be what she needs me to be. Just like it was before I opened my stupid mouth and put her in an uncomfortable position. I won't do that again, and I won't let her try to apologize for how she feels."

Lanna barked a laugh. "Oh, so you get to decide how she feels about it?"

"She doesn't want more than what we had before, Lanna."

Her lips bubbled as she blew air out of her mouth. "Whatever happened between the two of you back in Felgren, she's had time to think about it now. Whatever ridiculous confession you said to her with that silver tongue of yours, she's been able to sit with. So, if she has more to say, let her say it."

"I don't want her to pity me and start something she'll later regret."

"Thevin, you are a fool."

I frowned, crossing my arms and turning my back on the balcony, staring down at my boots.

"In the accumulated mere hour I've been in Saelyn's presence, there was one single person on her mind. Can you guess who?"

"The Viceroy?"

She laughed, pulling her head back and grabbing her chest. "A fool indeed, Thevin of Felgren." She slapped a hand across my back. "Part of me hopes she doesn't tell you her true feelings for a little while longer because Pining Thevin is much more fun to tease than Runner Thevin."

I huffed a laugh. "Speaking of, any news from the Blight Line?"

"Yes. The news is, it's been quiet. Strangely quiet. It's got the Wieldwryns spooked. We head out there tomorrow to prepare for the Dimming, but something feels…off."

"Do you know our assignment?"

"It depends." She scratched the back of her head, loosening the golden braid pinned there. "Shit," she mumbled as her braid toppled down her back. "I'm about ready to take my own blade to all of this," she said, holding up the long length of her locks.

"Depends on what?" I pressed.

She sighed, dropping her hair and mimicking my stance with

her back against the railing. "Depends on the Baron." She nodded toward Sae who had just stood, adjusting her gossamer gown and looking around the room. "Saelyn is rumored to have immense power. Enough to change the tides."

I nodded slightly. "She's more powerful than anyone realizes. We need her. As much as I hate to admit it."

"What have you seen her do exactly?"

"I'll let her explain. Tonight. At the gathering."

"Hmm. Not spilling her secrets to your commander? You're worse off than I thought."

I chuckled, smiling at Sae as she headed toward us.

Folding her hands in front of her, she said, "Next up is the Ceremonial Dance to the Song of Remembrance. Is that right?" Before either of us could answer, she turned her back to match our casual pose, leaning in to whisper, "How'm I doing?"

"Perfect," I whispered back.

Lanna pushed off the rail to complete a circle of the three of us. "I must say, Saelyn of Felgren, I'm impressed with how well you know our customs already. The dress, the shoes, the eating of the Rudismar, and now the Ceremonial Dance."

Sae visibly gulped. "The Rudismar was a bit difficult for me, but Thevin gave me hope." She elbowed me. "He ate his in one bite."

"The Rudismar?" Lanna asked in disbelief. "I've never seen Thevin even attempt it."

I didn't remember eating it. I'd never been one for raw seafood, let alone topped with powdered pearls. "It wasn't so bad," I replied.

"I'm glad I tried it," Sae continued, "but I'm not sure it's to my taste."

Lanna made a face. "It's to no one's taste. It's a stupid tradition."

A low hum echoed through the room, signaling the start of the dance and song.

"It's starting!" Sae said giddily. She pulled my hand from where I'd crossed my arms at my chest. "Will you dance with me?"

Lanna waved a hand dismissively. "Thevin doesn't dance."

I glared at her. "I don't mind it."

She huffed and shook her head. "I've never once seen you dance at these gatherings. You always stand here like this."

"Maybe I just don't want to dance with *you*."

Sae's eyes darted back and forth between us as we bickered.

Lanna pretended offense, patting her chest. "How could you offend me so?" A smile tugged at her mouth. "And in front of my new friend, too."

"You'll get over it. Besides,"—I pointed across the room to the Viceroy's daughter, Malla—"I see someone who could stand dancing with you for more than two seconds."

Lanna's face fell as she followed my point. "She's no longer interested in dancing with me."

I smirked. "Now who's not trying hard enough?"

She rolled her eyes, winked at Sae, and left, headed to the musician at the front of the room.

I turned my attention back to Sae, only to see her gnawing on her lip repeatedly.

"Hey." I rubbed her shoulder. "You alright?"

She was silent for a moment, watching Lanna join the Viceroy at the front of the crowd as the singer I recognized as Pynth stepped onto a box laid down on the floor. She was a talented woman and it was true what Lanna had said. I preferred to keep to the back of the room and listen to the Song of Remembrance alone. But if Sae wanted to dance, then we'd dance.

The music began and couples flowed out to the cleared floor. The first lyric lifted through the room, accompanied by a single violin.

> *"A song to give voice to those we've lost, a song to take*
> *time to remember them."*

I pulled Sae out of her trance, leading her onto the dance floor where I took her hands, placing them on my shoulders, grabbing her waist.

She laughed nervously, avoiding my eyes, still chewing on that lip and watching the musician as Pynth sang,

> *"Their lives at a cost, their stories at end, and a song*
> *to take time to remember them."*

"It's a beautiful song," she murmured.

"What are you thinking about?" I tilted my head, recognizing her hesitancy as we danced.

She cleared her throat, finally meeting my gaze. "You and Lanna…you're close?"

I shrugged. "Yes. We've been friends for many years. She commands the Runners, and I've been conscripted into that army since I was fifteen."

She nodded and the song continued,

> *"The mountains, the forest, the seaside, and plains,*
> *we sing a song to remember them."*

"And have you ever…" She hesitated and I pulled her just a little closer. "Have you ever been more than friends?"

I tilted my head back in laughter, instantly disturbing the peaceful quiet of the song and murmuring my apology to those around us. "No, Sae. We're friends. That's it. Lanna prefers women in that regard anyway."

"Oh," Sae said, her cheeks reddening. "I just thought that because you seemed so close that maybe there was something more there."

"Never," I assured her. "She feels like a big sister, really." I shrugged again. "Or what I imagine a sister would be like."

Her shoulders relaxed. "I've enjoyed this day." A wide, toothy grin swept over her mouth. "Almost drownings and all. Thank you for taking me out. It's helped to keep my mind off of my father."

I squeezed her waist. "You're welcome. I enjoyed our day, too."

I couldn't help it. My eyes lingered at her mouth, and I stepped imperceptibly closer as the song came to its last line.

> *"We cannot reverse what's come at great cost, but we*
> *can take the time to remember them."*

The last note sounded and everyone in the room turned to clap. Everyone except Sae and I. We held each other still, the sound of cheers surrounding us. I hardly heard them. Our eyes were locked, our hands on each other's bodies, refusing to let each other go.

I told myself to take my hands from her waist, to turn and clap with the others, but I simply didn't want to.

She opened her mouth and took a deep breath, her eyes a sparkle of deep blue. "Thevin, I—"

*BOOM.*

A rupture beyond the tower rumbled, and I pulled Sae down to the floor, covering her huddled body with my own. Screams flew through the room and people began to run as great black clouds billowed in on the orange glow of the sun entering the dining hall. Haunting snarls bellowed through the air and great black vines slithered over the arched balconies, quickly followed by the beasts who climbed them.

I grabbed Sae under her arm, yanking her up and heading for the stairwell that led down the Spire just as blood cut through the air in a familiar tang of iron and salt. Cries of pain and fear drummed through my ears, and I ignored them all, my sole task to get Sae to safety. Her tears tracked down her cheeks as she looked back in horror at the massacre behind us. I caught a quick glimpse to assess the level of danger, counting no less than twenty Blight beasts that tore through the room, followed swiftly by the one woman we all feared most.

The Blightress had come for Saelyn.

# CHAPTER 34
# SAELYN

Clothed in a black gown with sheer black panels that ran high up along her neck, I caught the eye of the woman who had started all of this. Her blood red lips curved into a smile and her eyes, somehow catching multiple colors at once, glinted, offering me a glimpse into her great well of power.

I saw it there, surrounding her in a colorless void. The dark abyss of hatred and wrath swirled around her pale skin and blindingly white hair that ran in long, lush trails down her back. Even through the din of screaming and pain around me, I heard her speak.

*"Hello, Little One."*

"Get her out of here, Thevin! To the stairs! Now!" I heard my mother's shout just before she erected a great ball of green light, pulling long swaths of power from it that wrapped around two of the Blight beasts, pinning them to the floor where Lady Lanna swept in to slice off their heads.

Without a word, Thevin pulled me to the staircase. I looked back to watch the Blightress lift the Viceroy from the floor and shred through his chest with sharp black nails, his blood sputtering over her lips, matching them in color.

"Saelyn!" Thevin cried in my ear. "Move!"

"Wait!" I yelled back. "I can fix this!"

His face furrowed as he all but dragged me across the floor. "We need to leave, now! Get to your mother's portals on the staircase!"

"Stop!" I begged as he bent and lifted me over his shoulder. He didn't heed my shouts as he began our descent down the staircase that wound around the outside of the Spire. I pleaded with him to let me down before we hit a wall of black, the inky vines crawling up the side of the Spire, thick with thorns. He cursed and lowered me finally as we witnessed even more Blight beasts bounding up the sides of the stone along the vines. My mother's waiting portals flickered just a few feet away, but still beyond the horrors the Blightress had brought to annihilate everyone in that dining hall. With each jump, the dark creatures' lumen-like bodies would bind with the vines, allowing the monsters to gain footing up the vertical surface.

Thevin cursed, slashing at the growth woven over the stairs with a dagger I'd never seen before.

I grabbed his shoulders, calling, "I can warn them!"

His response was on his lips, but too late as I spoke under my breath, "*Revertayden en tepiore.*"

In a flash of white, Thevin squeezed my waist. "You're welcome. I've enjoyed it, too."

I stumbled and blinked, my breath coming in rapid bouts. My skin was no longer marred with the spray of blood, my hair still pinned tidily on top of my head. The Song of Remembrance was ending, and I had just seconds to get this timing right and undo the course of events that would arrive soon.

"Sae?" Thevin placed his hand at my neck. "What is it?"

"The Blightress," I started, my eyes darting to the edge of the room where the boom would come at any second. "She's here!" I pointed and Thevin's head darted in the direction they'd come.

"The Blightress? She wouldn't come here. She wouldn't risk—"

The song ended and the room erupted again and for the first time in applause. "Everyone out!" I shouted. "Get away from those windows!"

*BOOM.*

I wondered for a split second what the boom actually was before I saw it. A portal had opened in the sky just as the black vines of what Thevin had called the Blight crawled over the ledge of the balconies, oozing their thick massive trunks over the white stone, trickling into the room smooth as water.

Thevin pulled me instantly, once again repeating that we needed to get out. I hadn't been quick enough. I hadn't done enough to give them time to stop this.

Her voice resounded in my thoughts as I was pulled away through the panicking crowd. *"I thought that might be you, Little One. How is it that you can reverse time?"*

I shuddered, refusing to respond. *"Revertayden en tepiore!"*

"You're welcome. I've enjoyed it, too."

I flew from Thevin's grip on my waist, running wildly through the crowd, the last line of the song on the slight breeze that drifted through the room somehow smelling like iron and salt.

> *"We cannot reverse what's come at great cost, but we
> can take the time to remember them."*

I found my mother at the edge of the room, weeping silently, the tracks of tears down her face a mirror to the ones I would shed in less than a minute if I couldn't stop this.

I grabbed her shoulders. "The Blightress—she's here. She's coming from there." I pointed to the south-facing windows and it took all but a moment for my mother to take action. The room erupted for a third time in applause, and my mother ran through the crowd, erecting a wall of green that spanned from her outstretched hands, encasing the domed, round room in a shield of her light.

The boom sounded as I'd heard twice before, its thundering rattle not nearly as loud behind my mother's protection.

Thevin found me, pulling me to him as we watched the Blightress step out of her portal onto the very edge of the stone balcony, nearly touching the Baron's wall of shimmering emerald.

The screams still poured through the room as the crowd backed away to the northern balconies. The Blight slithered up the sides of my mother's shield, unable to penetrate her power. The Blight beasts followed in vicious growls, muffled through the green haze. My mother watched them carefully, then shot her hand through the air, impaling each one with a spike of solid green power.

The Blightress's gaze caught mine through all of it, and once again she spoke in my head. "*This little power of yours is quite the irritation, Saelyn of Felgren.*"

I gulped a breath, refusing to break her stare and responding in my mind. "*You—you can remember?*"

A brilliant smile lifted her crimson lips. "*I've remembered every time you've done this, Little One. All the way back to three years ago, when you discovered this unique part of you. I can show you more, if you'd like. All you have to do is reach out your hand to me, and I'll show you the extent of the power you wield.*"

She opened her hand to me and my mother whipped around, fear gripping her face. "No!" she screamed, turning back to the Blightress.

"*Where is my father?*" I begged. "*Please, I want my father back.*"

The ancient woman's eyes darted to my mother and she spoke in a harrowing voice that resounded through the shielded room. "Oh, *Little Sprout*," she started with amusement. "You have not told her the truth?"

Her cold laughter filled my body down to my bones, and I feared I'd never be warm again. Thevin pressed me even closer to his chest, his arms wrapped tightly around me, ready to bolt at any second.

The voice I'd never forget sounded once more as the Blight released from the shield, pulling back into the dark abyss of the portal behind the Blightress. With another of her saccharine smiles, she nodded to me, calling, "Until we meet again, Little One."

In flash of dark power, she was gone.

# CHAPTER 35

# THEVIN

"How long has she spoken to you?" The Baron of Felgren paced at the gathering of the Four. Or the Three, in this case. We were missing one of the leaders.

"Tonight was the first time I'd ever spoken to her," Sae responded, shifting in her seat and watching her mother move back and forth across the low light of the room.

They had placed her in a red chair the color of fresh blood, and her gown clashed horribly. She looked frightened and confused, but that same determination I loved allowed for the slight raise of her chin after every inquiry as to how she knew the Blightress was coming and saved us all.

The council of the Four sat at the long table across the dais of the room used solely for these meetings in the Spire. The Viceroy, Lanna, and Lady Lamoral sat at the center of the table with the Madame of the Mountains and Clairannia at the ends. The medicus conduit had introduced herself at the gathering as a commander in the Wieldwryns. A seat had been left for Baron Karus, but she had refused it, preferring to pace in front of her daughter instead.

"Saelyn, we are trying to understand," Madame Zoreyah said

softly, folding her hands in front of her. The brilliant gold tattoos across her brown skin almost glowed in the flickering light of the candles lit in sconces along the walls.

This circular room was windowless, lying somewhere in the middle of the Spire. There was one door in, one door out, and I'd seen my fair share of inquiries take place within its sandstone walls. I leaned against the stone, carefully watching Sae in profile, observing her reactions to the questions directed solely on her.

The Madame leaned forward further. "How is it exactly that you knew the Blightress was coming if you had never spoken to her before this night?"

Sae's chin lifted once more and I bit down on my tongue. I'd been allowed in this meeting by the Baron's command, though most who usually attended had been turned away. My parents, too, had been allowed to stay, standing quietly behind the long table. I watched every one of Sae's expressions as she tried to hold together the turmoil that kept sweeping across her face. Not a single tear fell down her cheeks, though I knew they threatened to by the occasional tremble of her chin.

"I—" Sae started, her eyes flickering over the faces at the table, landing on her mother who had stopped her pacing, waiting for the explanation we needed.

I didn't understand it either. How *did* she know?

One moment we'd been dancing, the next, she had sprinted from my grasp, finding her mother first to warn against the Blightress's attempted onslaught. By the look of how many Blight beasts she'd brought with her, most in that room would have been slaughtered, if not all.

Sae straightened in her seat, heaving in a big gulp of breath before stating, "I felt her presence before she came. I don't know how. I've never felt it before."

She was lying. I knew her tells, and the white-knuckled grip of her hands across her lap was one of them. Her nostrils flared slightly—another sign.

I frowned. I didn't understand why she'd lie.

Lady Lamoral's voice came haggard, harsh, and slow as it

drifted quietly in the silence of the room. "How could you predict the presence of the Blightress if you've never seen nor spoken to her?"

With her gray hair, sunken eyes, and drooping lips against her wan skin, she looked as if she'd just left her deathbed to attend. Though, the truth was, I'd never seen her any different.

Lanna placed a hand over her mother's, amending, "What my mother means to ask is, what was it that correctly made you believe it was the Blightress who was coming?"

"I don't know," Sae replied. Another lie.

I glanced at Baron Karus, curious if she also realized her daughter was not telling the truth. As if in a trance, she stared without blinking, standing still as a statue and just as silent as one. Her eyes narrowed slightly and a feather ticked in her jaw, transfixed at a blank wall.

"You can understand, my dear," began the Viceroy, "how we find this ability of yours to be…curious." His gentle smile lifted, easing the tension. "Such a power as to be able to track the movements of the Blightress could be supremely beneficial in this war, especially as the Dimming draws near."

Sae cleared her throat. "I cannot track her. I just…I could feel that she was coming."

Madame Zoreyah addressed the rest of the council. "The Blightress would not have come unless she knew Saelyn was here. She would not have expended so much power."

"Agreed," Lanna said with a nod. "I've already sent word to the Blight Line to hold outside of Lythglyn. I've asked for a reprieve for the Wieldwryns and the Runners for a week which will allow us to settle when we arrive."

The Viceroy countered, "Perhaps this is the time to push for the Dimming instead of hold, Lady Lanna. The Blightress has weakened herself and will struggle for a short time to siphon enough power to replace all of the Blight beasts she lost. Not to mention the portal she created to get them here. Baron Karus,"—he turned to address Saelyn's mother—"will your shield hold the Spire for the time being?"

"It is already up and holding."

"Good, good," he replied. "She certainly won't be able to cross through—"

"Excuse me, but," Saelyn interrupted, "what do you mean when you say she would not have expended such power unless she knew I was here?"

Clairannia shifted in her seat, her eyes on the Baron rather than Saelyn.

Lanna answered as if reciting from a book, "The Blightress has limits. Ever since your father sacrificed his life to diminish the strength of her heart, she has been unable to neither portal nor produce her Blight as quickly as before, according to your mother and those in Felgren who interacted with her seventeen years ago."

Sae frowned, glancing to her mother, but again lifting her chin. "And what exactly is the Dimming?"

I rubbed my hands across my face, my stomach dropping. I'd avoided telling her, hoping to find the right time, not even sure I was the right one to explain.

The Viceroy cleared his throat, adopting a soft tone. "It is the day our armies amass to invade the Blightress's lands and render her power useless. We are nearly ready, but have been waiting for some time." He gave her another slight, simple smile. "We have been waiting for you, Saelyn. For when Baron Karus has deemed you ready to join our forces with your great power and defeat the Blightress and her evil once and for all."

Sae's eyes flicked to her mother in shock. The Baron, catching on to what had been said, reached out to her daughter, cupping her hands over Sae's. "You are seventeen, Little Love. You are more than ready."

She stood, pulling out of her mother's touch. "The Dimming relies on me?" Her voice seethed in a rare temper, but one that was quick to ignite. She addressed the table, "And has she told you *who* is in the Blightress's lands?"

"Saelyn," her mother warned.

"My father is there. Alive."

Gasps and frantic looks pierced the air. I watched Lanna,

knowing how she'd feel about the news that the hero she'd idolized and looked up to her whole life still lived.

Her voice cut through the shock first. "Baron Revich is alive?"

"Yes," Sae answered. "And we must save him. That is my real reason for being here. I will not return to Felgren until he returns with us." Sae's voice quivered slightly and my body begged to go to her. To hold her and let her cry in my arms as she'd done the night of her seventeenth birthday.

"Is it true?" Madame Zoreyah asked, addressing the Baron directly.

A single tear fell down Baron Karus's cheek, though she raised her chin high, just as her daughter tended to do. "What my daughter says is true."

The raspy cough of Lady Lamoral came next. "How do we know the Baron is telling the truth? What proof do you have?"

"It's true," Clairannia answered swiftly. "I was there, seventeen years ago on the day Saelyn was born." Her lips pursed. "And I confirmed it. I can feel their bond through Baron Karus. It is intact, which means he still lives, though I do not know of his condition."

"He is well," the Baron interjected. "Through our bond, he promises he is well. And he is waiting."

Lanna's fury echoed through the room. "You've hidden this from the isle for seventeen years?"

"I did not do it easily, Lanna."

"Then why?" she pleaded, rising from her seat. "Why did you hide this for so long? We could have saved him by now," her voice faltered. "We could have had him back."

The Baron shook her head, staring at her daughter. "Saelyn does not know the whole truth yet, and she will be the first to hear it, not this gathering." She turned back to the table. "This council is adjourned. With Lady Lanna representing the Spire, I move for it to reconvene at the Blight Line when the Four represented can be gathered to discuss the change in the Dimming."

"Agreed," the Madame murmured, followed shortly by Lanna and the Viceroy.

"I would hear your explanation before you go, Baron Karus."

Lady Lamoral glared across the room, and I wondered at the icy tone she'd used.

The Baron nodded once, continuing, "It's settled then. We leave at dawn by way of portal to the Blight Line. Thevin,"—she turned her black eyes to me—"please escort Saelyn to our rooms. I will be there shortly."

I uncrossed my arms, lifting myself from the wall, following Sae out the door. Her head was low, watching her own feet shuffle in those ridiculous shoes. We entered the short hallway that led to the outer staircase around the spire, and without a word, she grabbed my hand in hers for balance, lifted a leg, and unstrapped one silver shoe before doing the same with the other. Barefoot, she swung them between us, never letting go of my fingers that wound through her own.

The night breeze wafted through the staircase, and the sky was littered with clusters of stars, though a shimmer of green power hid their true light. The Baron's shield would protect the Spire as long as Saelyn was in it. Through the glassy magic, a half moon shone down, casting a soft glow across Sae's cheek.

I knew because I stared. I let myself stare as we descended, wondering at this friend whose secrets I thought I knew. I would have sworn I knew all of Sae—her hopes and dreams, her past, and what her future might become, but I did not know how she warned of the Blightress's coming.

As we neared the hall that led to our rooms, I panicked, my mind racing for any excuse I could think of to keep our hands entwined—to keep her there with me where she was safe, and we could just be like *this*.

We left the staircase, turning down our white stone hall lit in flickering copper sconces. I opened my mouth to ask if she wanted to sneak down to the kitchens when she cut through our silence first.

"Thank you." All anger from her gone, her gaze was instead of sadness, a woeful blue in her eyes when she looked up at me. "Thank you for saving me."

My brows furrowed and I frowned, squeezing her hand. "It was you who saved me. All of us. I didn't do anything."

A slight smile crossed her lips. "But you would have. You would have pulled me away to safety."

"Yes."

It was all I could say, all I could answer, my eyes dropping to her lips as they parted slightly on her mouth.

She lifted her free hand, her fingers tracing my jaw, traveling up my cheek and tucking a curl behind my ear. At her touch, her nearness, her scent of forest and sea, my heart thudded in a racing counter to every training I'd had on staying calm in any situation.

I hadn't been prepared for this. I hadn't felt the want, the need and longing as I did now to keep her here with me. To somehow keep her just like this, cupping my cheek, lifting her head, her eyes flickering from mine to my mouth rapidly, repeatedly.

I lost any sense of who we were and what we'd discussed in her room, dancing on that day before she turned seventeen. I'd told her then that I couldn't lie. I couldn't pretend I did not love her, pretend I didn't need her smile like I needed air in my lungs. I'd tried. I'd tried so hard to keep our friendship what it was, to give her the same Thevin she needed, but she was so close to me in that hall. I could feel her breath, warm and sweet over my mouth as she looked into my eyes in question.

I had no answer. I had no will other than to stand there, a man waiting for his love to love him back.

"Sae," I whispered, but she ended anything else I'd have mumbled, pressing her lips lightly to mine as if asking whether I wanted this, too.

I swear the air sparked. The sconces flared and the wind howled as she continued, my own lips moving with hers, her fingers tightening through mine, pulling my hand behind her to bring herself closer.

I didn't know much, but right then, I knew her.

I didn't know our future, her limits, or my role to play in the fight to come, but I knew Sae.

I knew the shape of her lips. I knew the sweetness of her tongue as it brushed against mine, deepening what she'd started into something from which we'd never recover.

Never once in my life would I heal from this kiss, the roam of her hands along my neck, the press of her body against mine, the taste of her on my tongue, her breath leaving her lungs so beautifully in rapid succession, matching my own.

She lifted herself further, the sound of her shoes dropping to the stone the only sound after the hurried range of our breath, the parting of our lips only to meet again, hungry, demanding, both of us discovering for the first time what it really meant to be kissed by someone you *knew*. Someone you'd met every summer in a forest that lived and thrived in its paths that led to yellow fields and golden sun.

That was Sae.

A glorious sun in a blue sky, lighting the world in her brilliance, her clever words, and playful laugh.

I gripped her waist as her fingers shifted through the back of my hair, pulling, scraping, urging me to give her more, take more, become more with her.

She finally broke from my mouth, tilting her head back to breathe, still pulling herself closer, wrapping her arms around me as I moved my lips across her jaw, down her neck, willing to bury myself within her skin, never parting, never experiencing another winter without her warmth.

The smallest moan lifted from her lips and sent me reeling, struggling to pull back from her as I should.

Clarity hit me like a punch to the gut, and I broke from her embrace, my lips just as swollen as hers. I stepped back, touching my mouth, my body urging me to go back. "I'm sorry," I whispered, watching her struggle to regain her breath, same as me.

She shook her head, her chest heaving, a smile spreading across her red lips. "Don't be," she said, breathless. She shook her head again and stepped forward in a laugh. "How could you be sorry for *that*?" Her eyes glittered and she touched her own lips, a wicked smile underneath her fingers.

I regained my breath and said, "I'm sorry I let it get that far."

She scoffed. "As if I wasn't the initiator here?"

"Saelyn?" The Baron's voice rose through the hall behind me, and I turned, ever the soldier in her army, ready to hear my next command.

Sae sighed and shuffled to where she'd dropped her shoes, farther away than I realized we'd moved in our kiss. She pressed them to her chest and walked to the door of her rooms. "Goodnight, Thevin," she said, pressing her red, swollen, and obviously kissed lips together and opening the door.

"Goodnight," I returned, barely audible, but loud enough for her to hear as she twisted her lips in a coy smile.

"Be ready at dawn," was all the Baron said to me, no doubt noticing my lips in the same condition, my face flushed just as well, and my hair run through by the long, beautiful fingers of her daughter.

I nodded once, turning across the hall, shaking, utterly destroyed, living on a cloud, the grin rising within me as I allowed it for just a few moments more before I opened the door to my rooms and let that memory stay with me for the rest of the night.

# CHAPTER 36
# SAELYN

Kissing Thevin was all I wanted to think about.

I wanted nothing more than to fall into bed, smiling at how natural it had been to reach for him, pull his hands around my waist, and taste his lips.

Too tired to explain how I loved him but feared losing him, I chose instead to just be with him. No words, no heavy burdens of wrapping our heads around how much our friendship was changing—just my lips on his. My body pressed to his, and his hands…

I took a heavy breath in an attempt to chill my heated blood and bring my heart back down from where it soared in the revelation of everything we could share in the future.

My mother shuffled to her room, exhausted, pulling at the disheveled braid she'd woven across her head and letting her long white hair flow down her back.

I hadn't known her hair matched the Blightress. I didn't expect to see their similarities—powerful women dressed in black with long white locks and red shades on their lips. While my mother's eyes were almost always black, I couldn't explain the variety of colors that came from the eyes of the Blightress.

I hurried out of my gown, stepping into a midnight blue nightgown that had been left for me. I knocked on my mother's door and at her quiet answer, I stepped inside.

She sat at the small desk, tracing her name over the carved wooden box I knew played a song about the sun and the moon. She wiped her eyes before she turned to me, and I was surprised to see their bright emerald hue returned.

I hurried to her, falling on my knees and taking her hands. "Mama?" I squeezed her cold fingers, all my anger for what she hadn't told me gone. I didn't know where to start or what she had left to share with me, so I waited for her reply.

"You look so much like him." She sniffed and gave a stunted laugh, shaking her head. "I'm sure you're tired of hearing that, but…" She brushed the side of my face. "I know these eyes. This hair." Pulling a strand forward, she flattened it against my shoulder, stalling in what else she needed to say.

I bent my head in silence, struggling to find the words to ask. But I needed to know. I needed to know what happened that day my father left us. I needed to know why. I chewed on my bottom lip, the questions forming in a list in my mind.

She slipped off the chair, kneeling down to the sandstone floor with me, pulling my hands into her lap. "Before I tell you how he left and where he is now, I—" She choked, her voice halting as she pressed the back of her hand to her mouth.

"It's alright, Mama. However long it takes, I'm listening." I gave her an encouraging smile. "I'm only here to listen."

She took a long, shuddering breath, her gaze steady on me. Still green. Green as the trees of Felgren in early spring.

She lowered her hand back to mine, clearing her throat and starting, "The first thing you must understand is that your father loves you very, very much."

# PART FOUR

## SEVENTEEN YEARS BEFORE

# CHAPTER 37
# REV

The rhyzolm hummed.

Roared.

Slid across my fingers while I attempted to peer into the oblivion of the Blightress's portal. The dark abyss would lead us straight to that cavern where she kept her heart from the world.

I dropped the stone back into my pocket with one name on my mind.

Saelyn.

This act was for Saelyn, the children on the isle, and those who would come to be.

Our home had its measures of issues, but it was peaceful. This woman, this ancient being, would continue to disrupt that peace. She'd already harvested channelers into macabre trees, siphoning their power for what?

She had a purpose. One I believed we did not yet see or understand.

One I feared.

So there we stood, two Barons, three channelers, and one centuries old lapis conduit, sister to the woman whose heart we sought to destroy.

The black portal swirled as an inky wall at the end of the dark tunnel. Karus had led us here, underneath the forest, where the Blight had permeated Felgren before she destroyed part of it the first time. This is where the Blightress had taken her months ago, and where her path led once again.

Karus pushed her hand through the portal, pulling it back quickly and confirming, "Ilyenna, we can go through this. It's not like a Baron portal."

I bit down so hard, the force of it rippled through our companion bond. I didn't know how to make these portals. Whatever portal magic that had been taught down the line of Barons was not what the Blightress could produce. Her portals allowed anyone in, regardless of how many hearts were within their bodies, whereas mine allowed just one. Her portals could remain open when a person went through, whereas mine would close.

Karus touched my shoulder, addressing all of us. "Remember, to leave this portal, show your truest, innermost desires. Your emotions must be faced. When I was trapped, I left by giving into my anger." She heaved a sigh. "I don't know how long we'll be inside, but we wait. We wait for everyone before moving forward. I'll go first."

"You will not," I countered, finding her hand in the dim tunnel and pulling her toward me. "I will go and meet you on the other side."

"I'll go first, Baron Revich," Lia spoke, pushing her way forward. "I understand my sister's magic better than you. I will go to the other side and meet all of you there."

Karus nodded and Lia stepped forth, disappearing in an instant into the endless black.

"How long do we wait?" Philius asked.

"We don't wait," Karus said, attempting to take her hand from mine.

"Let me go before you," I murmured. "Please."

Her shoulders slumped. "Alright. I'll see you on the other side."

I cringed. It had been the exact thing my mother had said to me before her death. Karus, realizing this, squeezed my fingers with a sorrowful look. I took a deep breath and kissed her softly. Without another word, I let go of her hand and stepped into the portal.

~

"*ILLUMINARE.*" M*Y* *ORB OF BLUE LIT THE SPACE AROUND ME WHICH* held no substance. No grit, no earth, no walls, nor anything to ground me. I walked on air if I walked on anything at all.

This is where Karus had been.

For who knows how long, she had wandered through this existence before screaming her way out of it.

I felt for the rhyzolm in my pocket, curious if I could still feel our daughter. She was there. Just a small hum like a beacon in the far distance, pulling me back out of this place.

"*And what is it the Baron of Felgren desires most?*" The voice of Adaynth came to me in the dark, sounding as if he was there, next to me in the space that was not space.

I shrugged, taking one more look around at the absence of everything. Squeezing the rhyzolm and thinking of my family, I said, "I simply desire to love them. To keep both of them safe. Of any future I'll live, I'll live it for them."

I stepped out of the portal easily. No shove like Karus had described, but a light force of wind at my back, my boots landing on wet stone of a dim cave.

Karus was already out, wrapping her arms around me, her cheek pressed to mine as she spoke low into my ear. "I said us. I just want the three of us together."

I held her tightly. "I voiced the same."

She pulled away to kiss me. "You took a bit longer to get out."

I swept a hand through her white hair. After that last *Simulair Solum* spell, which rid the entirety of Felgren from the Blight, we'd never get her chestnut color back. "I just wanted to know what it was like for you. What you went through in there last time." I shook my head and kissed her again.

Philius all but flew out of the portal, Lia ready, catching him at the back of his vest and holding him steady. "Fuck, that was awful."

Karus chewed her bottom lip, whispering, "C'mon Ilyenna."

But it was Talon who came next, catching himself before he hit the wet stones of the cave we'd all entered.

"By the…" Philius murmured, standing in a stupor at the pulsing heart hanging from the cave ceiling.

It was difficult to ignore the steady beat that filtered through the dank air, but I managed, waiting for Ilyenna to join us.

Talon paced in front of the swirling black with one long dark braid swaying at his back.

A minute passed, then five.

"I have to go back in there," he said.

"No." Karus grabbed his vest, jerking him from where he'd started to force his way back in. "She can do this."

"I'm not waiting two weeks for her out here."

Karus visibly winced.

I stepped in front of him. "Ilyenna is perfectly capable of getting out of there. Give her more time."

He stared me down. "Would you wait for your companion? The mother of your child?"

We both knew the answer.

"You wouldn't find her in there anyway," Karus explained. "She has to leave of her own accord. It's why none of us saw each other. We don't exist in there together."

I jostled his shoulder, bringing his focus back to me. "She's going to figure it out, Talon."

Nodding, he stepped out of my grasp to set himself against the wet rock.

Karus slipped her fingers through mine and we turned our backs on the portal to behold the cave together. It was just as she had described—a vast underground cove of damp rock, and a crimson pulsing heart, wide as the dining hall, which hung from what looked like a dozen arteries at the top of the cave. I noted the staircase that led upward to a small opening. It had to be the one Karus had climbed to get out of this place and wander through the Blightress's lands just months ago.

"It's grown," Karus said, gazing out into the open cave,

watching the pulse of the heart which she could find in herself any time she wanted to.

"It grows?" Philius mumbled in disgust.

Lia hovered behind him. "It was once the size of a human heart. She's been feeding it for a century."

Philius's face scrunched. "Feeding it with what?"

Lia's tired gray eyes shifted to Karus.

Karus didn't return her gaze, instead replying, "Fear. She feeds this heart with fear." She let go of my hand and stood at the outcropping of rock that led down to the cavern floor. "Her wrath is fed by what she fears most."

A stale breeze sifted through the air, pulling at her white hair and bringing a sharp trill as it drifted over the hole above.

Philius asked in a whisper, "What is it she fears most, Karus?"

She didn't turn, didn't drop her shoulders at her answer, she only looked on at the crimson heart, sharing a beat with hers. "Being alone…forever."

～

"So," Philius started, breaking the silence. "What was your favorite century?"

Lia huffed in a chuckle, and Karus rolled her eyes.

The four of us sat, our backs to the rock wall at the portal's exit while Talon stood, still staring into the swirling surface.

"Many of them blur together," Lia began in answer, "but I do remember certain times, certain people who were special in my life."

"Did you ever have a family?" the Prince asked next. I tuned in to listen, also curious about Lia's centuries on the isle.

"Children? No." She held up her left wrist, displaying the curved *l* still inked on her skin. "I never wanted children, and when the *liberum* mark was created, I was first in line."

Philius nodded, glancing at his own mark left on the stub of his wrist. "Has it been lonely, then? Never aging, everyone you love around you growing old and dying?"

A numbness crept over my skin. I slid my arm around Karus, pulling her tighter to my side so she could lay her head on my shoulder.

Lia thought for a moment. "At first it was difficult to endure. I loved, I lost, and then I'd love again only to lose once more. So, I started leaving before the end."

I narrowed my eyes. "You just left the people you loved?"

"It was easier on all of us."

"Or was it easier for you?" Karus murmured.

"You do not know the pain of watching someone you love wither in body and mind, Baron Karus." Her voice came sharp, a lesion meant to dig deep. "Though, maybe someday you will."

Karus sat up at that. "What do you mean?"

"Only what you yourself already suspect. The Blightress gave some of herself directly to you. It may be long life she gave as well."

Karus froze and her face paled.

"What about Barons?" Philius questioned. "Karus told me a Baron's power comes from the first Baron who got it from the Blightress. Wouldn't a Baron live forever then, too?"

I shook my head, having already asked myself the same question. "Adaynth was able to find a way to pass on his power, Baron to Baron. He *does* continue to live"—I tapped my temple—"in here. Barons have unnaturally long lives, but the power does not allow them to live forever."

"You're saying the first ever Baron of Felgren lives in your head?" Philius looked stunned. He huffed, awkwardly folding his arms at his chest. "My sister might live forever and has an ancient man in her mind."

"He doesn't like me," Karus admitted, picking at the edge of the rocky floor. "I don't hear him often, not like Revich."

Lia swallowed hard. "Adaynth speaks to you?"

I leaned my head back against the cold rock. "Sometimes. And only recently."

"He is coherent?" she asked.

"Yes."

"How did he diminish her power before?"

"He said it doesn't matter. It won't work the same again. He kept this heart contained with the *Simulair Solum* spell under the Fortress for centuries. It dampened her power until she convinced a Baron to bring it to her."

"Ereyth," Lia finished.

I nodded.

"So how do we destroy that thing now?" Philius asked.

"We pierce it," Karus answered, "We use our power to cut it down, let it bleed and die, your flames to burn it." I squeezed her waist at the words of violence, but she continued, "She's lived long enough. Destroyed enough lives. As soon as Ilyenna is out of the portal, we—"

A gust of wind poured from the wall of black, shoving Ilyenna to the rocky floor, panting with tears streaming down her cheeks. Talon was there a moment later, pulling her to him, shaking as he held her.

Talon soothed her tears, rubbing her back and whispering repeatedly to her that she was out. We all stood, readying our nerves for what would come next.

Ilyenna's eyes rose to Karus. "I—I don't know how you endured it. I don't know how long I was in there, but it felt like days."

"You got through it. You're out," Karus said.

Ilyenna fell into his chest once more. "I didn't want to say it. I didn't want to admit it, Talon, I'm so sorry."

He soothed her again. "Whatever it was, it's alright now. You did it. You're here."

"It's not alright!" she cried. "I didn't want to admit what I desire most. I didn't want to *say* it."

"What was it, child?" Lia asked, pulling a handkerchief from her pocket.

"Our baby," Ilyenna started, wiping her eyes, "I don't want our baby to have magic. I don't want our baby to go through any of this." She wrapped her arms tighter around Talon's shoulders. "I don't want the Blightress to have a reason to make our child into one of those trees." She wiped at her face. "And I am sorry for it. I don't want our baby to share this gift, and—"

Talon shook his head, kissing her cheek before she could continue. "You wish to protect our child. There's nothing to be sorry for. There is nothing to forgive."

Philius jumped to the highest rock that looked over the expanse of the cave mouth below, leading to the heart. "I hate to be the one to say it, but we've been here an hour and have pushed our luck already."

Talon moved to interject, but Ilyenna stopped him. "He's right." She wiped her eyes and nose one last time. "Let's get this over with."

Karus flicked her fingers, her green tendrils of power forming half of a longsword, sharp and deadly if she willed it.

I was not a violent man, but violence I would embrace, if it meant we'd be free of that ghost.

My own longsword, a deep blue, aligned to complete the other half of hers, forming the weapon we'd use together to cut down the heart that haunted us.

A golden hunting knife took form at the end of Talon's swirl of power, a serrated knife at the end of Ilyenna's. Philius flicked the stubs of his wrist, pulling bright orange sparks of flame and Lia's power misted around her in sharp, silver wisps.

Karus instructed, "We cut it down and leave when the pulse is silent. Run back to the portal, and we will wait for everyone to get out from there."

Nods coincided all around and we began our descent down the rocky path leading further into the cave and closer to the heart of the Blightress.

# CHAPTER 38
# KARUS

My feet fell steady, my heart in sync with the one we'd come to bleed. This was the path the Blightress had chosen for us. This was the outcome she had risked by not backing down.

The scent of my first homeland wafted through the cave. I caught the familiar smells of the marketplace, the crisp green of fresh grass that I had rolled down on the hills surrounding Hyrithia.

I ran a hand under my nose, leading our party closer to the heart, trekking across the damp stone floor. The deadly sword Revich and I had made together hovered in front of us, waiting for our command to cut down the abscess growing from above.

A wind shifted through the cave, drifting over my skin in a frigid touch, smelling of the farmland we had come upon as we had traveled to Radyx. Then salt. The salt of the sea wafted under my nose as well. I paused, hesitating in the spell I seemed to be under.

"What is it?" Rev whispered at my side.

"Do you…" I wiped under my nose again. "Do you smell that?"

His frown deepened and he lifted his head, drawing a deep breath through his nose. "I don't smell anything unusual."

I continued forward, my skin prickling in the chill of a frozen heart. Where I imagined I'd feel warmth in the glowing beat, I was instead left with an empty cold.

There. Again. The slight breeze with no real origin swept more urgently across my face, pulling at the long white strands of my unbound hair, shifting across my skin and bringing with it the scent of home.

Felgren's trees, moss, fresh blooms of spring and the dew that settled in a meadow of golden flowers… I closed my eyes for just a moment, imagining I was back in the forest I loved.

"Something's wrong," I whispered low, only loud enough for Rev to hear.

"Can you feel her? Is she coming?" he said hurriedly, his eyes darting to the hole in the top of the cave.

"No, I don't feel her. It's just…" I shook my head, shaking the sense of Felgren away. "What does the Spire smell like?"

Revich opened his mouth slightly, his eyes narrowing. "It smells like the sea. Salty brine." He squeezed my hand. "Tell me why you ask."

"I—"

"If we need to leave, you need to tell me right now."

I shook my head. "You don't *smell* that? The snowy drifts of the Attatok Mountains?"

He gave me a short shake of his head.

"The salty air of the Spire?"

Again, a short no.

I tried to swallow, my throat suddenly dry, deprived of moisture from the rapid bouts of air I was inhaling. I shivered again as we reached the point where our magic could slice down the heart in one fatal swoop.

"The…" I began, watching Lia's silver slivers of magic rise to the arteries hanging from the cavern roof while Talon and Ilyenna's power poised at the side of the cold organ above us. Flames encircled Philius's wrists, the most power I'd ever seen him wield at once. "The earth of Felgren, Revich." I shook my head, too late in my understanding of what had been true in my own heart for so long.

Lia let loose her power over the heart with the slash of flayed flesh resounding in a sickening clean slice throughout the cave. My hand shot to my own heart, and I grabbed at my vest, pulling at the fabric. "*Wait*," I gasped, too late and too quiet. Talon and Ilyenna took Lia's opening as the cue to plunge their glowing knives into the pulsing tissue, piercing the side. A spray of blood, thick and cold, splattered onto the rock of the cave walls.

I screamed, my cry echoing off the stone as I fell, and in the moment my body hit the floor, I caught Lia stumbling with her hand at her own chest.

My heart had been cut just as deep as the one above us, same as all the other magic wielders in that cave who cried out in unison. I had been too late to recognize what the cavern wind had tried to convey. The Blightress was a part of every crevice of this isle, and we had just flayed what fueled us all.

Revich pulled at the back of my vest, heaving me up off the ground. Blood trickled from the sides of his mouth, and he winced as he wrapped an arm around my back, hauling us toward the portal. "Get up!" he yelled in a bloody cough that left him wheezing. "Back to the portal! Now!"

I moved my feet toward Ilyenna, despite the push from Rev in the other direction. I held my hand out to pull her up from the ground, Talon unconscious beside her.

I yanked on her cold fingers. "We have to go!"

Philius rose with a long gash spilling dark blood down his face. "Talon! Get up!" He fumbled, hitting Talon's cheek with his wrists. Talon's eyes shot open, and he blinked rapidly, finding Ilyenna resisting my pull toward the portal, reaching for him instead. Bolting from the ground, he coughed, spitting blood and rushing to Ilyenna's side.

"Take them out!" I screamed, clutching my chest with one hand, pointing to the glowing knives jabbed in the heart with the other.

Talon and Ilyenna pulled back on their power. Blood oozed from the clean cuts, pouring in a steady *drip, drip, drip* onto the stones below.

"Sh-she's here," I stuttered at the same time a cackle of laughter ricocheted off the cavern walls.

Revich had me in his arms instantly, hauling me over his shoulder in an agonized grunt.

Her voice lifted through the iron-tinged air for all to hear. "How foolish you have been, Daughter of Felgren. Did you not wonder at how easily the Blight fell? Did you really think I would not guess at your next thoughts? Do you still not see how well I know you, regardless of how defiantly you shut me out of your mind? I'm beginning to enjoy my dark corner there, Little Sprout."

Revich raced over the stone floor, waving his arm in the shape that would produce a portal. It formed instantly, a bright spot in the dim of the cave. "Philius! Go!"

"I can help!" Philius called just as a low growl swept through the cavern and two Blight beasts prowled down the stairs behind the Blightress.

"I can't get her out quickly while worrying about you!" Revich boomed. He lowered me to the ground, grabbed Philius's arm, and shoved him toward the portal. Anger overtook the fear on Philius's face as he fell, disappearing in an instant. The portal dissipated along with him and Revich made another, calling to Lia who stood at the base of the heart, watching her sister descend the stairs.

"It's been too long, little sister," the Blightress cooed, finding the last step.

"No…" I whispered, getting a closer look at the beasts prowling low behind her. One was not fully black, its legs short and ears still covered in a gray fur I knew well. "Parvus?" I trembled. The beast swept its head in my direction. The eyes of the monster the Blightress had created flashed red toward me, and I knew where Parvus and Rauca had gone.

"No," I whimpered. Revich, unwilling to hesitate, picked me up over his shoulder once more. "No!" I screamed this time, reaching for my loyal friend, my lumen for over seven years, turned dark and distorted by the Blightress's magic.

"You will not leave, Karus." With a wave of her hand, the Blightress cut off our exit, sending a tremble through the cave. An avalanche of rock fell over our path back to the portal.

"Go!" I cried to Revich, scrambling down from his shoulder. "You go! Take Lia and Talon with you!"

He ignored me, pushing me behind him and backing up, facing the Blightress as Talon and Ilyenna did the same.

Lia spoke to her sister for the first time in centuries. "Let them leave, Visalia. You can have me instead."

The Blightress crept forward with our lumens turned Blight beasts growling low behind her. "Why would I want you, Thalia?" she sneered, drawing out her sister's name in mockery.

"Because you seek to reclaim the power you've given." Lia wiped at the blood on her face. "Here it is, in me."

The Blightress tilted her head back to laugh in a flush of long white hair, her fingers ending in pointed black nails lightly touching her throat.

I didn't miss the quick shift of Lia's gaze to Revich which he returned with a subtle nod.

I was weak, barely able to stand, my heart heavy as if it was pooling blood inside my chest. I coughed again, spitting up a mouthful. My head swam in a haunting pulse that mirrored the one still echoing in the cave.

Revich murmured, just loud enough for Talon, Ilyenna, and I to hear. "Be ready to run back to the portal."

I turned my head, confirming in my dizzy state that it was still blocked by impenetrable black stone.

Rev called, "Each one of us felt those wounds through your heart, why not you?"

It took me a moment to realize he was speaking to the Blightress, and I blinked rapidly, doing what I could to stay conscious.

She displayed no sign of weakness from our destruction of the Blight in Felgren. There was no gripping of her chest as her heart bled profusely above us. We had slipped right into her trap. She flashed him an amused smile with her crimson lips. "I ripped my heart from my chest precisely so I would no longer be weakened by such a useless thing."

"But it's not useless," he countered, unfazed by her answer and taking the time to continue backing us up towards the fallen rock.

Revich was stalling.

"Your heart is the pinnacle of power on this isle. Felgren is just a tool. It's your heart that feeds it. You are a part of everything—the mountains, the sea, the grasslands, the forest." He gripped me tighter, pushing me back further. "It's not that magic and its wielders do not exist without Felgren. They do not exist without you."

"What a clever Baron you've ensnared, Little Sprout." Her iridescent eyes swept to me while I struggled to keep mine open. "I did wonder what had you so enamored. I should have taken you when you dallied with that soldier in Hyrithia. He would have been no obstacle." She laughed in unrestrained cruelty. "Now hand her over, Revich of the Hallow Marshes. You know I will do her no harm. I only seek to return what is mine."

I filled my lungs with a ragged breath, swallowing the blood sliding down my throat. "Why didn't you come for me then? For all those years in Hyrithia, why didn't you just take me?"

Lia's hands formed a ball of silver light behind her back, readying her power.

The Blightress only had eyes for me, her face cool and calm. In my rapid blinks, I thought I saw her face soften slightly. "Because, Karus, I wanted *you* to come to *me*." She drifted past her sister, drawing nearer. "I wanted you to reach out your hand and ask for mine because *you* needed *me*. I have always held all the answers you needed. I have always been the only one in this world who could understand you because I made you what you are. And we will be great rulers in our reign." She lifted her fingers toward me, her palm outstretched. "Mother and daughter, reunited to choose the fate of our isle together."

Revich shifted, his hard body covering me further, but I saw her face over his shoulder. The face of longing, of loneliness. The face of a woman who had forgotten that love could never be taken by force.

Stepping forward, her hand still outstretched, she admitted softly, "I did not foresee Heimlen's deceit, but I did what I could to keep your mind intact. I kept it quiet, hidden away until the day you were ready to feel again. Keeping you safe in Felgren is the one thing to be thankful to your lover for." Her eyes flashed to Rev then back to me. "Karus, come. Revich can join us if you must have him." Her lips pulled into a hopeful smile. "It is time to come home."

Lia's ball of light grew behind the Blightress, shaping into a wall of brilliant silver.

I shook my head, my heart in my chest bleeding for what she asked of me that I could not give her. "I cannot love you."

"Your life is long, Little Sprout, and time is healing."

I shook my head again, losing strength in my legs, adding, "I do not want to love you."

Her nostrils flared and her chest heaved under her sheer black dress. "I grow tired of this defiance. If you will not come willingly, then let me be clear. I will not make the same mistakes with your daughter that I did with you. I will take her for myself, and she will be raised under my love, my rule."

In a flash, Lia struck. The boom of rock hitting rock behind us thrummed through my ears and Revich scooped me into his arms, turning from the Blightress and her sister without another look back.

Talon and Ilyenna ran just behind him, and my eyelids drooped as I struggled to keep them open. A mound of the stones blocking the path now piled on top of where the Blightress had stood. Her dark shadows wove under the rock and her scream of rage echoed through the cavern as black magic wrapped around Lia, gripping her throat.

I cried her name, my voice hardly more than a whisper, blood still trickling down my tongue.

Revich reached the portal, ready to shove me in as I heard Lia's choked words stumbling on another phantom breeze through the cavern. "I should n-never have left her. I won't leave her now."

Rocks continued to fall, blocking our path back to the heart, trapping her in the cave with the Blightress.

"*No.*" The cry I meant to scream escaped my throat in a pathetic whimper, the sound ending in an abrupt cough.

Rev pushed me into the portal where I lay silently in the abyssal dark.

Alone and afraid.

~

SAELYN STAYED WITH ME IN THOSE MOMENTS THAT MOVED. The ones I could not feel as they passed.

My child's heart beat with mine, wounded as it was, and we lay, suspended in time, place, consciousness. My mind woke and faded, brought me back to awareness before drifting again, not ready to wake, not strong enough to leave.

But Saelyn stayed, living and growing.

I felt her presence there in time that was not time. In space that was not space. In darkness that was not dark, for light did not exist on its own in this place.

Saelyn would not rest. Saelyn would not be still, kicking endlessly at my ribs, shifting endlessly across my growing belly, refusing to rest with me, refusing to give into the dark.

She kicked me again, jabbing herself under my left rib and I started, jolted back to consciousness again, but different.

I blinked, I assumed. I felt the movement of my eyes, yet the darkness continued. "*Illuminare,*" I rasped, and the smallest spark of green light flickered at my fingers. It faded out, and I gulped, my tongue sticking to the roof of my mouth in a coating of iron. "*Illuminare,*" I spoke again, this time using the spell as an anchor, catching myself on the comforting glow of power I knew.

Saelyn planted another kick, and this time, I grunted, the force of her little limbs in my belly much stronger than anything I'd known before. I lifted my hand, hovering over my womb to confirm my revelation. My belly had grown fuller, rounder, spilling over the band of my skirts, the hem of my vest pulled back to reveal my skin stretched taut.

The sight pulled me to more clarity, and dread pooled in my

spine as the creeping fear of just how long I'd been inside this portal reared its head, stark and vicious.

My breath came in heavy rasps as I tried to sit up, my body limp and useless on the floor that was not a floor.

My light burned brighter. I lowered my head, closing my eyes again. The faint glow behind my lids gave me enough hope to focus on what I needed to leave this place.

My desire, my current, innermost want in this world would let me leave.

My eyes too dry to cry, I let the memory of how I got here slip back in, let it brighten as I heard Lia's last words to me in that cave.

She wouldn't leave her sister again.

The Blightress was alive. I felt her there, lingering in that space of my mind, still shoved in the dusty corner. I knew what that meant for her sister.

I bit down and focused on what I needed to do to leave the portal.

My desire.

What did I want most?

Rev.

Saelyn was well, better than well, it seemed. She thrived, not missing a beat and kicking me from the inside yet again, pushing me to get us out of the place that was not a place.

I took a deep breath, pulling that truth forward between myself and my love.

You breathe, I breathe.

You live, I live.

*Rev.*

I wanted Rev safe. I wanted to go to him. To be in his arms again, holding me and telling me that everything was going to be alright. I repeated my desire over and over again, and then, I heard his voice.

"It's alright, Karus," he whispered somewhere above me, cradling me in his arms, pushing my hair back from my face.

I blinked.

Once. Twice.

There was my love, sitting on the other side of the portal, in a tunnel lined with dark roots on which brilliant blue blooms littered the walls. His face had changed, covered in rugged black hair over his jaw, and chin, and lips. But his eyes. I knew those eyes. Those eyes of which I'd never spend enough time gazing into. The soft blue of a rolling ocean surface, wet and salty tears streaming down his cheeks.

He shifted his hand into my hair, pulled me to his chest, and wept.

# CHAPTER 39
# REV

I watched Karus with a smile across my face that must have been something to see, for I would no longer weep. I would not worry, nor falter in my hope. I would not give into that pacing dark which waited for me to break.

I had shed enough tears to last a lifetime in the dank tunnel underground, awaiting her return. Waiting just as I always did. Patiently *waiting* for my love and our growing child to come back to me.

Karus lay asleep in our bed as she had since drifting out of that portal the day before. The rhyzolm had saved me again and again from falling to my wretched despair, proving that she lived, that our child lived, and had grown stronger in the four months I'd spent alone.

When Pompeii had last visited me in the tunnel, bringing more supplies, forcing me to the surface to breathe fresh air for only a moment, I'd hardly registered how long it had been.

Four months was nothing.

My smile grew to see her belly rise and fall, so much bigger than before that tunnel. Before we learned that there was no destroying that heart without ending the lives of every magic wielder on Arcaynen Isle.

Lia had not returned, nor would she.

I knew it in my heart that she was gone from us, and there was still no sign of what had happened to Mychael and Rell. I had portaled Philius and Renn back to the grove of syphoner trees along the Tectus Trail. They'd reported there was no sign of either missing channeler and that most of the trees had been burned away, though some remained in their spectral glow.

The Blightress must have survived.

In those months below the roots of Felgren, I had pondered what it meant to be tied to the source of magic for the entire isle. Maybe Ilyenna had been right to wish for her and Talon's child to be born without magic, which was another thing Pompeii had come to inform me.

Their baby boy was born in Felgren. Healthy and unusually long, it would be a while yet before we knew if Thevin possessed any magic.

I hadn't gone to see them.

I hadn't gone to check on Renn or any of my channelers.

I had done nothing but wait.

"*She breathes in a deep sleep.*" The voice of the first Baron rose again through my mind. "*You should stretch your legs. Get something to eat. Look after your people, Revich.*"

"You can go now," I mumbled on my hands, balled into fists at my mouth as I leaned on the bed.

"*No, I cannot go.*"

"Then be quiet," I snapped. Then added softer, "Please."

"Baron?" Pompeii's voice drifted through our rooms.

I jerked, startled to see him there.

"Yes?" I answered.

His lips pursed in a thin line. "I thought I heard you speaking to someone just now."

"No," I lied, turning back to Karus. "I wasn't speaking to anyone."

He came closer in a careful glide, setting a tray of Karus's favorite foods on the nearby table, arranged with everything but cinnamon buns. "I can stay with her if you would like to see how baby Thevin fairs. And Renn has been asking after you. I kept them all away from the tunnel as you wished, but it might be time to—"

"Not until she wakes." My voice came, colder than I'd meant.

"*She will not wake for hours yet, Revich. As I told you, she and your child are in a deep sleep.*"

"The faerie has been…a nuisance," Pompeii continued, pulling my black chair from the fireplace to sit beside me. "I'll admit, I've been no match for her. Indeed, only the Prince has been able to console her. Surprisingly so." He chucked, sitting back. "He took her to see Thevin. She was fascinated by his cries."

"*You should go. Let him watch over her for a little while. Get some fresh air. I can alert you when Karus wakes.*" The voice of Adaynth echoed again as it had done over the four months of waiting in that tunnel. Sometimes it had been the only thing to keep me sane, to keep me from stepping back into that portal where I would have wandered forever searching for her.

Other times, I loathed the sound. A cruel reminder of our fates. Of what befell two people who wanted only to love. It's all we'd ever wanted, and we'd had so little time together.

"I will not leave until she is awake," I repeated to both of them in the dim light.

Pompeii leaned forward, grabbing my knee. I looked to him at that with surprise.

"At least go bathe." He clenched his jaw, the muscles tight on his face as he pleaded, "Show me that much, Revich. Show me you have not gone too far down the path of despair that I cannot convince you to clean yourself up." A smile tugged on his mouth that did not reach his golden eyes. "She will not much like the smell of you, especially in how far along she has come."

"Alright," I said, leaning in to kiss her forehead. I shuffled to the washing room with sconces already lit for me. A bath had been drawn as well, and I wondered just how long Pompeii had been in that room before I noticed him.

I did question at my sanity then.

*"You have not lost your mind, Baron Revich,"* the voice scolded. *"You are barely conscious half the time and don't allow yourself a reprieve."*

I nodded to the voice, shuffling out of my clothes, noticing fresh ones on the chair near the door. I swirled the minty paste at the basin around in my mouth and stepped into the enormous tub, ignoring the memories of her which formed there, choosing instead to grab the soap and attempt to scrub.

It was hard work, and forgoing a much needed shave, I instead rose, drying my skin and hair quickly, donning my fresh shirt and pants before stumbling from the washing room in record time.

"Has she—" I started.

"No, Revich," Pompeii answered, filling a plate with fruit, cheese and a soup I recognized, but could not remember from where. "She has not moved a single inch in the seven minutes you took to bathe."

I leaned against the bed, hand in my pocket to feel Saelyn again. I smiled down at her, promising myself I would continue to smile, for she was here. She was safe. She was alive.

"Now show me you can eat, Revich." Pompeii set the plate down on the bed and gestured to the black chair he'd risen from.

I sat and ate.

The meal felt heavy in my stomach and my eyes fluttered closed. I opened them again, flicking my head back in surprise at my body's attempt at slumber.

*"You need rest."*

"Rest now, Revich." Pompeii pulled the blue quilt back from the bed, gesturing for me to lay down next to her.

I all but crawled into the bed, pulling her body closer to mine, wrapping my arm around her rounded belly, scenting her skin which still smelled like her. That unchanged scent of pine and lavender. A forest and field of flowers calling me to sleep was the last thing I remembered as two voices said something to me and my thoughts drifted away to nothing.

# CHAPTER 40
# KARUS

Voices drifted through my head.

A man I'd met in a grove of maple trees, determined to convince me of…something.

A woman, a ghost, a piece of me, and I a piece of her whom I could not escape.

Without my conscious mind to force them to their dark recesses, they warred within me a fight I struggled to understand, but a battle I could hear all the same.

My body ached, my head pounded, and my daughter kicked, restless within my womb, bringing me back to the surface again.

I knew this room.

I knew this bed, these walls, this man beside me.

My eyes fluttered continuously as I tried to pull myself fully awake.

I lay on my side, my hand in his as he slept, his other hand spread over our child.

It took a moment to pull myself back to what had happened. I remembered the cave, the truth of the Blightress's heart I did not comprehend until it was too late.

I remembered Lia's sacrifice to get us out.

I remembered waking in the portal to Saelyn's swift kicks and leaving, finding myself in Rev's arms, right where I most desired to be.

The growth of hair on his face along with how much Saelyn had grown, confirmed that I'd been in that portal for months.

Just as before, I'd been kept alive by the Blightress's power.

I needed food.

I needed water.

I needed to move, to get up and walk.

I heaved breath into my lungs, attempting to swallow the panic that loomed as the voices of two ancient beings faded into faint echos, crawling back to their corners.

I wondered why they left so easily.

I wondered if they'd chosen to pause their eternal war to let me live. They needed me to live.

"Rev," I rasped, hardly more than a groan from my lips.

His eyes shot open and he rose, reaching out to my face, his breath a rush of air as he held his forehead to mine.

"Karus," he choked. "Pompeii is on his way here with food and water. Are you hurt? Can you feel Saelyn?"

I pried my tongue from the roof of my mouth, choking on an attempt to swallow. He reached for a cup at his beside table, helping me sit up and holding it to my lips. I basked in the cool water as it flowed across my tongue, barely strong enough to take a few sips.

He pulled my limp body to him, his hand moving across my belly, feeling for our daughter.

"She's healthy," I managed to whisper. "Our daughter is strong."

He huffed a sigh of relief, rocking us back and forth on the bed. I felt his chest shaking, but I did not hear him cry. I felt his anguish down our companion bond, tethered with relief and joy.

My arms limped at my side, but I tried to raise them to hold him, too.

"You don't need to move, Karus. I'll hold you."

A rush of air filled the dark room and Pompeii entered, carrying a tray of food. A flash of iridescent wings caught my eye behind him, and I tried to grin as Moira kicked off his shoulder, flying to us on the bed.

She attempted to shove Rev's face away from mine, screeching, "Get her up! Now!"

He swatted the air, replying, "What are you doing? Stop that!"

She maneuvered around his hand easily, fluttering to my shoulder and tugging at my dingy shirt. "Karus, get up! You need to come with me!"

"Moira!" Revich roared as I all but fell out of the bed at her tugging my sleeves. "Explain yourself or leave!"

He caught me easily, pulling me back to his chest where I wanted to fall to sleep again, too tired and weak to do anything but stay still.

"Do I have to do *everything* for her?" she spat, flying to Revich's face. "Get her up, now! Get her into Felgren!"

I heard Rev's attempt to keep his cool, replying through gritted teeth with, "*Why?*"

She released an exasperated growl. "Because she's almost *dead*, you hairy-faced behemoth! Can you not feel her life fading? I've felt it since you brought her here! Felgren feels it, too!" She put her hands on her hips over petals of red roses. "Get her outside now!"

"Why would Felgren—"

"Because she's part fae, for toadstool's sake!" She spat each of her next words. "Listen to me!"

Revich halted a moment in silent question to Pompeii.

"I will help you lift her," the Overseer offered, setting the tray on the table and moving to the bed, pulling one of my arms around his shoulder.

A sigh of relief came from Moira, her enormous violet eyes steady on my face. "I've got you, Karus. I know what to do."

She flew to the door, waiting as Revich and Pompeii helped me limp to it. I stumbled at the doorframe, my head lolling forward. Moira snapped her long sage fingers in front of my nose, a twinge of something floral bringing my focus back and my eyes wide.

"Stay with me," she commanded.

I blinked wide, stumbling forward, my eyes entranced by the

shimmer of every color of her wings as she darted around the foyer and through the Fortress door out into Felgren.

I blinked again at the glow of the setting sun, wondering if this was just a bizarre dream. A line of Growers had planted themselves into the edge of trees that marked where the Fortress ended and Felgren began.

"Lay her down here." Moira pointed to a grassy bed of moss and soft petals dug into the earth and shaped just my size.

Revich voiced what I myself was wondering. "When did you make this?"

He and Pompeii carefully laid me down in my Felgren bed as she answered, "I can feel her in the many branches of this forest. Ever since she presented herself as fae in the Great Stream, all of us have been able to feel her life source."

I closed my eyes for just a moment, promising myself to open them again.

"You can feel each other? All the fae?" Rev asked, bending to my side, pulling my hand in his.

I sensed Moira's eye roll without needing to see it. "*Barons*, leaders of the forest, humans who know nothing." She coughed and added, "No offense, Karus."

I felt the tug of a smile at my lips.

"What now?" Revich asked.

"Be quiet and let Felgren replenish what she has lost."

I felt the roots of trees grow over my legs, the pop of blooms opening around my head.

Pompeii questioned somewhere nearby, "Baron Revich, do you think this wise?"

Rev squeezed my hand once, refusing to let go even as long blades of grass swept over our fingers, growing from the earth beside my arms. "Moira kept her alive and well for seven years through the darkest winter this forest has ever seen. I won't question her now."

Moira huffed and murmured under her breath, "Smartest thing *you've* ever said."

The forest hummed. It grew its roots, its flowers, its grass over my skin, my rounded belly, my chest, sending with it that whisper of my name on the wind—the one I'd known and first heard years ago across the sway of trees on newly unfurled leaves in that first spring.

Felgren lived in me and I in it. Our fates linked, our lives sprung from the same source of power. Terrible, endless power, but we would decide what to do with it. We would decide our own fates and paths.

Another smile tugged at my lips as a bloom burst open at my chin, tickling me and I laughed.

Rev squeezed my hand tighter and the silence was not silent at all.

It was warm and many sounds at once.

I felt the scurry of something small racing through the underbrush nearby.

I heard the creaks and groans from the ancient trees above me, who fed me their life through the roots woven over my legs.

I smelled the late spring air, wondering if it had yet turned to summer, the season our daughter would be born into this forest, healthy, and new, and loved.

With her perfect timing, she kicked and I choked out a groan.

My eyes opened to see the wall of flowers, purple, blue, and pink surrounding the shape of my head. Moira's long pointed face came into view, and I grinned, matching her own.

"There you are." Her lips pulled to the side. I recognized her sharp canines and the flicker of light and color as her wings buzzed in a rapid hum.

Another face shifted into view, his eyes a worry of black that melted to blue at the sight of my glow.

For glowing, I was.

A radiating green washed over my skin. I could see it there, following the swirl of power as it drifted, unbidden but a part of me just the same.

Revich smiled, a laugh escaping him. "Moira," he started, not taking his eyes from mine. "Thank you." He touched my cheek. "Thank you for loving her, too."

# CHAPTER 41

# REV

Holding her hand tightly in mine, I twirled Karus around as she laughed. The sound of her voice lifted through our rooms in a bright call that would always guide me home. She stepped back to me and I caught her at my chest, one arm wrapped round her back to pull her close, the other holding her hand over my heart, so she could feel the joy that she gave to me.

Our daughter, heavier and only a few months away from joining this world, separated us more than usual and Karus looked down, knowing my thoughts.

After Karus had been replenished by Felgren, we'd gone straight to the dining hall where Jesslyn had provided Karus with an endless amount of food. We sat, eating our first meal together in months, and I caught her up on everything that had happened in the time I'd waited for her in that tunnel.

But now was the time for dancing. Now was the time for holding her close to me, relinquishing my dark despair into joy, for she was there, and I would never let her go.

I pressed my forehead to hers as we swayed to the music, produced from something Pompeii had delivered from the Spire in honor of our first child. A cylindrical turner, he'd called it, explaining how the long gold tubes were inserted and the handle was wound to play music.

"A child of summer," I said, before kissing her lips and pressing my hand to her belly. "We'll never get Saelyn out of that forest to go to bed."

Karus laughed again, adding, "I'd imagine not. Just think of all the trouble she and Thevin will get into over the years."

I chuckled at that.

It had quite the impact on me to finally hold Talon and Ilyenna's child. The first one born in Felgren in hundreds of years. He was beautiful with long legs and a mass of yellow curls on top of his head, looking just like his mother.

I scooped my hands underneath Karus's full belly, easing the weight of everything she grew inside her.

She stopped and tilted her head back in relief, letting a long breath flow loose into the air. "I never expected motherhood to be so heavy."

I kissed her forehead, lingering in her hair. "I can't wait to hold her, Karus." I adjusted my grip, lifting our daughter higher. "I can't wait to see her beautiful face. To sing to her the song of my mother. I hope she looks just like you."

"That's funny because I was hoping she looks like you." Her eyes, a vibrant green, sparkled and she bit her lip in a smile. "I hope she has this hair." She tucked my black waves behind my ear, pulled haphazardly back into a ribbon at the top of my head. "I hope she has this nose." Her finger slid the straight downward slide of my nose and I laughed. "But most of all," she continued, her fingers drifting, "I hope she has these eyes so that I can see you in her every time she's in my arms. Every time I hold her close, I'll be reminded of where she comes from and who loves her just as much as I do."

I shook my head, my face crumbling as I attempted to hold back my tears of happiness there with her, on the cusp of becoming a father.

"I love you," she whispered, her hands trailing over the rough hair on my face that she'd insisted I keep for a little while longer.

I met her lips with mine in a soft kiss. "And you'll love me still."

She gave a snort, agreeing, "And I'll love you still."

~

"About two months, give or take a week, and Saelyn will be here," Clairannia all but squealed, her hands glowing a soft red over Karus's belly. I had gone to retrieve the medicus conduit the day after Karus healed. I picked up Figuerah to join us as well.

Clairannia pulled Karus's shirt back over her belly. "Tell me more about this fae healing Moira put you through."

Karus grunted in our bed, reaching out a hand for me to help pull her up from Clairannia's examination. "I don't understand it myself."

"But it worked," I added.

Karus nodded. "Whatever fae healing that was, I needed it without knowing I did."

Clairannia placed a hand over Karus's heart, murmuring "*Vennae*," checking the pulse of two heartbeats within her. "And do you feel any different? Any noticeable changes? Violet eyes? Vines growing from your hair? The relentless need to stick petals to yourself?"

Karus huffed a laugh. "Nothing like that. I could tell when I was healed, though. And it didn't take long. When Rev pulled me from the earth, I was hungry."

Clairannia brought her hand back to her lap, satisfied. "Well, all we have to do now is wait." She shrugged. "It could be eight weeks, it could be six. Your body will decide."

Karus bit her lip and glanced to me. "But not longer than that? You won't let me go too long?"

Clairannia took her hand. "No, Karus. Don't think on that for one moment. What happened to…*her* will not happen to you. I promise."

She nodded, giving a small smile. A knock came at the door, and I rose to let Figuerah into the room.

She held up a vase of golden sunflowers. "I thought this room could use some color," she said, placing them on Karus's bedside table and leaning down to give her a quick hug. "Is everything going well?" she asked Clairannia.

"Perfectly well."

"So, she can come with us to *The Sun Which Does Not Sleep*?"

"Yes, but nothing too wild."

Karus drank from her cup. "Moira says a human has never been to the celebration. So we don't really know what exactly to expect. Besides the face paint."

"And the most beautiful fae we've ever seen," added Figuerah. "Moira won't stop talking about how unprepared we are."

"How are we supposed to prepare for a fae festival humans have never seen?"

I kissed Karus's hand, rising to leave them to discuss what Karus and I had decided were our plans moving forward.

I too, needed to explain our next steps to our channelers, so I headed to Viridis to meet them.

*"It's quiet."*

"I know." I turned down our hall corridor into the foyer.

*"Don't trust the silence."*

"What else would you have me do?" I replied in a low whisper, nodding to Jesslyn as she scurried around the halls, taking over Lia's duties.

*"She will not wait the twenty years it will take to gather an army to subdue her. Your plan is not good enough."*

I stopped in the empty, dimly lit corridor. "Again, Adaynth, what would you have me do? Unless you plan to tell me what you did centuries ago to dampen her power, I don't want to hear your warnings." I continued down the labyrinth that was the path to Viridis. "It's all we have. We cannot destroy her heart without killing us all, and even then, who knows if she'd still survive. My guess is that Lia merely bought us time in that cave. We know the Blightress survived, but we don't know if she's been hurt. Our only option right now is to find a way to contain her power and that answer may lie in Viridis."

*"You don't have twenty years to train enough channelers to help you in this task."*

"THEN WHAT WOULD YOU HAVE ME DO?" My bellow echoed through the hallway, amplified by my power as Baron and snuffing out every sconce along the walls. Darkness fell and I pressed my hand to the cold black stone of the Fortress, taking my breaths deep, holding back my desperation from spilling out of me again.

A figure loomed in the dark. A man. His back against the wall, his head tilted as if he gazed up at something I could not see. I didn't relight the sconces, preferring the dark to regain my composure.

He spoke, his voice no longer contained to my mind. "I left Visalia. The last one to stay, the last one to leave. That's why it won't work again. Nothing heroic. No last stand against her. I finally left her for good, and she stopped her spread of darkness upon Felgren."

I stood upright, facing him. "You gave up on her."

Even in the dark, I could see his features from some distant flicker of flame far down the hall. The Blightress's companion, her lover and childhood friend, stared into the space behind me, unmoving, no more than a ghost haunting the halls he built, speaking warnings of the woman he'd scorned.

"How could you do it?" I asked, sliding my hands into my pockets and clenching the rhyzolm in my palm.

"She had become something else entirely from the woman I loved. I kept her heart safe and warm. That was where I loved her. In a tiny room under this Fortress, I loved her still."

"You left her with nothing. No hope, no way back into the light." I scoffed. "I pity you, Adaynth."

"Why? Leaving destroyed all of it—the Blight she had grown, the dark creatures she had dreamed into reality—all of her hate and anger fell away the moment she understood I was gone and not coming back."

"I pity you because even now, you do not accept your role in the path that has led us to this moment. This point in time where my companion is on the verge of bringing our daughter into this world, and yet, the woman you loved still walks this earth even more capable of devastation than when you left her. It's you who has played a part in all of this, and I am sick of hearing you in my head."

I stepped back, regaining my composure. "I am done listening to your warnings of Karus, of your long lost companion, the fate of this forest—all of it." I ran my hands through my hair. He watched me with dark hazel eyes. "You want to know the worst of it?" I laughed. "I'm not sure you're real. I'm not sure if this is all a dream or if I'm still in that fucking tunnel, waiting for Karus to find her way back to me. I wake every day, unsure if I will see her there beside me. I fall asleep every night, unsure if she'll be gone by morning, if she'll be taken by this woman you left because you didn't know how to love her at her worst. I feel my daughter moving in her womb, unsure if I'll ever get to hold her or some next great tribulation will befall us before I can, so I ask you again, Adaynth, what would you have me do?"

I wiped my eyes, sniffing and standing tall. "No more warnings. No more suggestions on what I should or should not be doing for myself because none of that matters. What matters is Karus. Our child. *Their* future. Whatever I must do, I will do it to ensure that they are safe. There's the difference between us, Baron." I shook my head. "I would't have left."

"I left and saved Felgren," he snapped.

"You left for the wrong reasons."

He cocked his head at that, turning to look down the corridor, unfolding his arms from his chest. His stare sent a chill through my spine, and I followed his gaze, squinting in the distance at the flicker of light down the hall, seeing nothing.

"I'm sorry I cannot be of further help, Revich, but I am trying." He stepped closer. I could see through his wispy form, no more than a figure who lived with me in my head since the day I had accepted the power of Baron, bargaining with him to let me share it with the woman I loved.

He reached out as if to put a hand on my shoulder. "Whatever happens next, remember that I am trying to fulfill the promise I made to Karus and keep you happy, and safe, and loved—just like she asked the night she took half of this power." As he began to disappear from my sight, he repeated one more time, "Revich, I am trying."

# CHAPTER 42
# KARUS

Pompeii stood at the kitchen sink, sleeves rolled up with his arms elbow-deep into warm, soapy water. He scrubbed at the many dishes that had piled up each day without the help of Lia.

Her kitchens had always been tidy and organized—a song and dance she alone conducted and without her…everyone needed time to adjust.

Jesslyn kneaded dough in one corner, silent tears falling down her cheeks that she ignored, taking the reins as the cook in the Fortress and directing tasks for the kitchen maids.

I rolled my own sleeves, having forgone my Baron's vest, choosing a flowy cream dress instead that fit my growing body much better.

I stepped up to his side, plunging my own hands into the water, scrubbing at a pot that had something burnt stuck to the bottom.

"I would tell you that you needn't work here in the kitchens, Baron, but I doubt you'd listen." Pompeii continued his scrubbing, adding a plate to the sink next to us filled with clean water and clean dishes. He grabbed another few plates, added them to the sink and continued to scrub.

"If the Overseer of this Fortress is called to help in the kitchens, then one of its Barons can do the same," I replied.

"If Baron Revich—"

"Do not coddle me, Pompeii. You are one of the few I can rely on for that. I can clean a few dishes and live."

He huffed in a laugh, and we worked quietly for a few minutes more.

"I am sorry." I broke the silence, something breaking in me as well.

"I do not wish to speak of it," he replied, adding more dirty pots to the sink.

"There is a chance Mychael and Rell are still alive."

He let the dishes fall back into the water, gripping the edge of the basin. He stared down at the suds, his nostrils flaring, his grip tightening.

I'd never seen him angry. I'd never seen him lose his composure, but I heard it as he swept into my thoughts where our connection lie. *"Which do you think is worse? A life cut short or a life lived inside a tree, the power you hold being siphoned from you for the rest of it."*

I flinched at the disdain in his voice clearly masking the pain of a man losing the man he loved. *"I do not know."*

*"Will Mychael age if he is alive, being used as a power source? Will you promise to find him one day when I walk with a cane and greet my lover, old and withered, my hand shaking as I take his?"*

My tears dropped into the suds, but my hands kept their pace. *"I tried."*

*"You tried."* He returned his hands into the water, picking up a cup. *"Thank you for trying, Baron Karus."*

I bit back a sob. He didn't want my apologies for not bringing his love back home. He wanted Mychael's life to be out of the hands of the woman who had as much access to his thoughts as I did. I cleared my throat, moving forward with what I needed to know and speaking aloud again. "Has she spoken to you?"

"No."

"But she is still there?"

"Yes."

"We cannot risk it."

"I will leave then, if I must. Alas, I cannot cut my lungs from my chest as Philius cut his hands from his wrists."

"We cannot risk her taking over your mind, but what if I have another idea on how we can cut that bruise from your chest?"

He finally turned to look at me then. "I am listening."

~

"I can't believe you convinced me to do this," Clairannia muttered under her breath as she helped guide me to build the right shape and capacity of the lungs I formed.

Pompeii lay on a blanket of grass in a clearing in Felgren, rendered asleep by a spell. Figuerah cradled his head in her lap, agreeing to come in case we needed her help reviving him.

"But you do believe it could work or you wouldn't be here," I responded, adjusting the length of the verdant lungs I grew, matching the size of the model Clairannia had woven in front of me. I pressed my hand further into Felgren's soil, drawing the power I needed to form the perfect pair of working lungs for Pompeii. They would replace his and sever the mind connection the Blightress and I shared with him.

Clairannia shook her head. "Magic replacing one's toe or ear is one thing, but I have never heard of magic replacing a much-needed organ and the patient living to talk about it."

Figuerah winked my way. "Karus is a litany of firsts, aren't you, love?"

I smiled back, continuing to reassure my friend. "We all heard him. He'd rather try this than have to leave the Fortress indefinitely."

"Maybe he could leave and practice shoving her from his mind," Clairannia suggested in a frown, eyeing my creation as I worked on the long branches of flesh that would circulate air through his new lungs. She added, "You've been able to keep her out. Why not give him a chance to do the same?"

I shook my head, waving my hand over the surface of the small tubes I'd created. "I've had my whole life to keep her out. When we practiced keeping me out of his head, he failed every time. He knows the risk, Clairannia. He has made his choice, and we certainly can't do this without you."

She wrung her hands on her white skirts which denoted her as a medicus conduit. "It's not that I don't believe you can do this, it's what it means if you can. If this replacement of his diseased lungs with ones of your creation succeeds, then this will be a break-through of magic the likes of which we've never seen."

"What are you doing with the Looking Man?" We all jumped at the sound of Moira's high-pitched voice coming from a branch of the ash tree above us.

Figuerah recovered first, cocking her head. "Looking Man?"

"Overseer," I mumbled, continuing my task.

She fluttering to the ground, pulling one of his eyes open wide. "Does an Overseer not look or see?"

"Stop that!" Clairannia chided, ushering her away from our patient.

Figuerah laughed. "An Overseer is not called such because he sees, Moira. It is a title given to the one closest to the Baron to help in his or her duties."

"Well, it's true he's always looking, this one," Moira said.

"What do you mean?" I asked, biting my lower lip to hold back my laughter.

Moira shrugged, fluttering a few inches off the shaded grass. "He speaks little, looks a lot. He seems to know everything going on in that black fortress. He seems to know all of you as well."

I flicked my gaze to Clairannia who sighed in an agreeing shrug.

"So, what are you doing to him?" Moira asked again.

"I am growing him a new set of lungs to breathe," I answered.

"Why?"

"Because the lungs he has were contaminated by the Blight trees I grew in Felgren, and now he has a mental connection to both me and the Blightress, which we cannot have."

"Why?"

"Because Philius had a similar connection to her due to the

Black Fever Heimlen created from the Blight, and she took over his mind, which in turn lost us Mychael and Rell."

"Wh—"

"*Moira.*" Figuerah rubbed her face. "Karus and Clairannia are doing something that has never been done, so watch quietly or leave."

Moira stuck her long pointed tongue out at Figuerah who rolled her eyes, but they both stayed silent while I put the last touches together on the lungs that would fit into Pompeii's body.

Clairannia murmured her adjustments to me and I made them, my heart racing, my lip a messy red splotch on my face as I bit at the corners again and again.

Clairannia finally gave her approval with a nod, and I shifted on my knees, taking a deep breath, the lungs hovering over my hands. I blew into the tube at the top, and with my breath, they filled, no longer a haze of green magic, but green flesh instead, pumping air of their own accord.

"Well,"—Figuerah let out a breath—"they seem to work. I hope."

"The hardest part is yet to come," Clairannia added, unbuttoning the shirt across Pompeii's chest, his breathing deep in his spelled slumber.

My stomach churned seeing what had been left in the wake of the disease that would have taken his life if I had not destroyed the Blight trees in Viridis with fire. It spread across the shape of his chest in a mottled black and purple, stopping at his throat.

Clairannia drew her power into a thin, sharp blade above the sternum of his chest, shimmering in bright scarlet. She had brought with us a sizable porcelain platter, intending for his current lungs to lay there while we replaced them.

"What are you doing now?" Moira asked, tilting her head to the side. Her violet eyes grew in size as she watched Clairannia's glowing red blade slice across the center of Pompeii's chest. Blood pooled at the cut, but Clairannia was ready, capturing every drop in a deep bowl she had formed with her power.

All of us sat in silence watching Clairannia pull back skin, breaking the bones of his ribs in disturbing cracks to access the horror of what had lain quiet in Pompeii's chest for months. His breath still came, unhindered by his torso being flayed open. The inky black flesh he held within his body smelled of decay, just like the trees I had grown in Viridis.

Moira covered her mouth, turning to the side to retch onto the forest floor. Her body's reaction to the popping bits of lung that burst in succession ended with her passed out on the ground. Figuerah was not far behind and had to turn her head, squeezing her eyes shut, her nostrils flaring to breathe any fresh air she could.

I wanted to hurl all the contents in my own stomach, but bit down on my cheek instead.

I could do this for Pompeii. I got him here. I could get him out.

Clairannia looked on in fascination, her rich brown eyes wide, her mouth slightly open as she leaned down to inspect the diseased lungs. "He would not have survived this in the end," she stated easily.

I could guess that even without all the medicus experience she had. He may have been cured enough to live, but these lungs would have become useless before too long.

She continued her work, some of which I saw, some of which I could not stomach, turning my head away at the pull of black flesh that fell onto the tray in a heavy wet slap I would not soon forget.

My stomach roiled, my effort spent trying to breathe fresh air rather than dampen my disgust. I knew that Revich would soon be able to feel what I felt, if he was not on his way here from Viridis already.

"Get ready, Karus," Clairannia said to me. "I need one side at a time. Starting with the lung on his left."

I did as she instructed, maneuvering what would become his left lung into place as she used her power to fuse the flesh to flesh, seamlessly providing a seal. His left lung expanded with his diseased right lung still intact.

Clairannia wiped her forehead. "One down, one to go, Figuerah. Just hold on."

Figuerah nodded, letting out a breath in a puff of air, breathing back in a fresh gulp.

We followed the same steps, replacing his right lung with the one I had grown with my power. Clairannia sat back for a moment, her hands covered in his blood, the rest of it pooled in her magic bowl, her power sending a line of it to trickle back into his exposed veins.

His breathing was steady, the same deep sleep keeping him from witnessing any of what we had done.

"I think it worked." Clairannia's smile was wide across her small mouth. "Time will tell, but I think you did it."

"*We* did it," I corrected.

She made quick work replacing all the blood spilled from his body, closing his chest and murmuring words of healing over his bruise. She had tried it before to no avail, the black marring of his skin indicating that he had been inflicted with a disease directly from the Blight. But now, the color of his golden-hued chest returned, the bruise subsiding at her words.

"Figuerah," I muttered, watching Clairannia in awe. "Look."

She did, one eye open, her head jutted back as if she didn't dare see any parts of Pompeii that resided inside of him.

She gave a huff of a laugh. "Well, Clairannia," she started, "looks like those medicus books will have to be amended."

~

"I'VE SEEN YOUR INSIDES."

"*Moira*," Clairannia snapped, listening to Pompeii as he took another deep breath for her.

I held the tray of my Overseer's rotted lungs in one hand, just waiting for Clairannia to give me permission to burn them. I held it by my palm, letting the platter balance in my hand, ready to upturn my stomach the moment I could.

Clairannia held her ear to Pompeii's chest as he inhaled. "Does it feel any different when you take a deep breath?"

"Yes," he responded, a shaking smile spreading across his mouth. "Yes, I don't ever remember breathing this deeply." He looked at me, his chin rising. "Thank you, Baron Karus." He turned to Clairannia, her hand pressing lightly on his chest. "And thank you, Conduit Clairannia."

Moira jabbed a thumb at Figuerah. "She held your head the whole time."

A deep laugh came from his chest, which Clairannia smiled about, and he turned, thanking Figuerah as well.

"Can I?" I asked, raising a fist to my mouth.

Clairannia nodded. "Burn them. They're dead now anyway." She took one last look at the seal of skin running across the width of Pompeii's chest before pulling his shirt closed and letting him button it. "Your lives and magic are linked." Her gaze caught mine as she scrubbed blood from her hands. "You have more than one life in your hands now, Karus."

I locked eyes with Pompeii. The angle of kohl across his lids was smeared on one side. It brought a sense of imperfection to his usual perfect golden skin and immaculate mustache and beard. I attempted to force my way into his mind, searching for that connection the Blightress and I had shared. Met with silence, I smiled wearily.

His chin rose and he swallowed, repeating, "Thank you, Baron Karus."

I brought my lips together and bit down, my heart broken for this man who did so much for us. My heart broken for his lover, a young channeler who may never see her sister again, and an ancient cook who had sacrificed her own life to save ours.

I twisted away, unable to speak, taking with me the remnants of flesh displayed in fresh blood upon a porcelain painted platter.

IT FELT GOOD TO BURN.

I felt the pressure of a woman's voice beginning her speech of something I did not want to hear, and I pushed it away, forcing her dark presence back into her corner.

I allowed myself to enjoy the sight of the Blight, bonded with human flesh, burning on a pyre of my making.

The pops and crackling of whatever underlying atrocity his lungs had been formed into lifted through the air at the small stream fed from the tower of black rocks leading to the charred maple tree. Only now, the new life of regrowth wound its way over the blackened bark, confirming that it was not dead, but in the midst of rebirth.

"That was quite a feat."

I jumped, taken out of my trance of watching the flame lick over black flesh. Adaynth leaned against a rock, his arms folded across his chest in the exact image I had first seen of him all those months ago.

"I did not invite you here," I stated, folding my own arms across my belly, adding, "and I am not dreaming."

"You spent all your effort forcing Visalia away from your mind just now, so I thought it prudent to take advantage and try to talk some sense into you."

I scoffed. "You could leave me instead. You're good at that."

His jaw slid to the side and his eyes narrowed in what I recognized as malice. "This is my last attempt to convince you of anything. The longer you are quiet, the sooner I can leave."

I bent to the clear stream, running my hands through the cool water and rinsing them of any remnants of Pompeii's blood. "I shall be silent as the grave then."

He lifted one leg over the other in a casual grace. "Your plan to spend twenty years building an army of magic wielders to subdue the Blightress will not work."

I continued to rinse, keeping to my agreement of refraining to speak.

"She will not wait that long to strike, and the next time she comes, she will not fail."

I nodded, rising to face him.

He watched me in strained silence.

I shrugged. "Is that it?"

"I was hoping you'd agree with me."

"And if I do, what solutions do you bring? What should we be doing instead?"

He gritted his teeth and spoke through them. "I do not know."

I huffed a laugh, stepping closer. "What a resource we have then. A centuries old Baron who comes as a harbinger of doom with no ideas to replace the ones we have." I nodded my head to him in mock respect. "Thank you for your concern, Baron Adaynth. I look forward to your silence in my thoughts and dreams here on out."

His anger burst forward as he closed the gap between us, confirming what I suspected. His body shifted in an unnatural sheen because he was no more than a hazy figure born of my Baron power. "Revich will not survive it."

The hair on my neck rose. "Explain."

He pointed a finger at my chest. "If you are taken again, if he loses you one more time, he will fall to madness."

"He won't," I started, "I won't leave ag—"

"You will!" His words lifted in the breeze, sent across the trees of Felgren as if in assurance that what he said would come to pass. "Once she has you again, she will not let you leave. She will not let your daughter leave. She will wait as long as it takes for your own madness to overcome your senses, and you will fall beside her just as broken as she has become."

I opened my mouth to protest, but he wasn't done.

"And Revich will not survive it." He raked his fingers through his brown hair, some of his longer locks falling into his face. His hazel eyes pierced me with unearned hatred, and I knew he believed what he said. "I was there with him those months in that tunnel waiting for you to return. For whatever reason, for whatever nonsensical hold you have on him, his sanity hangs by a thread. If you or Saelyn are taken or harmed, the man you know will not survive it."

My chin trembled, but I bit down, refusing to cry, refusing to let him see how much his premonition affected me. I sniffed in a deep breath and replied quietly, "You care for him."

"Yes."

"Why?" I shot back immediately. "Why Revich? Why care for

him? Of all the Barons' minds you have occupied, you have not intervened. What makes Rev so different to you?"

His mouth slackened and I didn't miss his glance down to my growth band, now with seven moons embroidered across the emerald silk. He blinked at me for a few moments, and I waited. "He is not like the others. His thoughts are not occupied with power or the legacy he leaves. He thinks of you. Your child. Your channelers. The people of this isle who could use more magic in their lives to make them easier lives to live. I admire that in him."

"He is more worthy of this power than any Baron who has ever lived," I spat.

"Of that, we are in agreement, Baron Karus."

I nodded. "I will speak to him. We will listen to other ideas moving forward, but there is little we can do with Saelyn's birth approaching quickly. We are combing through Viridis for possible solutions, but have found nothing. After Saelyn arrives, Revich will reconvene with the other leaders on the isle for solutions and gather more channelers to bring here." I stepped back to the stream, washing the delicately painted platter and rinsing the embers of ash —all that was left of Pompeii's Black Lung.

"I tried, Karus."

His words, so similar as mine to Pompeii hours ago, frightened me. "You tried *what*, Adaynth?"

"To give you what you asked for that day you took half of the power of Baron."

"I asked you for the power to keep Revich happy, and safe, and loved."

"And I tried to give it to you."

I pressed the platter to my chest. "What did you do?" I whispered.

"You may never know, but you should know that I tried."

"I am done with your cryptic fucking answers," I seethed. "Tell me what you did!"

He began to fade, the Baron whose role in our lives could not be ignored. "I cannot. The path forward is set. I cannot change it. Do not let her take you, Karus of Felgren. Do what you must. Revich will do the same."

The wind swept him away, and the platter snapped under the force of my grip. My hands sliced open from the break, bleeding down the length of my arms and dripping a dark stain of red across my womb.

~

I DID WHAT I COULD TO CLEAN MYSELF UP. I HEALED THE WOUNDS OF my hand and attempted to pull the blood stains from my dress. If I had paid more attention to certain halls of Viridis, I would have known the spell to change the color of my dress completely or the spell to remove blood from linen.

Lia would have known.

Instead, I walked silently back to the clearing in a stained dress with a broken platter I hadn't thought to mend.

Rev was there, as I knew he would be, laughing with my friends and pulling at long stems of grass to chew on the sweet ends.

I leaned against a nearby tree to watch. Pompeii was pulling up wide pieces of grass and blowing into them across his thumbs. A shrill whistle blew into the breeze and Moira laughed delightedly, immediately asking him to do it again.

"I haven't been able to do that in years!" Pompeii laughed delightedly, picking another piece and handing it to Revich to try. He pulled the blade taut and blew, a dull sound winding out.

I could have stood there for hours admiring the people I loved as they sat in moments of carefree happiness that were too few and far between as of late.

Rev glanced between the trees, likely feeling me there. His smile could have knocked me down in its beauty. He jumped up from the ground, jogging to me to lift and twirl in the air. I let the platter crash to the forest floor, burying my face into his neck as he whispered at my ear, "You clever little weaver of lungs, you. How on earth did you do it?"

I smiled into his neck. "I pulled from Felgren. Those lungs come directly from this forest. Is he doing well?"

Rev pulled my head back to look at me in his swirling gaze of blue. "Better than well. He can breathe easier than he has in years." He took my hands and brought them to his lips, finally noticing the stain across my dress. "Is this blood?"

"Yes. From my hands. I tried to get it out." I pulled at the fabric.

"Pompeii's blood?"

"No, it was mine."

He turned my hands over, looking for wounds. "Why were your hands bleeding?" His eyes dropped to the broken platter fallen to the ground nearby.

"I accidentally broke the platter and cut myself."

His eyes met mine, still holding my hands up to his face. "He spoke to you, didn't he?"

"How did you know?"

"I've come to understand Adaynth better these past few months. I can think of two ancient beings in this world who could make you as angry as I felt you were not long ago. What did he say?"

I glanced to the conduits and Overseer as they gathered themselves to head back to the Fortress, Moira hovering in Figuerah's shadow. "He told me what he told you. Waiting will not work. She will come and take me, and you will not survive it."

He stared down at the grass behind me with a pain I hated to see crossing his mouth. "We have resources. We have Viridis, even in its repairs. We will spend all of our time there, searching for something that might help us and practicing."

"Practicing?" I asked.

"Shields and portals." He drifted a hand over our growing child. "At some point, you will be able to enter a Baron portal again and make some of your own. Pompeii was able to bring some books on shielding out of Viridis while I waited for you to leave the portal. I want you to read them. I want you to be practicing every spare moment you have."

"*Every* spare moment?" I rose my brows.

"If we—" He sighed in a heavy pause, bringing my knuckles

back up to his mouth to trail with kisses. "If we can shield this forest, we might be able to keep the Blightress out of it."

"Truly?"

"I believe it can be done. You'll start tonight. I want you pulling on all three sources of your power to perfect your shielding ability."

I stepped back from his touch, a haze of green light engulfing my body, sheer but strong. "We'll practice now."

He smirked, holding a hand up to the wall of power and pressing hard. "Good, Karus." His smile grew across his face and his eyes lit in a promise I knew was coming.

I lifted my chin, backing up to a tree. "Just try to get through, Baron Revich."

He tilted his head, his eyes flashing in the challenge as he slowly stepped forward, his body on the other side of the power I held. "Are you practicing or teasing, Baron Karus?"

I closed my eyes, breathing deep, allowing myself to send my love for him down our tether. I would not spend my days in constant worry. I would not forsake the time we had. Each day I woke up next to him was one of joy and happiness that he was near. Opening my eyes, I grinned, letting him feel all I could feel. "I love you, Rev."

He shook his head, pressing on the shield with his power, melding my walls of Felgren green with his deep blue into a swirling teal I'd seen before. "No," he started. His hand fell through, and I widened the shield to bring him in, too. He cupped the back of my neck, his thumbs running along the base of my jaw. "No, you don't get to say it like that if I can't touch you."

"I love you," I said again.

He huffed, shaking his head. "I would say you cannot know what those words do to me, but you do." He brought my hand to lay flat over his chest. "You breathe, I breathe."

I nodded, fighting back the tears. "You live, I live."

He bent down slightly to reach my lips with his, and I closed my eyes, fueling the shield around us with more than the power of Felgren, or Baron, or Blightress.

I fueled it with my love for him.

And it grew.

It grew as he lifted my chin, as he ran his hands along my cheeks, slowly sliding them down to my neck, never breaking our kiss, never letting go.

Tears streamed down my face because I could not hold them back. I didn't want to.

I cried for loving him. I cried for what we would have and what we'd already missed together, what fight we still had left to endure, but that we would endure together.

My power shifted from the soft haze of soul-bound love into something burning. Something hot and destructive, insistent and raging in an endless flame that consumed us both there in that forest. Our clothes were soon discarded, our bodies soon joined as the crackling shield of green flame lit in a cage of my making, enclosing two Barons, two lovers, two lives bound as one.

# CHAPTER 43

# REV

"Just a little higher. Like this." I took Karus's hand, raising it far above her head, stealing a quick kiss on her nose to make her laugh.

She did. It was beautiful.

She chewed on some fermented cabbage she had found in a jar tucked in the cellar of the Fortress. Her cravings the last few weeks had been…surprising.

"This high?" she asked, pulling her right hand up in a cupped shape.

"Right there," I confirmed. "Now this one down in a quick movement, like this."

I showed her the movement again, a portal of my making sparkling under a birch tree in Viridis. She pressed her hand to its surface, staying put.

"Just checking," she chuckled.

I stepped through instead, catching her around the waist when I appeared behind her instantly.

She laughed in a cough, turning in my arms. "Revich!" She pushed herself out of my grasp halfheartedly, and returned to her jar, scooping another spoonful of the wet cabbage.

We were only a few weeks away from when Clairannia predicted Saelyn would arrive into the world. Karus had blossomed into this gorgeous creature. She'd always been so beautiful, but motherhood gave her a rosy glow in her cheeks, a sparkle in her eyes I had never seen before. Her body had adjusted well to growing another human, and I admitted to myself that I had very much enjoyed her new curves.

"So, I just think of a place?" she asked, covering her mouth in her chewing.

"A specific place. The better you know where you want to be, the more accurate you are. If it's just a quick thought, you might end up smacking into something."

"But I can go to a place I've never been?"

"Yes, but again, the more you know about it the better. For example,"—I spread my hands again, another portal forming—"this will take me to Radyx, right to Madame Zoreyah's courtyard. I've been before, so I know the layout of the gold columns and the pattern of mountains and streams on the tiled floor. I know exactly where to land. But this,"—I created another one, glowing next to the first—"will take me to a peak in the Attatok Mountains. I've never been to the top of a mountain, but I can guess at what it's like. I might land on a Horned Vintras, for all I know." I made a step for the second portal, and she shot out a hand, pulling me back by my vest.

Laughing with me, she said, "You wouldn't leave me for a mountain top, would you?"

"Mmm," I hummed, winking. "Convince me to stay."

She wrapped her arms around my waist. "All I have to offer is a cabbage kiss."

I tilted my head back and laughed, closing both portals behind me as I reached down to pull her face to mine, taking my reward for staying.

She broke our kiss, going back to her coveted jar of the fermented vegetable. "I'd like to try to send you somewhere. Then you come back here and tell me if I got it right."

"I'm happy to be your test subject anytime, Baron Karus."

She finished chewing and straightened her back, pulling her hands apart in the motion I'd shown her a dozen times. The portal, emerald and buzzing, flickered to life under the tree.

"Perfect," I said.

"Let's hope it goes where I think it goes," she murmured.

I smirked and stepped inside.

I arrived immediately into tall grass around a copse of nitor trees. The sun's heat grazed across my skin, and I took in the fresh forest air.

"Ah, Karus," I murmured aloud, shoving my hands in my pocket and taking a moment to remember.

It had been around eight years ago now since I had brought her here for the single purpose of kissing her and secondary purpose of kissing her twice.

She had allowed a few dozen more as we lay under the night sky. The nitor moths' journey to the nitor trees occurred only on nights of the full moon, and on that night, I had been a young man forsaking any kind of life without her in it.

I took one last look at the grove of trees and left that place to memories. I stepped back into Viridis through my own portal, landing right in front of where she'd been.

I pressed my forehead to hers, finding her hands in mine, pulling them to my shoulders. "Can I…" I whispered.

A blush flushed to her cheeks. "Kiss me?" She leaned forward, pressing all of herself into me. "Why, Baron Revich, I was hoping you would ask."

~

Leaning against the wall of the circular room under the foyer, I stared at the pedestal which had once held the Blightress's heart. Adaynth had kept it suspended over the stone, caging it in the warmth he claimed was his love still burning for who she had been. I had maybe twenty minutes before I needed to get back to Karus, who would be waiting with the painter from the Spire. She had commissioned our portrait as Barons, again insisting we needed one along the winding staircase to the tallest tower, adding to the long line of Barons of Felgren.

"I don't like it here." The first Baron appeared as a faded image on the opposite wall, leaning against it in his usual folded arms and cold grace.

I took my hands from my pockets and rubbed my face, scratching at my beard which I had kept for several weeks because Karus seemed to like it.

I had seen Adaynth in this form every day for weeks now. He'd appear for a few minutes at a time, saying something somber and cryptic before leaving like a whisper of magic in the wind.

I cleared my throat. "I came because I was curious how you did it."

His eyes flashed to mine. "How I kept my companion's still-beating heart alive or how I subdued her power with it?"

"Both."

He crossed one leg over the other. "Her heart will always beat as long as it's preserved. I truly do not know what would happen to her if it was somehow destroyed."

"And her power?"

"That's an interesting question, Revich." He glared down at where her heart had been hidden for centuries. "I didn't know at the time that keeping her heart warm would suppress her power. I only meant to love the woman I remembered in the only way I knew how."

I shifted, careful in my next words. "But the *Simulair Solum* spell…that's what you used?"

He nodded. "I used some of the power of Baron to set the spell inside her heart. It didn't burn it. It never hurt her. I—" He stopped, a rare occurrence of pain crossed his eyes. "I just wanted her to be warm. I could not hold her and give her warmth of my own, so I held her the only way I knew how. That had the secondary effect of stifling her rage, and therefore, the power she possessed. I don't know why."

"Lia's hair was black," I stated. "Was Visalia's hair black when you knew her?"

His lips upturned slightly. "Finding more correlations to Karus, are we?"

I shook my head, pulling myself from the wall and walking to him. "No, I asked you if your lover's hair was black before you left her and suspended her heart in a simulated sun, Adaynth."

He slid his jaw to the side before giving me a silent nod.

"Show me how you did it." I jerked my head to the pedestal. "Show me how you kept her warm."

# CHAPTER 44
# KARUS

My eyes drifted closed again, and I jerked back in response, blinking rapidly.

The books Rev had taken from Viridis lay in haphazard piles on our bed, the one I'd been trying to finish lay open on my lap, held up by my enormous round belly. I added a length of gold ribbon to the page and closed it, setting it on Revich's side of the bed. I pulled myself up further onto all four of my pillows, ignoring my need to relieve myself for the fifth time in the last hour.

Our fire crackled low in our hearth, and I watched the flames from our bed, rubbing my sides to relieve some of the pressure. I could tell Saelyn slept as she was not twirling around in my womb like a dancer across a ballroom floor.

Giving into my needs, I slid my legs over the bed and shuffled to the washing room. Too tired to bathe, I slipped out of my dress and stepped into a sheer green nightgown.

The Queen had sent clothes as soon as I had written to her of the child growing in my belly. She had outdone herself with two trunks of dresses and nightgowns that I truly did not need. They had arrived along with the cradle Clairannia and I had chosen, carved from dark walnut with bright yellow linens.

I washed my face and cleaned my teeth, stumbling back to our bed, only to find Revich there reading *The Guide to a Safe Homestead*.

I adjusted my pillows, hitting them into submission and slid under the sheets. He continued reading, flopping his left hand out next to me, palm up for me to take.

I combed my fingers through his without a thought, reaching with my free hand to the plate of lemon slices I had snuck from Jesslyn's kitchen.

I scooted toward the bottom of the bed and picked up a book from the piles, opening to the marked page, pressing on the spine to keep it flat and popped a quarter of lemon into my mouth.

"What's the latest treat you've brought into our bed?" he asked, squeezing my hand.

I sputtered, spitting out the sour fruit into my hand and said, "Close your eyes and stick out your tongue."

"I like where this is going," he murmured, doing just as I asked.

I laughed and pulled some of the flesh from the wedge. I settled myself at his side, facing him as he lay back against our bed frame. Rev coughed and his face puckered when I squeezed the lemon over his tongue.

Laughing, I wiped the bottom of his lip. "What is it I've brought into this bed on this night?"

He smacked his lips, eyes still closed. "I cannot tell."

"Really?" I huffed in surprise. "Seems like it would be obvious!"

He hummed a low sound. "Perhaps I need to taste it in a different way."

"How else would you—" I cut myself off, noticing the smirk forming on his mouth. A rumble of laugher came from my chest as I fell into his. He wrapped his arms over my back, holding me to him.

"Well?" he questioned, opening his blue eyes and watching me with raised brows.

I laughed on his lips, bringing myself up to his mouth. The tartness on our tongues eased into something sweet and familiar and he lifted himself off the bed, keeping one hand wrapped around my back and sliding his fingers to my neck with the other.

I swept my hands through the rough hair on his face, breaking from his kiss. I crossed the straight line of his brow with my fingertips, down his cheek, ending at the fullness of his lips. "You really are beautiful, Baron Revich."

He took my fingers and kissed them. "And lemon has never tasted so sweet."

I pulled my lip under my teeth, my hands traveling lower on his torso.

"Have you read all of this book?" He held *The Guide to a Safe Homestead* in front of him, stalling my advances.

I unhooked the first button on his vest. "I've read some."

He ignored my wandering hands and opened to the page I had marked. "You've read through this?" he asked, pointing at the chapter titled, "The Most Important Part of a Tree is its Bark".

I skimmed the first few lines and nodded, remembering how I had read this theory in a half-doze a few hours earlier.

"What did you learn?" he continued, sliding one hand up my leg, bunching the soft sheer fabric with it.

A thrill of excitement ran through my skin, settling low between my legs in anticipation. I leaned in again, kissing him harder than the last.

His hand reached the heat that pooled at my core and I gasped, breaking our kiss.

He didn't miss a beat, asking again, "Tell me what you learned, Karus."

The smallest moan left my lips and my eyes drifted closed as I began to fall to the strokes of his fingers, winding in tight circles at the center of where I took my pleasure from him.

"Something about trees and bark," I answered, gripping his arm in earnest to keep up his pace.

He stopped his movement, and I gave a whine which he returned with a smile. "What else?"

In an exasperated huff, I squeezed high on his thigh. "I can't remember what exactly it was about, but I'm happy to reread it *later*."

He shook his head, pulling his hand away from under my night-gown, replying, "Of all the books here, I believe these few pages hold a deeper secret than one would assume just by reading this terrible chapter title."

I pursed my lips, adjusting my body and clenching my legs together, longing for more than his fingers to touch me.

"Let's practice your shield," he instructed.

A bit of a smile crossed my mouth as he donned the same tone and language I remembered from being a channeler under his tutelage.

He continued, "You form your shield around yourself, and I will read this passage to you. I will stop reading when you successfully keep me out. Then I will let this book fall to the floor and mix the lemon on my tongue with more of what your body has to offer."

I bolted from the bed, my shield up instantly with the ache between my legs painful in the promise of what was to come if I could just prove this one thing to him.

He gave me a smug smile and stood himself, pressing lightly on the shimmer of green that surrounded my body in a bubble.

His hand didn't press through, but the shield bent at the shape and he began to read, "Passing through the thicket of trees in Felgren Forest, one might believe that these ancient towers survive mostly due to their dense root systems or the leaves they grow in spring to soak in the warmth of the sun, but I have come to understand their secret."

I gasped as Revich's hand fell through my meager attempt to keep him out and he tsked, unbuttoning his vest fully and tossing it to the floor.

I swallowed and tried again, the formation of a green shield circling me once more.

"Listen carefully," he said, continuing where he left off. "The trees in Felgren survive due to their protective layer of bark. Without such a feature, they would succumb to the harsh rains of spring and the frozen bite of a Felgren winter. Not to mention the dry heat of summer, which would shrivel the trees to mere stubs without such a protective layer."

Rev stepped forward, pausing and pushing again on the shield I wielded. I instinctively stepped back, my body begging me to hold my power so we could move on from such a dry reading about trees.

His first attempt a failure, his chin rose and he pushed harder. I cocked my head in a silent challenge, crossing my arms at my chest. Pulling his white linen shirt from his waistband, he lifted it up over his head, somehow keeping his place in the book, and tossed it behind him on the floor.

I backed up once more, my back hitting the blue chair by the fireplace. He took advantage of my surprise and pressed on my shield again, this time shifting through its weak surface with relative ease. He traced his hand lightly across my collarbone.

I pulled on my power and forced him out again, complaining, "It's not fair. I can't focus while you distract me with all of *this.*" I gestured to the definition of muscle across his bare torso.

He shifted the book in his hand. "At the time when you will need a powerful shield the most, how will you focus if you do not practice first? You will have distractions, you may at times not wish to shield at all, but you cannot let anything through, Karus. Promise me you will try."

I knew he meant *her.*

I understood then his real purpose in this exercise. He believed this book held the key to holding my shield for longer and stronger than what I'd been able to produce before. He believed I'd be able to keep the Blightress out.

I nodded, straightening my back against the chair, focusing on my intent to keep him out. The muscle at his chest rippled as he pressed a hand to the back of his neck, the book open in the palm of his other hand and he continued, "The most fascinating truth about this layer is that it is continually renewed from within." Rev's eyes rose from the page and he stared at me for a moment. I nodded, taking a deep breath and focusing on the magic that radiated from within my body.

I could pull power from the forest floor, but there would always be this spark of channeling magic I had been born with. And combined with the power of Baron, it was strong, whole, a charred maple tree in a grove, its verdant leaves swaying in the breeze. I closed my eyes and continued to listen.

"Layers of these trees, grown from the nutrients of the sun and the earth, eventually become bark, thus dying off to add protection and promising the tree's survival."

I peeked an eye open, not much liking that last line, but he kept his head to the page and continued. "Like the bark of a tree, so must you protect the life you build with a layer of your own in the form of a magic shield. These are easy enough to produce, harder yet to strengthen. No spell has been found to aid in the shield you can form around yourself just by thought alone. Perhaps it is the fact that your power comes from the trees of Felgren themselves that any channeler is able to achieve this feat with nothing more than a simple instruction from their Baron."

My eyes flicked open at the snap of the book shutting. He tossed it to the bed and closed the gap between him and my power radiating in a thicker haze than it had before. He moved his hands to the top of his waistband, unbuttoning them at the same time he pressed again on my power.

I crossed my legs, clenching them together and attempted to focus. I dwelled in that place inside of me which held my strength in magic, a tall tree of life, marred by the destruction my power could bring. Taking a deep breath, I watched his hand as it pushed on the surface in front of me. It didn't bend to his will, and the surface didn't break. I exhaled in relief.

Then, his power flared.

An azure light blazed across the surface like wildfire, closing in on my power, my shield shrinking toward me.

"This won't work," I breathed, pulling what I could to keep the shield from collapsing. "I want you in here with me too much to keep you out."

He pressed harder and I heard his soft reply, "There may be times you want me in there with you, but your shield must hold. You protect yourself and you protect her."

Glancing down to my belly, I placed a hand over it. "I don't like this conversation, Revich."

"I told you we'd stop as long as you can keep me out." Another flare of blue light lit the room, engulfing his hands in a swirling mass of the power of Baron. He leaned forward on his hands, pushing into my shield. It began to bend, sinking inward toward my chest, but I would not allow it to break.

Anger coursed quickly through my veins.

I would protect him. I would protect all of us. There was no choosing to be had. I carried the strength of the most powerful place and beings on this isle, and I would not fail in this task he presented to me.

I reached from within, just as he had instructed, letting fill the well of power inside that charred tree of my mind before it spilled over and over again, green layers forming continuously from me, pushing Revich back.

Pushing even harder, he began to slip, my power growing, engulfing not only me but the chair, the small table beside it, soon flowing over half the bed and pushing Revich against the wall.

He took one last lunge forward, my power giving slightly to his own before I siphoned again from that well, pushing him back up against the black stone.

I let the shield fall, breathing heavily and holding onto the chair for balance.

He was there, taking me into his arms and kissing the top of my head. "I swear, every day we discover more about your power. You have no limits, my love."

I pressed my forehead to his neck. The cool skin of his bare chest eased the heat from pulling so much power forward.

He lifted my chin, pressing a kiss to my lips, his hands roaming my shoulders, pulling at the straps of my gown.

"Wait," I breathed.

He stopped, pulling back to hear me.

I swallowed hard, regaining my breath. "Again," I panted, "I want to try again."

# CHAPTER 45
## REV

"Looks like a lumen."

I jumped, almost cutting into my hand with my whittling knife. Adaynth sat in the blue chair across from mine, bent forward and watching as I shaped a piece of pine over a basket.

"That's not your chair," I responded, adding, "Move."

He lifted his hands in defeat, his shadowy form standing and shifting to the fireplace which I had kept burning bright as Karus slept on our bed, exhausted in more ways than one.

"Do you…" I started, jerking my head to the bed where Karus and I had spent a long, lazy hour enjoying the promise I had given her for her shield work.

He cringed. "No. Any inkling of desire in your head sends me far, far away. And she doesn't let me in regardless."

I nodded, tilting my head and continuing my work. "She can contain a shield to the corners of this room."

He frowned.

"And," I added, looking up at him, "she can keep me out of it."

"How?"

"You know how," I lashed. "You are constantly reminding me how it is that she holds so much power."

"And what do you plan to use this shield for?"

I cleared my throat softly. "She might need it."

"I see."

I worked in the quiet, shaving away at the wood, carefully shaping the features of the head. Minutes passed and nothing stirred in the quiet crackling of the fire.

"It is a lumen." I broke the silence, knowing he was still there.

I rose from my black chair and brought it to the cradle which would rock our baby to sleep in a few more weeks. My first gift to Saelyn, shaped from the hands of her father. I tossed the shavings into the fire and set the basket back on the floor.

"Are you staying here all night?" I asked. I waited for the answer that didn't come, looking up to see that Adaynth was gone.

My jaw tightened and I crossed my arms at my bare chest. I tried to smile. I tried to fill my heart with the joy I had felt every day as Karus lived with me, growing our child, challenging what she could do with her power.

The smile did not come.

I glanced once more to the empty cradle and admitted in the silence that I might never see it filled.

# CHAPTER 46
# KARUS

Moira cupped the white bloom of a morning glory in her hand, dipping her finger into the red paint she had made from the petals of a demorte flower. She traced swirls of scarlet around my eyes and along my neck, repeating what she'd helped me do a thousand times on my lips.

"I remember this," I chuckled under the tickling of her long fingers.

"You didn't hold still then, either, Karusss." She drew my name out, and I laughed, hindering her progress.

She finished her work and fluttered back, cocking her head to one side then the other. "Hmm. It's missing something."

I looked down at my sheer paneled dress, draped in a golden fabric I was fairly sure a fae had woven. Two panels fell across my newly large and cumbersome breasts, tying at the waist before spilling over my enormous belly to my toes. Two long slits at my side rose to my hips, displaying more skin than was used to showing.

I took a glance in the mirror of the washing room, admiring the designs she had painted on my face in preparation for *The Sun Which Does Not Sleep*. She flew out of the room, yelling something at Revich who waited for her to be finished with me so we could get ourselves to the fae festival. I heard his exasperated call back to her, all the words just mumbles from where I stood, adjusting the fabric at my chest.

"This is what you needed!" she squealed on her return. She placed a crown of sunflowers across my white hair, and I guessed she'd torn apart the vase of them at my bedside.

"It's perfect, Moira." I knocked my forehead to hers and she grinned, all sharp teeth and wide eyes. She herself had been painted in an intricate pattern of lines across her green skin and wore no flower clothes at all.

"I must go. They won't start without me, and I've been gone too long already."

I nodded, waving her out the door. I took a last look in the mirror, adjusting my conduit ring on my finger, tight as it was from my swollen limbs.

Stepping out of the washing room, I scrunched my face, closing my eyes and waiting to hear what Revich had to say about my faerie festival attire.

He said nothing for too long, and I peeked an eye open.

He sat on the edge of the bed in his usual black pants and a creamy soft shirt. Moira had told him to lose the Baron vest to make the fae more comfortable with his presence. He looked me up and down slowly, and I felt that pull on the line between us. I followed it, walking toward him. The golden panels of my dress shimmered in what might have been actual sunlight as far as I knew.

I stepped up in front of him, tossing my hands in the air and down to my sides, saying, "Well?"

He let slip a breath from his lips in a puff, looking me up and down one more time. He took my hand to his lips and stood, begging, "Please tell me there are more faerie festivals in our future."

Giggling, I bent my head to his chest where he caught me and lifted my chin. "No, no, Karus. We are not smearing this…masterful artwork. You are a glorious sun goddess, and I will not allow even the slightest smudge until I get you back here in my hands tonight."

"Promises, promises, Baron Revich," I cooed.

He squeezed my hand, bringing my knuckles to his lips once more for a teasing kiss and wink. "Shall we?"

WE MET CLAIRANNIA AND FIGUERAH IN THE FOREST, BOTH OF THEM dressed similarly in a gown of red and a gown of silver.

"I wish Nyeimah could see this," I called to Figuerah as she turned to show the movement of her dress.

"I plan to bring it back with me when I return." She held her hands out to me, and I kissed her cheek, then Clairannia's, careful to avoid smearing their paint.

"How are you feeling tonight?"

I shrugged, squeezing Figuerah's hand in reassurance. "Heavy and hungry. Same as usual."

"I am very much looking forward to finding out just what these faeries eat!" Clairannia exclaimed, grabbing my other hand, guiding us onto the path that would lead to *The Sun Which Does Not Sleep*. The three of us followed the path that wove deep into the trees, glowing in a display of warm, golden sun.

Revich followed close by, giving us time to predict just what we were about to see. Moira had told us at least a dozen times that humans were not allowed to join in the festivities of *The Sun Which Does Not Sleep* and that we'd been given special permission by the Growers due to the decimation of the Blight in Felgren.

We trekked deep into the forest, and I was thankful I had worn the simple sandals Figuerah had brought me to fit my swollen feet. We heard music and laughter up ahead, rifling through the trees in a joyous revelry.

"Karus," Revich mumbled in a reminder. I nodded and sent my shield of green power around us, letting the haze of it dim as it blended with a blue shield of his own.

"We can't see everything if we're like this," Figuerah complained.

"No more risks," Rev replied, then moved in front of us to lead the rest of the way.

We reached a wide field of tall grass where the sun indeed was not sleeping in the sky as it poured its heat and rays of gold down onto the various puddles of water cut into the clearing. Each body of water was circular in shape with a circumference of summer blooms. The sun reflected over every glassy surface, illuminating a glow over the span of creatures who danced, sang, and laughed before us.

I'd never seen so many bodies at once in every shape and size imaginable. A flutter of pixies, even smaller than Moira, flitted by while sprinkling something behind them in their wake. An enormous tree with the bodily shape of a woman swayed nearby to the beat of the drums, her hair forming as the branches of the tree, blooming in white flowers. More Growers than I had ever seen at once moved languidly around the open space, two of them tossing what looked like little sapling children into the air.

The music came from fae in the center of the field covered in green vines blooming in purple, pink, and yellow. They sat in a circle, playing on instruments they must have built from the forest. These fae looked the most like humans with similar shades of skin and long flowing hair.

"The fae warriors," Revich whispered in my ear as we gawked at the celebration and the creatures dancing in celebration of the longest day of summer.

"They look like us," I stated in disbelief.

"They most surely are not human," he replied, pulling me to the long fallen tree draped in fae foods.

Clairannia and Figuerah were already there, filling a stiff green leaf with fruit and what I could only guess was a nut paste. I hurriedly joined them, filling a leaf the size of my head with a little bit of everything. The four of us humans sat on a log, facing the dancers near the fae warriors as they played their songs hard and fast, the branches and legs of the fae moving to the rhythm with a mesmerizing ease.

I dipped a rolled flower into the paste, my tongue delighting in its smooth texture with the crunch of dried petals. Rev brought an enormous crimson strawberry to my mouth and I bit down, its juice trickling along my chin. He caught a drop on his thumb, bringing it to his mouth to lick. I laughed, the sound a common theme in the celebration which honored the sun descending slowly toward the horizon.

Hours later, I leaned into Revich's shoulder, watching Clairannia and Figuerah dance together, holding hands and twirling around to avoid the puddles of water still glinting in the last glow as the sun began its sleep.

We swayed slightly to the song, and I rubbed my hips, an ache settling in deep and unrelenting. Revich rubbed my back, turning toward the sun setting low in the sky, murmuring in my ear, "So I will see you at dusk, said the moon to the sun." He pointed into the darkening sky above us, the moon showing her silvery face already in the hazy blue of twilight.

I hummed, pushing on my belly where I could feel Saelyn's body, tight and heavy.

I heaved a breath and he placed his hand over mine asking, "Are you ready to go? You're shifting around quite a bit tonight."

I scrunched my face, a tight pull racing across my taut skin, squeezing my insides before releasing. I took another deep breath. My face flushed, even through the cool breeze of a summer night.

"I'm suddenly very uncomfortable," I admitted, taking more deep breaths in and out. Revich reached into his pocket, pulling out the rhyzolm. It vibrated across his palm, convincing us both that Saelyn was well and healthy inside my womb.

Another stretch of tightening drew across my belly, and I yelped, bending to relieve the heaviness.

"Clairannia!" Revich called, cupping his hand at his mouth. She couldn't hear us in the echoes of laughter and strings being pulled and plucked with the beat of drums in the shape of mushrooms.

"Sit here and do not move," Revich ordered, guiding me to the stump of a tree. "Shield up. I'll be right back."

I did as he said, pulling from the well of power at my core and producing a haze of green, like emerald glass.

Yet another pull raced through me, and as I caught my breath, I finally admitted what would happen this night. My body was ready for Saelyn to arrive, regardless of where I was or what creatures I was with. I breathed in through my nose and steady out of my mouth, just as Clairannia had shown me days before in preparation of bringing Saelyn into the world. Another pull, this time more like a vice across my belly, squeezing and yanking in a pain I could not escape. I cried out, the sound lost in the din of the celebration.

*BOOM.*

A shattering explosion of black blocked out the last of the sun, the sound rippling through the puddles around the clearing.

The music stopped and I looked up.

"No," I gasped, my cry barely escaping my lips.

The Blightress sauntered out from a portal of abyssal black, scanning the fae of her making with a few dozen Blight beasts following behind her.

My hands gripped the sides of the wood stump, and my breathing became erratic, filling my lungs with air, but not nearly enough. The tallest fae warrior had risen in the arrival, her skin dark as night wrapped in vines the shade of green grass. With a steady voice, she addressed the Blightress. "You are not welcome here, Visalia, Endless One."

The Blightress stepped forward out of her portal. "Come now, Nova, I bid you no ill will on this evening of celebration. I come only to claim what is mine." She pushed forward, ignoring the Growers gathering behind her back. Her glowing eyes darted to me. "And what is mine is about to enter this world. Isn't that right, Little Sprout?"

"She is our guest and a friend to one of us." The fae warrior, Nova, stepped forward, dismissing the menacing growls from the Blightress's beasts.

"Neither of those things dissolves the truth that she is mine to take, and the time has come to leave." She reached out a hand in the waning light. "I give you a last choice, Baron Karus. Come with me now, or forfeit their lives, and I take you with me still,"—she paused as a crimson grin grew across her face—"just a bit more bloodily."

A battle cry rose from the five fae warriors as they drew swords of steel, running across the field toward the dark stain on the dusky sky. I heard her laugh drawl through the clearing as another forceful pull shifted across my belly. I stumbled from the stump, keeping my shield steady, searching for Revich. A fist pounded at my power behind me, and I turned to see him there, pressing a hand on the glassy surface. I spread the green light around us both and he took my hand, pulling me into the tree line away from the cries and roars behind us.

"Keep your shield up and keep moving!" he shouted, calling to Clairannia and Figuerah already in the trees.

I shifted my light again, enclosing the four of us as we tumbled through the underbrush and into the growing dark.

Clairannia held my other hand, huffing, "Is Saelyn coming?"

I nodded, unable to speak through my timed breathing, gritting my teeth through the pain, slightly bent as we ran.

A light beamed ahead, not the blue of Rev's, but a hazy purple wrapped around wings I knew like the back of my own hand.

"Through here!" Moira said in a harsh whisper, leading us onto a different path unburdened by bushes and fallen leaves.

I slowed, crying out in the swift pulse that shifted through my womb as if it were being torn out of my body.

Without missing a step, Revich pulled my arm over his shoulder, baring more weight and guiding me down the path. Figuerah loomed behind me, screaming, "*Fulgyren!*"

Lightning struck the ground behind us, and I turned to see the line of Blight beasts darting down the path. The scent of burned Blight followed us as we pushed forward, Clairannia joining her in an attempt to keep the beasts at bay.

"Fall back with me, Clairannia!" Figuerah shouted, stepping out of the shield that flickered and bent to allow her leave. Clairannia pressed my hand to my belly, saying, "Keep going. We'll meet you at the Fortress."

"No!" I fought to keep her hand with mine, but she pulled from my grasp, leaving my protection to join Figuerah.

Laughter filtered through the dark, confirming what I knew to be true. The Blightress had followed us out of that clearing and wasn't far behind. Tears, hot and flowing, slid down my cheeks as I tried to gauge where in Felgren we were.

"This way!" Moira called and Revich followed, pulling me with him though my legs shook profusely. I fumbled, almost hitting the ground, but he was there, lifting me back on my feet, my sandal broken and useless on my foot. I kicked it off, limping through the underbrush.

Clairannia's scream pierced my thoughts somewhere behind us, and I cried, "Revich! We cannot leave them!"

"Keep that shield up!" he ordered, urging me forward to follow Moira's guiding light.

A bodiless voice of malice echoed around us. "Oh, how I do wish you had come when I called, Little Sprout. You should have taken my very first offer, and we could have brought the heroic Baron Revich with us."

More screams flew through the darkness, followed by distant shouts and the groaning of wood. I fell to my knees, out of Revich's grasp, heaving and covering my mouth to dampen the sound of my cries. A warm stream of liquid trickled down my thighs in another signal from my body that Saelyn was coming very soon. I dug my nails into the forest floor, my knees sunk into the earth as I looked down at my belly, giving myself a moment to breathe.

"Karus." Revich grabbed my face, and I saw him clearly for the first time. His tears had not come, only the anguish of his pain fell on his face in a resigned acceptance that radiated through our bond.

"I just…need…a minute." I heaved, gulping down air.

"Now, I'll have to kill them all," her voice called. "Your friends, your lover. Oh, Little Sprout, I am sorry to inform you that Thalia's sacrifice was in vain. You still cannot stop me, nor should you try."

The taunting in her words frightened me beyond any fear I'd known before. I struggled to rise from the dirt, begging for Revich to help.

He did not.

"Help me!" I cried, reaching up for him as he stood, staring into the dark forest behind us. I twisted my head to look. Moira's violet light cast a haunting glow on what prowled our way, illuminating two Blight beasts.

I knew them both. The Blightress had brought what remained of Parvus and Rauca, both of them patched with remnants of their fur, even through the black vines of the Blight digging under their skin and around their jowls.

Moira shot forward in a purple stream without a word, bouncing off of their maws as they snapped at her in the air, jumping high to reach her with their black teeth. The beast which was once mine bit down on her wing, shaking her tiny body, and flicking her across the path where she landed in a sickening slap against a tree and lay still as death.

"Moira!" I screamed, then turned to Revich, pulling on his arm again. "Help me up! We need to get to them!"

He bent instead, meeting my face with his, his hands holding my head as he stroked my tear and paint-stained cheeks. "Give me twenty years, Karus. I know how to stop her for that long. I know what to do with her heart, but you need to give me twenty years."

A stumbling laugh escaped my lips. "You cannot be serious. Our friends are hurt! Help me up right now!"

I gripped his shirt, now smeared with red paint of a demorte bloom. His lip trembled. "I have loved you since the moment I knew of you." He reached down to my belly, pressing a hand there and murmuring, "*Remolyn.*"

The pain subsided and my body relaxed. Blue swirls of power spread over my belly, but I did not look away from his face, gripping his arm harder. "Help me up, Revich!" I screamed through gritted teeth. He pressed his lips to mine in a hard kiss that was no kiss at all in my cries.

Her voice echoed through the wind again, closer this time. "Why do you draw this out when we could be gone from all this death and pain?"

Revich moved to rise, but I refused to let go, my nails pressing into the chilled skin of his arms. "We can both go," I reasoned, my voice a stutter as my teeth chattered. "We-we can make it back to the Fortress, and I will bring our child into this world, and then we can follow your plan."

He took a deep breath through his open mouth, murmuring low, "Saelyn must be shielded at all times. You are strong enough to do this. I can keep her heart subdued and weak, but neither you nor Saelyn can leave this forest until it is time."

I pulled at his shirt, his pants, his skin, slicing a gash across his neck. I tore at anything I could grab, trying to rise with him, falling back down to the earth, keeled over in another wave of pain. His hand shifted over my hair before he turned away, forming a glowing portal of verdant green.

"You won't do this," I breathed, crawling toward him. "You would n-never leave me like this." My body shook even as I felt the undeniable pressure to push our child from my womb.

He stood over me, the blue of his eyes piercing my soul, opening a wound I feared would be the truth of each of my days if he left. "There is only one reason I would leave you. Tell me you know what it is."

I called out in pain, reaching my hand out to him as I fell with my back to the wet earth, pleading for him to take it.

He did. Instantly, he was there. The tears had finally come, spilling down his face as it crumbled. He kissed my forehead, whispering the spell of easing the spasms across my womb once more. He took my face in his hands. "Tell me you understand why I have to go."

I shook my head, denying it. "No. No I will not understand. There must be another way. There—" I grunted, holding my breath through the wave of pain. "There must be—"

"Two decades is nothing," he lied, his voice shaking as he sniffed, squeezing my hand tightly in his.

"You won't do it," I cried. "You won't leave me."

"I must. I can save you and stop her from taking our child. There is no other choice." His voice wavered, "She'll be so perfect, Karus. You'll bring her into this world beautifully."

I stifled my scream, the haze of my shield breaking in the agony. I heaved in and out rapidly, gripping his hand with all my strength.

"You can go for *one*," I bargained in a whimper. "You will come back in *one* year, and I will have s-something new planned. I-I'll spend all my time in Viridis looking."

"Saelyn deserves a life, too. She deserves her mother for all of it."

"SHE DESERVES HER FATHER!" I bellowed, my own voice echoing through the trees, carried on the wind.

"Seventeen years then," he promised. "Seventeen years—how old you were when I first saw your face, and then you'll have an army trained and ready, just like we planned. Tell our daughter I am dead so she does not grow up fearing for my safety. Give her a life of peace and sanctuary until the day comes where you can fight for what we've tried to build. Give her a future, Karus. This is the only way she has one."

Sobs wracked my body in disbelief. In my desperation, I ripped his shirt sleeve, pleading, "Do. Not. Leave. Me."

He bent once more, kissing my temple and then my hand, forcing his rhyzolm into my palm, releasing his fingers from my rigid grip. He stood as a shadow swept forward in a void of any kindness or love. The Blightress walked toward us on the path, a true symbol of the darkness I feared was my future. Her black skirts flowed behind her as she lifted the hem of her gown, stepping in casual footfall over bushes and leaves.

Rev's comforting presence left my side as he stepped to his portal, murmuring back to me, "I love you, Karus."

"Don't you *dare*." I wailed, trying to raise my body off the ground. "Don't you say it like that and leave me!" I dropped the rhyzolm and dug my fingers into the soil in a feeble attempt to crawl my way to him.

"What's this?" her voice cooed. "You leave the mother of your child as she labors?" She reached my legs and bent, her hand pressing lightly on my belly, murmuring the same words to soothe my muscles. "How utterly disappointing, Baron Revich. I shall find you and bleed you dry myself. You cannot hide in this world."

I ignored her, dragging my body toward my love, my companion, my every reason to fight and live. "I-I," I stuttered, gulping and shaking my head with tears that left me blind. "I will *never* forgive you for this!"

I heard the finality in his voice as he stepped forward. "I will never forgive myself."

The portal closed and he was gone.

"Do not fret, my child," the Blightress soothed, stroking her pale hand over my womb through another bout of pain, "You will learn at my side that the love of men is—" She stopped, pressing her hands to her chest. Her black nails dug into her gown, ripping and tearing, exposing her porcelain skin with streaks of red that coursed down her flesh in trails of blood. "*Where did that portal lead?*" she raged. Her iridescent eyes flashed red and her body began to fade into the darkness. "NO!" she screamed, slumping to the ground and flicking her hands at the space between two trees. She summoned a black portal just before her face fell into the dirt.

"I will *kill* him!" she coughed. Blood seeped from her lips as she crawled away from me. The two Blight beasts Revich and I had loved bounded to her side, tugging at her sleeves, pulling her unconscious body into the abyssal void. In a flash, they fell into the inky black, and I was met with cold silence.

In a desolate cry, I fell back into the earth of Felgren, reaching a hand toward the space where Revich had left me.

Alone and afraid.

～

I CAME TO OCCASIONALLY. ENOUGH SO TO PUSH AS FIGUERAH HELD my legs bent at the knee and Clairannia, draped in a wash of fresh blood, knelt, ready to catch my child. I heard a cry, a scream from healthy lungs fly through the night, my daughter's first cry fitting with my latest in the night breeze of Felgren.

I wept, howled, screamed until my voice had nothing left to give me to release the torrent of pain that ravaged through my bones, my heart shattered in the acceptance that he was not coming back.

Figuerah wrapped our wailing child in the fabric of her skirts and held her close while Clairannia mended my body.

I had no strength to stand, no strength to move as I lie, gazing up at the starry night sky, my body longing to fade back into the earth where I could live forever. Where I would live on, growing trees and flowers, providing shelter for the creatures of the forest, feeling nothing but the breeze, the sun, the damp chill of winter.

"Karus, you must get up." I heard Pompeii's voice, followed by my brother's.

"Don't do it," Philius seethed, his face appearing above mine. "You are getting up and we're taking you back to the Fortress."

"No," I rasped.

"Help me lift her," my brother called. I felt the hands of Pompeii slide under my body to scoop me upright.

"No," I whispered again, forcing my shield around me and pushing them back as I sank deeper into the earth. The roots of the trees crawled over my legs and the scent of freshly turned earth lifted under my nose.

"Karus!" I heard the shout, indistinguishable to my ears form who it came, and I settled further, ready to relinquish my body to the forest because I would not be living in the home we'd made without the man I loved.

A harsh wail sounded at my ear, and I turned my head, catching sight of Pompeii in the haze of green, holding my baby toward me. She cried in the night, just as I did. A tearful plea to be comforted, to be warm, to be with the one who did not hold us.

I reached out my arms and my shield dropped as he settled her onto my chest. Figuerah lifted my back, fitting me onto her lap deep in the ground. Clairannia pulled a warm blanket up over my body as I looked down at Saelyn's face for the first time. A mess of black hair sprouted from her head in every which way, and her round cheeks bloomed to red as she squeezed her eyes shut and wailed again.

"Shh," I soothed, rocking her in my arms.

She was perfect, just as he said she would be.

She settled slightly, but whimpered still, her traumatizing emergence into this world deserving of such fierce cries.

My voice was a useless thing, but I tried anyway, singing into the dim glow of the conduit lights around me,

> *"Sweetly does sing the wren to the tree, calling into the*
> *summer breeze."*

Voices hummed somewhere, but I ignored them, focusing solely on my daughter, the child Revich had promised away years of his life to keep safe.

I let my shield spread, understanding dawning on me of what he had meant. The power to protect came from within. And I had our daughter to protect now, just as he, at the heart of the Blightress, protected the isle from her full force of wrath.

I didn't know how he planned to do it for seventeen years. I didn't know what he had just done to cause the Blightress such pain. But a warmth drifted on the wind through the trees, and I felt him through our bond. He sent me love, he sent me loss, and he sent me the feeling of a peaceful calm.

I swallowed, wishing I could send him this image of our daughter, her deep blue eyes lulling as I sang to her in my arms, continuing the song that came from her grandmother, sung long ago in a little cabin in the Hallow Marshes.

> *"Softly does hum,*
> *The bee to the sun,*
> *Flying into the summer breeze.*
> *Shyly does bloom,*
> *The babe in the womb,*
> *Arriving into the summer breeze."*

# PART FIVE
## SEVENTEEN YEARS AFTER

*The only thing I can grasp is the cold.*
*It beckons me through the years in the silent chill that is the absence of him.*
*When we are ready, when the frost has burned with the fury of our loss, she*
*will pay.*
*And I will save him.*
*I will save him.*
*I will save him.*

# CHAPTER 47
# SAELYN

My mother, my strong, beautiful mother, did not let go of my hands as she told me the story of my birth.

She spoke of the pain, the trauma she and others had endured, and the lives lost that night.

She spoke of my father.

For the first time in my seventeen years, she spoke of his love, of his kindness, of his sacrifice so that I may live a life in peace, never looking over my shoulder for the Blightress to descend.

She spoke of the months after and how she wouldn't let anyone near me. She had carried me everywhere, even in the meetings where she would project herself from Felgren to the Queen, the Lady, and the Madame to discuss building an army of channelers and conduits trained in warfare against the Blightress. She spoke of how she conjured her shield through the depths of the roots of Felgren, keeping the Blightress and her monsters out of the forest for all seventeen years of my life.

She spoke of how she manipulated the seasons with her line of fae magic, forcing them to begin or end, syncing as well as she could with the time that passed outside of the forest to ensure that my seventeen years were approximately the same years my father spent in the Blightress's lands.

She spoke of how she lied, just like my father had asked her to, telling everyone on the isle that Baron Revich was killed by the Blightress on the night of my birth. Everyone had believed her, though there were four who knew the truth.

She spoke of the hardest days, glimpsing his face in mine, hearing his laughter and his humor in mine. She spoke of the woman she used to be, the woman I did not know.

"When we find him, we will return to Felgren and all will be as it should have been," she promised through her tears, squeezing my hands as we knelt on the floor of her room in the Spire.

"How do we find him, Mama?" I cried. "How do you know he is truly still alive?"

She tapped her chest. "Here. Our companion bond remains, and I feel him here."

Taking my hand, she pressed it to where her heart beat.

"How—" I thought for a moment, wording my next question carefully. "How could he be alive in the cavern of her heart for so long? How could he survive such a thing?"

"I do not know. I…I tried to leave once." She lowered her eyes from mine. "In a moment of weakness, I convinced myself I could leave you just for a moment. Just long enough to return him to Felgren without the Blightress knowing I was not there to continue the shield. I attempted a portal into that cave. You were three years old."

"And?" I urged.

She lifted her head, meeting my eyes once more. "He kept me out. I cannot portal there. He uses his own Baron power to fuel a shield around the cave. Neither the Blightress nor I can break it."

"Then what do we do?" I persisted. "How do we save my father and stop her?"

"That's the Dimming, Saelyn. It will take hundreds of magic wielders and those who carry swords to break through the Blight Line and put her to sleep."

I shook my head and huffed. "To sleep? You're going to save the isle by making her fall asleep?"

"We cannot kill her without killing all channelers and conduits on the isle. She is connected to everything. So, yes, we will force her into a deep sleep, and the power of Baron will be used to subdue her in a room underneath the Fortress. The Baron power will pass on eventually, but she will continue to slumber."

I thought for a moment, a sweep of exhaustion settling in. Finally, I nodded, resolute to do what I must in this war and reunite my parents. "I see now why she wants me, but I would never be hers. I would never love her, so why does she still try?"

My mother brushed my hair with her hand. "She sees you as her granddaughter. As the only family left who could possibly love her. You are young and she is ancient. She believes that with time, you could love her and shape the isle to her creation. She has gone mad after centuries alone in this world. It has nothing to do with who you are, Saelyn."

I nodded at that, rubbing at my eyes and smearing the kohl swept across them.

"Come." She rose and pulled me up with her. "Let's get some rest. There's much more to discuss tomorrow."

She folded down the yellow quilt across her bed, and I fell into it, overtaken by the day and night's events. Slipping in beside me, she bent and kissed my cheek as she'd done on the good nights when I was a child.

I closed my eyes, plagued by the sorrow of my father's last words to her that night.

*I'll never forgive myself.*

# CHAPTER 48
# THEVIN

"Early morning swim?" I asked, watching Lanna sweep her blonde wet hair into a plait.

"Every morning at dawn," she replied with a wolfish grin.

"At the Hatchery?" I asked casually, wondering if she'd heard of my interlude with one of the aurum fish.

"It's the strangest thing," she said, confounded. "One of the attendants informed me that swimming in the Hatchery will be closed for a few days to settle the fish from some brute who attacked them."

I nodded in agreement, keeping my arms folded at my chest and looking down at my boots.

She continued, "Something about a man riding alongside one of them then—*smack*! Another one knocked him out clean and his lover had to dive in to save him."

My cheeks burned. "His lover?" I questioned in a narrowed squint.

She flipped her braid behind her back, hands on her hips, grinning in delight. "His lover."

"That is *not* what happened," I mumbled, shifting off the wall and checking my baldric for the third time since I had woken.

Lanna flicked her favorite dagger between her fingers, running her tongue across her teeth. "Enlighten me, fish rider."

I sighed, rolling my eyes. "Alright. It's all true except the lover part."

She keeled over in laughter, grabbing her knees for support.

I chuckled alongside her. "Sorry you had to swim in the canals."

"No, no," she started, wiping at the tears in her eyes, "the full story from you will be worth it. What I wouldn't pay to have seen that."

"I almost drowned, thanks," I reminded her, slapping her back as she coughed a laugh.

"I'm glad you didn't. It's interesting though, isn't it? Why would the attendants assume that you and Saelyn are lovers?" She tilted her head back to the pillar in the room at the top of the Spire where all of our launches to the Blight Line took place.

I shrugged, tightening one of my straps.

"You are in deep, my friend," she huffed, leaving my side to fill a plate at the sideboard of breakfast foods.

I didn't tell her about the kiss.

I didn't tell her about how I had gone back to my bed afterwards, debating what I should or should not do next.

Saelyn had kissed me.

*By her breath*, I didn't stop it.

Perhaps I should have.

I didn't know what I'd do when I saw her again. And as I had fallen asleep, I'd tried to memorize the feel of her lips and body against mine. The feel of her hand in my hair and the way she had gasped at my mouth on her neck.

I decided I'd ignore it.

I'd treat her the same as if it hadn't happened.

If she felt it was a mistake in the light of dawn, that would give her the easy way out. Besides, we had a lot to do in the next few weeks, and we didn't have time for confusion in our relationship.

I meandered toward the array of foods, knowing I should eat.

"You should eat." Lanna echoed my thoughts, stuffing her mouth with a vanilla custard pastry.

I plated a sausage and a few cherries. Summer was in full swing outside of Felgren, evident in the variety of colorful fruits which lined the table. "What's our destination?" I asked between bites. "Lythglyn?"

She shook her head, wiping her mouth. "The ruins. We're joining the Wieldwryns this morning in the push back to the castle, since the Blightress has depleted some of her power with that attack last night." She paused for a moment, cocking her head to the side and narrowing her eyes. "Do you know how Saelyn knew the Blightress was coming? You said she was more powerful than anyone realized."

I sighed, glancing toward the doorway to the top tower room where we expected the Baron and Sae to join us any minute. Clairannia and Madame Zoreyah were already there along with my parents, the Viceroy, and some other important figures I recognized. "I truly do not know. We were dancing and talking one second, and the next, she bolted to her mother to warn her."

"It's a good thing she did," Lanna noted. "A second later and Baron Karus would not have gotten her shield up in time."

I hummed in agreement.

"Do you think Sae knows more than what she said at the gathering last night?" Her words were careful as she studied me. She was one of my oldest friends, but she was also my commander in this war.

"No," I lied, spooning some of the egg and seafood dish onto my plate. "I don't think she does."

"Well, that's a shame because I do think she is hiding something."

My gaze rose to her steely blue one and she tightened her jaw, speaking low for me to hear. "Baron Revich is alive. His daughter can somehow sense the Blightress's power. Both of these truths go hand-in-hand, though neither I nor the council understand exactly how. Whatever power Saelyn holds that can predict the movements of our enemy is not one we can afford to let her keep to herself."

I glared. "What are you saying, Commander?"

Her face softened slightly. I never used her title so seriously.

"What I'm saying is that you are her closest friend. She likely trusts you even more than I do and that's saying something." She clapped a hand at my back. "I only mean to win this war and bring Baron Revich back from wherever he fights in her lands. I only mean to return peace and safety to this isle." She shook my shoulder, adding, "You know that, Thevin."

"Aye, I do."

"So talk to her. Get her to help us. *By the Baron*, I don't know why she would hide something like this in the first place."

"She's never seen war. She didn't know the extent of what was happening until two days ago, Lanna. Give her time."

"We don't have time," she burst. She shoved her fingers through her hair, unbinding the yellow strands as she did so. "All the cards are on the table. The Blightress knows our hand. We have yet to fully understand hers and she is unpredictable at best, all-consuming death and destruction at worst."

"I know all of this," I gritted through my teeth.

"Then get Saelyn to help us. Do what you need to do because we can't wait for her to catch up on what's going on here." She dropped her hand from my shoulder and crossed her arms at her chest. "She's lovely, Thevin. But she does not understand the sacrifice of war like we do. No matter what you explain to her, she has been hidden away in that forest for the entirety of her life, blissfully unaware of what raged outside of it. Show me you understand what needs to be done. For her sake and all of ours."

That pressing truth settled in at her words. We needed Saelyn's power to win this war. And I was going to have to be the one to help her see that.

# CHAPTER 49
# SAELYN

The Baron of Felgren watched me in the mirror, pulling my dark locks into an intricate braid, securing my hair for the trip across the isle to the Blight Line.

She did not study me as my mother. She looked me over as a leader of the isle, silent and staring, thoughts flickering across her brow in confusion and deep thought.

I was nervous. Not to see Thevin again after our kiss in the hallway, but to get to the Blight Line and witness the real toll of this war that raged because of me.

I took my mother's hand in mine as she finished her work, securing my hair with leather ties at the back. "Thank you, Mother. I'll go get dressed."

She stopped me, squeezing my hand and speaking to me as we both looked into the mirror. "You felt the Blightress coming, but I've been wondering how she knew you had arrived here in the first place."

I gulped, truly unsure of how the Blightress knew. "I-I don't know."

Her black eyes shifted across my face in assessment. "I have not trained you in magic, though I know you possess it. A great amount of it, in fact."

I bit down on my lips, keeping her stare.

"Did you…use any magic yesterday?" she asked carefully, tilting her head to the side. "When you saved Thevin from drowning, how did you do it?"

My brows furrowed. "I saw him sinking in the water and dove after him."

"And? Did you try your hand at magic to get him to breathe again?"

"No, but I—" I thought back to my split decision in the water. When I had realized that massive fish was coming for him, my instincts told me to follow in the footsteps of my mother and create a portal—the last magic I'd seen her use. "I did try to create a portal…like the one I saw you form before we left."

She closed her eyes in a grimace.

"I'm sorry!" I turned around in my chair to face her. "I didn't know I wasn't supposed to, and I just saw another fish coming for him, so I just pulled my hands apart like you did and—"

"It's alright," she murmured, stroking my hair, "just tell me what happened when you tried."

"Well, there was a bright white light—just like how my magic presents itself. But the fish avoided the light at the last second, and I grabbed Thevin and got to the surface."

She nodded.

"Is that how she knew? She felt me use my power for something big?"

"I am sure of it. You and I along with your father have power that is connected to the Blightress more than any other magic wielders on the isle. I don't doubt she's been waiting to feel you summon yours in full force."

"I am truly sorry then," I murmured.

"Don't be, Little Love." She lifted my chin, kissing my forehead like she used to do. "You were saving your friend, and that is the best reason to use your power."

"But I shouldn't try anything else, right?"

"I have not taught you magic because I did not want her to know the extent of what you hold. Your own father wondered at the power you possessed even growing in my womb. I have feared all your life that she would take you and use you to return the power that was once hers. All magic on this isle comes from her, but that does not mean she gets to take it from you. When we reach the ruins, we will convene as the Four and you will have options with how you would like to proceed in this fight for your father and the isle."

I squared my shoulders and rose, taking a last look in the mirror and heading to the closet to get dressed. "These ruins are at the Blight Line, correct? Where we'll meet the last leader of the Four?"

She pulled her black vest over her chest, fastening the gold buttons down the front. "Yes. We arrive today at the ruins. You will stay back while the Wieldwryns and the Runners push the line to the castle."

"The ruins of what?" I asked, pulling on my tall black boots.

She twisted the emerald conduit ring at her finger and said, "The ruins of Hyrithia. It is there that we will meet your uncle, the last of the Four."

My head sapped to hers. "My uncle?"

"Yes. They call him the Handless King."

~

FOLLOWING MY MOTHER UP THE WINDING STAIRS OF THE SPIRE, I studied the hazy green shield that now covered the city. I'd known that shield all my life, never getting much glimpse of a clear sky because of it. But now, seeing the subtle glow, I missed the sky as it had been when we'd arrived. I felt the guilt slip in of leading the Blightress right to us with my attempt at a portal to save Thevin at the Hatchery.

We entered the arched doorway to the very top room of the Spire—the same we had entered from the portal in Felgren. With my bag slung over my shoulder, I searched the room for Thevin. He was easy to spot, biting a sausage at the end of his fork and speaking with Lanna and his parents at the breakfast table.

"Are you hungry?" my mother asked.

"Not really," I replied in truth. My stomach was in knots for what was next.

"Doesn't matter," she countered, "The first rule for where we're going is that you eat when there's food. I cannot guarantee when our next meal will be."

Clairannia drifted toward us in a swish of white. "Baron Karus! Word has arrived from Felgren. Pompeii and the other channelers' combined shields are currently intact. There have been no attacks on the forest."

My mother let out a sigh of relief. "That is good news then, thank you."

Clairannia reached out a hand to squeeze her arm. "Figuerah will be there. When we arrive, I mean."

"I know."

"You should speak to her. There's nothing wrong with you both apologizing for what was said a long time ago."

My mother gave me a small smile. "Please go eat. We'll be leaving within the half hour."

Seeing it as the dismissal it was, I nodded, and headed toward Thevin, glancing back to see the old friends continuing their conversation away from everyone.

I approached Thevin from behind, tapping his shoulder, greeting him with a happy, "Good morning!"

He swiftly turned, and at my presence, Lanna winked and walked away, quickly followed by Thevin's parents.

He opened his mouth to speak and then shut it tight, doing his best not to let his eyes roam over my ensemble.

"It fits nicely, doesn't it?" I stepped back and gestured to my loose white shirt tucked into my tight black pants, complete with boots that rose to my knees. I had picked it out the day before to match what I'd seen Lanna and other women of the Spire wearing.

"It does," he admitted casually, setting his plate down on the table.

I nodded slowly, clasping my hands in front of me. The strange stiffness of his body had my stomach plummeting. I was sure he was thinking of last night, but based on this awkward first conversation after, I worried he had regretted it.

"Well," I started, gulping, "about last night—"

"You mean last night when you saved everyone in this room from a sure death, or last night when you kissed me after?"

"You kissed me back."

"You kissed me first."

I huffed a nervous laugh. "I did, didn't I?" I could see him struggling not to smile and I continued. "Listen, I know our emotions were high and that I didn't actually ask if that's what you wanted, but—"

"I shouldn't have let it get as far as it did, and for that I'm sorry."

I frowned. "You already said you were sorry last night."

"I meant it then, too."

"Just because you're sorry doesn't mean I am, and—"

"You really don't have to explain, S—"

"Thevin!" My voice echoed louder than I had meant and several pairs of eyes darted to us. I felt the heat rise to my cheeks. "Would you please let me finish a sentence without cutting me off?"

He blushed as well, opening his mouth.

I poked him in the chest. "Don't you dare say you're sorry one more time. I just need you to listen without talking."

"Saelyn, you can talk and eat. Please get something in your stomach." My mother's tone caught me off guard as she grazed over the food on the other side of the long table. I fumbled for a plate, the rising frustration within me begging to boil over in what would be a highly embarrassing confession of love for the man next to me.

I wanted to tell him.

I was determined to tell him.

I did not know when to tell him.

My mother grabbed some pastries and left, heading to the middle of the room. I tossed some fruit on my plate, barely noticing what it was. Thevin plopped three strips of bacon on as well—my favorite and he knew it.

"Please accept my peace offering."

The corner of my mouth tilted higher than I would have liked. "For now," I agreed, though my entire being begged me not to. "But I would like to speak to you." I glanced around. "In private."

He shrugged. "I don't know when we'll next get a private moment. We're about to go into battle."

I hesitated with bacon perched on my lips. "Battle-battle? We're going right into fighting?"

"Pretty much. You'll be protected though. And Baron Karus is with us now, so we should have the power to push the Blight Line back and retake the ruins."

I dropped the bacon onto my plate, my stomach refusing food entirely. "You'll be in the front? Facing those creatures?"

"Hey," he mumbled, reaching under my hand to raise my plate back up to my face. "The first rule of war is to eat when you can. I'll be fine. I've done this a few dozen times. Lanna is a great commander and knows how to maneuver her Runners to allow space for the Wieldwryns to take action."

I frowned at my plate and instead picked up a strawberry, biting the red flesh off the green stem. "Will I be able to see you fighting?"

"Why? Looking for pointers?"

"No, I'll be looking for blood."

"Sae," he laughed. "I'll be perfectly fine. We all will."

I twisted my lips back into a frown.

"Look." He pointed to where his parents spoke to the Viceroy. "My own parents are not even slightly worried. Don't you think they would be if they thought their only child to be in serious danger?"

I huffed a sigh. "I suppose so."

"And look at the Baron." He pointed again. My mother was in the cleared space of the room, maneuvering her hands in that way I had tried, spawning one portal after another. "Do you think she'd be so calm if she thought her own daughter in danger?"

I shook my head, nibbling on a piece of bacon. "What will I do then?"

"You get to sit back and watch me cut through beasts and Blight. I'll be sure to add some flourish to the end of my slashing."

He smirked, and I chuckled, reaching out to the knives strapped across his chest. "You'll use these?" I traced my fingers over each hilt, three small ones in total, no longer than my hand. I followed the leather down to the sword strapped to his side.

"Will you really use this many?" I studied the cold metal, but glanced up at him when he didn't answer.

His gaze was haunting. His clear blue eyes flicked down to my mouth once. Twice. I straightened, the air between us shifted, though I was unsure why. I was absolutely sure, however, that I didn't mind it.

"I think it's time to go," he whispered, still staring me down, still emitting that same spark of what I'd felt the night before when I'd pressed my lips to his.

I brought my hand back to my side, not daring to touch him further. "Alright," I said, keeping his gaze.

I wondered briefly if this was it for us.

If we'd never recover from what we shared in a dim hallway midway up the Spire, on the cusp of the looming end to this war that, for me, had only just begun.

I wondered if I'd be able to correctly explain my feelings for him when the time came. Maybe he wouldn't believe me, and we'd live like this all our lives, never touching, only staring, our bodies humming in a synchronized tune that we'd have to deny forever.

"No," I whispered to myself, shaking my head slightly. I wouldn't let that happen. I had been the one refusing to risk losing him, but now I'd be the one refusing to keep our friendship the same.

"No what?" he murmured back.

I swallowed. "I—"

"If I could call to order, please!" My mother's voice rose through the room, demanding attention.

We faced the line of nine portals glowing green as a Felgren spring.

"With the attack on this great city last night, we leave you now to approach the end of this war with the Dimming." She glanced to me and continued. "The Blightress has haunted our lives for long enough and we are ready to descend upon her lands and put a stop to her tyranny." Pausing, she took a deep breath, closing her eyes and exhaling long and slow. "I tell you now, there is much hope. Baron Revich is alive."

The room hummed with murmurs and gasps. I was suddenly filled with a cold I couldn't name and stepped closer to Thevin.

"This comes at a great shock, I know, but please believe your Baron when I tell you, it was not a secret I held lightly for seventeen years. The Dimming is no longer just to end this war, it is to make Felgren whole again." She held my gaze. "And bring home the father of my daughter."

She stepped up to the line of portals. "Please spread word of this wonderful news. Let it reach from the ocean to the mountains that all will be restored." She put a fist to her chest. "Hold onto hope. Defy the Dark."

An echo of agreement shifted through the small crowd. Thevin mimicked the movement beside me and softly smiled down at me.

Madame Zoreyah was the first to enter the portals. Alongside her billowy golden pants padded a black muri, its face fading to white in old age. Surprised, I watched with raised brows as she entered one of the portals while her enormous cat followed through another.

Lanna was next, followed by Clairannia. Ilyenna and Talon nodded to my mother before stepping through their portals at the same time. My mother reached out her hand, beckoning Thevin and me to join her.

He did not let go of my hand as we walked through the crowd to face the last three portals.

"Thevin will go next, followed by me," she instructed. "You will be last, Sae, and you will stay back. I will protect you. There is nothing to fear."

I nodded, untangling my fingers from Thevin's. He smiled at me and left, his portal of brilliant light closing with him now hundreds of miles away.

"Be well, Baron Karus," the Viceroy spoke and my mother

nodded once before stepping into her own portal. The green haze over the Spire disappeared instantly, leaving the room to brighten in the morning midsummer sun.

I looked around, all faces on mine, all thoughts likely on the fact that I had a father who still lived and that this war had begun and would end with me.

I didn't know if I should say anything, but felt the urge to leave them with hope. "I will return with my father back to Felgren. I promise, I will bring him home. And I will do what I can," I continued, stumbling slightly on my words. "I will do what I can to end this war and return peace to this isle. I am sorry to be the cause of so much suffering, but it will not continue. Everything I have to give will be spent to end it."

The silence sat, quickening my heartbeat. In my nerves, I took a step toward the last remaining portal. A clap sounded and I glanced to my left to see the Viceroy, tears in his eyes and hope on his face. Cheers continued throughout the room as onlookers, people I had never met, but had known of me all my life, hugged each other in hope and the joy that comes from such a thing.

I nodded, forcing back tears of my own and stepped through my mother's portal.

**CHAPTER 50**

# THEVIN

"Right side, rank up!" Lanna's voice boomed in the fray of war. My sword was already drawn, slicing through a black vine, thick as my leg, as it crept over the decayed soil.

The Baron had been true to her word, portaling us only a dozen yards from where the Blight Line coursed over the tall green grasses of what once was Hyrithia.

But the city it had been was no more. We had fought over its ruin for years, pushing the Blight Line back and forth over the hills and city gates. Just weeks ago, it had been taken again, the Blightress sending an endless army of her Blighted creatures, capturing no less than eight of our Wieldwryns to turn to syphoner trees.

I gripped my sword with both hands, slicing up and through the Blight beast jumping toward me with a maw of grotesque canines dripping in black ooze.

"Runners, forward push!" Lanna called.

We joined the line of them already assembled, ready to descend upon the ruins as soon as we arrived. Saelyn would be here by now, but I couldn't turn back to look. I could only move forward, swiping long thick cuts across the beasts and vines that would consume the isle without those left to defend it.

Cut, turn, jab. Slash, duck, run.

It was always the same. A never-ending torrent of black flesh falling to pieces before more would rise again from the desiccated earth. Where we mourned our losses and searched far and wide for more to commit to our cause, the Blightress need only extend her hand and pull forth more of her dark monsters from the Blighted land.

Our only successes were born from clever tricks and distractions, wearing her power down and pushing forward as we did now.

The city walls half crumbled to the ground, and what was left of the Castle of Hyrithia remained tall in the distance, now covered in Blight since last I'd seen it.

It had been difficult to leave the last time the ruins had been captured. My parents and I had been a part of the last attempt to hold the city. At the dismal end of that last battle, I felt as if I fell with it, watching my friends patch up their wounds, several of them missing on the battlefield.

My father had patted my back, reminding me that we would not give up, that hope did not elude us. I had thought of Sae then, sunning somewhere in Felgren, safe and happy, waiting for her best friend to come back home.

It had been so hard not to tell her everything. Everything I knew, everything she was missing. I hadn't been able to hold back that night when we danced, no more than I'd been able to step away from her lips pressed to mine last night.

"Thevin! On your left!"

I heard the warning before the prowling beast struck, this one not a creature formed of the Blight, but one long-dead muri, pinning me down to the blackened soil. Its mangled jaw exposed white bone with strips of flesh flapping in decay, slick with black blood.

I grabbed its throat, holding back its sharp teeth with one hand, reaching across my baldric for one of the daggers with the other. The palm of my hand sunk through dead flesh and skin, cutting on a broken bone at its neck. Ignoring the pain, I sliced into its chest, then up, stalling its force of claws like knives at my shoulders. Lanna was there before I could finish the job, one swift movement of her sword across its head and it fell from its body—right onto my face.

"Fuck," I coughed, pushing the corpse from my chest and wiping the black blood from my eyes.

"Keep your head on what's in front of you, not behind you." She breathed deep with a grin on her face and a hand out to pull me up.

I took it, rising to see the field covered in an emerald light domed above us, pushing toward the castle.

Lanna huffed a laugh, grinning wide as she looked over my shoulder. "Baron Karus just lit the sun."

I turned, shielding my eyes in the golden, blinding light, barely able to make out the Baron crossing the field with it held high in front of her.

The *Simulair Solum* spell was the first to be taught to the channelers that would one day enter the force of Wieldwryns, though I had never seen it so large and emitting such a heat as this.

The hiss of receding Blight was a sound I'd never get used to. I cringed hearing the death of what had brought destruction over these lands. I looked around for Sae, unable to see her as the Baron moved swiftly across the field with her army of Wieldwryns. As Runners, our job was almost done, making a cleared path to the castle gates. We would continue forward to cut down any more opposition, but we'd meet little push back, the Blight and beasts of its nature unable to withstand the light of the glowing sun for long. A lick of fire began to burn along the castle towers, no doubt produced somewhere by the Handless King himself.

"Runners!" Lanna called with her sword held high, beaming in the light of the Baron's spell. "Tighten the line! Push to the castle doors!"

I spit black blood to the ground and wiped my mouth, gagging at the distinct taste of rotted flesh and bitter remnant of the Blight which had consumed the animal. I wrapped my bleeding palm in a strip of cloth Lanna handed to me, tying it at the back of my hand. Thankfully, it wasn't my sword hand that stung like fire.

Glancing down the line of Runners, I counted around forty of us, recognizing plenty of faces who had seen the same amount of war as I had. A few of them more, a few less.

Lanna marched forward, the sun from the Baron's spell directly overhead, shining a light into the black abyss and destroying all in its path. Of all the battles I'd fought, this was turning into the easiest to win. After seventeen years, we really might just have the power we needed to complete the Dimming and bring peace back to the isle.

We pushed on, meeting little resistance. With each swipe of our blades across the vines and creatures that dwelled under the city gates, ash soon followed, destroying the Blightress's dark forces to nothing but a coat of dust on the land.

The westward city gate, only twenty feet away from our line, remained broken and open since Hyrithia had first fell to the Blight ten years ago. I had only been a boy, hearing my parents' hushed whispers about the fall while we searched for Runners and Wieldwryns in the Attatok Mountains.

The Blight vines on the walls fell in tremendous crashes, torn from their purchase by the heat of the sun that hovered into the city. Lanna entered first, cutting through the vines and thorns like warm butter, their resistance muted in the power we now held on our side.

"Runners," she called, "pair off and surround the castle!"

We did as our commander ordered, Lanna and I running into the city to find it empty, the growth of Blight receding as we raced to the castle doors.

"She's pulling her forces back," I huffed.

"Don't let your guard down."

I nodded, flexing my left hand, tightening it into a fist to ease the pain of my wound.

"We need a Wieldwryn," she mumbled directly to me before amplifying her voice to reach through the city. "This is Commander Lanna. I need a Wieldwryn Commander at the castle doors."

I caught my breath, focusing on the formation of Runners who stood in pairs around the black-stained stone, swords at the ready.

A portal opened beside us and Clairannia stepped out, already focusing her power to form a sun of her own over her palm. It glowed a glittering crimson, the size of a dinner plate and nowhere near the enormity of the one that still hovered above us.

Clairannia stepped toward Lanna, speaking low, "The Baron cannot hold this and the shield much longer." She pointed above us to the flickering sun and glassy green dome. "I've been ordered by the King to empty the throne room first, and then we will send the rest of the Wieldwryn forces inside to inspect the rest of the castle."

Lanna nodded, replying, "The Blightress is pulling her forces back. We've met little opposition."

Clairannia glanced to me, and I gave her a short nod, lifting my sword again. She flicked her fingers, sending her simulated sun toward the castle doors. The hinges groaned and flew open. I stepped in front of Clairannia alongside Lanna, who gave a sharp whistle to the dozen Runners nearby to follow.

The castle was empty. Though stains of black painted the once gray-blue stone walls and tables, there was little sign of the Blight.

We stalked quietly through the foyer, turning left down a long hall. Clairannia sent her glowing light through the broken doors of the throne room, illuminating the mosaic of thistle on the floor. A spread of Blight roots recessed immediately, disintegrating into ash and staining the floor in a spread of black lines. The intricate tiles had been uprooted near the grand dais, now a gaping hole into the earth where the Blight had sprouted from underneath the castle.

I studied the domed glass ceiling, surveying for structural damage that could fall and kill us all. "Call for the Lapis Wieldwryn, Ilyenna," I ordered, turning to Flynn, a Runner I recognized and trusted. He nodded, sprinting back down the hall to give the order to the army catching up to us.

Clairannia pulled her sun back to her hands, instead sending a shield of red to encircle the domed ceiling to prevent any possible debris falling onto the soldiers arriving into the throne room.

"Thevin's wounded," Lanna noted and Clairannia, regaining her breath from the effort of holding the sun so long, reached out her hand to take mine.

"It's nothing," I replied. I pointed across the hall to the Runner holding a torn shirt at her side, her head tucked between her legs as blood dripped to the floor. "She's first."

Clairannia nodded, hurrying to the dais.

I sheathed my sword and ran my fingers through my hair. "It was too much for her," I commented, watching the throne room doors as Lanna did. "The Blightress's failed attack on the Spire was a loss for her hold on Hyrithia as well."

"I don't trust it," she said, sheathing her own sword and crossing her arms. "Why would she give up Hyrithia so easily when she used so much force to take it back only a few weeks ago?"

"She wouldn't be able to hold it. Not with Baron Karus fighting now."

She let out a weighing sigh. "She just backed off entirely. Not a single casualty or stolen Wieldwryn on our side. It was too easy."

Unsettled at her words, I just nodded, inspecting the gash on my palm. It wasn't looking good.

"Get to someone who can heal you," Lanna said, cringing at the open flesh, "That's an order."

# CHAPTER 51
# SAELYN

Nothing Thevin had explained to me in my room, safe and warm, could have prepared me for the fighting. The moment I arrived from the portal, spit out again into the tall grass like something discarded, I paled at the sound of war. My mother had bloomed forth a sun, raging and hot into the clear summer sky. At just its presence alone, the Blight faded away from the line of black that rooted to the earth, turning to little more than ashes.

I rose from the ground, searching for Thevin, but unable to see anyone I recognized in the chaos. Screams and orders emitted from the frontlines and a mass of the Wieldwryns, dressed in varying colors of what their magic could produce, followed into the city. Casts of colorful magic glowed every which way, though it was hardly needed with the damage my mother had done.

Her domed shield covered us all, descending on the city ruins which stretched as far as my eyes could see. My mother ordered me to stay behind her, and I did, following the trail of her black skirts as she raced across the tall grasses and into the black earth, a clear line of delineation of where this battle had been fought before.

I was thankful I didn't have my usual skirts to hold, instead keeping up with the mass of Wieldwryns in their sprint to the city gates. I hesitated, my heart hurting as I looked upon the destruction of the city my mother had come from. Wide streets and tall buildings were now little more than rubble inked in black stains across every inlaid stone, every storefront, and upturned carriage.

The city of Hyrithia had been completely consumed, and I shuddered to think of what had happened to the people when the Blightress's forces had taken hold.

Lanna's voice rang through the streets calling for help, and I watched my mother speak to Clairannia before she suspended the sun and opened a portal.

As soon as Clairannia was gone, my mother faltered, only slightly and possibly not enough for anyone else to notice, but I did.

I fisted my hands at my side, useless in this battle for which I had no training and would be more collateral than warrior.

Instead, I followed closely behind my mother, watching for any sign that she might fall as she lifted her simulated sun even higher on the horizon, a mirror to the rising sun to the east.

We neared the castle doors, catching the shouts for Ilyenna to come hold the castle stone, her lapis magic able to repair the structure from further destruction.

A tall man approached my mother, glinting in silver armor at his shoulders with a woman at his side who also glowed in flaming red curls, shaved on one side.

His handsome face broke into a grin, and he swept his arm across the dark skin of his brow. But it was not his golden eyes that beamed with joy upon seeing my mother which made me gasp—it was his hands, no more than brilliant orange flame shaped into long elegant fingers. His arms encircled my mother, bringing her into a shaking embrace. He murmured something in her ear, guiding her slowly to the ground. Her enormous raging sun above the castle dissipated in a flash along with the emerald shield over the city. I reached her side just as the man who must be the Handless King, lowered her unconscious body to the ashes.

"Mother!" I cried, taking her hand.

"She's alright," the King murmured, a sorrowful smile on his lips. "She'll come to in just a minute."

I nodded, relying on the people who knew her power to help me understand.

The woman with red curls and freckles stared down at me in disbelief. "She's the spitting image of him."

He murmured his agreement and huffed a laugh. "It's good to meet you again, Saelyn." He held out his swirling flame of a hand for me to take. "I am your uncle, King Philius of Hyrithia."

I took his hand, awed with how his flame did not burn my skin but held a warmth that felt something like comfort.

"The shield," I said. "We need to replace the shield. The Blightress came last night to the Spire and my mother's power was the only thing that stopped her."

I swallowed the lie, remembering the deep rumble of the Blightress's laugh as I had reforged time to change the ending to what would have been a massacre.

"Renn." The King didn't even turn to the woman before she was up, calling out to the Wieldwryns.

A dozen lights rose from the hands of the powerful channelers and conduits around us, forming into a dome of colorful magic rolling over the city.

"How long until she—" I started.

"Saelyn?" my mother's voice called to me. I heaved a breath of relief, helping her sit up.

The King patted her shoulder and said, "It's clear. We've taken back Hyrithia thanks to you, Baron."

She nodded, accepting his glowing hand to help her stand.

"Are you sure you're alright?" I asked.

"Yes. That spell affects me like this every time I've used it. Let's get to the castle and rest a moment."

I smiled quickly, taking in a deep breath and telling myself I could be useful here in some capacity and get the Baron into the throne room.

She didn't let go of my hand as we entered through the doors, the King ahead, letting out a long whistle at the destruction of his home.

"Fucking Blight," he cursed under his breath, tracing the black remnants across the stone walls with his glowing fingers.

He led us toward the throne room, and I wanted so badly to ask how he had lost his hands but kept quiet, instead observing the reactions around me. Cheers and laughter rumbled lightheartedly through the room.

Ilyenna summoned her power in the corner, reshaping the stone walls and glass dome above into one that could hold its structure. The floor was covered in soot over an intricate pattern of tiles.

I scanned the room for Thevin, eyeing first the few soldiers on the floor healing from their wounds by the medicus Wieldwryns. Clairannia was among them giving orders, and I sighed in relief, confirming Thevin was not one of the wounded.

The redhead rushed to the King. "No casualties, no Wieldwryns taken. The halls are clear and Hyrithia is ours."

He pulled her to his side for a lingering embrace. "Hold the eastern wall. I want a camp of soldiers guarding the Blight Line with the heaviest surveillance tonight. Find the rest of the Four and all of the commanders. They are to convene for a council meeting in the map room in one hour."

I continued to scan the room and my mother leaned in, whispering, "Go find him. I'll bring you to the meeting in an hour." She patted my hand and let go.

I didn't need more encouragement. My heart beat wildly as I wove through the people speaking in relief of their easy victory this morning.

I soon found him sitting on the dais, wrapping his hand in white linen. "Thevin!" I exhaled, rushing to kneel in front of him. "You're hurt?" I took the hand bound in cloth, peeking under the bandage.

"I haven't made it to the healers yet," he said, dismissing my concern.

I frowned. "This looks bad."

"It's just a cut."

"Like these?" I reached out to his right side, patting where I knew three long slashes scared his chest.

"Like those," he murmured in barely a whisper.

I huffed in reply, carefully removing the bandages to expose the raging red gash across his calloused palm.

"What are you doing?"

"Healing your hand."

I thought he'd refuse, insisting how small of a wound it was, but he didn't. He held his palm up to me, and I closed my eyes, sifting through the healing spells I knew from reading about them in Viridis.

The truth was, I didn't much like the Medicus Conduit Hall. I found it stunningly boring. I had spent most of my time in Viridis studying the words of the magical language instead.

He chuckled in my long pause. "I really don't think it's as bad as you're—"

"Hush, you," I retorted. Instead of trying to remember the specific word that would close his skin, or even going to ask Clairannia for help, I focused on what I knew. I'd pieced together the language of magic many times before, weaving it into something useful. I could do it again.

The words came to me, and I placed my right hand over his left, gripping it tightly. He gasped through his teeth at our touch, but remained silent as I murmured, *"Cutis Mea, Cutis Tumn."*

My skin fused over his wound. I could feel the stretch of my palm thinning, giving what I had to offer to close the gash with my flesh. A soft white light glowed under our clasped hands, and I grinned wildly up at him, pulling my hand from his to show that he was healed.

The cut remained in a white scar down his palm, still covered in red and black blood. He grabbed my hand, flipping it over to see a twin scar to his own.

"You've got one, too."

I shrugged. "I don't mind."

He traced his finger down the puckered line, and I shivered, the slightest breath leaving my lungs. He brought my palm to his lips, leaving a kiss and mumbling, "Thank you."

He kept my hand near his face, holding it with both hands, and I wondered if he was remembering the kiss we shared just hours before, like I was.

I cleared my throat. "I've been meaning to tell you, Thevin—"

"There he is!" A booming voice overtook my words and Thevin looked up, smiling and pulling me up with him as he rose to greet the man.

They embraced, clapping each other hard on the back, the man laughing and saying, "Thought you'd be gone longer than only three weeks! What brings you back so early?" Noticing me for the first time, I gave him a polite smile.

He was almost as tall as Thevin with dark hair cut to the scalp and a wicked looking scar that began on his left cheek down to the olive skin of his neck. He glanced from Thevin to me and then back again, a brow raised.

"Mavryn, meet Saelyn, daughter of the Baron of Felgren."

He jerked his head back, scanning me from head to toe. I raised my chin, offering my hand. "It's nice to meet you, Mavryn."

He took my hand in a sly grin and shook it with a firm grip. I imagined he was somewhere around Lanna's age—only a few years older than Thevin and I.

"The daughter of the Baron leaving Felgren after all these years to join us in Hyrithia," he remarked. "I'm wondering why."

Thevin stepped closer to my side. "That's for the Four and the commanders to discuss, not for you to wonder."

"My time spent fighting this war would say otherwise," he countered, flicking his gaze back to Thevin.

I felt the tension strike quickly between them, curious if the subtle animosity was from my leaving Felgren or something from their past.

I broke the silence, folding my arms across my chest. "Are you also a Runner, then?"

Mavryn nodded, tilting his head and giving me a wolfish smirk. "That I am. And I must say, it is good to learn that you are real, and we do have a reason this war has been raging for so long. All over a pretty girl who smells of—" He casually leaned in, taking a big whiff through his nose. "Pine and sea, is it?"

Shocked at his words I huffed a nervous laugh, but Thevin's anger rose swiftly.

He pushed Mavryn back, stepping in front of me. "That's enough. You reek of Blight, Mav. Get something to eat and wash up because your manners are fucking terrible."

Mavryn held up his hands in defeat, falling back and laughing, "I meant no offense to the girl. Just as happy to see her as you are." He winked at Thevin and gave me a sweeping bow before walking away, greeting others in the crowd.

"Fucking asshole," Thevin mumbled, watching him go.

"Hey," I called, pulling at his shoulder to face me. "I hate to say it after you just defended me, but,"—I ruffled his dirty golden curls at the top of his head—"you don't smell so great yourself."

# CHAPTER 52
## THEVIN

The cleverly named map room was indeed a room of maps. One enormous one lay across a wide table, providing the topographical elements of the entire isle. More maps were rolled up and shoved into baskets along the walls, sharing shelves of books about Hyrithia's history.

The Blight hadn't touched a few rooms in the castle, this one included, though that didn't save it from the ravaged dishevelment of becoming a council room in a time of war.

I heaved a sigh, waiting for the council to begin the meeting which would provide us higher ranking officers with our next tasks before the Dimming.

Saelyn spoke quietly with the Handless King—who turned out to be her damned *uncle*—next to the tall fireplace. My parents had left out that little detail, including that they had trained with him when they were channelers in Felgren.

Everyone important to the cause was here, myself likely the least important one of all. Lanna conversed with Madame Zoreyah and a beautiful woman with the same umber skin and the same tattoos. I assumed it must be her first daughter and heir.

There were a few more faces of commanders I recognized. One

woman I did not know spoke with Clairannia, stealing glances at Baron Karus who stood near the topographical map, chewing on her bottom lip relentlessly.

The Baron's black eyes rose from the illustrated trees of Felgren Forest, and she caught my stare. Tucking her hands into the pockets of her skirts, she stepped around the table, joining me in the shadowed corner.

"Thevin," she greeted kindly. Though we rarely interacted, she'd always been pleasant to me and welcoming in my arrival at her forest every summer to steal her daughter away on adventures.

I inclined my head, straightening my posture and forcing my own hands into my pockets. "Good afternoon, Baron Karus."

"I am happy to see you unharmed from this morning."

"You as well," I responded, squeezing my scarred hand in my pocket and stealing a glance at her daughter.

The Baron didn't miss it and turned her head to Saelyn as well, saying, "I didn't thank you…for staying with Saelyn after I told her about her father."

I cleared my throat and said, "She's my best friend. I would do anything for her."

The tiniest glint of humor crossed her face before disappearing altogether, and she continued. "I know you would. It's why I need to ask something of you."

"As a Runner under your command, I follow your orders."

She shifted on her feet in unease. Taking a deep breath she met my stare, softly replying, "I do not ask you as Baron, I ask you as Saelyn's mother."

I frowned. I didn't like where our conversation had led, and I stole another glance at Sae. She laughed at something the King had said, and he chuckled along with her. "What do you ask of me, then?" I questioned, looking back into her eyes, black as an abyss.

"It has been…difficult to relay the dangers Saelyn will face with us in the Dimming. I will push during this meeting to allow her the choice of if she wants to join us after what she's seen, but,"—she grabbed my forearm—"promise me you will protect her, even if I cannot. Even if every last one of us is down, you will not let the Blightress take her."

Once again I focused on Saelyn, the harsh desperation from her mother's request sending ice through my veins. Sae caught my stare, smiling and giving me a short wave. She pinched her nose closed and raised a brow toward me.

I wanted to laugh, but couldn't seem to, resigning to just a slight nod instead, confirming that I had in fact bathed and cleaned up from the battle. She must have noticed the fear I could not hide on my face and said something to excuse herself, walking toward us across the room.

The Baron's grip tightened, and I covered her hand with my own, now sharing a scar with her daughter. "I will defend her until my last breath, and even then, I'm sure Death allows compromises."

She gave me a tight smile and nod, letting her hand slip from my arm as Saelyn joined us.

"Hello, Mother. Thevin," she started, her grin bright and beautiful. "This room is lovely, isn't it?" She glanced around and spoke to her mother, "I was just speaking to my uncle about how charming it is, and he had quite the story to tell of the time the both of you stole some of these maps and trekked northward to establish a new city."

The Baron hummed a laugh and replied, "I believe we were about seven at the time, so it certainly was not a successful journey."

I watched the Baron speak to her daughter as if she had not just warned me of what may come to pass. As if she had not just told me that she expected I could be her daughter's last hope against the torrent of wrath that was the Blightress.

"It looks like we're all here," the Baron started. "Whatever is asked of you in this room, Saelyn, you are the one who will decide your future. That future may come with risks, and we would understand if—"

"It's alright, Mother." Sae brushed a hand down her arm. "I know the risks, but I am done hiding from them." She smiled at me, once again stealing a piece of my heart.

The Baron took a deep breath and nodded, stepping into the middle of the room.

Sae leaned in, sniffing at my clean white shirt. "Much better."

Her mother's words still haunted me, and instead of my usual flirtatious reply, I gripped Sae's hand in mine, regardless of the room we were in or what our roles were to be in this war.

She squeezed my fingers. "What is it?"

"Something doesn't feel right here," I responded, studying the faces in the room, especially the ones I had not seen before.

"I admit, I don't know how this is going to go, but I'll stay here beside you." The corners of her mouth turned upward, and I bit down hard, feeling the solid strength of my teeth, wanting to pull her away from all this discussion of the Dimming and the Blightress and just run through the fields of Felgren to kiss her in long grass blooming in yellow flowers.

"Where did you go just now?" she asked, leaning into my shoulder.

The deep blue of her eyes pierced my soul, solidifying that there was only her. There was only everything I wished we could share together, despite the fact that from her existence alone, death and souls siphoned for power haunted the isle since we were mere babes in our mothers' arms. "Just…" I started, reaching out to brush the sharp line of her jaw with the back of my fingers, "a place I wish we could be."

She caught my hand and didn't let go, her eyes flashing to my mouth.

"I call to order the council of the Four and the commanders of the Wieldwryns and Runners." The Baron's voice, slightly amplified, silenced the room. All eyes of the most important people on the isle turned to her, and she addressed them with her stout bluntness. "The Blightress has attempted to steal my daughter once already since we left Felgren. She arrived at the Spire last night to massacre the guests of the party and take Saelyn to her lands, where she would poison her mind over decades and all hope for this isle would be lost to a new, darker future."

I quickly glanced around the room, looking for shock and acceptance. I was met with mostly tired eyes and folded arms.

The Baron's jaw ticked and she swallowed, hesitating on her next words. "Baron Revich is alive."

The gasps in the room changed the mood, several commanders turning to each other, several more with deep frowns across their mouths.

"I have held this secret for seventeen years. A final request from her father before he left to weaken the Blightress's heart. He has been there all this time, stifling her power, allowing us to grow our army until the day we would be ready to embark on her lands and silence her forever."

A young man stepped forward, one I didn't recognize with bright red curls and freckles across his wide nose. "We could have used Baron Revich these past years, and yet you let him face her lands alone? Why couldn't we send help? Why does his presence there diminish her power?"

The Baron turned to him, her face softening, "Ashton...it is good to see you again."

He spoke through his teeth, "Why? Because I remind you of my father? If it's him you're wishing to see, I'll point you to his grave."

Sae looked at me and then back at her mother. I leaned into her ear to whisper, "Commander Geyrand was killed a year ago at a northern battle. His son has taken up his duties along with his daughter." I paused as the Baron said something softly to the man. "Your mother had history with Commander Geyrand. Before she met your father."

Sae squeezed my hand and nodded, focusing back on her mother.

"Regardless of what you think, Ashton, I cared for your father. I care for your family and this fight is for them." She waved a hand around her. "This fight is for all of us. The Dimming comes due and we need your soldiers in the north for this final push."

"And Baron Revich?"

The question came from the back of the room. A woman stepped forward, her dark skin complemented by the golden iumenta conduit clothes she wore. Her long hair was swept back in dozens of intricate braids, golden beads patterned into each one. I recognized her as the woman speaking with Clairannia earlier, but did not know her name.

"What state will we find him in when we arrive in her lands? What horrors have you left him to face alone?"

Her words stung. Even I could feel them as the air in the room grew taut. Baron Karus's chin trembled the slightest before she gave her answer. "I do not know, Figuerah," she murmured softly, flexing her fingers at her side. "I have tried once before to get to him, but he has shielded the cavern where her heart beats. I cannot see him. I cannot get to him."

Figuerah stepped closer, her face full of anguish. "And what does Adaynth have to say? What does the source of the power of Baron have to tell you about where one Baron fights alone for seventeen years?"

Lanna stepped forward, hands on her hips. "Baron Adaynth? The first Baron of Felgren?"

Figuerah nodded. "Karus has not been forthcoming in her power's source. Not only does she hold the power of Felgren and some of the Blightress, her power as Baron comes directly from the first Baron in history." She took a deep breath, adding, "And that Baron lives inside hers and Baron Revich's minds. He can speak to them both, so I ask again, what does Adaynth have to say about Revich's fight?"

More whispers filtered through the room at the second secret brought to light. I watched Sae as she frowned at her mother and Figuerah. I could only imagine what she felt from hearing hostility towards her mother.

Baron Karus murmured something low and Figuerah's lips pursed in response.

"What does she say?" Lanna asked.

A swirl of green tendrils, bright and solid, wrapped around the Baron's fists at her side as she broke her calm demeanor, her rage spilling forth in a wind that swept through the room. "He does not speak to me!" she stormed. "I have begged, offered my own power back to him, done everything I could think of to get Adaynth to speak to me! He is still there, in the dark corners of my mind and will not tell me how my companion survives in the Blightress's lands!"

She took a step toward Figuerah, who stood her ground, though Clairannia rushed to their sides. "Do not ask me what I have done for Revich because I have done everything but give my own life!" Her power broke from her hands, wrapping around the three in a swirling mist. "And the only reason I have not done that is because Rev wanted his daughter to live safe and happy in our home. I would have given my life a thousand times over to save him." Her voice broke and Figuerah reached for her hand, tears running down her smooth cheeks. "I would have given up everything but our daughter to bring him back, for that is the one thing I cannot do. So I have *waited*. Seventeen years I have loved and raised our daughter the best I could with my heart bleeding in my chest every moment he is there alone without his family, without the two he loves most, and I will bring him home, Figuerah, because I am *done* waiting. He has given enough for this fight." She gestured around the room. "He has given years of his life for all of us to hope. To defy that dark, and it is my turn to save him." She paused, taking a deep breath. "I will save him."

The silence was cold. It filled the room in an uncomfortable stillness. The only sound was the crackle of fire at the hearth, the only movement was the swirling green mist around the three powerful women, trapping them in unspoken words, years of the weight they held hanging heavily between them.

At the Baron's words, my throat tightened, and I saw I was not the only one in the room who struggled to keep their tears in check.

Before I could pull her back, Sae took three steps forward. "Use me as bait," she offered, loud and clear. "The Blightress can feel when I use a vast amount of my power, so use me as bait and get to my father. Plant your army around me so that when she arrives to steal me away, your forces can attack and hold her."

"No," I hummed low.

I knew she heard me, but ignored me anyway, continuing, "I am the cause of this war, and I offer myself to be the end of it."

The King stepped forward. "The Blightress knows when you use your power?"

"Yes. It is how she knew where I was outside of Felgren. I...I used some of my power impulsively while I was there."

"And how did you escape her? Baron Karus hasn't explained how that didn't end in a slaughter." King Philius glanced to the Baron, who now held the hands of both Figuerah and Clairannia, her power easing into a single glowing circle around them.

Sae lifted her chin and her knuckles whitened. "I knew the Blightress was coming and warned my mother so that she could erect her shield and protect us all."

"You can track the Blightress's movements?" He uncrossed his arms, his flaming hands falling at his sides.

"Maybe...I-I don't know for sure how I knew she was coming."

Lie.

The King addressed his sister. "With Saelyn using her power to attract the Blightress and Sae's ability to know if she's coming, we have a chance to implement the Dimming. I have one hundred Wieldwryns practicing the sleeping spell on each other every day. They're ready."

Lanna added, "And with the aid of Commander Ashton's northern Runners, I have four hundred soldiers to fight through to the cave where Baron Revich waits."

The Baron nodded, stepping out of the glowing mist. "Saelyn, this is your choice alone. We can find another way if you—"

"I am tired of fearing to make a choice, Mother. I want to train with you and play my role in the Dimming." She turned her head, smiling at me coyly over her shoulder as she finished. "I choose this risk. I choose *this* future."

My chest would cave from the beauty of it—watching her offer all of herself and everything she had to end this war. And I'd stay by her side through all of it. Just as I had pledged to her mother, I would fight for her to my last breath and beyond.

"Are we in agreement as the Four to pursue this new plan for the Dimming?" Baron Karus looked around the room at Madame Zoreyah in the corner, slowly petting the head of her muri while her daughter bit her fingernails in agitation. She nodded once, then everyone looked to the King who sighed, murmuring his agreement.

She turned to Lanna, who had nervously run her fingers through her hair so much during the council, her pale waves were almost completely unbound from the braid around her head.

"If Saelyn agrees, then I agree. But if she changes her mind at any moment, we do not force anything upon her. Baron Revich would not want that for his daughter."

The Baron nodded, holding her palm out to Saelyn. "As Baron of Felgren, this is my Offering to train you in the magic of the Forest that flows through your veins from the roots of the trees to the new leaves in spring. Do you accept?"

Sae reached out her hand, placing it in the palm of her mother's. "I accept this Offering, Baron Karus."

At their touch, her clothes transformed.

I'd never actually seen the customary acceptance of an Offering, but I'd heard of the conduit in training being given a conduit ring and formal clothing they would subconsciously choose.

Instantly, Sae became taller, her feet wrapped in high-heeled shoes similar to those she wore the previous night. They were a pine green, the top wrapping around her delicate ankles, trimmed in what looked like rhyzolms.

The sheer forest green length of her gown hinted at all of the shape of her legs, flowing downward from her waist where she wore a velvet bodysuit that ended high along her hips to show off her creamy skin. Her sleeves billowed in the same shimmery sheer material, ending at her wrists in cuffs of gold lace.

I could only imagine what the front of her gown looked like if this was the back, and I shifted uncomfortably against the wall.

"Runners," Lanna called, "you're with me to the eastern gates. We will inform the rest there and prepare a timeline to invade. Move out."

I swept a hand through my hair, following orders like a good soldier instead of pulling Sae into my arms to dance to the music I heard when I looked at her. Lanna caught my eye and my hesitation as if she expected it and jerked her head to the door.

I didn't look back as I left.

I was a Runner in the Four's army on the front lines.

I didn't get to dance.

I felt the clap of Lanna's hand across my back. "I did what I could to make sure she always has a choice."

"Thank you," I muttered, heading down the blood-red carpeted stairs, now stained with veins of black. "I will follow orders." I stopped her on the last step as the other commanders left us, hustling to the eastern wall. "I will follow orders until I can't. I go where she goes."

She chuckled and jostled my shoulder. "Then I think she has a real chance to do this right."

# CHAPTER 53
# SAELYN

A ring wove over my right forefinger the moment my gown formed over my body. I held it up to the flicker of firelight, in awe of the representation of my power.

A silver band was topped with a teardrop shaped stone in a hazy white to the point of becoming almost clear, with long streaks of black lines running through the stone every which way. It was chaos, it was beautiful.

"Runners, you're with me to the eastern gates. We will inform the rest there and prepare a timeline to invade. Move out."

I heard Lanna's call and turned around too late, watching Thevin leave with the rest of them. My heart sank as he left, but I assured myself he was in no danger joining the forces at the new Blight Line.

"It is beautiful, Saelyn," my mother said, taking my hand back in hers to admire my conduit ring.

"I've never seen such a stone," Ilyenna whispered, having silently slipped up beside me.

"Never?" I asked, holding it up to the light again.

"Never," she replied, glancing to my mother and her friends. They shook their heads in a solidified no.

"It doesn't have a name?"

"If it does, I do not know it."

I twisted my lips to the side, lowering my hand and finally taking a look at my gown. It held a similarity to the style I'd worn in the Spire. But instead of a powder blue, I was draped in the green forest of Felgren. Intricate gold designs woven into the sheer fabric wound up the front with slits in the side that left nothing of my legs to the imagination. Long sleeves billowed around my arms down to my wrists and a belt of metal golden vines tightened across my waist. The neckline of the gown was open and daring, curving downward across my chest in a deep V. I gasped at my shoes, which I admitted I loved most, regardless of how my feet arched uncomfortably. They extended my height at least three inches off the ground. I pulled back the sheer fabric to admire them.

"Are those…" Ilyenna bent, squinting at the band around my toes and ankle. "Rhyzolms?"

Everyone crowded in to look. Even Madame Zoreyah left her corner with her daughter and squinted to comment on the Offering clothing I had summoned somehow deep in my subconscious.

"I would have thought blue," I laughed nervously, running my fingers over all the details I wore.

My mother explained, "Every channeler who accepts their Offering is draped in varying shades and styles of green. It's a tribute to the forest that fuels you." Her smile lit her eyes in a shade of Felgren. At this height, I finally reached hers. She pulled me into her arms, squeezing me tightly while whispering in my ear, "He would be so proud of you. I am so proud of you, Little Love."

"I—" Thoughts raced through my mind of how I had lied to her. Of how I let her believe I did not know how I could predict the Blightress's next moves or how I had never told her I had the power to create my own spells and could turn back time. "I will try to bring him home, Mama." I kissed her cheek. "I promise, I will try."

She squeezed me tighter as if she needed to hold on. As if I was that anchor, keeping her in place and keeping her from falling to her grief, her pain of waiting seventeen years for her love and father of her only child.

I just hoped I was strong enough to save them all.

❧

I WANDERED THE RUINS OF THE CASTLE WITH MY UNCLE WHILE THE armies set up their new base. He told me stories of his childhood with my mother and with his mother, the former Queen of Hyrithia. She had fallen during the battle of her city ten years ago —her death a sacrifice to buy time for her people to escape. Many of them had not. He spoke to me of his time in Felgren, training under my mother and father and how it had taken the tides of war to bring him into his power.

"And so you cut your hands from your body to sever the connection to the Blightress? Did it work?"

"Yes. The Blightress had no hold over me after that."

"And the others? You said there were others who carried the black hands of the Black Fever. What of them?"

We looked out at his broken city. He gripped the gray-blue stone of the tower—the only tower left intact. "She either called them to her lands to siphon their power through those trees... or..."

I frowned. "Or what?"

"Or," he lifted his head to the east where tents rose along the Blight Line. Dozens of soldiers monitored the clear delineation of black, standing guard over the forces gathered in the city. "Or, they could have their hands cut from their wrists."

"That's a terrible choice."

"It's the choice I gave them. They could walk into her lands, or they could sever their connection to her. Most chose the latter."

"And these syphoner trees..." I bit my lip, searching the line of soldiers for one familiar face. "Do they kill the channeler?"

"I don't believe they do."

"But the people within them can't be severed from the tree?"

He looked down at me with the pain of grief I knew well from my mother. "That we don't know. We have never...successfully released a channeler from those trees alive."

He was quiet for a moment, staring out at the northwestern peaks where the Attatock Mountains lay hundreds of miles away.

"You know someone," I started. "You know someone trapped in those trees."

"I am the reason two people are trapped in those trees," he spoke softly. "Renn, my guardswoman, has a twin sister. The Blightress stole her from us years ago. I fear she has become a syphoner tree and that one day her sister will find her, molded to the wood as a source of power for the Blightress."

I nodded solemnly. "And the second?"

He met my gaze then. "Do you often speak with Pompeii? The Baron's Overseer?"

Taken back at the question, I smiled in missing him. "Of course! I call him Pah-Pah." I laughed, turning my head south. "I could never get his name right as a child, so it stuck. He is the closest to a grandfather I'll ever have, and I love him dearly." I shifted on my feet, feeling the ache from the shape of my shoes. "He was always there to raise me when my mother…when my mother couldn't."

"Your mother loves you."

"I know my mother loves me," I snapped. My cheeks flushed and I gave a nervous laugh. "Sorry. I-I know she did her best. And I understand why her best wasn't more of what I needed."

"You are astute in your conclusions of people, Saelyn. A trait I believe your father gave you."

I nodded, having heard our similarities my whole life.

"It's a terrible shame," he continued, "that I got to know your father and you did not."

"He was your friend, my father?"

He laughed, deep and hearty. "I wish I could say it was so. I didn't make it…easy to stay in the same room with me for more than a few minutes back then. I was a foolish Prince of Hyrithia, though hopefully, not a foolish King."

"You don't seem so foolish to me," I said.

"Thank you, Saelyn. I have tried to make amends for the mistakes I've made."

"And the second?" I asked again, catching a glimpse of Lanna's golden hair, walking the Blight Line and pausing every so often to speak to the soldiers at their stations.

"The second?"

"The second person you know trapped in those trees."

He hefted a heavy sigh. "Mychael," he said with rasp in his voice. "My loyal guardsman and Pompeii's love."

I gasped. "Pompeii's companion is trapped in a syphoner tree?"

He shook his head, explaining, "They were not companions. Perhaps they would have been if they'd been given more time. All I know is that they loved each other, and I tore them apart."

I placed my hand over his orange flames, cool to the touch. "The Blightress tore them apart, not you. I have only just met you and I see that you love your people. Please do not hold the guilt of something you could not control. Pah-Pah is happy in Felgren, and if there is a way to return Mychael, you'll find it."

He hummed, nodding. "I'm glad you came, Saelyn. Now, let's keep exploring. There's a hidden staircase near the throne room that leads to the guard tower. Care to see if it's still intact?"

~

We walked the castle for a few hours. I could ignore the ache in my feet for a few minutes at a time, but the stairs were killing me. My mother joined us eventually, laughing with the King about their misadventures as children. I didn't complain even once about my shoes, loving the sound of my mother talking about her life.

"Where did my father grow up?" I asked finally. It was a question I'd been longing to know for years, but was too afraid to ask.

My mother perked up in an unexpected happiness. "In the Hallow Marshes." She pointed to the stones on my shoes. "His family mined rhyzolm. The people still do there. It's the only place on the isle where you can find it."

I jabbed my foot forward, pulling the length of my gown up to see. Five green stones adorned the wrapping at my ankle. "Is that why you send lapis conduits there?" I asked, stepping back down on my foot and grimacing at the pain, wondering when it would be appropriate to take them off.

"You're sending lapis conduits to the Hallow Marshes?" my uncle questioned.

She lifted her chin, replying, "Yes. We don't need them. They do."

"Karus," he scolded, "we need *every* conduit."

"There are just a few, Philius. With the war, Revich's people have had very few buyers to sell to. The lapis conduits help find rhyzolm with less danger to themselves. The amount of orphaned children has plummeted in the last decade."

"You didn't run this by the Four—"

"I will not give up on his dream."

"His dream was to allow us to win this war and without all of the—"

"*Don't.*" The lash came with a black glare at her brother. "Don't tell me about what he wanted for all of us. Don't tell me what he would think or say." She shook her head and turned around, headed toward the throne room where the Wieldwryns gathered. "Just don't, Philius."

We watched her storm away in a flood of black skirts and white hair.

"She doesn't like to talk about him much," I offered. "She... struggles sometimes. To keep it all in."

"I see. Her temper doesn't help either. It never really has."

I chuckled. "Now *that* I'm sure I did not get from her."

He rubbed his short black hair. "We can all be thankful for that, Saelyn."

WE ATE A QUIET DINNER IN THE DINING HALL, SURPRISINGLY NOT AS grand as the one I knew in the Fortress. Its walls had once been a midnight blue with a pattern of purple thistle painted along the doorways. Now, the walls were a blackened mess of ash and dust.

Our meal was a simple spread of bread and cheese. Philius

had explained to me how Hyrithia used to be known for its fish, but since the Blightress had spread across the entire east coast down to the boarder of Felgren, they could no longer access the sea.

I ate in silence, listening to the details of the Dimming they planned, needing only a few weeks to gather all their forces to Hyrithia and march into the Blightress's lands, where I would use my power to lure her there.

"Which spell do you think most likely for the Blightress to sense?" Madame Zoreyah asked, tossing a bit of cheese to the giant cat at her feet.

My mother glanced to me, and I waited to hear if she'd tell them about the portal I'd attempted.

"The sun. We'll practice *Simulair Solum* this week. It's the most likely to get her attention."

"What about the aftereffects?" my uncle questioned.

"We don't know if that will happen to Saelyn as well. I will explain tomorrow." My questions were already on my tongue when she rose from her seat, finishing with, "For now, I am exhausted. Saelyn, shall we head to our rooms?"

She held her hand out for me, and I pretended a yawn. "I'd like to say goodnight to Thevin first if that's alright."

"Alright," she agreed, moving toward the doors. "But please have him escort you back into the castle. He will be sleeping out in the tents with the other Runners until the Dimming, so you will not get to see him as much as you're used to."

I wanted to frown and disagree. I would see him. I'd find a way to see him everyday, regardless of her warnings.

Instead, I nodded, plastering a contented smile on my face. She left and I rose, curtsying slightly and excusing myself from the room where my uncle struggled to hold back a grin as he watched me go.

I passed his guardswoman, Renn, in the hall, but she didn't meet my eye, ignoring me completely as she headed to the dining hall behind me. I picked up my pace, hurrying as fast as I could in the high heeled shoes I looked forward to getting rid of.

I passed people in the streets of the city ruins. I lost count at fifty campsites, all of them raised for the soldiers in both armies, some of which would be joining us in the next few days from all over the isle.

Guards stopped me at the warped metal gates that led to the eastern side of the castle walls. Two men, clothed in the black garb of a Runner looked me up and down before one of them asked, "You lost?"

"No," I replied curtly. "I'm going to see someone."

"You've found me," said the other. They both broke into laughter at the jest on my behalf, and I caught the stale stench of bad ale on their breath.

I blew air out of my lips, wishing I was wearing my pants and shirt from the Spire instead of formal clothing that certainly did not belong at the Blight Line. "Thevin," I interrupted. "I'm looking for Thevin, second to Commander Lanna. Please point me in his direction if you would be so kind."

"Wait, wait," the first one said, gesturing to his partner to quiet. "You're Saelyn, aren't you?" He laughed again. "Nym, did you hear that? This is the Baron's daughter. The one Thevin doesn't shut up about." They broke into new laughter, making me rethink what I had told my uncle about my temper.

"If you're not going to help me," I called, "then let me pass so I don't have to speak to you two idiots any longer." I stepped to the side to leave them.

The second blocked my path with his body. "We're just having a laugh, sweetheart. It's been a bit dull around here until you showed up in this." He gestured to my gown with greedy eyes. I had the unsettling urge to hit him across the face—something I'd never once done in my life.

He reached for my arm, but I pulled away just as he said, "Maybe if we lead you to Thevin, you'll think about taking us back to Felgren every summer."

My rage boiled in my blood, and just as I turned to punch the first one in his big nose, he fell to the stone, keeled over and holding his side in pain.

I looked up in surprise as Lanna kicked the other in the back, knocking him into the wall.

"Flynn!" she called with her hands cupped over her mouth. A young man rushed over from the tents that lined the outside gates. When he arrived, the two guards were still down, clutching body parts that I felt hadn't been damaged quite enough yet. "Relieve Nym and Temmor from their duties. I want them digging latrine pits for the rest of the week."

The man she addressed as Temmor cursed loudly, and she bent to his face. "You are so very lucky that conversation did not go any further. You almost sent yourself to Dremstone." She rose and addressed Flynn once more. "Inform their commanders of their leave of duty from the Runners. And tighten up the barrels of ale."

Flynn nodded, calling out to more Runners to help lift them up off the ground. They limped away, Temmor more so as the heel of my shoe had somehow found its way slammed into the top of his boot.

Lanna smirked at me, folding her arms.

"What's Dremstone?" I asked.

"A prison in the Attatok Mountains. There aren't many prisoners there, but enough that everyone knows of it. I'm sorry you had to endure that."

"Thank you for cutting in. I don't think my punch would have been as effective as yours."

She reached out, squeezing my bicep. "I don't know, Sae, I think with some training, you'd have a place in the Runners."

I laughed with her and she jerked her head to the southern side of the city walls. I followed her, adjusting my gait so the thin heels of my shoes didn't sink into the ash covered dirt.

She paused and touched my shoulder. "Just…don't tell Thevin about that if you don't mind. I'd hate to have to officially reprimand him for what he'd do about it."

"Noted," I replied. "How are things going out here?"

"Better now that we have a solidified plan." She stopped, her eyes trailing the long line of tents outside of the city. "I meant what I said at the gathering. If you change your mind—"

"I won't," I assured. "Thank you for sticking up for me in there." I scoffed, rolling my eyes. "And back there."

"You're welcome," she said, but her smile faltered. "I truly hope your father is found and saved from…wherever he is."

"You…you remember him fondly, don't you?"

"Yes. He was always so kind to me, though I'd only met him twice. The last time, he promised to fight monsters in Felgren with me someday."

"Monsters?" I kept at her side as we moved on. "There are no monsters in Felgren."

She shrugged. "He wasn't sure if there were or not. But he spoke of great fae warriors who fought them. Maybe they killed them off—I don't know Felgren history. Even if it was just a story, Baron Revich spoke kindly to me and admired my desire to fight instead of trying to drown it like my mother did. I don't doubt that he left because he felt he had to. And that is worth something in itself, Sae."

I choked down my tears, stopping her and pulling her into an embrace. She didn't laugh or deny me what I believed we both needed and hugged me back.

I swallowed and squeezed her tightly. "It is obvious to me why Thevin has chosen you as such a close friend."

She did laugh at that, replying with a tight squeeze. "And the reason he chose you for a certain role in his life is clear to me as well."

"Did he tell you—" I started, pulling back from her arms.

She held up a hand. "He hasn't said a word. In fact, he refuses to tell me anything, even though I can read him like a book I wrote myself." She shrugged. "His feelings for you are obvious to anyone who gets a glimpse of you two side by side for five seconds."

I grimaced at that, thinking of all the times we'd laughed care-free together, danced together, held hands for no reason other than to just be touching.

She continued, "All I'm saying is that he's been…moody and a bit more…defensive of you since you left Felgren. Don't get me wrong, he talks about you constantly to anyone who will listen, but actually seeing him around you…"—she blew a puff of air from her lips—"it's a whole other thing."

I tilted my head back, wanting to scream my frustrations into the cooling night air. The stars above winked back at me, the moon a hazy green hue from my mother's shield she held all the way to the Blight Line a few hundred feet from us.

"Alright, I've said what I wanted to say about it. C'mon." She pulled me along and I chewed on my lip, my mind a whirl of what exactly I'd say to Thevin tonight and how I'd say it.

She brought me to a dark blue tent with a pattern of thistle hurriedly sewn across its flaps. "Thevin!" she called. "Someone's here to see you!"

He stepped out barefoot, obviously preparing for sleep. An unmistakable joy danced in his pale blue eyes as he reached for me with a wide grin. "Sae! What are you doing all the way out here?"

"Good question," Lanna mumbled and we both glared at her. "Fine, I'm leaving. I'll be right over there in my tent when you're ready to head back to the castle."

"My mother asked for Thevin to bring me back," I said quickly as she stepped away.

I heard her laughter, but she didn't turn around, replying loudly, "Interesting. I wonder why."

"Yes," Thevin started, "she's always like that."

I shrugged, laughing, "I don't mind it so much. I like her."

I shifted on my feet, a sharp pain lancing through the arch of my right foot. Thevin glanced down, then back to my face with one brow raised. Without a word, he knelt, swiftly pulling back the hem of my gown to unbuckle my left shoe around my ankle. My cheeks grew hot and as I reached out to his shoulder for support, I felt his fingers next at my right. He lifted one ankle, sliding the high-heel from my foot, then did the same for the other.

"Better?" he asked, rising from the ground.

"Much," I managed to say, taking the shoes from his hands and holding them to my chest.

I wiggled my toes and he said, "Come in. You'll get filthy out here."

He opened the flap of his tent, and I jumped toward it, skipping over the ashes and onto a purple rug that looked far past its prime.

He poured something into a mug and handed it to me. I took it, sipping gingerly and finding weak but warm chamomile tea. "How are things?" I began, sitting on his cot and patting the space beside me.

He sighed and joined me, taking the mug as I offered the rest to him. "As good as we could expect." He downed the rest and set it back on the small table. "The Runners are celebrating the win tonight with bad ale and high spirits."

"You didn't want to join them?"

"Not this time." He rubbed his face and I resisted the urge to push back the curls that fell into it. He leaned his head on his fist, looking at me. "Are you sure about this whole 'use me as bait' thing?"

I mirrored his pose. "Yes, I'm sure."

"I'm not."

"Why?"

"Because, Sae, you're offering yourself up to the Blightress without really understanding the risks."

"Maybe it doesn't matter what I understand. Maybe what really matters is that this is the best plan we've got, and I'm ready to be a part of this end."

"I'm not ready to offer you up on a silver platter."

"You don't get to decide what platter I lay upon."

"Maybe I should."

"Maybe you're afraid of the possible outcomes, and your fear is talking."

"Maybe one of us should listen to their fear a little more."

"Maybe——"

The ragged snarl of a creature raged outside of the tent. Thevin was on his feet in an instant, reaching for his sword by the opening. "Stay here!" he called and left, racing barefoot into the night.

I opened the flaps and gulped down a blood-curdling scream as a stream of undead muri crawled their way out from under the city walls. There were at least two dozen of them ravaging their way across the line of tents, some still pulling themselves out from the earth caved in under the stone.

A mob of Runners fought, their swords swinging through the air, cutting them down one by one. The sound of battle filled my ears, and I covered them, screaming into the chaos, *"Revertayden en tepiore!"*

"The Runners are celebrating the win tonight with bad ale and high spirits."

I heard Thevin's voice and inhaled sharply, grabbing my head and gritting my teeth at finding myself back in his tent, sitting on his cot. I didn't hesitate, though, rushing to the tent flap and screaming into the night. "Blighted muri! They're coming from there!"

At my scream, several more flaps opened and the guards at the Blight Line rushed forward as the undead beasts began their crawl from under the stones. Thevin pushed me behind him, sword already in hand as he ran forward, slashing through the head of the first one out of the ditch.

"I need a Wieldwryn now!" he shouted, and the call fell down the line, echoing from Runner to Runner until I saw the flash of red skirts from an agricola conduit flying out of a tent and coming to our aid.

I stepped back, wondering if I'd given them enough warning, wondering if I could somehow push myself to go back even further.

The Wieldwryn arrived, just as two more beasts flew through the air, jumping at an impossible distance, but pierced through mid leap by a wall of green vines that sprouted from the earth. The Wieldwryn enclosed the hole beneath the stone wall with more of her brambles, cutting off the path for the rest of them. *"Simulair Solum!"* she screamed, erecting a ball of yellow light and forcing it into the hole. Ash fell all around us as she destroyed the rest of the beasts, cutting the fight short before it had really begun.

I ran to Thevin, who held a hand out, keeping me behind him as we watched the ash settle. The Wieldwryn retracted her wall of thorns and, with Runners at her side, stepped forward, looking down into the pit.

"We're clear!" a Runner shouted, and cheers went up around us. Several soldiers patted each other on the back, dusting ash from their faces and hair.

Thevin backed away from the wide ditch under the stone wall and called to the Runners. "I want every available soldier inspecting the wall around the entire castle. Pair off and take a Wieldwryn with you. You're looking for loose soil that has caved in slightly. Shout if you find one and do not hesitate to cover it."

Calls of "Yes, sir!" followed his command and the soldiers moved out, repeating their orders down the line of tents.

He grabbed my hand, hauling me closer to the cavity where they had come from, peering down. "How did you know?" he whispered harshly.

I stood at the edge, getting a glimpse of leftover ash and what could have lost us good soldiers. "I-I just——"

He sheathed his sword and lifted my chin, forcing me to face him. "Lies. You've been lying since last night when the Blightress came to the Spire. I cannot keep you safe if I don't know how you——"

I heard the crumble of stone before he was done, and without a single moment to release any spell from my lips, I pushed him into the ditch, landing on top of him, and raising my hand above us. A brilliant white light formed in a dome, shielding the pit from the crumpling stones of the caved castle wall. Massive bricks tumbled down like a sea of water, toppling over the shield I held. He gripped my sides hard, attempting to turn me over and cover me with his own body.

I held his sides tightly with my legs, refusing to budge as the last of the bricks fell. Panting, I lowered my hand, though my shield remained, lighting the space enough for me to see his face.

I laughed in submission to my heart, my eyes brimming with tears as I shook my head in disbelief. "I love you," I confessed, upturning my hands and letting them fall back to my sides in defeat.

"Sae," he whispered softly, his grip on my hips tightening. "You don't have to——"

I covered his mouth, leaning over his chest and bracing myself with my other hand. "Shut *up*, Thevin."

His eyes narrowed, but I ignored whatever retort he wanted to say, keeping him quiet for just a moment so I could confess all of it.

"I have loved you since we were fifteen years old. I loved you the year after that and this year after that. And I should have said it then." I shook my head, a single tear falling from my face to my hand still covering his mouth. "I should have told you all of it that day we danced for the first time and you tried to tell me how you felt. I was so stupid, Thevin. You tried to tell me everything, and I was so scared of eventually losing you, I just…"

I huffed another laugh, releasing my hand from his mouth but continuing. "Whatever comes next, whatever we're about to face, I cannot go another moment without you knowing what is in my heart. What your smile does to *me*." I pressed a hand to my chest. "I feel you here as you've always been, and I refuse to lie and pretend like I do not ease with the warmth of you at my side. Like I do not crave your touch or the comfort of your embrace, or wish to be wrapped in your arms where I want to spend all of my time."

I leaned back, straightening over his hips, wiping a hand across my face. "I love you, Thevin, Runner in the Four's Army, Thorn in My Side a Good Quarter of the Time, and Horrible Lumen Rider." I lifted my hands in the air one more time. "I love you because you are brilliant, and funny, and kind. You live like you care more than you ever admit, and I don't want another three seasons without you. I don't want to return to Felgren, waiting for you to come home, waiting for the signs of spring's end so that I can see you again, pretending I don't want to keep you forever."

His eyes paled like a flash of lightning across a dark horizon. He swallowed hard, murmuring low, "You done?"

"Yes."

"Good."

He lifted himself to meet me, taking my face into his hands, and slamming his lips to mine. I wrapped my arms around him, seating myself fully in his lap, pressing my chest to his, my lips roaming his, pushing for his mouth to open so I could taste what I'd been craving since the kiss we shared the night before.

A low grumble came deep from his chest as his hands began to roam down the sides of my body, slowly and agonizing as I felt a tumble of aches deep in my soul. He lit within me a fire I hadn't known was simmering just under the surface of my skin. I urged it forth, ready to burn under his touch, under his fingers as they shifted across my backside, following the length of my thighs, pulling me further onto his lap.

I didn't know much, but I knew he wanted me, and I him, our mouths wandering, our hands exploring in a black pit of earth under fallen stones of an old castle wall.

"Is anyone down there?"

We heard the call, even through my high moans and the sound of our hearts pounding together in one harmonious beat, our breathing sharp and heavy all at once.

He slowed his kiss, one hand leaving the strokes of my legs to cup my cheek. He ran his thumb across my skin, a challenging smile on his lips. "A quarter of the time, huh?"

"At least," I replied, unable to contain my wide grin.

"Hello?" the call came again, followed by another voice which said, "I see magic. There must be a Wieldwryn trapped down there."

"We can't stay here," Thevin said, stealing another soft kiss.

"No," I admitted, kissing him lightly back.

"I didn't say that right." He tilted my chin upwards, breathing over my lips. "I would gladly stay here with you, like this, for as long as you'd let me, but I'm afraid they'll start shoveling these bricks away any moment, and I'd hate for them to see you as I get to…" A lazy smirk crossed his mouth. "Utterly beautiful and lush as this."

A heat, new and exciting, pooled within me—that flame bursting forth again, and I followed the urge to continue, settling my lips back onto his, relishing in his sigh of frustration.

"There! I see two of them!"

He lifted me off his lap in a hurry, his arm wrapped around my waist, pulling me as close to him as we could while voices shouted above us and the view opened up to reveal faces even in the hazy dim of my light. They cleared a path and I let my shield fall, coughing in the dust left from the slide of stone. A hand reached down for me, and I took it, heaving my way out of the hole with Thevin's help pushing me through. We exited coughing, wiping debris from our clothes, Thevin's hand sliding into mine.

"That was good thinking, Miss." One of our saviors nodded toward me. She clapped Thevin on the back and said, "Glad we didn't lose two of our highest ranks in one night."

"Two?" Thevin asked.

"Commander Lanna," she began, "she—"

Thevin didn't wait to hear, running to Lanna's tent with me at his side. He yanked the flap and I gasped at the blood.

"She's not—" I started.

A woman stopped me, bent over Lanna's body on her cot. "No. She is not dead. She has been badly wounded by one of those beasts. Apparently, a few had crept out from under the gates before we heard your call. One of them came here."

Thevin dropped my hand, stepping closer and grimacing at the open gashes on Lanna's leg. A pool of rosy power spread over her body.

"Will she be alright?" he whispered, watching the face of his friend. Her eyes were closed, blood splattered across her cheeks. "Will she walk again?"

"I believe so," the medicus Wieldwryn muttered, continuing her movements.

I swallowed my fear and stepped forward, my heart racing at the gaping torn flesh across her right thigh. The woman's power slowly staunched the blood, mending her tendons and muscle. I turned, ready to heave the contents of my stomach and cry all at once.

I'd been too late.

I couldn't go back and fix this, regardless of how much I wanted to. Too much time had passed.

"Have the Four been informed?" Thevin questioned.

"I don't know. Commander Ashton came to look her over. I assume he'll inform them."

Thevin squeezed Lanna's shoulder once, then turned to me, the passion we'd just shared in my confession now changed to something else on his face. His eyes were a piercing lance, seeking answers to questions I still had the responsibility to tell him.

"I'll be escorting Saelyn back to the castle and return soon. Thank you, Aeytah."

She waved a hand to him in dismissal, focusing on her patient. We left, Thevin grabbing a pair of Lanna's boots and handing them to me as we walked back to his tent. We stepped inside and he was silent for a moment, pulling his ashen feet into one of his boots and then the other.

I followed his movement, wanting nothing more than to rip my gown off in frustration, knowing it was ridiculous attire for the Blight Line. The green hue was nothing more than a dusty gray, and I paled in realizing I was a woman playing dress up in the midst of real war with real consequences for not thinking through my actions.

I should have noticed Lanna was not with us.

I should have ran to her tent first.

Instead, I'd fallen into a hole with Thevin, pouring my heart out and kissing him while she lay torn and bleeding from the undead muri which had crept into her tent.

Thevin rose from his cot, standing tall and stiff in front of me, forcing my head back to see his face. He brushed a thumb across my chin, no doubt wiping away a smear of ash, the same that lined his own skin.

"You've been keeping more from me, Sae. More secrets than that you've loved me since we were fifteen."

I gulped and nodded.

"Why won't you tell me?"

"It could change everything."

"It will not change my feelings for you, if that's what you fear." He pulled my hand from my side, pressing it to his heart. "You cannot change those. I could live my entire life loving you like this, only to beg for a thousand lives more."

I arched my feet, bringing myself up to his lips. I kissed him softly, once, just one more time before I changed both of our lives forever.

I stepped back, leaving space between us which begged to close and stated, "I have been able to reverse time since I was fourteen years old."

His brow furrowed. "Reverse time? How?"

"I…I don't know exactly, but just like with all the other spells I've made, this one works just as well. I can reverse time by one minute, and I need to prove it to you."

He folded his arms across his chest, nodding to me once.

I ignored the shiver that ran through me, ignored the ever-stinging jab of guilt I held about too much meddling with time. I wondered briefly what the Blightress would think of me reversing time twice in one night. "Think of a memory or a thought. One you've kept to yourself and only you know of."

He thought for a moment while I tried to keep track of the seconds that ticked by. He nodded once, confirming he had something in mind.

"Tell me what it is. I will reverse time to the beginning of this conversation and then tell you what you're thinking of."

He gave a grunt of disbelief. "Fine. I was thinking of the moment before I jumped into the Hatchery pool and you were lying in the sun, drying yourself across the white stone. I thought to myself then that I could get through every one of my days, every battle I had left to fight, if it just meant I got to see you at the end of it."

I smiled in my agony, most of me wanting to stay here, to go to him and hold him, promising he would.

I took a deep breath, murmuring, "*Revertayden en tepiore.*"

I blinked, focusing my gaze as Thevin asked, "Reverse time? How?"

I gulped, needing to recreate this conversation as closely to what it had been before. "I don't know exactly, but just like the other spells I've made, this one works just as well." I paused, thinking of what else I'd said. "I can reverse time by one minute and prove it to you."

He again and for the first time, folded his arms across his chest, nodding for me to continue.

"Think of a memory—" I choked for a moment, hoping he'd think of the same thing. "Think of a memory or a thought you've kept to yourself so no one else knows."

I waited for him to confirm he had it with a nod.

I shuffled closer slightly, my voice barely above a whisper. "You're thinking of how you looked down at me drying in the sun at the Hatchery pool."

His eyes narrowed and he tilted his head to the side, but I went on.

"You're thinking about how you thought to yourself that you could get through all of your days, all of your battles left to fight, if you could just see me at the end of them."

Disbelief crossed his face and he shook his head slightly. "You can't know that."

I stepped closer, closing our gap, reaching for his arms tightly flexed across his chest. "I do know that. I know because you told me."

"I've...never admitted that to you."

"You did," I persisted, slipping my hands into his, still tucked across his chest. "We've already started this conversation. I told you I would ask you this question, you'd give me your answer, and I'd reverse time, able to tell you the memory you had chosen."

"You...you've been able to do this for three years?" he asked low, the slightest hint of frustration in his tone.

"Yes."

"Who knows?"

"You."

"Not your mother or Pompeii?"

I shook my head. "I've never told anyone before now."

"The muri," he started, clarity reaching his eyes, "the Blightress...you knew she was coming because you had reversed time. You knew she would come, and you saved us all."

"It took me two tries, but yes. I had to stop what would have happened."

"Lanna..." he trailed, his face tightening.

My lips quivered. "I didn't know or I would have fixed it. I would have gone to her first, but I didn't know and then too much time had passed and there was nothing I could do."

"Hey…" He unfolded his arms, cupping my hands to his chest. "I refuse to believe that was your fault. You've been given this power, but it doesn't mean you will have the chance to fix everything that could happen."

"I would have, though."

"I know." He pulled me to his chest, wrapping his arms tightly around me. "How many times have you done this between the two of us?"

"Just that one," I mumbled, my face pressed fully into his shirt, which somehow still smelled of home.

His body shook in a chuckle. "You've done better than I would have. I think I'd repeat both of your kisses at least a dozen times more before I'd be ready to let go of them."

I tilted my head back and laughed when he caught my lips into another kiss. We swayed for a moment, the only two people in the world.

"I almost did it once. That night we were dancing and you told me how our relationship was changing at a pace we couldn't slow. And then you told me the risk would be worth it, and I almost did it. I almost reversed time to admit that you were right."

"It doesn't matter now," he started, holding my chin.

"It does," I urged. "It matters to me that you understand why. I've always been…afraid to lose those I love. I watched my mother grieve over my father all my life. I've been afraid every moment that I could also succumb to such a fate. That I could one day feel the depths of her sorrow, and so I've held onto everyone I love in a desperate grip, unwilling to change a single part of my life for fear of the risk of losing them."

He listened quietly, stroking my cheek.

I bit my lip and continued, "That day, I told you I didn't want to risk losing you. But by not telling you the truth, I risked losing you anyway, and I won't stand still any longer. I won't wait around, afraid to move for where my steps might lead me."

"I love you, Sae," he said.

I sighed contentedly. "I love you, too."

He cocked a brow. "What about that quarter of the time?"

I lifted my chin, rising on the tips of my toes to meet him in a kiss again, mumbling on his lips, "Shut up and kiss me, Thevin."

## CHAPTER 54

# THEVIN

"Don't look at me like that," Lanna grumbled, leaning one hand against the side of the castle wall with sweat beading down her face, trying to catch her breath.

"As if you'd look at me any different," I muttered.

"I'm fine." Her teeth gritted in pain as she returned weight to her right leg.

I quirked a brow. "If this is you at fine, we're in trouble."

"I have time to regain strength before Commander Ashton's forces arrive, and we push past the Blight Line. I won't recover that strength, however, if I do not keep training."

"Spoken like a stubborn ass," I huffed.

She rolled her eyes and limped toward her tent.

I followed her inside, irritated that her blood was still splattered over everything. "Someone from the castle is coming to get rid of this today." I gestured to the large dark stain on her cot with a cold fear of how close she had been to bleeding out.

"It's fine," she shrugged, gulping water and planting herself over the dried blood. "If anything, it makes the tale that much more heroic. I caught several Runners sneaking in here last night to see the carnage."

I hid my broken knuckles in my pockets and licked my split lip. "Yes, Runners are simply awful at keeping things quiet."

She rose a brow. "It's funny, you know? I saw the condition of Nym and Temmor this morning. I almost couldn't believe that they had gotten into a fight with each other and ended up such a bloody mess." She winked. "Almost."

"Lanna?" Sae's voice sounded from outside the tent. "May I come in?"

With a teasing smirk, Lanna called, "Please do!"

Saelyn lifted the flap and stepped inside saying, "I've brought you some—oh!"

Seeing me there brought a flush to her cheeks, one I certainly hadn't seen on her face when I'd kissed her last night outside of her room until our lips were a puffy, brilliant crimson.

"Good morning," she said lightly, twisting her lips to the side with eyes that sparkled my way.

"Morning," I returned with my own wicked grin on my lips, neither of us bothering to acknowledge Lanna's stifled laughter.

Seeming to remember why she had come, Sae shook her head and swiveled to Lanna. Holding out a basket, she said, "I've brought you some fresh linens. I'm happy to change the ones that are… soiled."

Lanna peeked into the basket, nodding and giving her thanks.

"I also wanted to give you this." She pulled a dagger the size of her palm from between the fresh sheets.

Lanna took it, looking up in surprise. "For me?"

Sae nodded emphatically. "I heard that the hilt of your dagger broke—the one you used to kill the muri that attacked you. Details get around quickly here."

Lanna eyed me. "Indeed they do." She studied the knife further, and I leaned in to admire the hilt, woven in a pattern of ivy, ending in a deep green stone.

Lanna traced the vines with her fingers, tapping the bottom. "Is this…rhyzolm?"

"Yes!" Sae cheered, taking a seat next to her.

I took a decent glance at the long length of her legs in the black pants she wore and did my fair share of thinking about how soft the skin of her neck had felt as I'd kissed it last night.

"My uncle showed me a hidden staircase in the castle. It led to the old castle guards' quarters and I found this. He said I could keep it and that it's a sturdy dagger."

"Truly, it is. Thank you, Sae." She bent forward in a wince to hug her. "I will cherish it."

Sae returned the embrace, laughing, "I'd hope you'd use it!"

"Commander Lanna?"

We turned at the unmistakable voice of Clairannia.

"Aren't I so lucky for such a visit this morning," Lanna mumbled then called, "Come in!"

Clairannia lifted the flap, surprised to see the three of us. "I've come to look at your wound and assess your state for duty."

Lanna huffed, rubbing the side of her leg. "Must I?"

Clairannia held up a jar of something pink. "And I've brought a salve to ease the pain and tightness of your wound."

Lanna tilted her head side to side, deciding, "Alright. That alone is worth it."

Clairannia shifted closer and I held my hand out to Sae. "Shall we? Lanna gets a little cranky if she hasn't stabbed something in the morning."

Sae took my hand, grinning broadly. "I'd say she deserves to be cranky after what she's been through." Then noticing the split of my lip, she lifted her hand to touch it. "What happened to you?"

"He claims he tripped on the way back from escorting you to your rooms last night," Lanna called, now lying back in the bed while Clairannia checked her pulse.

Sae lifted my knuckles up to the light. "And what? You caught yourself on these?"

"It's odd," Clairannia chimed in, "Aeytah complained about similar injuries she healed from two other Runners just this morning. Though their cuts ran deeper, and I believe some broken ribs were involved."

They all looked at me knowingly. Sae even put her hands on her hips.

I finally shrugged. "It sounds to me like this place is a bit hazardous for despicable men."

"Clairannia," Sae huffed, "remind me of the spell to heal a split lip."

"*Sarchio,*" she laughed.

Sae turned back to me, and I did little to suppress my grin, seeing her irritation at what I'd obviously done. I bent forward to murmur, "Is this part of the quarter of the time, then?"

She lifted her finger across my lip, reciting the spell and healing over my skin with her white light. "I'm so glad you can identify these times yourself, so I won't have to point them out to you."

"Oh, I'd still like you to point them out to me. If only to see this look on your face."

"There you go again," she retorted, but I saw the hint of amusement tugging on her mouth.

I hummed low. "I'm starting to wonder if your estimate of only a quarter of the time wasn't—"

"Do you two need a minute or something?" Lanna asked, lying back on her cot while Clairannia's eyes darted between us, her fist at her mouth to stifle her laughter.

"*Sarchio,*" Sae finished over my hands, healing my knuckles back to their tanned coloring.

Before she could pull them away, I took her hands in mine and brought them to my lips, leaving a light kiss on her own knuckles. "I think we've worn out our welcome." I kept my gaze on her, my eyes flickering from hers of deep blue to her parted lips.

"No," Sae started, "I think it's just obvious we do need a minute."

Lanna roared in laughter, calling, "It really is about damn time."

Clairannia rose from the cot, shooing us out of the tent. Hand-in-hand we sprinted back to my own tent where, as soon as the flap was closed, I had my lips on hers. She ran her fingers behind my neck, and up through my hair as I kissed her gently, avoiding falling into the passion we'd shared kissing outside of her rooms the night before. We had neither the time, nor place for anything else.

I delighted in the new sounds she made. Light moans of her

breath caught in her throat as I wrapped my arms around her back and along her sides, pulling her up to me.

"My mother is waiting for me to return for training," she mumbled, breathless between bouts of her bottom lip pulling at mine.

"I should already be back on the field in Lanna's place," I mentioned casually, nipping at her chin in return.

"Then it's best we spend our day as we must." She tilted her head back to look me in the eyes. "But I promise, you will see me again at the end of this day. For all your days."

I chuckled, pulling her in to kiss one more time. "That is a promise I insist you keep."

# CHAPTER 55
# SAELYN

My mother stood in the field of fresh green grass to the west of the castle, and I knew she'd grown it. I could tell it was her work that covered what was once the Blight Line because of the yellow buttercups that bloomed all around, mimicking what I knew was her favorite field of wild flowers in Felgren.

Her back was to me with white hair messily strung into a single braid, playing with the wind. She wore her usual Baron's black skirts and vest with a loose white top. By the deep wrinkles in the fabric, I knew she'd slept in it.

I sat myself in the tall grass, pulling at the base of a blade in search of one wide enough to whistle through. I kept my eye on my mother, training with five Wieldwryns—channelers she'd been working with back home. She had them take turns lighting a bundle of charred sticks on fire, shaped to represent a Blight beast. The flames would ignite for a moment and then the channeler would call the wind to extinguish or spread them to the next dummy, based on their Baron's instructions.

I had seen her train before, though it wasn't something I was invited to, but rather snuck closer to watch. With the Blightress able to feel large eruptions of my power, I understood more of why she wouldn't let me train in Felgren. After all, the Blightress knew where I was kept, but if she didn't know the extent of my abilities, she'd still be in the dark about who I was.

But it was all a farce.

The Blightress did know what I could do. Unlike anyone else I'd ever encountered, she did not forget when I turned back time. She could recall every single one of my uses of that power, and I feared what that meant between us. Perhaps the Blightress was more than just a dark entity on the isle who wanted my power, but a distant part of me I could not escape.

The wind picked up, blowing my hair across my face, and I watched my mother turn to the east at its origin, closing her eyes in a peaceful smile. I listened for my name on the wind as I watched her, but no whisper came as it had done so many times throughout my life.

"Saelyn!" my mother called, realizing I had come to join her.

I swept the grass clippings from my lap and rose, taking her outstretched hand as she brought me to her side, planting a kiss at the top of my black waves.

"Wieldwryns," she said, "move to the eastern wall. Commander Figuerah is there and will practice *Simulair Solum* with you over the Blight Line. Meet for lunch at noon and we will gather more Wieldwryns to practice some healing and lightning spells from there. Good work this morning," she added, grinning broadly at each one.

All five gave mumbles of thanks and agreement, walking together back to the castle, laughing in the morning sun.

"Will you teach me those spells?" I asked, stepping in front of her with my hands clasped behind my back.

"Those and more," she answered. "However, it is tradition that before a channeler enters Viridis, they must first pass a test of power."

"Oops," I chuckled.

"Oops," she returned, laughing with me. "But even though you've spent more time in Viridis than anyone here, I'd still like to challenge you. Just to see what your power is capable of."

She hesitated in the slightest moment, but I caught it having studied all her tells for years. She was feeling that deep sorrow again.

She continued, "What would you say is where your power truly lies? What type of magic calls to you most?"

I took a moment to look south, knowing the tree line of Felgren was miles away, but somehow feeling its presence all the same. "Agricola magic. I used to practice it. Secretly," I added with a rising blush. "Pah-Pah caught me once or twice, but I enjoyed those winter months when I could melt the snow and bring life back to the green leaves of Felgren."

Her smile broadened and she took my hand, guiding me to a certain patch of earth that looked the same as any other. "This used to be the Blight Line," she said with a simple directness. "Just this morning, I returned this blackened field to one of green grass again. This city used to be my home, and I will see it returned so that my daughter may enjoy its delights as I have."

I nodded, taking part of my lower lip between my teeth.

She laughed, though I didn't know why and continued. "I, however, did not heal this soil. I merely planted grass atop what was ash and death, giving it a new chance at life, but not one guaranteed to continue. That's where you come in."

"Me?" I gazed out at the field—acres of land that sprawled across green hills leading down to the crumbled castle walls.

"You, Saelyn. When I was just a few years older than you, I was asked to prove my power, and in attempting to disprove my worth, I instead further fueled my magic. It is not something you will ever be able to hide from." She patted a hand over my heart. "You will feel it here." She pointed to the warm sun, a brilliant glow of the purest light in a cloudless sky. "You will hear it there, a whisper of wind that refuses to deny the power you hold and the depth of magic you wield. When your name is called, hear it for what it is—a promise that you are a child of great power and fate, and your father and I believe in the path you'll choose for your future."

I felt the purest truth of her words about my name on the wind, more so than she could know. "But how can I choose my own path if I am fated for another?"

She drew an arm across my shoulder, pulling me into her side. "You are destined for greatness, Little Love. Of this, I am certain." She leaned in closer to whisper in my ear, "But how you choose to get there is up to you. Times will come when you must decide for those you love. It is not always an easy choice, and you will not make it for only yourself. Everyone you love will be affected, but"—she held up a finger, her smile beautiful, her eyes an emerald green— "the choice is still yours to make, and if there is anyone I believe in, it is you."

"I…" My voice wavered, swept away with the breeze across our faces. I thought of telling her everything. All of me I'd hidden from her, from Pah-Pah. The spells I could create on my own, including the one that had saved us twice now. I thought of telling her of what the Blightress knew, and that every time I had reversed one minute of the present, she had come with me to relive it.

I didn't know what that meant. I didn't understand how it could be possible. But looking into my mother's eyes of leafy green, seeing the crinkle of lines across her face, I only wanted to enjoy her rare company. I wanted to soak in her love, though always given, not always shown.

I cleared my throat and returned her grin. "I'm ready for your challenge, Mama."

"Sit with me." She folded her legs underneath her skirts, tugging me down beside her. "Now lay your hands down like this." She spread her fingers wide atop the deep verdant grass, much darker than what we had at home.

I mimicked her movement, spreading my hands. My conduit ring caught the sun, winking at me over its many facets.

"Close your eyes, Saelyn, and tell me what you feel."

Pressing my hands to the earth, I took a deep breath. The Blight was still here, just under the surface. I knew because I could smell its decay and sense its consuming desire underneath my fingers.

"I feel it. The Blight is under us. Dormant, but…here."

"Destroy it," she whispered, her voice nothing more than a command from a Baron to her channeler.

"I-I don't know how."

A few moments passed, but I kept my eyes closed, my hands pressed into the soil, sinking further, feeling the roots of the grass that ended just on the surface of ashen Blight.

Her voice wavered as she said, "What makes you so powerful, Little Love? Show me what you can do."

I nodded with determination. I nodded without fear, ready to acknowledge the depth of the well of power I held when I had previously only skimmed the surface.

I sent my magic down deep, tendrils of white coursing through the solid ground, maneuvering through the roots of the Blight. The resistance came, as I knew it would, as a push back, a shove away, and a challenge to retreat.

The clear truth was, it was no challenge at all. My power widened, shoved through the ground in a long, deep line that I was ready to push forward, replacing the consuming roots of Blight with what could thrive here in the grasslands north of my home. My mind swirled with visions of life, the speech of magic forming words I could use to bring this land into a new age of growth and beauty, forever changing this landscape to the one I desired.

My mother asked what I could do.

So, I would do it.

"*Cresere en silvam.*" My words, new and comforting on my tongue, spilled forth just as my magic grazed the land. A long, wide wall of white haze draped one hundred feet from each side of my arms stretched out wide. I stood, opening my eyes and taking my first steps forward. My wall came with me, buried deep within the ground while the roots of trees I could name sprouted from where I crossed the hillside.

Faster, I picked up my feet in a run. My magic was not something still, but wild and free, a pursuit of the warmest rays of sun across a forest I loved, and though I knew what grew behind me, I did not stop to look. I did not stop to see my spell come to fruition—

a spell of growing a forest of trees, able to give power to those born to wield it.

My feet carried me across the tall grass, my laughter piercing the air in accompaniment to the groans of thick trunks and sprawling underbrush sprouting from upturned earth behind me.

My mother wanted to know what I could do.

So, I did it.

I grew her a forest.

CHAPTER 56

# THEVIN

She grew a fucking forest.

It wasn't very big—a little over an acre, but the fact that there now lay what looked like a cutout of Felgren in the grasslands of Hyrithia caused an understandable stir in the ranks of Runners and Wieldwryns.

"She has more power than the Baron."

"She has more power than the damn Blightress!"

I leaned against the wall of the castle, listening in on the conversations without joining them.

"What does this mean?"

"I say it means we have a fighting chance."

"I say it means we'd better not piss her off."

I huffed a quiet laugh.

"Maybe she can return all the land taken from us. Maybe she's truly the one who can fight the Blightress and win."

"If she did this in minutes, imagine what she could do in hours —days. She should be at the Blight Line right now, shoving it back. It's time we show our strength."

"We don't have all our forces."

"Just look at that! We don't even need them!"

"Thevin, what do you think? You know her best."

I cut my stare from the line of trees to focus on the three Runners still gaping as I did at the miniature forest. "I think I understand better why the Blightress has sought Saelyn since she was born."

"But do you feel like we have a real chance now?" Flynn asked with a light in his eyes.

I nodded, pulling myself off the wall, headed into the new forest. "Hold onto hope!" I called behind me.

"Defy the dark!" the Runners returned in a rowdy cheer.

It smelled like Felgren.

It felt like Felgren—the tallest trees that reached the base of the sky, the ferns and bushes—even small paths were woven through the underbrush as if the forest floor had been trailed countless times by countless feet.

When I'd heard what had grown on the other side of the castle wall, I'd known exactly who it had come from. My duty to take over some of Lanna's tasks while she rested forced me to stay away, though I tempted myself a dozen times to forgo those responsibilities and see it for myself.

As the sun began its dip to the horizon, I had finally been able to excuse myself and the other Runners to race across the city ruins to see the forest which had grown from nothing.

When rumors were confirmed it was Saelyn, daughter of the Baron of Felgren, who had grown such a thing, even more whispers arose about the Dimming and how successful we'd be in our final push into the east.

Trekking deeper into the wood, I allowed myself to imagine this was Felgren and I was off to meet Sae at the little shelter we'd built beneath the grove of maple trees. I pictured one of the many summers we'd met there, sharing plans for the next day, laughing at something Pompeii had said or a new guessing game I'd learned, telling her nothing about my life shadowed by battles and war.

All I'd ever wanted, before I understood that I loved her, was to live my days in Felgren. But now, I could not distinguish if that was because Felgren was home or she was.

"Looking for me?"

Her voice called somewhere to my right. I scanned the trees, finding her sitting beneath one, sketching shapes in the dirt with a narrow pointy stick.

I left the path, careful through the bushes and ferns, doing what I could to keep the new life undisturbed. I sat down across from her, bending my legs so they encompassed hers. Gesturing above us, I asked, "This your work?"

Her laugh flew free and she tossed her stick, scooting closer, shifting her legs underneath mine. She grabbed the front of my shirt, pressing her cheek to my chest, and I folded my arms around her.

"What's everyone saying?"

"Nothing much, just that we're all saved now that we have you with us."

Her head rose to see my face. "I just wanted to show my mother what I could do. I didn't actually know it would be this until…until I did it."

I made a point to look around, nodding and admiring the thick trees and curling ivy. "I could live here."

She snorted, snuggling back into my shirt, saying, "You could not."

"No, really," I insisted. "If you made it, I'll cherish it. If you want to spend your days growing your own damn forest, I'll build us a home in it. Right there,"—I gently turned her chin, pointing across the line of trees to a tiny clearing—"can't you see it? A little cottage, just big enough for the two of us so we don't have to host any guests."

She laughed again, wrapping her arms around my neck as I continued. "You and me, Sae. We'll spend our days working the land, building a garden and a life. You'll travel into the city on occasion to do your magical miracles, and I'll fix up our home, dinner on the table when you return."

"Hmm, and what of the people who'd try to settle nearby?"

"I'll chase 'em off with a broom."

Her cackle of laughter shook her chest and with it, I couldn't help myself, finding her lips with my own, stealing her kisses to save for the worst times yet to come.

"You wouldn't miss it?" she asked, trailing kisses over my cheek. "The life of a Runner, I've discovered, is quite a thrilling one."

"No," I swept my hand across her hair, tilting her face. "No, I wouldn't miss any of it. I do what is asked of me because it is what I can do. It's this life,"—I nodded to the clearing where I'd painted a future for us—"that I'd miss if it never comes to be. And it doesn't have to be here. I would build a future with you wherever you want to take us. I am forever at your call. Where you go, I go."

Tears glistened in her eyes and she nodded. "I want this future, too. No matter what we have left to face, I will get us to that life."

I pressed my forehead to hers. "Promise?"

"Promise."

# CHAPTER 57
# SAELYN

A few more days passed in the same rhythm. Runners trained with their swords and Wieldwryns trained with their magic. I fit somewhere in between, often finding myself taking my breaks in Thevin's tent where we kissed, and touched, and held each other until duty forced us to leave, our lips puffy and red, an obvious tale to tell for anyone who cared to look.

My mother noticed, but never said a word. And Figuerah, whom I was starting to really like, lifted my left wrist just once, checking for the curved *l* inked there after I'd been gone a particularly long time, only to come back more disheveled than usual.

But Thevin and I hadn't ventured down that path yet, and though my thoughts often wandered to what it would be like, we had agreed to wait until the Dimming was over, and we could focus on the growing passion between us.

For now, we had dreams of our future set, ready to begin our lives together as soon as all of this was over.

I had told him about the Blightress moving back in time with me, and he had agreed that meant we should not underestimate my connection to her. We agreed that I should not respond if she tried to speak through my mind again.

Commander Ashton's forces arrived by the fifth day, a few days ahead of schedule, and he brought his sister, Commander Allyanna, with him.

Where my mother had been met with cold anger from Ashton and Allyanna, it was Commander Geyrand's widow who greeted her with warmth and friendship. I had been at the dinner when she arrived, dressed in the palest pink and ruffled skirts I'd ever seen. She had a full curvy figure and a friendliness that radiated around her.

She had hugged my mother for a long while, saying something in her ear which brought tears to both of their eyes before she joined us with her two children, whom I guessed looked more like their father than her.

More tents and more food had to be brought in for the growing army and more than a few times, I had overheard the new Runners discussing the odd forest that had grown to the west of the castle.

I used my spell to blend into the crowd more often than not when I was getting around, wishing to move unnoticed by the very people who were fighting a war that began over me.

My mother could not escape their glances and whispers, however, as the truth spread of the other Baron trapped for seventeen years in the Blightress's lands. Weary looks and sometimes downright glares crossed their faces as if by leaving Felgren and admitting where my father had been, she was not to be trusted.

Lanna healed slowly and my guilt at not saving her from such an injury, whether deserved or not, left me talking to her often and checking on her progress.

While we waited a few days more for Figuerah's companion, Nyeimah, to bring some Wieldwryns from the Attatok Mountains, I overheard my mother and Lanna speaking in harsh, but hushed tones.

"You know I am needed here," Lanna lashed.

I began to back away from their private meeting, deciding to share the fresh apples I'd found from a tree in my forest another time. But my mother's next words stopped me.

"I know you, Lanna. You would not abandon your mother like this. She needs you at her side."

Lanna huffed. "She will die within the week whether I am there or not."

"You will regret it the rest of your days if you are not with her when her soul departs. Both of my mothers are dead, and I did not get to hold their hands as their breath left them. I am telling you this as someone who cares for you. I would not wish for you to regret this."

Lanna paused a moment and I peeked slightly around the corner of the tent where they spoke. "You don't even like her," she mumbled, crossing her arms and shifting her weight to her left leg.

"That doesn't mean she deserves to be alone at the end." My mother reached out to squeeze her hand. "Go, Lanna. I will hold off the Dimming until you are ready to return to us. Not a soul will think your absence unjustified. We can wait a little longer for you to say goodbye."

"Alright," Lanna sighed. "I'll leave tonight and send word when I'm ready to return via your portal." Another long pause. "Thank you, Karus."

My mother walked away and I began to backtrack when I heard Lanna call, "You can come out now, Sae."

Heat flared across my cheeks and neck as I stepped forward from behind the tent, apologizing profusely that I had not meant to eavesdrop.

She shrugged, thanking me for the bright red apple, biting into the skin and saying, "I would have told you anyway. Your mother's right. I would regret not being there at my mother's death."

"I'm sorry that her life is ending."

"I wish she could have heard that we saved your father and the isle. She has always meant well for me, even if it didn't appear so."

"You'll leave for the Spire by portal tonight?"

"Yes. I'll ensure my commandment is settled with Thevin before I go. I'll admit I wouldn't mind a swim or two in the Hatchery to stretch my legs before I return."

"Do you swim there often?"

"Every morning I can."

"Then I wish you a peaceful time away. I have the strangest feeling that you are not needed here right now, but somewhere else entirely."

She laughed, slapping me on the back and leading the way to the training pasture. "How very cryptic of you, Sae. Perhaps you're right."

~

IT WAS LATER THAT EVENING WHEN A SMALL GROUP OF SOLDIERS watched her go. My mother's green portal flickered like firelight and the rest of the Four bid her farewell, asking to relay their wishes for a peaceful rest for her mother, the Lady Lamoral.

Thevin held my hand as he approached for their goodbye. "Go play Lady of the Spire for a bit and then get right back here," he said, letting go of my hand to hug his friend.

Chuckling, she squeezed him tightly, forcing a grunt from his chest. She stood back, gripping his forearms as he gripped hers. "Don't start any new wars without me."

He laughed. "Why do I feel like I'm the one who needs to say that to you?"

"Because it's true," she shrugged.

"Well, old friend, I insist you find some peace while you are gone. You need it, and you deserve it."

"Then peace I shall find. Though I don't think you can call me old. I'm barely seven years older than you."

"Practically ancient." Thevin winked and brought her in for another hug, this time squeezing her to a gasping grunt.

I moved to hug her goodbye next and she murmured in my ear, "Thank you for loving him back."

"Actually," I informed her, "I loved him first."

She hummed and turned, walking with a limp to the portal where she gave her final wave and stepped back to the Spire.

~

THE SIMULATION OF THE SUN WAS HEAVY.

My mother had warned me of its weight along with a truth I did not know; the spell had taken all the chestnut brown from her hair, leaving it a shadeless white. Therefore, I knew the risk when I'd first tried the spell. I also knew that she had never been able to break it without someone helping her—usually by forcing her to the ground before she was lost to it.

She had never told me the whole story of how she had lost seven years of her life to the aftermath of the spell the first time she'd tried to carry it on her own, and I didn't pry. Just as all of her life history, I'd listen when she was ready.

So, though the sun was heavy, it did not affect me in the same way. I had grown it, held its weight, and closed the spell with relative ease, and my mother was proud.

She beamed across the training pasture, watching her daughter build the sun over and over until I was so exhausted, I collapsed onto Thevin's cot for an hour at the end of each training.

She, Clairannia, and Figuerah were training the whole lot of us younger Wieldwryns, teaching spells of fire, lightning, and wind—anything that could harm the Blightress's creatures and the Blight itself.

A few days in, I received my official Wieldwryn pin. I had admired the red flower pinned to the vests and shirts of all the Wieldwryns, but hadn't yet studied them up close. I affixed the red flower to my shirt, admiring the garnets and black obsidian stones.

"It's so detailed! You said Ilyenna makes these?" I asked my mother a fortnight after we had arrived at the Hyrithian ruins.

"Mm-hmm. I asked her for this design to mark the Wieldwryns, and this is what she came up with. She is a very talented lapis conduit."

"Why this flower?"

"In honor of an old friend."

I watched her carefully. We were walking through my acre of woods, our orbs of green and white light hanging above our heads to brighten the way in the dark. "Someone you lost in the war?"

"Yes. A fae of Felgren. Her name was Moira and she was there with me through my darkest times until her life was taken long before she was due to leave this world."

"I'm sorry," I said quietly. "Was this flower her favorite?"

She nodded, adding, "Demorte. She would mix the petals into a concoction to paint my lips red. It was and still is very rare for humans and fae to interact, but Moira was…an extraordinary creature. I miss her dearly."

A hardened cold settled over my skin, and I folded my arms at my chest, rubbing my sides. A howl interrupted the silence and we both looked south, reminded of the lumens we'd left behind. "I wish I could have known her. I wish I could have known what life was like before I became the cause of all this."

"You are not the cause of all of this." She swept a hand down my hair. "You have done nothing but bring joy and love to all the lives of the people you meet. The Blightress does not understand love. This war is her doing and hers alone."

I waited a moment, wondering if I was ready to hear the answer to what I'd wanted to ask next. "Do you think this will work? The Dimming, I mean. Are we ready to face her?"

"Yes." She didn't hesitate. Not even a moment of doubt sounded from her voice.

"Alright then." I leaned into her shoulder and she put her arm around me. "Let's end this and bring my father home."

The Lady Lamoral was dead, and Lanna was missing.

Word was received three days later of the Lady of the Spire's passing, followed the next day by a letter from the Viceroy, explaining that no one had seen Lanna since her usual morning swim in the Hatchery. She was to report back to the Blight Line that afternoon.

I tried not to worry and tried harder to convince Thevin that they would find her and ease his own panic. The Four and commanders were gathered in the throne room, myself included in the conversation because of my role to play in the upcoming Dimming.

It had been planned that upon Lanna's arrival back to the Blight Line, we would descend upon the Blightress's lands, beginning our trek to the east and then north. There, I would use as much of my power as I could manage through the *Simulair Solum* spell and, hopefully, lure the Blightress to us. But with news spreading of Lanna's sudden disappearance, unrest began to flood through the soldiers in distant whispers and colder nights coming from the Blight Line. Our armies were at unease as the Dimming loomed ahead.

"We said we'd wait for her, so we should wait." Thevin, who usually remained silent and reserved at any gatherings, had been persistent and vocal in this one.

My uncle replied, "Our soldiers are restless. There's only so much training we can do before we must attempt this end once and for all." The Handless King's words were difficult to hear, but true, and Thevin knew it.

"Lanna has trained all her life for this." Thevin insisted, stepping further into the circle where we all stood. "We cannot just give up on her after one day. She wouldn't miss this for anything."

"Exactly," Madame Zoreyah stepped in. "Which means something more sinister is at play here. We cannot afford to waste more time than we already have gathering all of our forces. I motion we move into ranks tomorrow and leave for the Dimming the following day."

"So that's it?" Thevin scoffed. "You're all just willing to let this go? She is a missing Runner Commander and now officially one of the Four. What more could she be before you look for her?"

My mother chimed in, "We are looking for her. I spoke to the Viceroy directly today as soon as I heard. They are sending all the guards they can manage to find the heir to the Spire. We need to let them do this their own way. And Zoreyah is right. We cannot wait for long." Her mouth set into a frown. "I move to send our forces through the Blight Line in two days hence."

"Second," Zoreyah added.

They all looked to King Philius. He lowered his head as Thevin stared at him across the open space. "Third."

"It is done then," the Madame said, turning to the rest of the commandment. "Send word through your ranks. Gather needed provisions and begin packing up the camp. We leave at dawn the day after next."

A murmur filtered through the hall, and Thevin turned in a silent calm I knew was just a cover at the surface.

I shouted his name, rushing to get through the crowd and reach him.

A gruff voice behind me said, "Let him walk it off. It's what he usually does."

I spun around, recognizing the Runner I'd met on my first day at the city ruins.

He sheathed the dagger he was using to clean his fingernails and smirked. "Figured you'd know that by now."

"Mavryn, right?" I asked, remembering his name, but deciding to irritate him anyway.

His olive skin had darkened while training in the sun, and his dark eyes glinted as he stepped closer in a casual gait while the room cleared.

I didn't fear him.

I didn't fear losing whatever bullshit game he wanted to play, either.

"And you are Saelyn. Our Savior. The Daughter of the Great Baron of Felgren. The girl who has come to end the war she stepped her dainty toes into at the last hour."

My temper flared. I had no patience for this. "Think what you want. You can go back to whatever life you had before in two days, and I'll never have to lay eyes on you again."

His arm shot out to grab me as I turned to leave, and he pulled me to the shadowy corner of the hall. I hadn't realized how quickly it had emptied, and I dug my nails into his hand as hard as I could, yanking it from my shirt.

"Never touch me again," I spat.

"Good point. Your lover might pay me a visit and break some of my bones, too."

I flicked my hand between us, a raging white flame held above my palm, scalding to anything but my own skin. "I can fight my own battles, if you care to see. Don't speak to me again."

I spun in a huff, storming across the empty hall.

"I had no life before this war!" he called. His deep voice echoed throughout the empty throne room, stopping me in my tracks.

I refused to turn, but he continued, "I'm just a year older than you. This is the life I've known. I had parents—once. Once a long time ago, I had a sister, too."

I heard his steps echo, moving toward me, as the truth of his words held me still, forcing me to listen. He was at my back, this time murmuring low, ensuring I heard each word that seeped from his mouth like an illness I couldn't escape.

"Each one of them was murdered on the Blight Line. Not even the power my sister held could save her life and make her into one of those abominations they call trees." He leaned even closer, his face at my ear. "And you want to know something else, precious Saelyn of Felgren?"

I gritted my teeth and turned, my glare one of a fury I knew he recognized because he laughed in my face, his hand flying quickly to the curve of my neck, pressing a thumb into my skin, hard enough to bruise. "Thevin must be a better man than me because I would have fucked you and turned you over to the Blightress the minute I was through to be done with this war."

An inky black wave of power wrapped lazily around his throat, his mouth, trapping his arms to his side. He was held in a tight grip, all of him covered except his eyes.

His eyes I kept to see, to understand at what point he'd gone too far. At whatever point he'd tripped the darkness inside of me, emerging from the tips of my fingers in waves, squeezing, pressing on his chest, lifting him into the air.

I only wanted to hurt him, to watch him writhing in pain. I heard the crack of his ribs with the crack of my ring and glanced down to see the large stone fracture in lines of more black, more trails of darkness.

*"He doesn't deserve to live, Little One."*

I agreed.

Or did I?

I blinked rapidly, my breath caught at the man I had hanging from a dark power I didn't recognize as my own. Blood, bright against the dark wisps of my power, ran down his chin and his eyes bulged in red.

I dropped him, rushing back until I tripped on my own boots, falling to the mosaic floor in a pattern of dark thistle.

He didn't move.

I didn't move.

Only my breath broke the silence as it came rapidly from my chest along with the hard swallow at my throat, dry and sore.

*"Do him a favor. End his life because, as he said, he has none."*

"Go away," I whispered with tears running hot and free down my cheeks.

*"If he lives, I look forward to making a corpse of him first."*

"Go away!" I screamed, shouting into the growing dark.

"Sae?" Thevin's voice cleared my head, and I turned on the floor, crying with relief.

He was at my side seconds later, holding me close. "What happened? Who is that?"

I stole a glance at the body of the man I wasn't sure still breathed and said, "Mavryn. I-I didn't mean to! I don't know how I—"

He pulled me back against his chest, warm and safe, a place I probably didn't deserve to be but would stay in until he forced me away.

"I'm going to look, Sae. I'm not leaving you. I'm just going to see."

I clung to his shirt harder, but he gently pried my hand from him, rising off the floor to inspect the body.

I hadn't meant to play this game, and the blood that pooled around his head told me I had either won or lost.

"He's alive," Thevin called. "Come here. I need you to stop the bleeding."

My lips trembled, but I rose, stepping toward the man I'd almost murdered in cold blood because he said something so foul, I snapped.

"Right here," Thevin urged. "Close this gash."

"*Sarchio*," I whispered, my teeth chattering in a cold I felt to my bones.

The wound slowly closed, my magic returning to the hazy white I'd known all my life.

Thevin pressed his fingers to Mavryn's pulse. "He'll live, Sae. You didn't kill him."

I let out a pathetic sob of relief, my nails digging into Thevin's arm. "We have to tell my mother," I said, still staring at the pool of blood trailing through the grooved lines of the tiled floor.

He nodded. "We have to tell one of the Four. It doesn't have to be your mother. There's no one else high enough in rank to dismiss him and do so quietly."

"He'll be dismissed?" I asked, bleary eyed, my thoughts swimming.

"What did he do?"

I sobered at Thevin's tone.

"He was angry. He blamed me for the loss of his parents and sister."

"Did he touch you?"

"Does it matter?" I scoffed, "Look at him! I almost killed a man, Thevin! I don't even remember snapping." I gulped again, my throat scratchy as I said, "My magic turned black and…and I heard her speaking in my head again."

He shook his head with eyes of cold steel. "It matters. Did he touch you?"

"He-he grabbed me and pushed me to the shadows."

"But that's not what made you do this," he said low, rising and glancing toward the hall doors. "What caused this, Sae? What turned your power black and called the Blightress to your mind?"

"I-I don't…remember."

"Lie." He reached down for my hand and pulled me swiftly to my feet, catching my waist and lifting my chin. "I will not harm him further. Tell me what he said to you."

"He said"—a tear ran hot down my cheek—"he said you're a better man than him. And that he would have…he would have fucked me, and then turned me over to her when he was done."

Thevin blinked slowly, his jaw feathering in the force I knew he placed upon it. He moved his hand to catch the second tear falling in the trail of the last. "He deserved what you gave him and more. Let's find your mother and be rid of this."

"No," I stopped him as he tried to leave. "My uncle. He can help us. I don't want my mother to…I don't want to burden her with this or know the Blightress spoke to me again. She's barely hanging on as it is, and I don't know what this could do."

"Alright. The Handless King it is. But tell me you will agree to his judgement. Whatever he proposes as punishment for Mavryn will happen unhindered."

I nodded, taking his hand.

We left the hall, finding our way out to the foyer and taking the main staircase that led to the royal quarters.

I let Thevin do most of the talking.

My uncle listened, glancing at me in concern occasionally and following us back down to the empty throne room.

Mavryn stirred and was heaving himself up to a sitting position, gripping the side of his head.

"You are forthwith stripped of duty in the Runner's army," my uncle called, waving an orange flamed hand toward him. "At full dark, you will walk into the Blight Line where we leave you to your fate, or you will be escorted to Dremstone where you will spend the next two years working the mines."

Mavryn spit blood onto the tiled floor, tilting his head back against the wall. "And her punishment for the thousands of lives she has ended?" He laughed bitterly, adding, "Hiding away in her forest while good people were shattered beyond recognition? What judgment do you place on your niece, wise king? Or should I ask what judgement you place on your sister?"

An orange spark knocked his face back, sending him sidelong on the floor. He lifted himself in another laugh of malice, spitting more blood that pooled from his lip.

"You have a death wish, it seems," my uncle spat, glaring down at the man who had been a Runner just minutes ago, now nothing more than dead or a prisoner.

"You are all fools," Mavryn chuckled, wiping at his bloody face. "We've fought this war for nothing." He pointed a finger at me. I saw the tremble in his hand as he continued. "That fucking bitch should have been knifed in her mother's belly, and this never would've—"

The dagger flew straight and true, slicing through his black shirt, piercing the left side of his chest. I gasped, grabbing Thevin's arm still outstretched, his aim unmatched and deadly.

Mavryn slumped over in silence, no more than a corpse as if the Blightress had predicted he would be before long. The crimson pool flowed quickly, joining the blood already spilled from this man.

I turned to my uncle first, swiftly taking a step in front of Thevin as if I could protect him from any damning repercussions of killing in cold blood. "He wanted to die! You heard how he spoke, uncle, please don't. Thevin was only trying to protect me."

"I'm not going to punish Thevin, Saelyn."

I dropped my shoulders, but still stood in front of him as if I could take any of my love's blows for myself.

The King stared over my head, watching Thevin. "I'm going to get rid of this body, and we're never speaking of this again."

I felt Thevin's hands at my waist, attempting to push me behind him, but I wouldn't budge. I planted my boots solidly on the floor, ignoring his insistent tugs.

A glowing cage of orange light flickered over what was left of Mavryn, enveloping the corpse in a shield of flame. We said nothing as all three of us watched the swirling power radiating from the King, burning fast and hot.

Thevin wrapped his arm around my waist, pulling me toward him as the fire receded, and all that was left of the Runner was a pile of dark ash across the ruined tile of the castle floor.

# CHAPTER 58
# THEVIN

I killed a man.

The worst kind of man.

It didn't matter that he seemed to want to die, I'd given him that end without hesitation.

I stared up at the pale blue stone that made Saelyn's ceiling in the castle ruins, one hand tucked behind my head, one wrapped around her as she still slept on my chest. Dawn wasn't far away based on the dim light of the room she'd been given to use, next to the Baron's.

King Philius had forced us to leave as soon as the body had burned. He had ushered us up to Sae's room, saying food would be sent, and we were not to leave until he retrieved us in the morning. I didn't know what excuse he'd made, but based on the dark circles under Sae's eyes and the bruise forming at the base of her neck, I didn't resist his orders, knowing a quiet rest would be good for us both.

We hadn't discussed it. We'd taken a few bites of mutton and fell into bed, both of us asleep within minutes of lying together, holding onto one another as if we'd never get to do this again.

I'd slept next to Sae before, but never like this, where I could feel her breathe.

I didn't know how the rise and fall of a chest could be so exquisite, but there it was in her. She slept on her stomach, one arm draped across me, one sprawled through the white sheets. Her black hair spilled over me in beautiful waves of a tangled mess, and I took a minute just to pretend. Pretend this was our cottage in the woods. Pretend there was a leak in the thatch I'd need to fix that morning, and that the potatoes were ready for harvest. Pretend we had planned a walk through the woods to gather mushrooms, and I'd gather bread and cheese and a blanket so we could picnic. Then I'd lay her down on a soft bed of grass somewhere, loving her as I'm sure we were meant to do.

It was the future I imagined for us. It was the future I wasn't sure we'd ever see.

Tomorrow we'd descend into the Blight Line, and Sae would be used to lure the Blightress to our forces and the Wieldwryns would act.

As with most things in my time as a Runner, I didn't want to do it.

With just one word from her, I'd run away, find Lanna, and leave all of this. We were young. We were born into this fight we didn't deserve to have to see.

I'd killed a man.

The worst kind of man, but still, I had taken a life.

I let that settle with me as I felt the tears fall down my face. I knew I would kill him all over again, but there it was, the hardest point to face.

I lived my life as a Runner in the Four's army.

I'd been trained to kill since I was fifteen.

Four years later, I'd done it.

What would another four years bring to my life?

I swallowed back the ever-present lump in my throat, careful not to wake her.

It didn't matter anymore.

Whatever fight came next, I wouldn't let her face it alone.

# CHAPTER 59
# SAELYN

Even the rising sun could not shine on the Blight.

The rays beamed over the endless black, but did not seem to touch its surface.

Not an ounce of light could filter to the depth of what lay east over the land.

A desolate silence beheld us—the entire army of Runners and Wieldwryns.

My mother and Thevin had argued for him to be at my side the entire way through the Dimming and they'd won out, eventually earning the support of my uncle as well.

Other commanders were chosen to lead the front line of Runners, all four-hundred fifty-six of them.

The Wieldwryns in their varying colors of vests were just above two hundred, and our three leaders in my mother, uncle, and Madame of the Mountains were standing at the tip of the Blight Line, waiting for the call of their commanders that their troops were ready to embark forward.

Thevin and I were a few rows back, listening to the shouts of confirmation. He held my hand tightly in his, dressed in Runner black, ready to blend into the landscape if he needed to. I wore my black pants and boots, but my mother had dressed me in a green flowing tunic to honor where I'd come from and what we were fighting for.

A howl broke the silence, echoing across the vast landscape, and I wondered if it was an omen of good or if it signaled our doom.

The command came from my mother, not in voice, but in the glowing sun she set before her, quickly matched by the King and Madame Zoreyah. The hiss began, immediate and eerie, as the Blight Line moved, forced back by the power which destroyed it.

The forward march began and we walked through the ash at our feet. The line of Runners widened, spanning into a semi circle around our leaders, swords drawn, ready for the inevitable defenses of the Blightress's creatures.

None came.

We continued on for a mile.

Two.

The Wieldwryns were given the signal and more simulated suns appeared in the wake of ash as the Blight continued to fall away in hardly more than a whisper of demise.

Despite the warmth of the many suns surrounding us, my teeth chattered.

Thevin gripped my hand with force, scanning all sides of us in constant surveillance.

I watched my mother. Or at least, I watched her sun.

I was too far back in the line to see more than an occasional glimpse of her white braid, but her sun I knew. It was the largest of them all, burning ahead, directing a path forward.

The plan had been to fight.

The plan had been to destroy as many Blight beasts and trees as we could before I would be given the signal to produce the sun, hopefully leading the Blightress right to us when she realized I was within her grasp, no longer protected by my mother's shield of power over the city ruins.

But the fight never came, and as the Wieldwryns slowly trickled out of power and word was sent down the line to rest, we stopped, the Runners wrapping everyone else in a tight circle, eyes open and swords at the ready for any sign of movement.

My mother made her way to the inner circle where I stood with Thevin.

"What do we do?" I asked her at first sight.

"We continue forward after a short rest," she answered, then addressed Thevin. "Your promise still stands?"

He nodded once. "Where she goes, I go."

"Good. Here," she held a skein of water to me. "Carry this with you for now. I need to speak with Clairannia and Figuerah."

Muttering my thanks, I took a long swig, handing it to Thevin before looping the tie on the end to my belt. Another howl arose and all of us tensed, scanning the wasteland of ash, partial Blight lying in wait to be destroyed.

"Something's wrong," I warned.

"What do you feel?" Thevin asked, tensing at my words.

Before I could answer, the cry boomed across the army with a call to close into tight formation. I heard *Blight beast* echoed across the lines, and I spun around, looking for the creatures which would surely be upon us soon.

I glanced up to the sky, clouded in gray, waiting for my signal to begin the spell. I was to look for a single flair of green above us, as if my mother would begin her shield. It was all to be a farce to urge the Blightress to act quickly and begin her attempt to take me.

The moment she appeared, my mother would feel her presence and call the Wieldwryns to her aid, forming a chain of Cosensian Magic which could allow them to siphon their power to her, enhancing the sleeping spell and suspending the Blightress into a sleep-like state.

We also had my power to reverse time if need be.

Thevin and I had discussed how best to use it, knowing the Blightress would expect it of me if plans went awry.

Another howl erupted and I finally caught a glimpse of the beast, rampaging through the ashes behind us, a great mass of black with silver eyes.

"Boros?" I called softly, unheard over the calls to hold the line.

My loyal friend pounded over the earth, something calling him all the way out here from Felgren to protect me. The same realization hit my mother as she called to hold the attack while I screamed to let him through.

From what felt like nowhere, true Blight beasts emerged from the ashes behind us, hundreds of them forming over the ground, endless vines of black shaping in twisted limbs of beastial claws and teeth that emerged from their elongated snouts of thorns.

"Reform the line!" I heard my uncle shout, the command echoing as we turned our back on the Blight yet to be demolished.

I could no longer see my lumen through the sprouting Blight beasts, prowling closer to the Runners in a slow, careful gait of predators assessing their prey.

The crack of tree limbs came next to the sides of the line as great creatures of bone-snapping jaws roared, swiping across the sea of Runners at our sides, sending them flying across the Blight.

"Steady back!" I heard over the screams of soldiers and the sound of the attack we knew would come. The Blight beasts launched forward, ripping and tearing into our front line. The command for the Wieldwryns' suns came next as the battlefield lit in the brilliance of hundreds of channelers and conduits syncing together to take down the threat that had finally come for us.

My mother's signal came in a flash of green brilliance, blinding me for a moment before I rose my hands above my head and screamed into the battle, *"Simulair Solum!"*

Reaching up to the sky to hold my sun, I saw the abyssal black portal, lying in wait behind us as our army retreated back toward the Blight's edge. Thevin saw it too, calling down the line at the danger as several at a time, soldiers fell into the illusory wall of mist, slipping into the portal the Blightress had formed to be rid of them.

A root shot through the earth behind my boot, and I yelped, falling backward. Before Thevin could right me again by his hand, I landed hard, my breath leaving my lungs completely. My sun fizzled out and just as Thevin bent to pull me back up and I drew in another breath to reverse time, wet roots shot from the earth, pinning my arms and legs. Several roots of Blight spread over my mouth, silencing me completely.

My eyes grew wide as I struggled and Thevin shouted my name, flicking a dagger from his baldric, slicing at the vines around my face.

The Blightress's power only dug deeper, pulling my entire body slowly into the earth. Shouts raged above me as Thevin pushed soldiers out of the way so they wouldn't trample my head and render me unconscious. The Blight over my mouth squeezed tighter and no matter how many he cut away, more Blighted roots wound over what remained.

My mind whirled in a panic, and I strained my eyes downward, hoping Thevin would understand my movements.

He caught on quickly, focusing instead on releasing my arms from my sides. With one precise swipe of his blade, my arms were free and he started on my legs as I formed my hands in the the long, circular shape I'd seen my mother do before she wielded a portal.

It hovered wide above me, not in the shape of my body, but in an ever-changing formation of white, hazy light. I reached for it with one hand, digging at the roots over my mouth with the other. I didn't know where it led—all I knew was that I needed to get through or I'd be consumed into the earth below, buried completely as the battle raged above me.

A boot knocked into the side of my head and the world faded in and out with screams and snarls, the snap of branches and the smell of burning. My hands fell limp to my sides as my own blood trickled into my eyes. Thevin's rage was a clear anchor in the screams of war. The last moment I stayed conscious for was the rip and slice of root, violently torn from my face before I was pulled to Thevin's chest and jumped with him into an oblivion of white.

❧

THE SILENCE WAS COLD.

It filled me in a thick chill that coursed through my veins, slowing my blood, and catching my breath.

I blinked slowly to see white, spread as far as my eyes could see, blanketed with drops of blood.

I lifted my head from something hard, understanding that though it was freezing, something was keeping me warm.

Black fur, matted and full of briars with frozen ends spread under me and a familiar whine sounded quietly in the stillness.

"Boros?" I muttered, blinking more, rising more.

Blood rushed to my head, and I felt for the gash. Frayed black fabric covered the wound, staunching the flow of blood.

My black lumen licked my arm as I sat up completely, finding that I had been nestled into his long coat of fur.

We were alone and I began to panic, memories rushing to me of what we had left behind.

I could only guess the portal worked, and I had delivered us somewhere else entirely—a land of endless white snow with black trees that rose spindly and emaciated into the gray sky, pulsing in various colors.

I searched the layer of snow for footprints, finding them leading away from us. I rushed to my feet, stumbling and gripping the back of Boros to steady me.

"Where's Thevin?" I asked and he whined again, offering his back to me.

I pulled myself up, weak and dizzy, and he trudged forward with layers of snow meeting the top of his legs. We followed the footprints, cresting a hill to find a figure in black standing atop.

"Thevin!" I called, and he turned, his shirt ripped and his cheek bloodied.

His eyes grew wide and he raced to us, calling my name as I tumbled off Boros, struggling to rise to my feet.

His arms wrapped around me tightly, and he puffed into my hair, his fingers pressed hard to my scalp as he squeezed me to his chest. "I was only gone a few minutes, Sae. I'm sorry you woke up alone."

I buried my face further into his shirt. "I wasn't alone."

I heard his sigh of relief and felt it under my cheek. He kissed the top of my head and pulled me back, eyeing my wound.

"Is it bad?" I asked, lifting a hand to touch where he'd bound it with cloth from his own shirt.

"You'll survive," he replied, peeking under the bandage.

"I think I can heal it." I opened my mouth to begin the spell of mending, but his hand shot forth, covering it.

"The Blightress doesn't know where you are. You portaled us here and any magic you use now could lead her right to us."

I frowned, taking his hand from my mouth and nodding. "Have you seen any of the others?"

His brow furrowed and he cupped my cheek. "Can you walk?"

I nodded and he helped me to my feet with Boros nudging under my rear to lift me. "Did he come through my portal, too? I didn't know I'd be able to bring more than one through. My mother can't do that."

"No, he found us over an hour later."

"An hour?" I cried.

He gave a short nod and grabbed my waist, helping me reach the very top of the hill.

A vast wilderness of white lay below, more trees blackened to mere husks of wood jutting through the snow like jagged teeth rotted and broken, but faint with varying glows of color.

A dome of blue caught my eye across the valley, and I leaned forward, squinting in disbelief.

The swirl of azure power covered what seemed to be a dark hole leading underground.

"Could that be…" I trailed, thinking of my father's magic and what I knew of it.

"I think you brought us to your father, Sae," Thevin began, then pointed across the land to a distant base of the hill to our left. A small party trekked through the snow, led by a woman in easily identifiable black skirts and vest. "And your mother has come to save him."

# CHAPTER 60
# THEVIN

**B**aron Karus was easy to spot. I counted at least a dozen Runners with her, dressed all in black and failing to blend in with the white landscape that should have been Blight covering the land. The rest of the party, around a dozen more, I could not identify except for the glowing hands of the King.

He trudged through the four feet of snow behind her and together they left a wake for the others to follow.

"We have to get down there," Sae said with chattering teeth.

I truly did not want to.

I had spent the last hour in a panic—no magic, no blankets, no way to tell if Sae would wake, no way to heal her wound that had spilled her blood all over this cursed snow.

If I'd been given the power of Felgren, we'd be gone by now, for I would have waved my arms every which way in an attempt to create a portal to lead us back home.

If I'd been given the chance to change our future with magic, I'd have wrapped her in a spell of warmth instead of holding her as close to my own body as I could, begging whatever forces would listen to keep her warm enough and keep her alive in this desolate, broken wasteland.

Whatever or whomever it was who watched over us, my pleading through frozen tears had been answered. Boros had found his way to us and through his mass and heavy fur, he'd been able to keep the blue from her lips better than I could.

I took Sae's hand at the top of the hill and helped her onto his back, jumping on behind her. I wrapped an arm around her stomach and bent us forward to shelter her from the bitter chill of this damned winter landscape. The Runners spotted us of course, silently signaling down the line at the black spot moving down the hill.

The Baron did not use her power to melt our way, and I suspected it was for the same reason I had advised Sae not to use hers. Baron Karus hesitated for only a moment as she pushed through the snow with her hands tucked under her arms. Her white hair had clumped into frozen crystals. She didn't call out. She didn't wave or gesture at seeing her daughter ride a lumen down the hill. Instead, she held Sae's gaze, her typically black eyes turning a piercing green. Her teeth chattered, but she continued on toward the swirling blue that rose a few feet from the layers of snow.

We caught up to the back line of Runners and Wieldwryns.

"What happened?" I asked Aeytah, noticing the long scratches down her ripped medicus skirts.

"They were o-on us so fast," she said through her teeth. "Before we realized…half the f-forces fell into the Blightress's black portal behind us. We didn't find them."

I hopped down from Boros and gestured to her torn skirts. "May I?"

She nodded, her entire body shaking. I ripped the top layer of her skirts, splattered in flecks of blood, and wrapped the fabric around her tightly as a makeshift cloak.

She stuttered her thanks and I continued my questioning. "How did you end up here?"

"The Baron called us to her portals. Sh-She could only make so many. She said if Saelyn was lost to the Blightress, our only hope would b-be to get to Baron Revich for help." She pulled her improvised cloak tighter. "Her portals landed us half a mile back."

"What happened to the Runners and Wieldwryns who didn't make it into one of her portals?" Sae asked.

Aeytah shook her head solemnly.

"Boros," Sae called, "get to my mother. Hurry."

She tightened her legs on his back, and I reached out a hand to stop him. "I'm coming, too."

Sae called to her mother as we neared the front of the line.

She didn't turn. She didn't even look back, but King Philius did.

His eyes were a golden blaze of light—fury and desperation across his features. "There's no reasoning with her!" he called. "She's doing this with or without our help."

Baron Karus reached the edge of the swirling blue dome, digging around her legs to see the ground. Sae urged Boros further before jumping off his back, forcing her way through the long line of people, frozen and huddled as closely together as they could manage for warmth. I followed, holding onto her belt as she made her way to her mother.

My future was in front of me, and I wasn't letting go.

# CHAPTER 61
# SAELYN

Reaching my mother's side, I wrapped my frozen arms around her waist. She held her hands up to the blue shield that flickered in thin patterns of swirls across its surface.

Without a word to me, she clutched my hands folded around her hip and pressed her forehead against the power my father wielded.

"Please, Rev," she whispered, her breath leaving her lungs in a puffy cloud of white. "Let me in."

Emerald light flowed from her fingers, easing in a languid haze across my father's blue, becoming something muted and teal, folding over and over again until her hand fell through. An opening, just her size, formed within the shield.

Her breath shuttered, and I gasped at the comforting warmth that welcomed us, instantly melting the ice crystals on our hair and clothes.

She finally looked at me with eyes wide and green, glassy from the few simple tears that fell down her cheeks. "I told you we'd save him." Her grin was wide, her cheeks blooming from pale white to a strawberry red. "Your father is here, Saelyn, and he's waiting to meet you."

I pursed my lips and nodded, my chin shaking, my breath short as my mother took my hand and stepped forward onto a rocky shelf, lowering herself down into a hole and finding the step below. She reached up for me, helping me follow her inside while Thevin slipped down right behind me. I felt the hand of him at my back, gripping the belt across my waist as if he wouldn't dare tempt fate and let me out of his grasp.

My mother didn't hesitate or stop to help anyone behind us, instead beginning our descent down the jagged stairs carved from rock. Her long fingers wound tightly through mine, and I had to watch my step, keeping close to the cavern wall. When I'd felt I found my footing, I let myself observe the place my father had hidden himself for seventeen years of his life, waiting for the time to be right, waiting for my mother to find him with an army at her back.

The cavern was vast, a shelter of black hewn rock, sharp and wet, dimly lit by the opening to the surface above us. A single glow of red let off a slow pulse at the bottom of the cave, too far down and too far toward the back for me to make out any figures.

It was the warmth that gave me hope. It blew freely all around, encompassing the three of us as we carefully made our way down the stairs. The heat was comforting, staggering even, as we neared the bottom, each wave of it pulsing along with the red light.

My mother jumped the last few steps, letting go of my hand and picking up her skirts, racing across the black stone without falter. She called my father's name over and over until her voice broke in a raspy cry that shifted off the rock through the dark. My heart splintered hearing the desperation in her last call before she reached the light, falling to the ground in sobs to destroy the silence.

Thevin took my hand and we ran. He caught me twice before I could fall, the glow growing closer and closer.

I realized what it was quickly enough, recognizing the shape of a human heart from the medicus books in Viridis. As large as a lumen's head, it pulsed, suspended off the rocky floor next to a man who sat, leaning against a short rock wall.

I stopped, suddenly afraid to move closer. Afraid to see what so many years alone had done to my father who had loved me enough to leave me.

My mother draped herself over him, sobbing and murmuring words over and over again. He lifted a trembling hand to her face, and I wanted to know why he didn't hold her. I wanted to demand that he take her into his arms and cry in joy that his companion had returned to his side to save him. I opened my mouth to scream, suddenly overtaken with anger at what she had been through to get to this moment.

The words would not come.

I stepped closer in rising dread, my footfall deafening to my ears, my blood pulsing now in a wicked urging to keep moving, keep getting closer to the truth of what had happened to my father while I lived my life in Felgren, blissfully unaware of his condition.

"Sae," Thevin warned softly.

I knew why.

A thin line of blood dripped from the side of the beating heart, flowing across the dark rock, directly to my father's withered hand, emaciated, but open, as if welcoming this lifeforce into his body.

Closer to the pulse, I felt the strain in my own chest, as if the small cut of her heart wounded me as well. I rubbed my chest in the ache, watching a bead of crimson slide down the flesh, falling to the ground in a splash and finding its way to his outstretched hand. My nostrils flared and my breath shuddered.

This was the heart of the Blightress.

And this was my father, draining it, wrapping it in the warmth I recognized was a melding of a simulated sun and love, allowing her blood into his body where it had sunken his skin, keeping him alive, but unable to keep him fed.

Drip.

Drip.

Drip.

I watched in inescapable trepidation as he blinked slowly, his eyes a familiar blue as he gazed into my mother's with the ghost of a smile.

His words were barely audible, but I caught them, spoken in a breathless rasp to my mother. "I can no longer see. But I held on to hear your voice one last time, my love, my beloved Karus."

She held his withered hand to her cheek, whispering something I couldn't understand. In those moments of seeing my father for the first time in my life, I knew they'd be his last.

"No," I whispered.

Thevin squeezed my hand, trying to pull me away, to pull me to his chest so I didn't have to see my father's body, already more corpse than life, lying across from the wounded heart of the woman who was responsible for all of this.

Like a sliver, the Blightress had festered her way into our lives since before I was born and here we were, at the end of the line, the end of the story, no happy returns, no easy whisk back to Felgren where my mother could love my father. Where I could love him, too. He had waited for us all this time. And now, he would die.

Shouting sounded somewhere behind me, but I didn't care to look. I didn't care to turn and face whatever tragedy was next for us, only able to stare as my mother sobbed, her words ringing in clarity, her voice hard as she held my father's face in her hands.

"YOU CANNOT LEAVE ME!" she screamed, even as his hand went limp at his side, falling back to the hard stone in a slap.

Drip.

Screams.

Drip.

Boom.

My name was called somewhere next to me, time moving slowly, as Thevin slid behind me, pressing on my back to face whatever terror he'd seen.

I stepped closer, unfolding my hand from his, following my boots across the rocks, only hearing my mother's pleas.

"You *cannot* go, Revich. You must come home. You must come back and see your daughter." She rubbed his cheek, stained with her stream of tears. "I've done what you asked of me, so you must come home now. You breathe, I breathe. You live, I live! This is our fucking lifeline! Our lifeline, damn you!" She pressed her forehead to his and his eyes fluttered closed as she whispered, "Do not go where I cannot follow."

Drip.

Flame.

Drip.

Clash.

She pressed her lips to his, holding his lifeless face in her hands. In the softest, broken words, she murmured amidst his last breath, "*I love you still.*"

The last words my mother would ever speak to the man she loved settled into my skin like a fatal wound across my heart.

My father was dead.

My mother's cry was anguish.

This broken woman—my mother, my kind, loving mother who did what she could for me. My mother, the bearer of the power of Baron, leading forces, training magic wielders, building an army to withstand the power of the Blightress and keep me safe my seventeen years from all of it. Every memory I held, every joy, and pain, and loneliness I'd felt, I'd done in the safety of her glow—an endless green across the borders of the forest which fueled us.

Her cries did not stop, did not ease, nor did the pain that ripped through my body as I watched my parents somehow love each other to the point of becoming broken things, forced into this path by the one power in this world who could have stopped it.

The Blightress could have ended all of this years ago. She could have ended her pursuit of me, of my mother, of whatever fury she'd waged across the isle, forcing her darkness into the earth and across the lives of many, killing, stealing, syphoning more power, more magic as her heart dwindled in this cave, weakened by my father set out to save us from the wrath she wielded.

Drip.

Bellow.

Drip.

Push.

I was shoved to the ground, shielded by Thevin's body from the rocks that flew through the air, crashing across the stone.

I lifted my head to see my mother kiss my father once, one single last time, her hands shaking as she rose from the ground, gazing upon his broken body.

I felt Thevin's heaving chest as he continued to cover me as a human shield, a man not born to the power of Felgren, but born to the gift of protection for those he loved.

My mother's face turned to rage as she spoke low in the din of battle, facing a force of power I could sense, but could not see.

"IT IS MINE TO WIELD!" she screamed. "GIVE IT TO ME NOW!"

I saw him then.

A man, or the shape of one, sitting beside my father in a ghostly form, staring up at my mother with hatred in his hazel eyes. His lip fell into a snarl and something oozed from his fingers, black and solid, folding across my mother's figure as she held her hands out before her, accepting the darkness into her skin.

His eyes flickered to me then, and I caught his stare.

I knew him. Somehow, I knew him.

"*I tried, Saelyn,*" he whispered through my mind. "*Your time has come.*" A wash of sorrow pooled over his face. He nodded once before fading into nothing more than a whisper of black smoke.

Thevin was yelling, but all I heard was the drip.

The heart continued to beat, continued to live, wounded, but strong enough to stay aloft, the slice at its side slowly closing, healing over as if my father's death meant its awaited salvation.

Drip.

Sae.

Drip.

No.

I watched the last bead of crimson splash into the puddle of blood at my father's side. Confused, I wondered where the black vines had come from as they tore through the rocky floor, upheaving the basalt and creeping across the ground around us.

I blinked at my mother as she stepped toward us. She looked at me once. Just one time with eyes fully black, dark pools of wrath that I knew were her own seeping from the rocks below her. I felt in my heart that the Felgren green of her power would never return, her soul too broken, too much asked of her to endure since the day of my birth and my father's leaving.

She stepped around us, black slicked over her hands in billowing oil, sliding down her skirts to her boots. She left a trail of ink in her wake, and I twisted under Thevin to see the chaos of battle behind me.

The Blightress reigned midway up the rocky stairs, her hair of white a mirror to my mother's, both of their robes black, both of them waging war and hatred, neither conceding to the other's demands. Neither of them ever would. This war would rage eternal.

The Blight was vicious—sharp thorns jutting from the thick woody trunks as they burst from the ground, growing tall and separating the soldiers who had followed us. They fought them off with swords and magic while Blight beasts ravaged through the maze, taking the few soldiers we had down quickly with unrelenting rage.

Two portals from my mother appeared beside us, black and flickering at the edges. Thevin had not retreated from covering my body on the ground, but added to the commands given by my uncle who lit a third of the Blight on fire. The torrent of vines fell to ash as three simulated suns lit the cave, causing even more of the Blight to fall.

"Sae!" Thevin shook me, rousing me from my daze. "We have to go! Your mother has ordered us out!"

I looked at the portals of black, understanding where they led.

Those portals led to a future of running.

A life of hiding—doing everything we could to escape the Blightress as she took her final steps to consume all of the isle for herself.

In moments of great suffering comes great clarity.

In moments of my name whispered on the wind, in a night of birthday check lists, and summers of running through the fields of Felgren with the friend I'd come to love.

And in those moments, I understood what I had to let go.

It was my turn to risk, my turn to deny the future I saw laid bare before me where everything stayed the same.

I was seventeen, and I'd been given great power.

The time had come to wield it.

Thevin hauled me from the ground, never letting me go, never wavering in his protection, choosing me over his duty as Runner to stay and fight.

"I can fix this!" I shouted.

The crackle of fire and death echoed around us.

"I can fix this!"

He shook my shoulders, pressing his hands to my face. "There's nothing you can do! We need to leave!"

He pulled me closer to the portals, and I dug my heels in to the slippery rock. "I need to get to the Blightress!" I called, ducking as shards of stone flew over our heads. "Please, Thevin! Help me!"

"No!" he screamed, urging me further. "I won't let her take you!"

"Please!" I took his face in my hands and kissed him hard. "I just need to take her hand, and I can fix this," I urged. "I need your help. We need Boros. *Please*, Thevin. This is me, fulfilling my promise to you." He jerked his head as if to deny me again, but I held onto his face, pressing the pads of my fingers to his cheeks, stroking the left side where his dimple would appear in every one of his smiles for me. "The life we want is ours, and I need you to believe I can get us there. I need you to believe in me."

His lips trembled and a cry left his chest. "I can't let you go," he shuddered, gripping me tightly, his voice broken in a repetitive, "I can't. I can't let you go."

I pressed my forehead to his, feeling my own tears slide down my cheeks. "I can show her. I can show her all of what she has done, and I can keep my promise to you, Thevin, please." I kissed him again. "Let me fix this."

His countenance shattered and he held my head so tightly as he pressed his lips to mine in a kiss goodbye. A kiss to tell me that if he believed in anything, he believed in me. He turned through his tears, calling to Boros who fought a Blight beast, snarling and ripping at its throat in one tear of branches that sprayed black blood through the air.

My loyal lumen heard the call and came, leaping over and under the Blight still winding its way along the walls.

We jumped on his back, and I leaned forward, whispering in his ear, "Get me to her, my friend. You're going to have to leap as high as you can."

He bolted toward the stairs, and I took in the battle in all of its finality—the last stand of the Four's army against the Blightress of Wrath.

Of Hatred and Rage.

Of a bloody heart that had been wrapped in the warmth of love my father held for me and my mother for seventeen years, draining her of her power, but keeping him alive.

The Baron of Felgren was unrecognizable.

My mother changed into something I'd imagine in a nightmare, ripping the head from a Blight beast's body, flicking her hand toward a thick vine of Blight only for it to snap, oozing a black puss and writhing on the ground.

Darkness surrounded her as she gazed up at the Blightress on the rocky stairs, who grinned with lips of a blood-red crimson.

Boros narrowly avoided a vine that burst underneath us, and he leapt over the swiping branch of an enormous blackened tree, its maw cracking under its cry of ire at our escape.

We closed in toward the staircase, passing bodies and upright Runners and Wieldwryns alike. Thevin slashed through branches and vines at our sides, ignoring the cuts on his arms and face from the sharp thorns that ravaged his skin. We passed my uncle as he dove over his guardswoman, Renn, shielding her body from the withered branches of the Blight tree swiping at them.

My mother rose from the ground, lifted by pulsing black trees, dripping with more of the black viscous substance that trailed from her hands. Fruit the size of plums grew and burst one after another, the flesh splatting to the wet rocky floor, only to sink down into the stone, emerging in saplings that rapidly grew into more of her own Blight trees.

"You could have been this all along, Little Sprout." The

Blightress's voice rang through the screams and snarls, hitting its mark.

My mother screamed in rage. The haunting black of her hands shot forth as she continued to rise from the ground, the name *Blightress* now earned by both of these women, set in a course of never-ending war.

*I can fix this.*

"I will make you suffer!" my mother snarled. "I cannot kill you, but I can bury you so far beneath the earth, not even your rot can reach you!"

*I can fix this.*

A grin of malice crept across the Blightress's face. "Then I will take you with me, daughter."

All at once, they summoned all of their power. Black trails of magic wrapped around my mother as wet trails of black sludge knocked the Blightress to the edge of the stone stairs, her body covered with the thick substance.

"*Look at me*," I called to the Blightress in my mind, finding her there in a thin, weak thread I could not pull too tightly for fear of severance.

Her eyes of many colors flashed my way as she scrambled, trying to regain her footing with the weight of my mother's seeping power forcing her to the ground.

Boros leapt again, flying through the air as we neared. The Blightress shifted her gaze and with a sweep of her magic, pulled my mother down from the abominations she'd produced with her own dark power.

The Blightress gritted her teeth and swept her hand at her legs, forcing the ooze from her gown, splattering it against the rocky wall.

"*It's over, Little One,*" she returned, pushing from the stair to rise again.

"*Give me your hand,*" I urged. "*Channel your power to me, and I will show you.*"

Time slowed, Boros leapt, bounding off a thick vine, ignoring the thorns raised across its surface. Thevin's words of love, of believing in me, came slow and sure as he kissed my head and grabbed my waist, lifting me further toward the Blightress.

My mother's scream of panic pierced the slow of time as she saw me reach high into the air, the Blightress's face easing into something serene. Her long fingers, tipped in sharp, black nails, reached down toward me as her question came without hinderance.

*"Show me what, Daughter of Felgren?"*

With Thevin's last shove, I flew from Boros's back, my hand reaching for hers, my fingers sliding over her open palm, grasping her hand as I answered, *"The life you've given me."*

Her fingers wrapped around my wrist as mine did hers, and I felt the speed of time quicken, my body beginning to fall and Thevin's scream matching my mother's as I said under my breath, *"Revertayden en tepiore."*

# CHAPTER 62

# SAELYN

## I WAS SEVENTEEN AND EMPTY

A flash of white blended into the soft glow of lanterns hanging across the trees of Felgren, decorated with brilliant colors of paper banners strung between them.

*"You've brought us back in time. To Felgren."*

I shuddered at her voice beside me.

The Blightress stood on solid ground, though she wasn't solid at all. I looked down at our joined hands, our skin blurred, my own tanned from summer sun, hers a pale white.

I brought my focus back to the clearing. The decorations were familiar. I'd made them and hung them not long before this day, weeks ago.

I took a deep breath watching my past self in a birthday dress of cerulean velvet, rising from Pah-Pah's side and heading straight through the crowd of people dancing. At the same time, Thevin left his tree, crossing the crowd towards me. We met in the middle and picked up the slow dance together.

I glanced around. No one noticed us.

No one knew we had ever been here.

I returned to her in my mind, *"I need you to see all of it. I need you to know about my life."*

*"So you've brought us here. To this day. Why?"*

Thevin and I had stopped dancing though the music still played. His mournful smile hadn't fooled me then, and it didn't fool me now.

*"This is the day I turned seventeen. The same day my mother told me my father was still alive. Do you see that man I'm dancing with?"* I pointed across the clearing.

She squinted and smirked. *"I recognize him. I've seen him in battle before, Little One."*

*"I love him."*

In silence, she turned away from the scene of Pah-Pah interrupting the dance to tell me to climb to the tallest tower to speak with my mother.

I nodded. *"I do. I loved him many years before this night. I love him now. But I cannot love him in the future you've given us. We cannot live the life we want because you've made it so."*

*"If this is what you wished to show me with that power you've been given, you've wasted it. Such love is a foolish thing."*

*"There's more,"* I pressed. *"We need to keep going. Give me more of your power to go back further."*

*"I see no reason to. I have you and shall not let go. Let us return to our time and be done with this."*

I gripped her hand tighter, solid to my touch. *"No."*

The tilt of her head frightened me, reminded me that this was an ancient woman full of a power I could not fathom.

*"I see your mother's defiance lives in you as well."* Her blood red lips turned to a frown. *"End the spell. Return us and I will leave with you."* She nodded to Thevin in the crowd as a clap of thunder rolled and my past self stepped around him to leave. *"I will keep your lover alive if you truly wish it."*

*"Say my name,"* I urged, watching my newly seventeen self bend her head low, following Pah-Pah back to the Fortress.

*"Why?"*

*"It's what will take us back,"* I said hurriedly.

Her eyes narrowed, but she followed my command, my name

leaving her lips and floating on the billowing storm in a whisper on the wind.

# CHAPTER 63
# SAELYN
## I WAS SEVENTEEN AND LOVED TO DANCE

"You pick one of these, and then you fit it in here like this."

My room in the Fortress flashed, and I held onto the Blightress tightly.

Her frown deepened as she looked around the room, both of us no more than dim shadows in the back of it.

My past self snapped the tube for the cylindrical turner into place and continued, "When it reaches a stop, you let go and listen!"

Thevin spun me around to the music. I had missed the joy on Thevin's face the first time, too willing to ignore the possibility that he had fallen in love with me.

"*That did not take us back,*" the Blightress spat, but continued to watch what unfolded before us.

"*I will not take us back until you have seen what I need you to see.*"

"*I am channeling my power to you. I can end this without your permission.*"

"*Please,*" I begged, "*please watch my life with me. It's the only thing I ask of you. We'll return and you'll win your war, but please know what you have done first.*"

"Ask me," Thevin said.

"Ask you what?" I had questioned with a blush across my cheeks.

"Ask me what I'm thinking."

"My dear friend, Thevin, what are you thinking about this very moment?"

"How beautiful you are."

Just as it had before, his answer struck me hard. This time, instead of fear for what I felt I could not risk, I was filled with fear of what the future held if I did not do this properly. I understood now who had spoken all those whispers of my name my entire life, and the time had come for me to use my power to convince the Blightress to help me reach the future the isle deserved to live.

She observed in silence.

Thevin and I argued.

He confessed what my smile did to him. What he knew brewed between us and what we could not deny.

He'd been right. All along he'd done the right thing to admit his love for me, and I'd just stood there, unwilling to push myself forward and take what I wanted.

"*You denied him,*" she started. "*You said you loved him years before this, so why not admit your feelings here? What risk do you speak of?*"

Thevin backed away, leaning against the door frame as the young woman I was just stood there, letting him go. "I don't know, Sae. The risk feels worth it to me."

"*I was afraid of losing him. I feared he would tire of me and leave me. My life has been lived in fear of losing those I love.*" I gulped, watching myself stare after him, the tines of the music clicking at the song's end. "*There's more. Say my name.*"

"*Saelyn,*" she murmured, and we left my room, leaving my past self alone completely in a flash of white.

# CHAPTER 64
# SAELYN
## I WOULD BE SEVENTEEN IN ONE DAY AND FRETTED OVER THE SILLIEST THINGS

We appeared back in Felgren at the same clearing where my party would commence.

I had been fretting, anxious that day for the party to be perfect. It would be the first party held in Felgren for the last seventeen years.

The Blightress watched Thevin and I hanging decorations across the trees. She saw us laugh, observed how I chastised him, resulting in Thevin's feigned offense. Even now, looking back at my life, I saw it.

He and I cared deeply for each other, and I hadn't understood until now just how obvious we had been.

"*You were in his company often,*" the Blightress mused as Thevin and my past self bantered while hanging lanterns.

"*He has been important in my life.*" I shivered, adding quietly, "*One of the only things I could depend on.*"

She frowned at me. "*And your mother? Where is she in this?*"

I shook my head. "*You won't see much of her in my past.*" I nodded to where Pah-Pah had come to greet us, offering lunch. "*You kept my parents apart for seventeen years. My mother struggled every day of her life. Why don't you see that?*"

"*It wasn't I who forced your father to leave, Saelyn. He left of his own will.*"

"*You gave him no other option.*"

She hissed, gripping my hand tightly. "*You do not understand what your father cost me the night he left. You do not know how I mourned you. How I mourned your mother. By the end of this, I assure you, you will.*" Black pooled from our joined hands. "*Saelyn,*" she shouted, and this time, before we flashed away, I watched myself look up into the trees. I remembered wondering who was haunting me.

And holding the hand of my ghost, now I knew.

# CHAPTER 65
# SAELYN
## I WOULD BE SEVENTEEN IN SEVEN DAYS, AND I GLARED AT THE CHECKLIST I'D WRITTEN

ack in my room, the Blightress flicked her hand from mine, crossing to the other side of my bed. Her spectral form stood behind my past self sitting at my desk, trying to fill the checklist of tasks to be completed before the party. I'd been stuck on the invitations, hesitating sending them because I still had not told my mother what I had planned.

"*Your mother told you of the night of your birth?*" she asked, tracing a ghostly hand down my hair at the desk.

I stepped further into my room. "*And of some…events that led up to it.*"

"*Events?*" she cackled. "*Such as what? That your parents came to that cave to kill me? That I murdered my sister to regain the power I'd given her? That I had grown the heart I'd ripped out of my chest years before into something that fueled me?*" Anger flashed through her eyes. "*You speak of the life I have given you, and yet, you do not know the life we could have had together.*"

I heard my mother's knock, and I moved out of the way as she came inside, passing through me slightly.

"*You are not my mother,*" I replied softly, watching the woman who was as she told my past self that she already knew about the party. I had rushed to her from the desk, so grateful she wasn't angry.

"*I could have been,*" the Blightress replied just as softly.

"Do you know just how much you are loved?" my mother had asked me.

"*I could have been* her *mother. I should have had her to hold like this.*" She gazed longingly as my mother and I embraced. I remembered the moment as a happy one.

The Blightress reached out her hand for me to take, but I watched in the mirror, gazing upon my past self who rushed to the desk, excited to show off her colored banners. She looked up to see me in the mirror's reflection.

She looked into my sorrowful face in the mirror.

I did not think this was working.

I did not see a change of heart from the Blightress.

Suddenly, the Blightress came into focus in the mirror, taking my hand, and my past self startled before the Blightress called my name. "*Saelyn.*"

# CHAPTER 66
# SAELYN

## I WOULD BE SEVENTEEN IN TWO WEEKS, AND I WAS CONVINCED I WAS THE MOST HIDEOUS CREATURE ON THE ISLE

"*Viridis,*" the Blightress lilted, stepping away from me again, scanning the courtyard and halls of the garden library.

My past self mumbled her way through a thick book, searching for the spell she needed to rid her face of the bright red blemish on her chin, just hours away from seeing Thevin again.

"*I've always loved it here,*" I replied, joining her at the balcony. "*I felt less alone in this place. The tall trees, the books, the birds…*" We watched as a dozen sky-blue birds flew across the great glass dome above. "*I used to sleep here. On nights when I waited for my best friend to return in the summer, I pushed these benches together to make a bed.*" I inhaled the familiar air. "*Viridis never let me down. Viridis never looked away because of who I looked like. Viridis never disappointed me or avoided looking in my eyes because my eyes were his.*"

She turned her head to look. The smallest hint of an upturned tilt to her lips emerged as she replied, "*You may have your father's features, but I see your mother in your spirit.*"

We heard my past self behind us in an excited squeal as the spell she'd found cleared her face.

"*Why her?*" I questioned, reaching for her hand on the rail. "*Why did you choose Karus to give your power to?*"

She stilled in her surveillance of the tops of the birch trees, dancing in their endless sway to a phantom breeze. *"I...felt her. When she was growing, I felt Karus in her mother's womb. Just as I had felt my own daughter all those centuries before."*

I swallowed my fear, asking quietly, *"You loved your daughter?"*

She squeezed my hand, her black nails pressing into my skin hard enough to leave marks. *"I would have done anything for my daughter. I tried to give my own life and cut her from my womb when it was clear one of us had to die."*

My past self rose to leave Viridis and I stated, *"You loved my mother, too."*

*"I still love your mother, Saelyn."*

With the whisper of my name, the light flashed and we left the day like any other, leaving myself behind, alone to my thoughts in Viridis.

# CHAPTER 67
# SAELYN
## I WAS ALMOST SEVENTEEN, AND I LIVED FOR VIRIDIS

"You're like a father to me, Pah-Pah."

"*The Overseer?*" the Blightress asked, raising a brow as we watched myself and Pompeii from months ago eating apples and cheese in my favorite Viridis hall.

I laughed, my eyes filling with tears upon seeing him again. "*Yes. I miss him.*"

We listened to the chatter and just as I had at the time, the Blightress did not miss the sudden stiffness in Pah-Pah's back at the mention of my seventeenth birthday.

"*Your father made Karus promise to raise you under her protection for seventeen years.*"

"*You know about that?*"

"*I heard his begging to your mother, yes.*"

"*And still you tore them apart?*" I fisted my hands at my sides, hearing Pah-Pah's words of what was worth risking in my life.

"*I care naught for your father. He is just a Baron.*"

"*Do you not see it?*" I pleaded. "*You are hundreds of years old and still you cannot understand what you have done. You broke my mother. She was happy. She was powerful and using it for the good of her people. You tore that from them. How can you call that love?*"

Pah-Pah finished his words of wisdom. Words that had stayed with me from that moment on. "The same, Sae. The same life we have always lived."

The Blightress lashed, "*She chose that life. She could have been happy at my side. I even offered for her to take your father with us if she was so attached to him, and still she refused.*"

I opened my mouth to argue, but she grabbed my hand and grinned wide, calling my name again.

# CHAPTER 68
# SAELYN
## I WAS FIFTEEN AND WORRIED I WAS IN LOVE

The blinding light of the summer sun flashed and even the Blightress winced, shading her iridescent eyes with her pale hand.

Past Thevin and I were lying in the field of yellow flowers and he had just called me "Pip", short for pipsqueak. I bristled, already beginning to admit how I loved him, irritated at being thought of as a child at fifteen years old.

"*You offered her a half life,*" I spat, continuing our conversation from the last scene of my past. "*She would have kept him at her side, watching you dictate her life and take everything from people of the isle. I see why she hates you,*" I continued, no longer caring to be careful with my words. They spilled from me like water gushing downstream, and I had no desire to hold them back. "*You are nothing but a selfish woman, unable to attain what you wanted in life, so you'll just take whatever you deem yours.*"

Her eyes flashed a shade of crimson and she waved her hand as if this was nothing more than a tiring charade she was done performing for. "*Saelyn,*" she called smugly, and we left, my time to convince her of what I needed running thin.

# CHAPTER 69
# SAELYN
## I WAS FOURTEEN AND I WAS CLEVER

Felgren winters were short, but unforgiving.

My younger self had been out here, practicing magic alone and unsupervised before Pah-Pah found me, giving me a scolding for using magic when I was supposed to wait calmly to learn.

*"My mother didn't let me practice my power,"* I admitted, folding my arms across my chest. *"She was trying to keep you from knowing anything about me."*

*"Unfortunately, she succeeded,"* the Blightress agreed. *"All I knew was that you had the power to reverse time."* An icy smile crossed her lips as fourteen year old me did just that, taking back the spell to heal the frozen plant and taking back the scolding Pah-Pah had warned would come if my mother knew. *"But only by a few moments. I guessed it was you who had discovered it within yourself."* She hummed. *"Adaynth always did have the knack for creating spells of his own."*

I started. *"Adaynth? The first Baron of Felgren?"*

*"Your mother has not told you everything, then."*

I bit my lip. *"What does he have to do with me?"*

Her eyes swept to mine, dark with secrets I didn't know were hidden. *"Adaynth was the father of my child. And I have long suspected he played a part in the power you've been given, Saelyn."*

Upon her voicing my name, we flashed away again.

My last chance loomed ahead.

The first memory I had of my name being called on the wind was coming closer, and I needed to make it count.

# CHAPTER 70
# SAELYN

## I WAS TEN AND I UNDERSTOOD WHY MY MOTHER STRUGGLED TO LOOK AT ME

Ten-year-old Saelyn and Thevin sat in the tall grass with Pah-Pah as he taught them how to whistle through the wide blades. I had been curious about my father growing up. We didn't speak of him. We didn't admit how much I was growing to look like the man painted with my mother in the portrait on the endless staircase. I had wanted to know everything about where I had come from, and Pah-Pah was the only one in the Fortress willing to speak of him.

"My mother misses him, too," I had said. Even at such a young age, I had been aware of the reasons she avoided my eyes at times.

"*Why would the father of your child meddle with my powers?*" I asked the Blightress.

She looked on with a slight upturn of her lips as a younger me pushed Thevin and threw grass in his face. "*He has lived in all Barons and you come from two with new magic unheard of. I do not doubt his part in what you have become.*"

My heart raced. "*That man…that man I saw beside my father…he is the Baron who lives in my mother?*"

"*And has since she accepted the power of the Baron of Felgren…*" she trailed and smirked my way. "*About seventeen years past.*"

I frowned, watching Pah-Pah throwing grass at us children as we rolled, each trying to pin the other.

"*Are we almost through with this magic?*" she asked me, holding out her hand for me to take again.

I shook, placing my hand in hers. "*There's just one more. The first time I heard my name called on the wind.*" A tear ran down my cheek as she echoed my name, and I knew that I had failed.

# CHAPTER 71
# SAELYN

## I WAS SEVEN YEARS OLD, AND I ONLY KNEW FELGREN

A little girl with long black hair, ocean blue eyes, and a slight splatter of freckles across her nose lay in the roots of Felgren. The warm spring sun shone down through the new leaves on the trees that danced in the breeze. She giggled, roots wrapping over her arms and legs, sinking her further into the earth where she summoned the power to grow the grass and flowers, tall and brilliant in an array of colors which matched the eyes of the Blightress.

*"I am asking you to give this girl a chance to live a life of love with the man who has been a constant at her side."*

The Blightress watched me as a young child who laughed at the grass that tickled my nose, both of us turning to hear Pah-Pah shouting my name somewhere nearby.

My chin quivered as I continued. I had taken the risk. I had taken the steps forward to change the path of my life, and now I was at the final call, the first moment of my life when it had been the Blightress who spoke my name, weaving her voice with the winds of Felgren. *"Please,"* I begged. *"Please see that my life has been a lonely one. I have been so afraid to lose those I love because I watched my mother struggle with her loss every day of my life. Don't make me lose him."* I stepped closer to her side. "*Don't let history repeat itself. You said you would have given everything for your child. My mother did. She gave everything she had to give me in this life, so let us return and leave us be. Let us mourn my father. Let Thevin and I start a life together and do what we can to heal Arcaynen.*"

She stared down at that little girl hiding from a half-hearted scolding, blending into the roots and soil of the earth to which she belonged. A muscle ticked in her jaw, and I held onto what little hope I had left.

She reached her hand out to me one more time, and I took it.

"*It is my turn to live the life* I *want. I will not harm your lover, nor your mother, but you,*"—her eyes flashed a flood of colors—"*you will be returning with me where* I *will give you love. Where* I *will show you the power you wield is endless. Time loses meaning when you share such power…and time is forgiving.*"

"*No,*" I whimpered, struggling to take my hand from hers.

She squeezed harder, yanking me back to her side, seething through clenched teeth, "*Saelyn.*"

# CHAPTER 72
# SAELYN

Her grip was painful. I flinched at the sharp point of her nails digging into my skin—the grasp of a woman determined to have the life she felt she deserved.

Felgren was in the midst of fall.

I recognized the orange and yellow hues from the trees. Leaves scattered around a very young girl's bare feet. She giggled, chasing them across the steps that led to the Fortress.

My mother leaned against the newel of the stairs, her cheek resting on her hands placed over the stone. A tear fell to her chin and she smiled, the faintest flicker of green lighting her eyes as she watched little Saelyn playing in carefree laugher.

*"What is this?"* the Blightress snarled. *"You said we were done."*

I stepped toward my mother, reaching out to touch the sorrow-filled face I had seen many times before. My fingers slipped through her, and she shivered, straightening her back and turning away from her child no older than three years of age. *"I don't know,"* I answered. *"I don't remember this."*

My mother made the movements I had mimicked before. A glowing portal opened and in the flash of light, my younger self pointed, shouting, "Mama! Green!"

My little legs ran, my black hair flying behind me, but she pulled me up into her arms, holding onto me as I reached for the portal.

"It's not for you, Little Love." She kissed my chubby fingers as I reached harder, repeating softly, "It's not for you."

I heard Pah-Pah's voice before I noticed him coming down the stairs. "You cannot go," he murmured.

My mother turned with me in her arms, and my little face lit in joy. "Pah-Pah!" I screeched, reaching for him.

He took me, bouncing me up on his hip and continuing his warning. "You leave and this leaves with you." He pointed to the dome of green that had shielded Felgren since the day I was born.

"I just thought you could—"

"No. No, I cannot, Karus. I cannot protect her as you can." He set me down on the stairs, pulling my wooden lumen from his pocket. I squeaked in joy, taking my favorite toy and running off to play.

"If I'm gone for only a few minutes, the Blightress will not know."

"She may, she may not. You cannot risk the former."

"It's been *three years*," my mother's voice cracked. "We have more forces. The armies are growing quickly." She wiped the tears from her cheeks. "He deserves to come home."

Pah-Pah shook his head. "They all deserve to come home."

The words visibly stung my mother. She shuddered, her face breaking as a sob left her lips. She turned again to the portal. "I'll only be a minute," she bargained. She pushed her hand through and stopped. "No," she whimpered. She tried again, this time pounding hard through the green surface, only to be met with a wall of blue light. "No!" she screamed and little Saelyn came running, crying and tugging on her mother's black skirts.

My mother fell to her knees in a puff of leaves, weeping into her hands. "He won't let me in," she cried.

Pah-Pah reached down to pick me up, and I fought him, kicking and screaming for my mother.

Her portal flickered out and she roared into the earth, her fingers scraping across the soil of Felgren.

In the midst of my mother's anguish, the Blightress yanked me to her side and called my name.

A flash of white and we appeared in my mother's rooms.

She was propped up against the headboard of her bed, staring at the empty fireplace. She stroked the messy black curls of a baby, no older than a year, sleeping against her chest.

The same tears I'd seen many times rolled down her face, pooling at her chin as she gazed off into nothing, softly singing the same song she'd sung to me for as long as I could remember.

> *"Softly does hum,*
> *The bee to the sun,*
> *Flying into the summer breeze.*
> *Shyly does bloom,*
> *The babe in the womb,*
> *Arriving into the summer breeze."*

Her voice broke on the last line and she bit her lips inward, her body shaking, holding in the cries of pain, doing her best to not wake her daughter.

The Blightress stared, her face a mask of eerie calm. I could only watch in silence, my heart in pieces as I looked upon moments in my mother's life she'd never meant me to remember.

"*Saelyn,*" the Blightress whispered and we were gone.

The cropping of black rock under a charred maple tree appeared, and we watched as I toddled through the small stream, babbling unknown words in my own language, picking up rocks and splashing my chubby fingers in the clear water.

My mother sat on the stream's edge, her face broken in despair, her eyes red as she quickly tried to rid them of her tears. She struggled to laugh and smile as her small daughter picked up a rock and let it plop from her fingers back into the water.

The Blightress shuddered, this time speaking in rising anger, "*Saelyn!*"

A forest path appeared, my mother cradling the wailing babe in her arms. Boros followed, sniffing into the air.

"Shh," my mother cooed. "Please, Saelyn." She lifted my forehead to her lips, kissing my head and pressing me to her chest, bouncing me softly, mumbling under her breath, "How?" Her voice broke as she spoke into the forest air. "How do I do this without you?" She knelt to the ground, her own sobs matching her child's as Boros lay down with her, resting his head on her knee.

"*Saelyn!*" the Blightress roared, and we left again, only to find ourselves back in my mother's rooms.

There I lay, a sleeping babe in her crib, bundled in a yellow swaddle, and there my mother lay, staring at the cold fireplace curled up into a ball, wrapping her arms around herself and crying her silent tears into the thick wool rug.

"*SAELYN!*"

I flinched, unable to do anything but gasp at the scenes that flashed before us over and over. My days as a baby had been spent with my mother in the depths of mourning, and we were witness to them all.

Again, *Saelyn*.

*Saelyn*.

*Saelyn*.

*Saelyn*.

The Blightress did not stop, soon shouting my name a dozen times, and then a dozen times more, each one leading to the next scene of my mother's torment, each one delivering my mother's tears, her desperate cries, her rage, all while I was so small, a babe born into this world of loss and lost love.

"*SAELYN!*" the Blightress gasped and fell to her knees across from my mother in the same position on the floor of her rooms. My mother's tears splashed onto the floor while her daughter kicked her feet in the air, gnawing on the wooden lumen.

"You have his eyes, Little Love," my mother whimpered, wiping her fallen tear from her baby's arm. "He loves you just as much as Mama loves you." She wiped a hand across her face and under her nose, taking in a shuddering breath. "You do not know just how much you are loved," she whispered, bending down to kiss my full red cheek. I cooed at her, kicking again.

"*Your parents loved you.*" The Blightress didn't stop the tear that slipped down her skin in a single stream of reflective light.

I sat on my own knees next to her, watching my mother brush at her baby's hair, holding her sobs at bay. "*Yes.*"

"*Your mother suffered every day away from him,*" she continued.

"*Yes.*" I placed my hand over hers. She looked away from my mother, instead meeting my eyes—my dark blue eyes that told a story of where I had come from and who had loved me enough to leave me.

"*I love her,*" she choked, inhaling in a shuddering gasp.

"*Yes,*" I repeated in a truth I understood looking at her face, recognizing the same sorrowful expressions I'd seen on my mother time and time again.

"*I don't want her to suffer like this,*" she managed, reaching out a hand to wipe the tears from my mother's cheek, unable to do so.

"*Then let's go back,*" I started, squeezing her hand again. "*You can help me fix—all of this—so that we can move on with our lives in the happiness we are ready for. My mother will always mourn my father, but without the threat of you taking me away, she can find some joy in her daughter's life. Please,*" I begged, "*let's go back and bury him. Give her peace and rid the isle of your Blight. Let our people be happy and prosper under the sun. Let them rebuild what has been lost and let my mother live out her days as Baron of Felgren.*" I inched closer, desperation in my voice, "*Let her no longer fear what can be taken from her.*" I paused, wiping the next iridescent tear that fell down her cheek. "*I know your fear. It is my own.*"

Her mouth pursed and her lips trembled. I saw the weight of what she'd carried for centuries reflect through her eyes. I knew her pain. I knew the sharp bite of loneliness like my mother. Like the powerful women before me, I too understood that empty chasm within and the fear of never filling it. I swallowed back the lump in my throat, remembering the words my father had started long ago. Words I knew he believed in.

Hold onto hope.

Defy the dark.

The dark was here, right before us. The truth of what my parents had been through to keep me safe. To keep me loved by them, growing up in Felgren where I belonged. "*We can do this together,*" I continued. "*We can let go of the fear of being alone.*"

She met my eyes then with hers and nodded softly. "*I can do more than what you ask.*" A genuine smile lifted her lips, the first I'd ever seen on her face.

She was beautiful.

"*One more time,*" she whispered. "*Release your spell one more time, and I will give you the life you've always deserved to live.*"

I took in a final breath and took her open hand. Glancing once at my young mother lost in her grief, I did what was asked of me. "*Revertayden en tepiore.*"

The dark flooded through me in a torrent of endless black. I gasped, afraid of what would be next, what the Blightress had meant in her words. I felt the grip of her fingers holding mine as we tore through time, and her power flowed through me, enhancing the spell tenfold.

I screamed as we landed, shielding my eyes from the golden glow of the setting sun.

"Stay behind me," she urged and drew a finger across my cheek. "Have a good life, Saelyn. Know that you are never alone. Know that you are loved."

I remained hidden, kneeling in the obsidian shadows that surrounded us like a cave. Glints of orange light shone off great puddles in the clearing. Marvelous tree creatures I'd never seen before halted their music and revelry, gaping at the Blightress. She rose straight, elegant, and tall in all her dark robes and dark power, dripping in shadows and calm as if she knew exactly where we'd gone to.

A figure stood with umber, bark-like skin and vines wrapped through her braided hair. "You are not welcome here, Visalia, Endless One," she called.

"I have come to offer you peace, Nova," the Blightress began. I could not see her face, but I noticed the swivel of her head toward the right. I followed her stare, recognizing the shape of my mother in a dress of gold through her thin green shield.

"What peace do you offer?" Nova asked, stepping to the side as if to shield my mother.

"A peace from fear." The Blightress slowly lifted her hand behind her, a last offering for me to take.

I placed my hand in hers.

It faded.

My skin, my hand, my arm—I began to depart, pieces of me lifting into the black swirls of her power as she continued. "From this day forward, I will no longer Blight this land. I will no longer seek any child to take as my own." I heard her shuttering breath before she called, "I will no longer seek to hold the life of Karus, Baron of Felgren."

My thoughts drifted.

I blinked, but my eyes did not close.

My mother rose, heavy with me in her belly. I saw my father then. He emerged from the gathering of fae near my mother, stepping in front of her.

If I had lungs to take a breath, I would have gasped.

He looked so much like his portrait come to life—so much like me. He was nothing like the withered man I'd seen in the cavern.

"Then leave now," he called. "Never return. Never seek out our child. Return those you siphon for power. Return Mychael and Rell to us unharmed. That is the peace we seek from you."

The Blightress nodded once and what was left of my hand fell through hers.

She turned her head back to me, and I faded, leaving this life behind for a new one.

One where I was no longer haunted.

One where my parents could thrive, raising and loving me together.

One where Thevin and I would fall in love again, this time with a brighter hope for our future together.

I did not fear it.

This was what I'd been born to do.

This was why I had been given such power.

I smiled as the part of me that was left lifted into the wind and the Blightress stepped back into her portal, smiling at me with tears in her glinting, colorful eyes. "You are never alone, Saelyn of Felgren. Remember that for me."

I left, drifting away in a summer breeze as her portal closed, and the world changed forever.

# PART SIX

# CHAPTER 73
# KARUS

With the same swiftness she had come, she was gone.

The Blightress left in a cloud of black, and I felt it. Deep inside my bones, I felt the shift, the world reimagined in a flicker of time.

"Karus," Rev called, asking to be let into my shield.

I dropped it and his arms were around me, his breath heavy, fear rippling through our bond. He had been so afraid. I felt it there between us.

But I could only stare over his shoulder at where she'd been.

I ignored the vice on my womb, the spread of tight spasms signaling Saelyn's arrival would be this night.

The fae began to fall back into the forest, leaving behind their celebration, but I could only stare.

Clairannia called, "We need to get back to the Fortress!" She pulled on Rev's shoulder while Figuerah called to the lumens in the growing darkness, her golden power of light trailing through the trees.

Revich spoke to both of them, but I could only stare.

*"What have you done?"* I asked, searching my mind for the Blightress.

No answer came.

No coy remark or threat of her power.

"*I don't believe you. Tell me what this is,*" I demanded to the silent corner of my mind where she had always been. "*Why can't I feel you anymore?*"

I was pulled away.

The fae warrior, Nova, said something to me, but I couldn't comprehend it.

I couldn't hear, I couldn't think, I couldn't process that my body was giving way to our child, I could only call over and over in my mind, afraid of what the Blightress had planned.

I had no reason to trust her.

I had no reason to believe her words of peace.

The next wave of pain, I could not ignore.

Clairannia was there, whispering spells to relax my womb, helping subside the spasms slightly.

Revich was speaking to me.

He held my face, his eyes a deep blue ringed with black. His shield around us was brilliant azure fire. I lifted my hands to grasp his, and I smiled in a laugh, blinking rapidly and coming back from the corner where I had just screamed Visalia's name in an echo of silence.

"Stay with me," Rev ordered. "Karus, look at me! Stay with me, my love."

"She's gone," I started, laughing again, tears streaming down my face. "I can't feel her there. Rev,"—I grabbed his shirt, shaking him—"she truly left."

He lowered his forehead to mine, placing his hands on my belly. "I believe you. Now, Karus,"—he lifted my face—"you need to bring our daughter into this world. She's not waiting to get back to the Fortress. Clairannia says she's coming now, and she needs you to focus."

I nodded, the sounds and light around us coming back to me as I was lowered to the forest floor. Figuerah sat behind me, propping me up, Clairannia knelt at my legs, helping me through my breathing, telling me when to push.

Rev stayed at my side, talking with me through every bout of pain, easing every spasm with the spells he knew to calm my racing heart and help me bring our child into the world.

Her cries lit the night, and I collapsed back into Figuerah's lap, closing my eyes, hearing the bliss of full, healthy lungs.

Figuerah shook, laughing and crying, wiping the sweat and tears from my face.

I blinked to see Revich holding our child in his arms, sobbing as I'd never seen, rocking her wrapped in his cream shirt, his chest bare, pressing our daughter to his skin. He whispered something at her ear before kissing her mess of black hair.

He leaned down to kiss me in a jumble of words of love and pride and admiration. He set Saelyn into my shaking arms and held the two of us, kissing my head repeatedly, beginning the song of his mother.

Time moved swiftly across the moments after and as my body healed from Clairannia's magic, I drifted to sleep, searching one more time for the Blightress, finding nothing but the silent, empty dark.

~

THREE WEEKS LATER, THEY CAME BACK TO US.

They all came back to us.

It began with the lumens. Revich and I walked the paths of Felgren, Saelyn taking turns in our arms, when Parvus and Rauca came bounding through the forest trees to greet us.

No vines grew from their skin, no red flickered in their eyes. They returned as the loyal lumens we knew with no evidence but our memories that they had ever been otherwise.

Mychael and Rell came next.

They arrived one evening as the sun sank below the trees.

Pompeii called to both of us through the Overseer bond, and we rushed to the foyer to find him there in Mychael's arms while Renn twirled her sister around and around in cries of relief and giggles.

I held Saelyn tightly as Rev rushed to Rell, asking if she was alright, looking her over for any signs of injury. When they both assured us they were unharmed, we headed to the kitchens to hear their stories.

"I don't remember anything beyond being pulled into that portal," Mychael explained. "The next I woke, Rell and so many others were lying in a grove of broken trees up north." He took Pompeii's hand into his. "It's why it took us so long to return. That was around three weeks ago, but Rell insisted on helping me return all of the other channelers to their cities. None of them remembered what happened."

"Can you tell us?" Rell asked excitedly. "How long were we gone?" She nodded to Saelyn in Revich's arms and then to Thevin in Talon's. "It must have been months if both babies of Felgren have arrived. What happened to the Blightress?"

Silence filled the kitchens and everyone looked to Revich and me.

"She is gone," I said. "She has released everyone she put into those syphoner trees, and she is gone."

Mychael asked softly, "Do you believe she's gone for good?"

I crossed my arms at my chest. "If this is some game she's playing, it's a convincing one."

THREE MORE WEEKS PASSED BEFORE THE QUESTION WAS ANSWERED.

Clairannia and Figuerah left Felgren, returning to their homes, promising to visit soon. Philius left as well, summoned by the Queen to meet with Lady Lamoral, whose young daughter, Lady Lanna, had gone missing one night in her bed. We asked Philius to represent Felgren and help lead the search for seven-year-old heir in our stead.

Revich and I had fallen into a routine. Parenthood was fulfilling and simple when we had a fortress of servants and friends who all wanted time spent with Saelyn, giving Rev and I plenty of much-needed breaks and quiet moments alone.

I had fallen asleep that afternoon on my blue high back chair, my hand still on Saelyn's cradle where I had rocked her to sleep. I dreamt of a black night lit with white shining stars. I dreamt of a forest bursting from the ground outside of Hyrithia's castle gates. I dreamt of a field of snow, high as my waist, cold and silent as I trekked through endless white seeking… someone.

I woke with a start, bolting upright and gasping. It had felt more than real. It had felt like a memory. I reached down to sweep my fingers across Saelyn's soft black locks to find that she was not there. I rose in a panic, whipping around to see a figure in black walking slowly across the room with a bundle in her arms.

"Please," I begged, reaching out. "Please don't take her."

The Blightress halted her steps, facing me with eyes brimming in tears. "I am not here to take her, Little Sprout. I am here to say goodbye one last time."

I dared not move. I dared not leap across the room to take my sleeping baby from her arms, knowing she had all the power to whisk her away in a mere second if she wanted to.

"You are here to say goodbye?" I whispered in a racing heart-beat. "To me?"

"To both of you." She smiled genuinely, stroking a long pale finger over Saelyn's cheek. "She has done more than you will ever know, Baron Karus." Her gaze lifted to mine as she finished, "I have loved you since I felt you. That, at least, will never change." She kissed Saelyn's head and stepped closer, handing her to me.

I took her quickly, backing away, already calling to Revich through our bond. He appeared seconds later in a flash of blue light.

The Blightress held up her hand, blocking the ray of power that shot from his hands. "I am not here for that, Baron Revich."

He stepped in front of me. "You said you would leave and not pursue either one of them."

She nodded, folding her hands in front of her billowing black gown. "And so I will. I wanted to hold her one time. Just once, I wanted to feel the weight of a babe in my arms."

I set Saelyn back into her crib as she stirred.

Moving around Revich, I asked, "Why can't I feel you? How have you gone from my mind?"

"You still hold my power as you will continue to do. But it was always my choice to stay with you." She took another step forward and Revich reached out to block me, but I lowered his hand, meeting her in the distance between us.

"I don't know why you've changed. But thank you. If there's anything you could have given me, it was this."

"I know," she whispered. "I love you, my Little Sprout."

I frowned, reaching out to her, feeling the pull of the thread between us that had been there since I had grown in my mother's womb. She faded into the black around her as nothing more than a trail of power that dissipated like the sound of a Felgren wind.

Months later we returned to the cave.

I needed to see it.

I needed to be sure and so did Revich.

Pompeii and Mychael assured us Saelyn would be safe with them and we returned, finding the massive cavern to be just that. Empty, wet, and dark.

The Blightress's heart was missing with no sign of where she had gone or what she had done with it. Word rumbled throughout the isle that the land was prospering, and I knew the Blightress must be alive, hidden somewhere, for we magic wielders could not survive without her. Revich and I portaled through her lands, searching for any sign of Blight.

We found nothing but a dead forest.

No beasts of Blight, no living trees to hunt us down.

Just empty silence and an abandoned palace of white stone.

That night, we returned to the Fortress, the three of us nestled in our bed. Rev softly sang the song of his mother to Saelyn, stroking her black hair as she slept. I watched with such love, my heart could burst from the overwhelming relief I felt having the two of them there—safe, and happy, just as I had begged all those months ago when I had accepted the power of Baron.

I held onto those moments then. I tucked them away to memory.

I reached out to cover Revich's hand, warm and soothing over our child. We held each other's gaze with Saelyn snuggled between us, and he silently mouthed the words, *I love you.* I did the same with a smile and promised myself I would never forget the love in that room.

# CHAPTER 74
## REV

Saelyn was three and wild.

Every chance she had, she'd burst from the doors of the Fortress, running down the steps and into the forest paths. It was a game we played. I'd chase her through our rooms and the foyer, and she'd run, giggling endlessly in her dresses of cornflower blue, a contrast against her black waves her mother or I attempted to braid each morning.

Saelyn was too busy for sitting down at three.

She wanted to know everything, explore everywhere. That year she lost her playmate for a time. Talon and Ilyenna passed the conduit trials, finding themselves ready to leave Felgren and emerge into the world as powerful conduits who could bring change.

Ilyenna insisted on setting up a home in the Hallow Marshes. There, she began her work on mining rhyzolm safely and more effectively while Talon used his iumenta talents to bring cattle to the marshes for the people to raise and sell.

We were proud of them both and ensured them they'd always have a summer home with us. Indeed, Saelyn and Thevin were two peas in a pod and the change was difficult for them.

But that year, Saelyn was adorably wild and three. And as I

chased her through the autumn leaves that fell in the grove of maples, her laughter sounded through the forest which she was born in—the forest which gave her the power we'd already begun to see.

I hadn't heard from Adaynth in three years. I'd probed that cavern in my mind a few times, asking after him, listening on the hard days for his voice.

Sometimes I wondered if I had dreamt it. I wondered if, in my desperate panic to hold onto Karus and our child, I had hallucinated all those conversations, all the warnings, the pestering to keep myself sane in my worry. Karus hadn't heard from either of the ancient beings, and we decided to let that be. We decided to live the life we'd been given to live with our love, our Baronship, our precious little Saelyn. That was enough.

No, that was everything.

"Watch me, Papa!" She twirled in the falling leaves and seeds of the maple tree grove. Her power pooled at her feet in whorls of white, and her laugh chimed along the Felgren wind.

I scooped her up, tossing her into the air where she screamed in delight before I caught her in my arms. "I see you, Little Love." I kissed her red cheek and she summoned an orange leaf to her hand with her power. "I see you," I repeated.

The rhyzolm did not lie.

Our daughter was powerful.

# CHAPTER 75
# KARUS

Saelyn was seven years old and as much a part of Felgren as any channeler would be. We lay on the forest floor, naming the flowers around us, calling to the birds which flitted across the sky in a symphony of white wings. Moira sat on my stomach, pasting new petals to her skirts as Saelyn handed them to her.

"But how do you *know* the roots of these trees give us power?" Saelyn was a curious child. And as we waited for the summer months to arrive and her favorite person to return to Felgren, we were in a constant state of answering all of her questions as best we could.

Moira's eyes widened in exasperation just before she rolled them.

Saelyn had already asked us what each flower's seed looked like.

She'd asked us why lumens grew so large, which had then began a conversation about the fae and what they were and where they'd come from.

Learning she shared some fae blood through me brought her to a torrential stream of questions for Moira, most of which the faerie had replied with, "You don't need to know."

I chuckled at my faerie friend. She had more patience over the years with Saelyn than any other fae would have. I was sure of it.

I took Saelyn's hand in mine and sat up. I pressed her palm to the soil, ensuring each of her fingers was covered with the fresh spring loam. "Call to the roots of these trees."

Taken aback, she tilted her head in a frown. "How?"

I shrugged. "Your choice. Do what feels right."

She chewed her bottom lip, and I shook my head in disbelief. Every day she looked more and more like Revich and my heart overflowed with the love I held for our child.

She closed her eyes and I caught Moira's stare as we sat quietly, waiting to see what Saelyn could do.

It began with the smallest sprouts of green crocus leaves—the first of Saelyn's favorite flowers because when they began to grow in clumps of purple and white, it was a clear sign that spring had arrived and summer would soon follow.

The striped leaves unfurled before the blooms shone in their spring hues, each with a brilliant yellow center. But Saelyn wasn't done. She pushed her fingers into the ground further and roots tipped the surface, winding over her hand, up her arm and over her legs. She laughed delightedly and I stared in awe.

Such power at such a young age was rare—unheard of except for two others in this world. One of them was myself and the other…the other had not appeared in years. Not a sighting, not a hint of the Blight that had coursed its way over this forest in a deathly embrace.

Saelyn was seven and she lived in Felgren while the forest lived in her.

## CHAPTER 76

# REV

Saelyn was ten and her paternal parentage was clear. She looked so much like me, I often wondered if this was what my mother had looked like as a child. Black hair, skin that tanned easily in the summer sun, eyes so blue they mimicked the depth of the sea.

That summer, Saelyn argued her way to my side every second she wasn't already off riding lumens with Thevin. Or receiving formal dance lessons from Mychael and Pompeii, who had apparently been hiding their talents all these years.

Saelyn, Thevin, and I were at the muddy lake where I was teaching them all I knew about mudfishing. They hadn't caught anything yet, but had made a game of it, each of them challenging the other to see who could catch a fish first.

Saelyn won when she pulled a copper tail from the mucky bottom, cradling the scaly beast in her arms, though it was no bigger than Moira.

"Ha!" she exclaimed, sticking her tongue out at Thevin who only smiled, his single dimple appearing on his cheek. "I caught the first fish! Now you have to kiss it!"

My chest heaved in laughter and Thevin called, "I'm not kissing that slimy thing! You kiss it!"

"I caught it!" she returned, "The hard part's over, now someone's gotta kiss it!" She made kissing noises, holding onto it tightly as she raced closer to Thevin.

"Gross!" he shouted, splashing her with the muddy water.

The fish slipped out of her arms, disappearing under the surface in a ripple.

She splashed him back, laughing and calling, "You owe me a fish, Thevin!"

He wiped his eyes, replying, "I can catch you a bigger fish than that anyway!"

I mucked through the water back to the shore, sitting on the muddy bank, letting the children of Felgren be just that—children.

Saelyn giggled again as Thevin reached down as I had taught him, though the water spilled over his shoulders and would make the pull more difficult. Soon enough, he did what he'd promised, yanking a fish half his size up over the surface by its mouth.

Saelyn squealed in excitement before the mudcopper flounced its body into the air, smacking Thevin in the face and knocking him below the surface. I rushed into the lake, but Saelyn was already there, pulling him up, helping him wipe mud from his eyes and laughing so hard, she held her chest.

He just smiled at her and shrugged. "Told you I'd catch the biggest fish."

# CHAPTER 77

# KARUS

Saelyn was fourteen and ready to train.

Her power had been manifesting for years, revealing itself in trails of white left in her wake.

Rev and I decided the winter she was fourteen that she was ready. We asked her what kind of Offering she wanted—a lavish party or a quiet celebration with just the people who loved her. She surprised us, confessing that what she truly wanted was a celebration in Hyrithia to end the Treaty between Felgren and the last city to refuse channeler Offerings.

She had met the Queen and her uncle once before, but through the years and all of our busy schedules, we had not visited the city. A part of me continued to fear Saelyn being taken from us. It was not the same pulsing dread it once had been, but I could not shake the feeling that the Blightress was there, looming in the background of every one of Saelyn's years of life in Felgren.

Revich and I agreed to the celebration, and I quickly wrote to the Queen. Saelyn could not have chosen a more welcoming benefactor for her Offering. The Queen made sure that this celebration would be as lavish as her coin could buy.

We officially dissolved the Treaty that night, ending the proclamation that channelers born in Hyrithia could not be given Offerings to train to become conduits in Felgren.

Everyone we knew attended, and as Saelyn took the hands of her Baron parents, her gown bloomed to one of shimmering Felgren green with sleeves that billowed long to her wrists. A simple ring of silver banded across her forefinger, topped with an almost clear white stone in a teardrop shape with five smaller stones above and five below. She gasped in delight upon seeing it there, leaping into our arms with joy.

Not long after, Thevin stole her away to watch Philius perform fire tricks with his power and end the night in a show of his magic as he had embraced it over the years, giving himself hands of flame.

Revich stole me away himself, covering my eyes with gold silk, leading me up to our rooms in the castle. He ushered me through the door and with a sweep of his hand and a kiss at my ear, my blindfold was gone.

I laughed in awe at our rooms. An exact replica of the night we shared for the first time as companions lay before me. All the details were the same, even down to the same mugs that steeped styris tea and the burgundy mums on the table.

"How much do you remember?" he whispered in my ear behind me.

I hummed, reaching for him in the candlelit glow. A few subtle notes of gray lined the black hair at his temples and graced the hair at his chin. He was still so beautiful with black eyes turning blue and that upturn of his lips always left for me to find when he loved me— just as he had loved me since the day he'd felt me through his rhyzolm.

"All of it," I replied, brushing my hand across his jaw. "I remember every night like this with you, and I'll never let myself forget them. Each day we have together is one I am thankful to keep in here." I pressed my hand to my chest. "To keep me warm. Because I know what could have been, Rev. I see it sometimes in my dreams, but that's all they are. I wake up next to you and thank whomever is listening that the life we wanted is ours to live. That you are happy, and safe, and loved."

"I love you, Karus," he said with a sweep of his thumb across my lip.

"And you will love me still, Baron Revich."

He huffed a laugh, unbuttoning my vest, whispering, "For a fucking lifetime." He kissed me hard with the same urgency, the same passion we'd shared since the night we'd bonded and the years before. He bent his forehead to mine, pulling on the back of my thighs to lift me to him, murmuring, "You live, I live. A lifetime with you is the *only* life I've ever found worth living."

# CHAPTER 78
# SAELYN

I was fifteen and convinced I was in love.

I was so incredibly flustered that summer, avoiding Thevin's persistent requests to swim in the Great Stream. What if I slipped and fell? What if Moira decided at that exact time to dive naked into the water as she loved to do? What if Thevin still saw me as just the child he grew up visiting a few months of the year and not the young woman I was blooming into?

Surely, I was blooming.

Hopefully. Probably.

My long, gangly legs were filling out along with my hips and chest, and I found myself staring at Thevin constantly that summer, admiring the pale blue of his eyes, the dimple at his left cheek when I made him laugh.

He wore me down eventually, chiding me the day before he and his parents were to leave back to the Hallow Marshes. I wasn't too unhappy about it, since I had convinced my own parents to let me visit his family in the Hallow Marshes. Then, I would get to see the Spire for the first time while we sold rhyzolm at the markets.

I would see Thevin again in three months, but I could not deny him a dip in the Great Stream that summer.

We stood on the edge of the bank while Boros splashed in the water, chasing a stick I'd thrown. My mother had taught me how to calm the stream just by asking—something to do with the fae blood we shared from the woman who had given some of her power to my mother.

"What are you waiting for, Sae?" Thevin asked, gazing out over the steady stream.

"You're the one who wanted to come so badly!" I scoffed, nudging his arm. "You jump in first!"

He smirked, looking me over and frowning slightly. "It's funny," he started, "I don't remember your eyes matching the color of this water."

He'd been saying more and more absolutely embarrassing statements like that all summer long, and once again, I felt the color rising in my cheeks, suddenly more than happy to escape his gaze and jump.

I dipped my foot into the stream, splashing him playfully. "I'm not surprised. You never notice anything right in front of you."

He took my hand, threading his fingers through mine, mumbling, "That's not true. I've always known your eyes were blue, Sae, I just…didn't know they were *this* blue." He gestured back to the water.

I gulped and bit my lip.

"Shall we?" he asked, bending his knees to jump.

"Yes," I answered, "let's jump in together."

With a synchronized shout, we leapt into the Felgren breeze and splashed into the Great Stream of Felgren.

# CHAPTER 79
# THEVIN

Sae was seventeen when I told her I loved her.

We were telling stories of the months we'd spent away from each other, having celebrated the longest day of summer and her birthday just the week before.

She tilted her head to the side as she added yellow paint to the buttercup flower she painted on the slanted ceiling of our fort in the grove of maple trees. Boros snored slightly at our feet while I added the long white stripes to the leaves of the crocus field she had painted as well.

I wrapped up my usual story of how my garden experiments had failed again in the murky Hallow Marshes. "So, potatoes are a no as well. I think next spring I'll attempt a cherry tree and write home to ask after its progress in the summer."

She wiped her cheek with her sleeve and dropped her paintbrush onto her tray of colors. "Potatoes grow here," she mentioned casually. "So do cherry trees. There's one not too far away in a little clearing. We can visit later if you'd like."

I sighed, dropping my own paintbrush into the bowl of water, saying, "I miss Felgren when I'm gone, Sae." I rifled a hand through my hair, adding, "I miss you."

She gave a hum and nod, wiping her hands on her apron. "I miss you, too." Her cheeks flushed a rosy pink when she caught my stare, and she added quickly, "You know, we might be able to convince our parents to let you stay a little longer this summer since I'm taking the conduit trials in the fall." She shrugged, wiping her face again, only to leave a smear of saffron paint across her cheek. "Maybe they'd let you stay on as a sort of…supportive friend to help me pass them."

I stepped closer and wiped a thumb across the streak of yellow, mumbling, "We all know you're going to pass them."

She turned her face to help me wipe the paint from her skin, exposing the soft lines of her neck. "I could pretend I want you here when I pass them."

I stopped, my hand lingering at her cheek. "What if you weren't pretending, and you did want me here when you pass them?"

"I—" She stopped, swallowing hard, turning her face to look at me.

*By the Baron*, her eyes were so blue. They'd haunted me for years now, and it wasn't until last summer that I'd realized why. I had fallen for my best friend and didn't know how to tell her she consumed my thoughts when I was away. How her letters once a week were never enough, but more of a bandage to stop the bleeding of being gone. How I tracked the days when we left each summer, counting them down until I'd see her smile and feel whole again.

Her lips parted and I stepped closer, closing what was left between us. She looked up to me in what I would call hope, her eyes lowering to my mouth more than once.

"Ask me, Sae," I whispered, sliding my hand down the soft skin of her neck.

"Ask you what?"

"Ask me what I'm thinking."

She closed her eyes in a laugh, lowering her head where I gently pulled on her chin in a request to meet my gaze again. She smiled in her beautiful way that was far more enchanting than any field of flowers the isle could produce, painted or not. "What are you thinking, my dear friend Thevin?"

"I'm thinking I'd like to kiss you. I'm thinking it's past time I tell you that I am in love with you."

She closed her eyes, lowering her head once more, but I gently tilted her chin once again. Her grin bloomed, hitting me square in the chest, and she shook her head, meeting my eyes and wrapping her arms around my neck, rising on her toes. "Oh, good," she said above my lips. "It's about time you caught up."

I met her in a kiss, the first of many we'd share in our little fort in the woods, dancing to no music, our hearts singing a song with no end.

# CHAPTER 80
# SAELYN

I was twenty-three and missing home.

"You have everything you need?" Clairannia asked, tucking a yellow flower into my black braid.

"What about the carrot seeds for Thevin? Did you pack those?"

"Yes, Figuerah," I said, hauling my bag over my shoulder. "Anyway, I think it's Mychael who would scold me more than Thevin if I forgot them. Something about needing purple carrots for his and Pah-Pah's anniversary dinner."

Figuerah pulled me in for an embrace, saying, "I hope they grow in Thevin's garden, then."

I kissed her cheek, saying my goodbye, doing the same for Clairannia.

"We'll see you on the first day of summer, dearest," she promised. "And give your parents a hug from us.

I nodded, assuring them I would, folding my paper with the names of the possible channelers we could bring to Felgren this summer and shoving it into my pocket.

"And one for Thevin, of course!" Clairannia called.

"And Moira," Figuerah added.

"Yes, Moira, too!" Clairannia pulled Figuerah into a hug. "Also, please tell Mychael thank you for the cinnamon buns he had you bring us. Tell him they were perfect, just like Lia could make."

"I will!" I called, waving and walking to the glowing white portal I'd summoned for my departure home from the Spire.

Figuerah called goodbye to us both, already stepping into the portal I had woven for her to return to the Attatok Mountains.

I took one last glimpse at the tall tower from which the city took its name, blew Clairannia a kiss, and stepped into my power.

I sighed in relief returning to my home, my bag dropped and forgotten on the steps of the Fortress, my arms around Thevin as I buried my face in his neck, taking in his scent of garden dirt and rain.

He lifted me off the ground, wrapping his arms at my back to hold me, speaking into my hair in a muffled voice, "Needless to say, I've missed you."

I slipped to the ground, rising on my toes to kiss him fervently. "Needless to say, I love you."

He nipped at my bottom lip. "Needless to say, I love you as well, and shall not let you go for a week."

I laughed, tilting my head back where he leaned in to kiss my neck. "Needless to say, I accept your offer and suggest we begin right—"

"If you don't need to say it, why do you keep doing so?" Moira sat on the stone staircase railing, plucking at the green ivy leaves which had once again wound up the sides.

"Here we go," Thevin muttered at my ear.

I giggled and pushed away from him, bringing a finger to the vine where a dozen new leaves unfurled. "It's just one of those things humans say, Moira." I watched her lick her hand, pasting her sticky saliva onto the leaf before patting it across her chest.

"Seems like a lot of extra words to me," she said, shrugging.

"Do you know where my parents are?" I asked. "They said they'd be here when I arrived."

Her violet gaze turned to me, and she grinned, displaying her sharp teeth. "It was *him*." She jabbed a thumb at Thevin. "He made sure they'd be gone when you got here."

I turned to Thevin with my brows raised.

He rubbed his faced, forcing a hand through his golden curls. "I tried to get rid of her, too, but she refused to leave."

Moira stuck out her long green tongue, shaking her head. "I was never going to listen to *you*. Besides," she added, "Karus tried to stay, too, but that hairy bog monster of hers folded her over his shoulder and carried her away." She rolled her eyes. "They've been gone for at least an *hour*. I was waiting for them to get back here to greet you."

I met Thevin's gaze, suppressing a grin.

He started down the steps, picking up my bag and taking my hand, saying "I think they got the hint you didn't, Moira."

She scoffed, adding another leaf to her chest and calling as we hurried onto the path through the trees, "Why don't you humans just say what you mean!"

We laughed with arms wrapped around each other's waist, unwilling to let each other go.

"I'll say what I mean," Thevin started. "I mean to show you something special."

I rested my head on his shoulder. "Please tell me it's a picnic and I get to eat. I was so busy with the Viceroy and her father this morning, I skipped breakfast."

He kissed the top of my head, steering us down a less trodden path. "You'll see. Is Viceroy Malla well? How goes the transition?"

"She is well. The people have decided to allow her to officially become Lady of the Spire and start a new matriarchal line with the caveat that her first daughter be named after the missing Lady Lanna."

"Sounds like a good compromise."

"It is. The people do love her, and she has great plans for increasing the number of medicus camps that travel through the less populated areas of the isle. I hear they are much needed in the north as more towns arise from the abandoned forests there."

Thevin hummed, turning us again. "You've worked your miracles even more in the month you were gone."

I huffed a laugh. "I wonder if I'll ever feel like I'm doing en—"

I stopped in my tracks.

He'd led us to a tiny clearing between the trees which once grew a few patches of grass and an enormous bed of purple crocus. Now, it hosted a cottage built of gray stone with sunshine yellow shutters and a sky-blue front door. A path of river rocks led to a few garden beds nearby, already filled with new growth I recognized as potatoes.

My mouth agape, I stared in awe, tears begging to spill down my cheeks.

"Welcome home, Sae," Thevin said, pulling me closer to his side and planting another kiss on top of my head.

"You built this for us?" I asked in shock. "How—when—"

"Did you really think I was just going to take you back to our rooms in the Fortress after our companion ceremony next month? To your childhood bed?"

"I-I didn't really think about it."

"That's alright because I did. We've always talked of building something a little bigger than our fort, Sae, so I called in some help and did it."

I stepped forward, wiping my eyes and nose with my sleeve.

"Do you like it?" he whispered behind me.

I turned on him, jumping into his arms, crying at his neck. "It's absolutely perfect! I can't believe you did this!"

He let me down and lifted my chin to meet his eyes of pale blue. "Needless to say, I want nothing more than to share this home with you, Saelyn of Felgren." He paused, tilting his head and squinting at our new home behind me. "I will say though, I really think those front windows could use some flower box—"

I reached up and covered his mouth with my hand, saying, "Shut up and kiss me, Thevin."

# EPILOGUE

At Saelyn's playful words, a tug pulls on my lips, forming into a smile.

It is clear the boy loves her, just as she assured me he would all those years ago in another life. I am finally contented with the truth of it after observing this latest act of devotion, watching him working through days and nights to build her this little dwelling.

Truly, it is not much, but the way her eyes sparkled upon seeing it, I can feel that she does not mind its size.

He kisses her and picks her up to carry her to the door. They laugh together at his fumbling to open it while keeping his mouth pressed to hers.

I hear their laughter cease as they step inside, and I can no longer find an excuse to linger.

I step back from the trees which have hidden me for years I have not bothered to count. Time is a construct built by those who will see its end. Time means nothing to me.

The only two I care to love have found their peace, and it so happens, I must find mine.

I trail over bushes and roots, brushing my hands along the rough bark of the trees, sharing an endless life with each of them growing in the forest I once woke on a night of a full moon.

When I arrive at where I must go, I wave my hand across the field of clover, opening the secret I've hidden in my patience.

I trail down the steps woven from the roots of the earth and enter my place of rest.

Like the little cottage the boy built, it isn't much.

I don't need more than this to sleep, however, and I don't need more than this to keep my heart safe so that all of my children may continue to live and prosper under the sun. Just as she asked.

I slip my shoes from my feet and set myself onto the bed filled with soft blankets and pillows. Enough comforts to keep me asleep for the longest my body will allow, for I am tired and weary of all I have done.

I lay my head of long white locks down onto the pillow and allow a single tear to slip off my nose.

I have done what they have asked and am ready to sleep. I have given my daughter her chance to be happy, and I have given my Little One what I promised her I would in that other place, in that other time.

I close my eyes to let the last trickle of fear release from my heart.

I may be alone, but they are not, and that is enough.

My daughters are happy.

My daughters are safe.

My daughters are loved.

# A Note from the Author

Hey, you.

Thank you for reading A Conduit of Light, A Baron of Bonds, and A Blightress of Wrath. What a ride it has been to show you this world. I would dearly appreciate if you would leave a review for any or all of these books wherever you like to review what you read. Reviews help authors more than you might think because the amount of reviews and ratings of a book help review sites learn to suggest them to other readers who may enjoy them.

So…

A Conduit of Light trilogy is over.

Karus, Revich, Saelyn, and Thevin's stories are over.

But what happened to Lady Lanna?

This fierce, sassy, and caring character demanded more time on the page and has woven herself into the history of Felgren.

How?

I will share her story with you in the future when we get to go back to Felgren and learn more about the fae warriors.

For now, join my newsletter and socials to keep up to date with my latest works in progress and new releases.

I cannot wait to share more stories and more worlds with you.

# ACKNOWLEDGMENTS

The amount of growth I have done in the last year and a half is astounding to me. I set out to write this story about a man who loved a woman who did not know herself. Through telling Karus and Rev's story, I have come to know my own self a little more with each romantic confession, each quip Moira has to say, each thread of darkness the Blightress weaves. She has been the vision of what it felt like to fall, and I hope this story can stay with you through the shadows you face.

Thank you forever to the readers who have found this series and stayed with it. I cannot express through typing these words what it means to me that you have laughed and cried with these characters, reached out to me in anger for what I have done to them, and giggled at those lighthearted times we all love. I hope this trilogy's end has left you with closure for these characters and a calming peace that they made it through.

Reed, my husband, thank you for being so damn proud of me through writing these books. You tell all the people you know, and tuck our little brood into bed extra nights because you support this dream of mine. Thank you. I love you.

W&V, said brood, you write your own books inspired by your mama, and I am so endlessly proud of the joy and creativity you produce. I love you forever and more.

Rachel and Elaina. Whatever it was that brought us together to share in the paths we have chosen for our lives, I am grateful. I will not question it, I will not dwell on how in the hell we three fell into each other, starting with a sparkling blue ring, but I will cherish your friendship and love. I will laugh with you, I will cry with you, I will build worlds with you, and I will not remotely consider that it was coincidence. Because it couldn't have been. My Dreamers that Do, my loves, my best friends, thank you for all you've done to help get these books into the world.

For my parents and family, thank you for your kindness and support through this new path I've taken. I can't wait to show you more of what I can do.

For Memaw, Kate, and Kelley: It has been so enjoyable to give these books to you that you somehow find time to read through motherhood, grandmotherhood, and busy schedules in your life. Thank you for supporting me fiercely and reminding me that actually, I am badass and can do great things. I love you dearly.

To all the Karuses, Saelyns, and Visalias, I leave you with this: It is the choices we make that define us. Not what has happened to us, but what we choose to do about it. And sometimes even more so, what we choose to do with our mistakes. I believe in love, and therefore, I believe in you. I believe that you are not born to be perfect, but oddly enough, become so due to your lack of it.

My dears, may you be happy.

May you be safe.

May you be loved.

# ABOUT THE AUTHOR

Chelsey Ann Tompkins was born a storyteller, specializing in tales of love and soulful romance. Her adolescence was spent reading countless historical romance novels, along with the classics by Jane Austen. However, *Jane Eyre* will always remain her favorite. When she is not dreaming up heartbreaking romance stories, you can find her brewing yet another vanilla latte, taking her kids to the park, or indulging in the blissful silence a bubble bath provides. She resides near Seattle with her husband and two children.